W9-CLK-348

A DARKNESS AT THE DOOR

BOOKS BY INTISAR KHANANI

The Dauntless Path
Thorn
The Theft of Sunlight
A Darkness at the Door

The Sunbolt Chronicles
Sunbolt
Memories of Ash

A DARKNESS AT THE DOOR

INTISAR KHANANI

Snowy Wings
PUBLISHING

Names: Khanani, Intisar, author.
Title: A darkness at the door / Intisar Khanani.
Description: First edition | Turner, OR: Snowy Wings Publishing [2022] | Series: [Dauntless Path; 3] |
Summary: Abducted by slavers, disabled country girl Rae effects a harrowing escape and vows to bring an end to the corruption infecting her kingdom—even if that means overturning the highest powers of the land.
Identifiers: LCCN: 2022904380 | ISBN: 978-1-952667-81-7 (hardcover) | 978-1-952667-82-4 (paperback) | 978-1-952667-80-0 (ebook) | 978-1-952667-83-1 (audiobook)
Subjects: LCSH Magic--Fiction. | People with disabilities--Fiction. | Missing children--Fiction. | Bildungsroman. | Fantasy fiction. | BISAC YOUNG ADULT FICTION / Fantasy / General | FICTION / Coming of Age
Classification: LCC PS3611 .H352 D37 2022 | DDC 813.6--dc23

*For all those who get up to good trouble
and keep fighting the darkness, within and without.*

CHAPTER

1

In the shadow-dark confines of the small room that serves as our prison, I sing a lullaby to the children huddled around me. The water laps against the boat's hull in a slow and sorrowful counterpoint.

Life is a river, it carries you to the sea
Distant is the land that has stolen you away
But I am the wind in your sail
I am the current you ride
So, sleep, my child, with your heart tucked close to mine.

My voice catches in my throat. Though I've sung this song a score of times in the days and nights that have already passed, I find I can't go on now. When I first swore to engineer our escape, it seemed only a matter of will. But the slavers who hold us captive are many and well-used to their work, and the opportunity we need to break free hasn't come. More and more, the lullabies I sing sound like lies on my lips.

To my left, a child shifts and then settles into stillness. There are six of us in this room, though I am the eldest by far. The vents built high into the wooden wall allow us a whisper of fresh air from the hold and a bare hint of light. Just enough to make out the shapes of the children around me.

"Do you have a plan yet?" a boy's voice asks abruptly.

I turn wearily toward the speaker. Fastu, I believe. "The same plan as before. We wait until the boat docks and escape under the cover of darkness."

"You're not going to do anything, are you, Rae?" he demands. "You tell us to trust you, but all we do is slip farther downriver with each hour. We're not getting out of here like this. I'm not waiting for you to decide to do something."

Definitely Fastu. At eleven years old, he is sure he knows best, and can't see past the fear blinding him. He's waited three days, and as far as he's concerned, that's more than enough. But the ship *has* to dock soon in one of the larger towns that line the river—for cargo or even just supplies.

"We need to wait until we're moored so we can get to land safely," I remind him. I try to imagine our prison from the outside, but my eyes were covered when I was first brought down here. All I know for sure is we're aboard a merchant galley—a wide-bottomed riverboat complete with a deck of oars above us for the crew to use when the wind drops. "There are at least thirty men in the crew. We'll have to slip past them and make it to land without their noticing—if half of them are already on land, it will be that much easier."

With my clubfoot and injured left hand—my littlest finger hacked away and my whole hand throbbing now, the skin tight and hot to the touch—I won't be much good against a single sailor, let alone half the crew, even with my knife. It's a truth that tears at me, because I *should* be able to do more. I press down on the desperation clawing at my throat; that won't do any of us any good. We can't eliminate the risks, just reduce them as much as possible.

"If it's night, half the crew will be asleep," Fastu argues. "There's no difference."

"There *is.* We need to be near other people, so that we'll be heard when we shout for help on deck. If no one's nearby, we'll be cut down before we make it to land."

"We have the buckets," Fastu says earnestly. "We can hit them with those the next time they bring our food, knock them over and take their daggers. And then we can run."

Buckets? Against armed men? Doesn't he understand these sailors are used to the desperation of the children they transport?

Our meals are brought by a pair of sailors, one of them standing guard with dagger drawn while the other passes around the small bowls of oats. He refills the bucket with its water ladle when he collects the empty bowls, and replaces the second bucket we use to relieve ourselves at the same time. There is *always* someone with a ready blade watching.

I wish—oh how I wish—I had someone else here with me. The last time I was on a slave galley, Captain Matsin escorted me with a quad of elite soldiers. All I have now is my own bruised and battered body and no idea how to save all six of us with just the bone knife strapped to my calf. Given Fastu's talk of buckets, there's no way I'm mentioning the one weapon I do have. He wouldn't be able to stop himself from doing something rash if he knew. My head throbs in time with my hand as I try to think of a measured response.

"Someone will die in that attempt," I tell him finally. "And you are forgetting that not all of you can swim."

"So they should stay behind! We can get help and come back," Fastu cries. "I'm not waiting till we're in a slave market to try to escape. We'll never get away then!"

"Listen," I say, my good hand curled into a fist, as if I could keep hold of my patience with whitened knuckles. "Once we escape, you'll need the Blessing to stay safe from the Darkness. We'll need the Speaker at the nearest town's temple to administer that—you can't just hope to stumble across a Speaker on the riverbank. Once you're Blessed, you won't remember enough to be able to help anyone you left behind."

He shifts, the movement short and angry in the gloom, but he knows the threat of the Darkness and the effect of the Blessing as well as I. Purportedly, the Darkness is a curse left behind within those who escape the slavers. It blooms when they escape, stealing the light of their minds and leaving them like empty husks.

But the truth is it's a magical attack. Only the wards the slavers have access to can protect against it, and the sash my sister Niya made me. Those, and the "Blessing" that washes the curse from a person's blood—and takes their most recent memories with it. The Darkness, the enchanted cup used in the Blessing, and the slavers' wards all have their genesis in the Circle of Mages, who use the gems they receive in payment as amulets, reservoirs of power needed for casting greater spells.

"I'll take whatever chance I can get," Fastu says now, not having heard a word I said.

I close my eyes, reminding myself that snarling at him will make no difference. He's young and scared and trying to save himself. I can't fault him for that. Though I wish to God he were less mule-headed.

To my right, I hear a faint shifting, drawing closer, and then a small, cold hand latches onto the sleeve of my tunic. I turn my head toward the child. From the size of her hand, the shape of her slight frame as she nestles against me, she can be no more than seven.

"You won't leave without us," comes the soft whisper. I recognize her voice: it's Cari. "Will you, Rae?"

I close my eyes, force myself to whisper back, "No."

"Promise?"

It's not a promise I should make. There's far too much out of my control to be able to swear such a thing, but still I murmur, "Yes."

Cari rests her head against my shoulder. I shift to put my good arm around her, hold on to her as if I could keep her safe when I have nearly as little power as she does.

Somewhere out there, people are looking for me. I have no doubt of that. I left home to discover what I could about the snatchers, fueled by my promise to my friend Ani, whose little sister Seri was snatched from the streets of Sheltershorn. I served as Princess Alyrra's attendant, investigating the snatchers on her behalf. I never expected to uncover a network of corruption leading to the highest powers of the kingdom: the Circle of Mages and the spare heir to the crown, Verin Garrin—whom Alyrra still doesn't know about.

Regardless, Alyrra will be furious and quite possibly devastated by my disappearance. Perhaps she'll send Captain Matsin after me with a tracking spell in hand, if she can acquire one. She'd need to source it from the Fae mage visiting the court in order to trace me past the ward shielding our cell from detection, but Adept Midael fashioned one for my friend Kirrana when she was abducted. His first attempt got us close to her, though not close enough to rescue her. He might do the same now. Perhaps, by the time we dock, Matsin will already be close at hand, waiting to come to our aid. And perhaps I'm only deluding myself.

Still, I can't help but hope.

With a faint creak, the door to our cell opens, letting in a fall of lamplight. It's a small door, no taller than a man's waist, easily hidden by the cargo in the main hold.

I squint against the sudden brightness. Cari scoots up against me, sheltering behind my larger frame. The lamplight brings our tiny prison into focus: the stained wooden walls, the children of varying ages, from six to eleven—the eldest being Fastu. On the other side of our cell, a bucket of stale water sits, a small metal ladle attached. Closer to me than I would like rests the bucket to relieve ourselves in, the floor around it sticky. The sudden rush of fresh air brings the stench of the room into sharp relief.

A sailor crouches down and peers in at us. He is short and built heavy, like a bull. His gaze comes to rest on me. "You, the old one. Captain wants to see you."

The old one, as if eighteen years were an eternity.

"Why?" I ask, fear building in my chest. There's no need for the captain to see me.

The sailor smiles, a twist of his lips that is more leer than anything. "Why not? Move."

Cari's hands clutch at my arm. I shift to my knees, try to tug myself free, but she holds tight. Whatever the captain wants, I can't avoid it. "Let go, love," I whisper, jiggling my arm. I'll only hurt myself if I try to peel off her grasp using my injured hand. "I'll come back. You have to let me go."

"Stay," she whimpers.

In the doorway, the sailor leans forward, even more like a bull about to charge. If he has to come get me, he won't be gentle about it. He'll yank me forward on my turned foot, and likely kick the poor girl.

I take a deep breath, not wanting to hurt her. But I don't have a choice—I have to make her let me go before the sailor acts. "Cari, let go. Let *go.*" I twist my arm free and scrabble away. Cari begins to cry, softly, but she doesn't follow. It's a sound that tears at my heart.

The sailor backs out of the door now that I'm moving. I ease myself out, my eyes half-lidded against the light. The second sailor

—because of course there are always two—sheathes his dagger before shoving the door shut and barring it. He has a scraggly beard that sticks out from his cheeks and chin like a thornbush.

"Move," the bullish sailor repeats, gesturing toward the ladder. I push myself to my feet and limp toward it. My whole left leg feels weak beneath me, leaving me slightly unbalanced. There isn't space to stand in our prison, not for someone of my height. My muscles ache now that I'm moving, my ankle still slightly tender from that last fight on board a different slave ship, when I slipped and fell, and the street thief Bren stepped over me to block an oncoming blade.

I force myself up the ladder, using my good hand to grip it and hooking my left arm around the rungs, taking them one step at a time so my turned foot doesn't slip again. There is no street thief to step in and help me, no ally here at all.

"Can you go any slower?" Bull demands.

I push myself harder, until finally I reach the top. There's another sailor waiting there. He stands back, watching as I pull myself out, my legs shaky beneath me. I crouch before him, the relative dark of the world a balm to my eyes after the too-bright lantern. That's a point in favor of planning our escape for night: after days on end in our prison, daylight will blind us.

It's late evening now, only a faint rim of softer blue left in the western skies, the stars bright pinpricks of light overhead. We're far downriver from the capital city of Tarinon, the plains stretching out to either side, not a soul visible. The breeze is cool and fresh, scented with early wildflowers and the green of growing things. It doesn't seem like a world that could hold the cruelty of a slave ship.

Somewhere across the plains is my family, possibly still unaware of my abduction. My parents, and my youngest sister who always gets into mischief—though I've now far outdone even her most impressive scrapes—and my middle sister, Niya, with her secret magical talent. She and I are a matched pair, meant to grow old together, be there for each other when everyone else has gone or moved on to build their own families—she because of her secret, and me because of my foot. I don't want to leave her alone.

Bull swings through the hatch, hauls me up by my arm, and starts forward at a brisk walk. I can't quite keep up, stumbling and half-trotting to stay beside him, my gait off-kilter. Even though he's half a head shorter than me, he's quick. Finally, we reach the captain's cabin, Bull knocking smartly upon the scarred wood of the door.

I glance back over the deck, trying to calm myself. At least I can use this opportunity to assess what we'll have to navigate to escape. The ship lies quiet, the sails full and the lower deck where the rowers sit empty for the time being—or not. I squint, making out movement, and realize that a good number of men are bedded down between the benches.

It will never be quiet on deck, not even at night with half the crew on land. For a brief moment, despair claws at me. Even if I could imagine slipping past the whole crew, how could I possibly sneak the children out with me? And yet there's no question of leaving them behind—they won't stay, and I gave my word regardless.

A voice calls for us to enter. Bull opens the door and pulls me in with him, never letting go of my arm. "This is her, Captain Morrel," he says.

The captain ignores us. He's seated at a table, the dishes before him near empty. The scent of lentil soup, fresh bread, and spiced potatoes lingers in the air. I swallow back a sudden burst of saliva.

The captain takes a slow sip from his mug—wine, I think, from the color. Or perhaps something stronger. He sets the mug down, eyes resting on me. "I see."

He's a strong man, lean with muscle, his brown skin darkened further by the sun. He wears a single silver hoop through his right ear, bringing to mind the rank ring Captain Matsin wears—only this has nothing to do with honor.

"We don't normally get older birds like you." Morrel leans back in his chair. His gaze travels over me, taking in the two messy black braids that frame my face, my stained clothes that, however dirty, speak of wealth. His focus snags on my hand. I look down and catch sight of it in good light for the first time since my finger was cut away by one thief lord to taunt another to violence.

My hand—and indeed my skirt and tunic near it—are caked in dried blood. The finger was severed at the joint, the skin there puffy and red, raw flesh still peeking out in the gap that should have been closed up. The whole of my hand is swollen, with red spreading across it, lines of crimson running up past my wrist and beneath my sleeve. I knew it was infected from how hot and tight the skin felt, how it throbbed. But this is much worse than I envisioned. It wasn't Cari who was cold—it's me who must be feverish. I take a slow breath, then another, but the world has gone strangely unsteady, my knees weak beneath me.

Morrel grunts and raises his gaze to my face. "I'm curious how you landed here."

I focus my eyes on the wide scar running across his knuckles. "Made a mistake, Captain."

He huffs softly. "Everyone down below made a mistake, birdie. What was yours?"

I grit my teeth. "I trusted the wrong man."

He doesn't need the details: that Verin Garrin, second in line for the throne and the lord tasked with overseeing the investigation into the snatchers, turned out to be the power behind them. That he laid a trap for me, and once he caught me, he nailed me into a crate himself and sent me on to the thief lord Bardok Three-Fingers to be shipped downriver. I don't know how I will get free, but I *will*. And I'll see Garrin brought to justice for all he's done.

"Hmm. I got orders to let you be. Strange, that. I never get orders for specific cargo. Why do you think that is?"

Because Garrin seemed to think that a word from him would assure me a happy, safe future as a slave. That didn't stop Bardok from taking my finger, and it's not going to stop Morrel now.

I shake my head stiffly.

"If even you don't know why you're special, I don't see any reason why you should get special treatment. I've got a whole crew of men who are delighted you're on board with us. *Thrilled*, really." He shrugs. "We've a rule with the young ones—they're more valuable untouched. And they tend to die if they get pregnant. But you? You're older and clearly already damaged. I'm not one to stand in the way of my men's pleasure when it costs me nothing."

I remember the leer on Bull's lips down in the hold, and my stomach seizes. "It's because of Red Hawk," I say, the words tumbling out.

It's a lie, of course. But Morrel won't care about a royal lord shut away in the palace—I've no doubt Garrin kept his role as secret to the average slaver as it was to the court. My only hope is that Morrel might be concerned about a thief lord known to take care of his own.

He scoffs. "You expect me to believe a thief lord—one who painted the streets with his own brother's blood—cares about some country girl in pretty clothes?"

"Yes," I say, my voice shaking. I don't know that story, but Red Hawk *is* a thief lord, and the stories sailors tell will be different from what country families share around the dinner table. I reach up with my good hand to tug on the thin gold chain hidden beneath my tunic. He watches as I pull free the hawk pendant Bren gave me.

Bardok Three-Fingers left it with me when he took my finger—I didn't realize that was a kindness until now. And maybe it wasn't. Maybe he simply didn't care.

Morrel swears and rises from the table, crossing to cup the pendant in his palm before lifting his eyes to me. "You're trouble, you know that?"

"You could let me go." As absurd as the suggestion is, I can't help the faint note of hope that slips into my voice.

He snorts and reaches out to shove the pendant back under my tunic, his hand brushing my throat. I jerk back and then catch myself, heart hammering. He smiles and settles his hand over my neck, his grip sending fear spiraling through me. "A smart man would just kill you and be done with it. There's a hundred different ways a slave can die on board a ship."

I wait, aware of the silent, loose readiness of the sailor next to me. Aware that there's nothing I can say to sway this man; he'll make his own decision now. The best I can do is not look like trouble.

The captain dips his head, his lips quirking. "But I'm a loyal man, and I'll follow orders. You stay below, I pass you on before that infection kills you, and we never see that pendant again." He drops his hand. "Take her back to the hold and keep her there."

CHAPTER

2

Outside, the sailor I've dubbed Bull drags me along, his expression disgruntled.

Something low and white flits by overhead. Bull looks up with a jerk. A great white owl settles on the wooden spar that holds the sail wide on the mast. The owl gazes down at us, golden eyes bright, its feathers pearlescent in the light of the moon.

Bull glances from the bird to me, his expression shifting to dislike tinged with fear.

"What's keeping you?" the sailor by the hatch demands. It's the one with the thornbush beard.

"She's brought an *owl* to roost here." Bull makes a warding gesture, as if anything evil would fear flapping hands.

"They're natural creatures," I say dryly.

"Shut up! No one asked you. Get down there and hopefully the thrice-cursed thing will go away." Bull shoves me the final distance to the hatch. I trip and stumble to my knees, a hand's breadth away from tumbling through. My left hand grazes the floorboards as I catch myself, pain flaring through my arm.

"Captain said no, eh?" Thornbush asks, tilting his head back to look for the owl. "Didn't think he'd mind."

"She's got Red Hawk's sign on her."

"Red Hawk?" Thornbush repeats. "There's a brute I don't want to meet. Heard he whipped a pair of men bloody and then strung them up in a public square not three months ago for crossing his laws, and they weren't even thieves."

"That and a dozen other killings, easy," Bull says, giving me a nudge with his boot. I gather myself, breathing through the last of the pain, and start down the ladder, trying not to think about their words. Bren isn't Red Hawk, I remind myself. At least, he's always insisted as much, despite my occasional doubts on the matter. Regardless, right now, whatever Red Hawk's done is protecting me. That can only be a good thing.

The owl hoots, a low gravelly sound that carries across the air. The men glance up, unnerved. At least it takes their attention away from me, giving me the time I need to descend safely into the familiar darkness of the hold.

"And she's got an owl to announce her death." Thornbush's voice floats out over the hatch. "I wouldn't want any piece of her, myself."

At the bottom of the ladder, I look around the hold carefully. I've been through it twice before. The first time, I had a sack over my head and was in shock from losing my finger, unable to count steps or notice anything else about my surroundings. The second time, I was too worried about not angering Bull. Now, I use the time the owl has bought me to study the hold. It's not particularly deep, but that's to be expected for a river galley. It is long and wide, filled with crates tied down for the voyage from the king's city to the port city of Lirelei, where the river meets the sea.

Perhaps we could hide ourselves in the crates and wait for them to be unloaded before we make our final bid for freedom. My knife may be made of bone, but it is Fae-made and was gifted to me by the Fae mage Genno Stonemane. It can cut through wood as easily as meat. I *might* be able to get us out of our room and hide us among the crates, as long as we time our escape for our arrival at a dock. Sneak out too early, and the sailors will realize we've hidden ourselves and search the hold until they find us.

"Move," Bull says, grasping my arm again as he reaches the bottom of the ladder. It must be his favorite word.

I shuffle along, glad that he doesn't choose to walk too fast down here. My leg is steadier now, but I want every moment I can outside of the cell. Thornbush follows behind us to make sure I get put away without any trouble.

I wait as Bull sets down his lantern and unbars the door, swinging it open. As he turns toward me, a bucket comes flying through the opening, slamming into his head and drenching him with filth. He falls backward with a shout, his shoulder thumping into a crate. I back up in shock.

No. No, no, NO. Not like this!

But it's too late to stop what's happening. Fastu leaps from the opening with the second bucket in his hand. Thornbush shoves me sideways against a crate, his dagger flashing in his hands as he passes me. Fastu doesn't stand a chance. He'll die, here, now, in front of me.

I yank up my skirts and grab my bone knife from its sheath, stumbling forward as Thornbush reaches Fastu. He seizes the water bucket and tears it from the boy's grip. Fastu shouts—*fool boy!*—and staggers backward, nearly stepping on Bull, who is still wiping filth from his eyes and trying not to retch.

My hand convulses around the hilt of my knife. If I kill a sailor, I won't make it off this ship alive. There's no way we'll make it out of the hold right now, not with the boy shouting and all the noise that came before that. But Fastu *chose* this when I told him not to—

Thornbush lifts his dagger, his gaze trained on the boy. "You shouldn't have done that, little friend."

I can't stand by and watch Fastu be killed.

He tries to twist away at the same time that Bull grabs him by the arm and yanks him back. I throw myself forward, reaching out with my free hand to shove Thornbush's shoulder, and pain explodes through my hand and up my arm.

Thornbush stumbles as I ram into him, a scream caught between my teeth. My knife slides into the fabric of his tunic, slicing a thin line of red down his back as I fall.

He twists around and kicks me square in the chest, sending me thudding against a wall of crates. I lie there, my breath frozen in my lungs and my vision edged in black as he scoops up my knife from the floor. There are other men in the hold now, and Bull has a dagger pressed against Fastu's ribs.

At the door to the cell, a girl crouches, frozen, staring out at us. Thornbush slams the door in her face.

My lungs start working again as he turns, my chest hurting with each inhale. Thornbush sheathes his dagger and grabs me, wrenching me up. I barely manage to keep my feet under me as he marches me back toward the ladder in silence.

The captain is waiting for us by the time we reach the deck, one of the sailors having gone ahead to alert him. He stands silently before the hatch, his face grim, listening as Thornbush explains Fastu's attempted escape and my stumbling support of him. A good dozen sailors have gathered at Morrel's back.

"How," Morrel asks softly, looking at me, "is it possible that we have had trouble from you already?"

I keep quiet. This wasn't my plan. I wasn't going to do anything now—and remembering Morrel's threats from not even a quarter hour ago, I don't want to take the blame. But Fastu's just a child. I can't let him be punished if there's some way I can protect him.

"She had a knife." Thornbush holds up my bone knife. "The boy came out of the room throwing buckets, and she cut me in the back with this."

Morrel's brows rise. He steps forward and takes it, turning the blade one way and then the other in the moonlight. In my eyes, the bright ivory blade is intricately carved, the handle inset with onyx and mother of pearl. To him, it will look like nothing more than a chipped kitchen knife. Still somewhat meditatively, he takes a step closer and whips it across my cheek, jerking my face to the side. I squeeze my eyes shut, praying the pain won't come.

It doesn't. I sigh in relief. It's nothing more than the pain a twig snapping against my cheek would bring, enough to make my eyes water and set my teeth on edge, but my skin is still whole.

I open my eyes to Morrel's furious gaze. He clucks his tongue in disgust and tries the blade on the pad of his thumb.

It cuts him. Deeply.

He swears, dropping the knife to the deck and grabbing a kerchief from his pocket to press against the thumb. The rest of the sailors have gone still, staring. Even Fastu, who has been jerking against Bull and trying to wrest himself free, pauses in his struggles to stare first at Morrel and then at me.

"Explain that knife," Morrel says, eyeing it warily.

"I can't." After all, I don't truly know how it works, nor do I want Morrel to think he can force me into making a gift of it to him, which he might if he knows it's Fae-made. "It's mine; it won't cut me. That's all."

His jaw hardens. "You're no mage."

There's no point in lying. He'll only put me to the test if I do. "No," I agree, my voice slightly uneven.

"You thought you could attack my men, and because of that necklace of yours, I'd keep you?"

I shake my head, not trusting my voice at all.

"Good. At least you're not stupid. Though I don't think you're going to need this where you're going."

He catches the hawk pendant in his hand and lifts it over my head, yanking at the chain when it catches on my braids. Not too hard, though—it's finely wrought gold, worth more whole than snapped.

It comes loose, and he pockets the pendant before turning his gaze to Fastu. "And you, did you really think a pair of buckets would win you your freedom?"

Fastu raises a trembling chin. "You won't make a slave of me," he says, as if his courage could save him.

"Don't intend to," Morrel says with a lightness that belies the violence in his eyes. "We keep our cargo undamaged, see? Unless it causes trouble. Then we've leave to dispose of it." He gestures to a pair of sailors. "Bring up the other ones. You, fetch a pair of sandbags and some rope."

My breath shudders in my chest. He's going to kill us. I've known it since the moment that fool boy came flying out of our cell, but hearing Morrel's words now takes it from abstract to immediate. I try to pull free at the same time that Fastu lets loose a yell and twists around, stomping on Bull's foot.

He gets no farther than I, one of my braids caught by Thornbush's hand, and a dagger shoved up against my throat. I go still, aware that I'll die now or in five minutes, and somehow, though it makes no difference, I want those five minutes. Fastu, barely visible from the corner of my eye, remains pinned against the bulk of Bull, an equally sharp blade nestled against his throat.

Above us, the great white owl hoots again, that same deep, rumbling sound, and more than half the sailors make warding gestures—as if God would be on their side. I let my eyes slide shut for a moment, breathe in the cool night air, and send up my own prayer.

I do not want to take the secrets I carry to the grave with me. The possibility that I have failed, that my truths will die with me, leaves me light-headed and numb. I should have told the children when I had a chance—told them everything I knew, so if even one of us survived, the story could be carried back to Alyrra. But the children would have to convince a Speaker of the truth of my story before receiving the Blessing to protect against the Darkness; they wouldn't remember me or any detail of what I told them after. It seemed unlikely any Speaker would believe them, instead chalking up their words to nightmares of their own making. But if one did, and sent word to the palace, such a message would no doubt be intercepted by Garrin. The Speaker would be silenced, and possibly the children targeted as well, and I would still be held prisoner.

I should have tried anyway.

I open my eyes, my gaze falling to my knife; it lies only two paces away on the deck, but it may as well be back in Tarinon. The pendant in Morrel's pocket can't save me, nor will the orders Garrin gave. My sash, the embroidery imbued with protections by my sister Niya, can only protect against magical attacks, not executions. I have nothing. So, when Morrel looks toward me as the children haul themselves up through the hatch, I part my lips to beg.

He raises his brow, and there's a dark amusement in his eyes. My tongue falters, as if suddenly knotted around the words.

"Want to say something, birdie? Beg my mercy, perhaps? This *is* mercy. I could do a hundred things with your body before I throw it overboard. I've knives and men aplenty. Tell me, what would you like?"

No hope. I know it, and he can see it in my face, for his amusement grows till it touches his lips. I say the only thing I can think of, my gaze falling back to my knife. "The blade is enchanted. It won't cut me. But it will turn against any who harm me."

He scoffs. "Will it? Even from the bottom of a river?"

He'll sink it with me; at least I have that much. A sailor binds my wrists, then loops a length of rope around my ankles and tightens it fast, the other end tied to a sandbag. But if the knife goes down with me, perhaps I can free us. It is a paltry hope at best.

To my side, Fastu is crying now, little gasping sobs as he is bound to his death. We are dragged to the rail, Morrel's voice ringing in my ears as he declares our crimes to the watching children. My eyes catch on the younger girl—I don't know her by sight, don't know any of them to look at, but she is about seven or eight, and she trembles as she stares back at me, brown eyes wide and shadowed, her cheeks hollowed and her hair tangled about her face. I remember her hand in mine, her panicked pleas.

I promised Cari I would come back, that I wouldn't leave her alone.

I promised.

"No one escapes alive," Morrel says, and nods toward Fastu and me.

A heartbeat later we are thrown overboard.

CHAPTER

3

The water closes over my head, the impact nearly tearing the breath from my lungs. The currents pull at me, tugging against the weight of my anchor. I jerk and twist, but the ropes around my ankles are well tied. The sandbag drags me down, down, down.

I bend my knees to bring the ropes within grasp, my fingers scrabbling past the ballooning folds of my skirts to find the knot. I cannot get a grip on it, not with my wrists bound together. Something collides with my head—it's Fastu, thrashing wildly, his air escaping him in a cascade of bubbles. Already, my own breath is trickling out of me.

My fingers slip on the ropes again. The sandbag has stopped sinking, and I bob at the top of the rope. The world around me is dark, the moonlight a faint memory.

I am going to die. There is no escaping this reality, the pressure of water all around me. My lungs burn. I tug desperately at the ropes because even without hope, I cannot give up. I don't want to leave Niya alone, or the stolen children, don't want Garrin to win, to continue—

Something white slices down through the water, swift and bright as a falling star. I lunge toward it, reaching, and impossibly my hand closes on the hilt of my knife. I try to slash at the ropes around my ankles, cutting away ragged bits of skirt as my lungs scream for air, but my grip is already going slack. I breathe in a choking lungful of water, my body convulsing, and try, try to slice through the rope, if I can only find it. The tip of the knife cuts through the rope with a jerk, and my legs come free.

Too late. My lungs burn with water, the river dissolving into a whirling darkness rushing past me. I flail, but I cannot tell which way is up anymore, cannot stop myself from inhaling again.

Air meets my lips.

I cough at the sheer shock of it. The sweet night air enters my lungs as my knees hit dry ground. I collapse, my cheek thumping against the moss-covered earth as I cough again.

How is that even possible? Am I dead? My lips gape open, but I can't seem to get enough breath, my lungs still heavy with water. I must be dying, this vision of air and dry earth nothing but a hallucination.

A hand touches my shoulder, and a stream of warmth flows from that point, cascading through my veins and closing around my lungs. My chest contracts, water spewing from my lips. After three great heaves, I subside, my body pressed against the good, solid earth, and find I am alone on a riverbank with a woman.

Wait—

"Boy," I gasp. "Boy!"

"What?"

"Water—*boy!*"

"Oh, shall I save him too? You will owe me for that."

I nod, half uncomprehending, and the next moment Fastu is there beside me, a sodden heap upon the earth, inert. The woman bends, a night-dark braid swinging down from her shoulders, and touches the boy's arm. His body seizes.

Magic. That is the only explanation—for his appearance, and mine, and the way each of us has been made to expel the water that would have drowned us even after we were taken from the river.

I close my eyes, listening to the sound of Fastu retching up water and moaning. I don't know this woman, haven't seen her among the mages of the palace. Whoever she is, she is powerful. And I'm grateful for her help.

The night air is cool in my lungs. My whole body is shaky and weak. I open my eyes and try to focus. Beyond Fastu, gasping now but still prone, lies the river. I lever myself up, following the fast-flowing waters with my gaze to where the slave ship sails, nearly out of sight. How is that possible? We were only just thrown from the ship and couldn't have been underwater long—no more than a minute, however long it felt to me. The galley couldn't have traveled that far already.

Then again, none of this is possible. Not my sudden arrival on this riverbank, and certainly not the woman who cared to save me but not the boy.

"Ready to speak, then?" She steps away from Fastu, regarding me steadily. As I turn my gaze to her, another shudder runs through me. She isn't human, can't be, not with those eyes deep as the river, and as filled with violence and beauty. I've met Fae before—obviously. All of them have eyes as unknowable as eternity, but hers are worse somehow, terrifying in their darkness.

"Your name is Amraeya ni Ansarim," she says with a smile as cold as death, "and you are the princess's attendant."

I don't know how she knows this, and I am beginning to doubt she is truly here to help me. There *was* a Fae mage at the king's court, but Adept Midael was very much male, and where his skin differed from the soft browns of my people for its very darkness, this woman's skin lies on the other end of the spectrum, pale as bone. Paler even than Genno Stonemane's. Further, she is clothed in a white dress with gray trim that reminds me vaguely of the fashions favored by the outlanders who live across the western mountains, with a tight bodice and layered skirts. Strange, that.

"Tell me, kelari, what have you done to end up here, thrown from a slave ship to drown in the river?"

I swallow to clear my throat, the taste of deep river muck still on my tongue. "If you know so much, you must know that."

She tilts her head, eyes gleaming in the moonlight. "I wonder, though, if you understand it all."

I glance toward Fastu. He lies with his eyes closed. He is either unconscious or clever enough to play-act senselessness. I return my attention to the mage—or ungoverned sorceress, as the case may be. "I knew the risks I ran in my work. This was the natural consequence of being found out."

"Found out?" she echoes. "Or betrayed?"

I start, staring at her.

She bares her teeth in a predatory smile. "What was his name, the one who betrayed you?"

"These are great secrets," I say, trying to keep my voice steady.

"I will make it easier for you. Was it not Garrin of Cenatil?"

I stiffen, and know at once I've given myself away. I say roughly, "What concern is it of yours?"

"Only that he has proven his character through his actions, and I have every intention of seeing him suffer for it."

"You know?"

"That he enslaves his people to enrich himself? Certainly. He is only following in his father's footsteps."

His father—? My brow furrows as I try to think. Garrin's father married into the royal family. His mother died a year later, shortly after his birth. His father died only a few years ago, in a riding accident of some sort. "If—if that's true, why did you not punish his father? Or stop him before now?"

"I have my reasons," the sorceress says. "As I did in aiding you."

I take a slow breath.

She smiles coolly. "You owe me a life debt twice over, once for yourself, and once for the boy."

Oh. Oh no.

It's not at all a good thing to owe debts to the Fae—not debts that haven't been given boundaries and limits and clear guidelines. I've traded in favors with Fae before—though with Genno Stonemane only, and he is more friend than stranger. And in the end, he would not accept a debt from me. I moisten my lips and decide I had better let her speak first. Never mind that I never asked her to save me; I'm not at all sure she won't throw me back into the river if I argue that.

She waits until it's clear I won't respond. "Tell me, Kelari Amraeya, what are your intentions regarding Garrin of Cenatil?"

That's easy enough to answer. "I intend to bring him to justice."

She laughs, a fearful sound, as clear and carrying as the cracking of ice. "Do you, child of the country? How will you do so when he is a noble lord, and nephew to the king?"

"I—" I shake my head. "I mean to speak with the princess first."

"She is one who requires proof."

"I have plenty of that." Not only can I testify that Garrin himself took part in my abduction, but I haven't forgotten the clue that connected him to the Berenworth Trading Company—which runs most of the slaves downriver and across the sea.

"What if your princess cannot bring him to justice? What will you do then?" she demands.

I don't know.

"Think on it," she says. The very gentleness of her voice raises the hairs on my arms.

How does she know so much about me? About what I was doing in the palace itself? I was discreet. Only a handful of people know that my true aim was to investigate the snatchers; everyone else thought me only the newest and least of the princess's attendants. Yet this sorceress seems to know everything. Including Garrin's betrayal.

I lick dry lips and ask, "What is it you want? Truly?"

"When you return to the palace, bearing the weight of your proof against the lord of Cenatil, call me."

"Why?"

"Because the debts you owe me will be due then," she says. "And I intend to collect."

She crosses the distance to where I sit in a heartbeat, her hand touching my brow before I can flinch away. A spark jumps from her fingertip to my mind, burning its way through flesh and bone, burrowing into my brain. I hear myself cry out, aware that I am clutching at my head, tearing at my hair with my good hand, but the spark is beyond my reach, burning, *burning*, and then—it's gone. No, not gone. Latent, like an ember asleep among burned-out coals.

"That is my name," the sorceress says. "When you need it, reach for it."

I look up at her, my face wet with tears and river water, my fingers still knotted in the tangles of my hair. There is no name I can sense, just the ember of her spell, sleeping.

I will tell the princess—about this sorceress, about her interest in Garrin. I don't actually have to reach for this spell in my mind, do I? What did the sorceress say? When I return to the palace? Maybe I can just avoid the palace proper.

The sorceress smiles faintly, still looking down at me where I crouch on the ground, as if she can read my thoughts on my face. "Let us be clear, kelari. You cannot escape this debt."

She flicks her fingers once, a quick, impossibly fast move, and taps my forehead. Magic burns through me, roaring along the same path as the ember she first laid in me, only this one sends tendrils of searing pain lacing their way through my body.

I open my mouth to cry out, and a whiff of smoke escapes, my tongue coated in ash. I mewl softly.

"I do hate to use a debt so quickly," the sorceress says, patting the top of my head kindly. "But you are just the loyal sort who will not keep quiet. That was your first life debt, transformed into a binding. Do you know what that means?"

I shake my head, my breath shuddering in my lungs. The pain is easing, but I'm still breathing smoke.

"It means I have bound you to silence, using your life as the counterweight. Should you speak of this encounter, your debt will come due, and you will die."

I want nothing more than to crawl away from this woman with her burning magic and her terrifying words.

"Do you understand?"

I nod jerkily.

"As for the second life debt, if you do not call me as we have agreed, then I will simply collect your debt from among those you love. Perhaps one of your sisters."

"You—you can't," I say, my voice rasping with horror.

She regards me with an air of mild bemusement. "Do you really think not?"

I don't answer. This creature is fully capable of anything she claims. I have no doubt of that. I've met enough monsters by now to know that what strikes me as horrifying is utterly irrelevant.

"Good. Do not forget."

She dips her head, takes one step away, and lifts her arms. They lengthen, fingertips stretching into wingtips, and with a single rise and fall she is transformed, born aloft now by magic and physics alike in the shape of a great white owl.

CHAPTER

4

"Hey," a voice says. "Wake up."
A small hand nudges my shoulder.

"Come on, Rae. Wake up. Please."

I open my eyes to gaze blearily at a scrawny young boy with a thin, foxlike face and short hair sticking out in every direction, the early morning light warming his features. Fastu.

I jerk upright, glancing around wildly, but we're alone on the riverbank, no slavers or sorceresses in the vicinity. I must have passed out after she departed, and slipped into a deeper sleep from there. It's a testament to my weakness that I slept through the night.

"We're alone," Fastu says, watching me keenly.

I take a steadying breath while he pushes himself to his feet. The scent of prairie grass is overlaid by my own stench, partially mitigated by my dip in the river, but still there, stale and slightly rancid. What I wouldn't give for a bar of brown soap and a goat-hair mitt to scrub myself with. And a meal.

"I wish we had some food," Fastu says, echoing my sentiments. "At least we have water."

"You didn't drink directly from the river, did you?" I ask, appalled.

He rolls his eyes. "'Course I did."

"Mmm." I reach out to gather my bone knife from where it lies on the grasses beside me, forbearing to mention that water should always be boiled first, unless it's from a well. I suppose he'll learn that lesson the hard way now.

My clothes are still faintly damp, clinging to my body in folds where I slept on them. It was just warm enough last night that I didn't wake from the cold, but I can't suppress the shiver that runs through me now. I slide my knife back into its sheath, trying to think ahead.

We're free. Unexpectedly, impossibly, alive and free. If indebted to a Fae sorceress, and who-knows-how-far from the nearest town.

My thoughts finally click together at that, and I look up sharply at Fastu. We may be alive and free, but we are distinctly not safe. Especially not Fastu. "We need to get to the nearest town," I say. "Before the Darkness can find us."

Fastu shudders, nowhere near as cavalier as he was about it yesterday. "It'll destroy us, won't it?"

"Not if I can help it. Stay close to me."

He looks me over with disbelief. My hand falls to my sash. The magical wards Niya sewed into the sash will protect me from the Darkness—as they protected another young boy a week or two past. They're impossible wards, because purportedly there *is* no protection against the Darkness. But Niya is self-taught, her magic unorthodox, and the gift she sewed me for my upcoming birthday is priceless.

"Come on." I stump across the low grasses, my muscles stiff and my left leg shaky. Somewhere soon there should be a road that follows the river—if not exactly, then close enough. If we move quickly, there's a chance we can reach the nearest town before the Darkness comes for us. If only anyone knew when it was likely to fall. The last time I saw it attack, it was late at night, but it may not be the same now.

"Staying together won't help against the Darkness, will it? It can't," Fastu asks, catching up with me.

I shrug. "Did you think anything could help you when you were thrown overboard?"

He twitches. "I saw her, you know. That sorceress lady. Couldn't hear her, though."

She must have cast a dampening spell to keep our conversation private.

"She looked scary."

I nod, fairly certain it's not worth testing her binding to chat with Fastu about her. There's a faint line in the grasses ahead that suggests a break in their growth. A road, if I'm not mistaken.

He squints, looking ahead as well. "But there's nothing that protects against the Darkness, is there? Not even magic."

"I know we've always been told that, but the Darkness didn't attack us on the ship. There *is* a protection."

"Maybe," he says slowly. "Whatever it is, though, we don't have it."

My turned foot catches on a clump of grass roots and I stumble, right myself. It gives me a moment to decide my next words. "Just stay close. Our best option is still to find the nearest temple for the Blessing."

That is how the Darkness is usually dealt with—the Speakers at every temple in our land have learned how to administer the Blessing. It protects those at risk from the Darkness and wipes away their most recent memories, making the snatchers themselves almost impossible to track down. It's a brilliant system, really, however immoral. At least Bren and those I was working with found no evidence that the Speakers themselves know that they're involved with slavers. They're most likely just being used by the Circle, who provide the engraved—and ensorcelled—cup used in the Blessing.

The line in the grass resolves itself into a road. I pause a moment to study it, but the tracks left behind indicate a relatively even amount of traffic going in either direction. With nothing else to help guide us, I turn to follow it south, traveling the same direction as the river. I made a promise to Cari, to all those children on board the slave ship. I don't know if I can keep it, if there's any hope at all of catching up with the galley, but I have to try. If I turn back to the palace now, by the time I rally help and come after them, they'll have long since reached Lirelei and been transferred on, no doubt to be sent overseas. If I want to help them, I need to follow after them now.

Fastu strides ahead of me. Despite my resolve, I can't keep up on my turned foot. "Slow down," I call.

He pivots, bony elbows sticking out as he sets his hands on his hips. "I know you've got that sorceress lady, but the Darkness is fast. Maybe faster than her." He hesitates. "It's my fault we got thrown overboard. I'm going to go ahead."

"No, you can't," I say sharply.

He shakes his head, small face set. "The Speakers can protect us, and I can get them. I promise I'll come back for you—or send them."

If Fastu goes ahead, the Darkness could take him while I'm too far away to help. I can lie about where I got the sash if I must. "No, Fastu, listen. I have a ward that protects against the Darkness," I say, but he isn't listening.

He turns and darts down the road.

"Fastu, *wait*!" I start after him, pushing myself into an uneven run. With each thudding step, a sharp pain shoots up my left shin. My muscles have weakened more than I realized.

"I'll go as fast as I can!" he shouts over his shoulder, breaking into a sprint and proving he doesn't even know how to pace himself.

"*Fastu!*"

He ignores me. Even running at my fastest, I only manage to keep him in sight for a short time before he disappears over a slight rise in the road.

I slow to a stop, bending over to catch my breath. The *fool boy*, trying to save us. My body vibrates in a symphony of discomfort and pain: my still-tender ankle throbs from my short run as do my shins; my hand with its shorn finger pulses with pain with each heartbeat; even my belly aches. I rub my stomach, unsure if it's hunger that ails me or dread. Perhaps the two together.

I need to keep going. Fastu won't run forever. Perhaps if he drops down to an exhausted walk I'll manage to catch up with him. I've walked long distances over the plains many times before; the road will make things easier now. I work myself up to the long, steady stride I used through the lands near my home, ignoring the sweat already dripping down my back, the ache in my ankle and leg. I miss having a walking stick, but there's no way I could hold one with my injured hand. And my right foot isn't the one that needs the support.

A half hour later, I still haven't sighted Fastu. I've managed to find a few spring greens to chew as I walk, pausing only a moment to gather them from alongside the road. The greens are hardly filling, but after days of the same miserable sludge we were served in the hold, it's sharp and bitter and delicious on my tongue, and helps me ignore my growing thirst.

The walking also gives me a chance to think back to a remembered conversation with Genno Stonemane about the Darkness, and the marker it seeks out in the blood of the snatched. And then to the favor he provided me by trying to track my co-investigator

Kirrana after her abduction, and the archer's journal I gave him to read in return.

I discovered the book half-hidden in the Black Scholar's library, and read its account of the Fae Attack to distract myself from the horrors of what I was facing at the time. Now I think of the sorceress in its pages, who demanded the king's life in return for the end of the war. On the final page of her journal, the archer recorded the sorceress's name: Sarait Winterfrost.

It's a name Stonemane did not allow me to speak—a name he begged me never to give voice to. I squeeze my eyes shut, thinking of the sorceress who saved me from a watery grave. I think of her demand that I call her when I return to the palace and face Garrin, slaver that he is and second-in-line for the crown. I think of the name nestled deep in my mind.

I have no doubt what it will sound like on my lips.

I top a slight rise and see the skinny form of Fastu just disappearing into a dip in the road. Oh, thank *God*. There is one worry at least that I can do something about. I pick up my pace, stooping to grab a handful of greens to tempt him with. I don't call to him yet —better to wait until he'll be able to see the food in my hands.

As he reaches the top of the far rise, he stumbles and falls, a strange, graceless tumble. And I know, *I know*. I shout his name, running as hard as I can, littering greens behind me in the road. Pain throbs through my ankle each time my foot comes down.

"Fastu!" I cry again, gripping my skirts with my good hand, but I can't run any faster. This is all I can do—I am too late, too slow. *Please*, I gasp out, a prayer that is only that one word. *Please*.

Ahead of me, Fastu lies in the dirt, his body jerking. My fingers catch on the knot holding my sash tight around my waist, tugging it loose as I reach him. I drop to my knees before him.

He's still now, his gaze blank and staring. He blinks at me without recognition. No, no, *no*. I pull the sash open, bracing myself for the Darkness to slam into me as I wrap my arms around Fastu, the ends of the sash in my grip—but it doesn't.

I let out a whimpering cry, pulling the boy into my lap, but he makes no answer, and the Darkness doesn't brush against me. It does not touch me at all.

It makes no difference whether I hold my sash closed around the two of us or let its ends go.

The Darkness has already left, and taken Fastu with it.

Eventually, I retie my sash and cajole Fastu into standing up. Having gained his feet, he stands with his head strangely bent, as if it is a little too heavy to hold straight. His gaze is far away, his expression too still.

"Fastu," I say, my voice cracking. "We need to keep walking."

He makes no response. I take his hand in mine, grubby and half-small, and step forward. He stays still until our arms are stretched out between us, and then, at my urging, he takes a step. And then another. By the time we're walking steadily, me limping and him shambling along in my wake, I am crying, tears spilling down my cheeks.

I wipe my face roughly, looking ahead to the town that must be there. Maybe the Speakers at the town temple will be able to help him. But that's a false hope, and I know it. The Speakers have no cure for the Darkness. No one does. The damage it does is irreversible—or so we've been told. I have no proof otherwise.

How could I have let Fastu get ahead of me? I should have convinced him that I could offer him some safety. I tried to—I *told* him I had a ward that would protect us. But he knew better. And now it's cost him everything.

"Fastu," I say, my voice rasping. "Fastu, can you hear me? Do you remember me? Fastu?"

He turns his head slowly to regard me. I can't tell what he's thinking, if my words reach him at all, or if he's only responding to the sound of them.

"Fastu?" I repeat and squeeze his hand gently. He was foolish and hotheaded, but not unkind. Just young and scared.

He dips his head in a semblance of a nod and then looks back at the road, taking another step.

I wipe my nose with my sleeve, sniffling. I've seen one young man before who was touched by the Darkness. He could perform simple tasks when gently guided, but there had also been an absence to him, as if part of him had been stolen away. Just as there is in Fastu now.

A white-hot anger flares inside of me. I grit my teeth, my left hand throbbing as I begin to curl it into a fist. Which I can't do, but *oh* I wish I could beat something, break the slave ship to pieces. I *hate* the mages of this land, sworn to protect us and instead betraying us so deeply—for what? More gems to make amulets to store their power when they're already the most powerful group in the kingdom? More gold when they're already rich? And with them, Verin Garrin, a lord in his own right, profiting off the slave trade, protecting the snatchers and Circle alike. And Berenworth Trading Company, whose galleys transport children to slavery through our land and away, to foreign mines and brothels and who knows what else. I want to see them all *burn*.

My breath comes in great heaving gulps, as if my lungs were bellows to fan the fire of my rage. I have already sworn to stop them, sworn it when I sat in the belly of a slave ship, my finger cut away by a thief lord, my freedom stolen with gentle words by a nobleman. But now that oath burns through me again, and I know that I will never give up this fight. Not until the Circle of Mages is brought low, and Garrin destroyed, and every last slaver clapped in irons.

Fastu stumbles. I pause, helping him to catch his balance. "You all right?" I ask, foolish, empty question that it is. He doesn't answer, and after a moment I say, "Let's keep walking. There you go, take a step. Good job."

I lead Fastu on, and with each step my rage cools and tightens within me, hard as a diamond. Nothing but death or the Darkness can take it from me, and I don't intend to let either have a chance.

I need to get Fastu taken care of, pass him into the Speaker's care here, and continue on to Lirelei as quickly as possible. I'll have to hurry if I want to have any hope of catching up with the galley before the remaining captives are transferred to a seafaring ship to be sold in other lands. I won't be able to find them once Morrel passes them on.

Eventually, as morning creeps toward noon, we reach the outskirts of a small town. A farmer's wife spots us from her garden and comes to the road, her expression shifting from curiosity to grief as she realizes what ails Fastu. She gives me directions to the temple at the center of town, and sends a child running after us with two great slices of bread a few minutes later.

I try giving Fastu's slice to him, but he only holds it forgotten in his hand. Instead, I break bites off for him and brush them against his lips, and then he eats.

The town is larger than my own village of Sheltershorn, though hardly a city. Still, the road changes from dirt to pavers, and the center of town contains a few large streets and squares. A middle-aged woman with an iron gray braid, a market basket over her arm, attaches herself to us. I shake my head at her questions, saying only that I was traveling and came across Fastu fallen in the road. I keep my left hand hidden in my skirts.

She tsks and leads us through the streets to the small, well-made temple along one of the quieter streets. It is built of yellow bricks, as are most buildings on the plains, and plastered with a smooth adobe finish. An arched outer entry provides a small roofed space to remove one's shoes, and then a proper door opens into the main sanctum.

An old man steps out to greet us, his back bent and his skin wrinkled, age spots showing dark against the gentle brown of his skin. His flowing sky-blue Speaker's robes give him an elegant look, the open front allowing a glimpse of the simple tunic and pants he wears beneath.

"Please, come inside," he says, focusing on Fastu. "He's been touched by the Darkness, hasn't he? We'll give the boy the Blessing."

I look at him sharply, his words breaking through my fury and exhaustion. "What good will the Blessing do? Can it help him?"

The Speaker glances at me, his lips pursing as he takes in my appearance. "There's nothing that can undo what has been done. However, the Darkness does not always finish its work in its first visit. The Blessing can protect him from losing what he has managed to hold on to."

"We should be quick, then," I say, my heart aching. "In case it returns."

Fastu allows his arm to be taken by the Speaker with only a slightly confused look.

"Speaker Lui, the young lady needs her hand seen to as well," the woman says firmly.

The Speaker, Lui, drops his gaze to my left hand and winces. "May I see, daughter?"

I hold my hand out. In the bright sunlight it looks even worse than it did in Captain Morrel's lamplit cabin, my whole hand inflamed, the empty knuckle showing red and black both, long streaks of red disappearing beneath the hem of my sleeve.

Lui shudders, looking suddenly nauseous. "Didn't you have the sense to say something, child? You'll need a mage to save that hand. I'll send for Mage Ehelar at once."

"No." I drop my hand, trying not to think of Niya's sash, not to look at it. Genno Stonemane is the only magic worker to have seen it before, and he knew the wards to be different at first glance—although he seemed to think that a human mage might not recognize it unless the wards were actively working. But they will work against the Darkness, whenever it might come, and I can't risk a mage discovering Niya's work. Especially not when the mages are behind the slavers. "I'll see a regular healer."

"What can you mean?" the woman protests. "A regular healer cannot do what a mage can."

"Even so," I say steadily. "Shouldn't we take care of Fastu first?"

My companions exchange a glance, and then Lui says, "Very well, we'll see to the boy and then decide."

"I've a spare room, should you need it, daughter," the woman says, nodding toward me. "My own daughter just married and moved out. It's quite livable."

It's such a country thing, her offer—a kindness proffered because you can, because that's what you do: take care of people in need, keep your community strong. I smile at her gratefully. "Thank you."

She nods and takes her leave a moment later.

CHAPTER

5

Lui leads Fastu and me across the sanctum to a doorway that opens into his own attached living quarters. There is a small kitchen space to the right along with a low table to eat at, and to the left there are a few cushions set out before a series of wall cabinets. They must house his few belongings along with his sleeping mat, put away for the day, and whatever items he keeps for the temple.

A young boy putters about the kitchen—one of a group of volunteers who share out the days of the month between them, no doubt, just as it is done at home. Together, they help with the work of the temple and assure their Speaker is cared for.

Lui seats Fastu on one of the cushions before the table, then watches with lowered brows as I limp around the table to sit opposite. Is he really only now noticing my foot?

Shaking his head, Lui moves to one of the cabinets and rejoins us a few moments later carrying a tray with a familiar set of items: a small cup with an inset stone and etched design, a velvet pouch that no doubt contains a white opal, and a small pitcher of water.

"The Blessing is quite simple on the surface," the Speaker says, setting the tray on the table. "I can explain it to you, though even I don't know all its secrets."

"I've seen it before," I say to save myself the lecture he's preparing.

"Have you?" Lui says, disgruntled.

I suspect I know more about the Blessing than he does: the opal will bring forth a person's most recent memories. The enchantment that wraps the cup is fueled by the magic stored in the inset stone; it will erase those memories at the same time that it washes away the marker that identified Fastu to the Darkness. A marker that must be in me as well, though I cannot guess how it was put there any better now than I could before.

Was it in the water we drank? I inspected the ladle and the bucket in the hold by touch, but found no sign of a stone or carvings. Nor did the bowls containing our food offer up anything but dents to my study. There was nothing else I could detect, no clue as to how we had been marked for the Darkness to find us. But I could have easily missed something in the dark.

I watch in silence as Speaker Lui presses the opal to Fastu's forehead, mouthing prayers, then helps him to drink from the cup. He is gentle and slow, and Fastu drinks obediently. The Blessing makes no difference that I can see, but then, it wasn't meant to.

Lui sets the cup down with a sigh. "I am afraid that is all I can do."

With the Blessing done, the helper boy approaches with bowls of curried spring vegetables, slices of fresh bread that were no doubt sent from a neighboring kitchen, and a plate of brown olives. It's a veritable feast. While I eat, the Speaker feeds Fastu and asks me for everything I know about him. I can't admit to being on the slave ship with him—that would imply I need the Blessing as well, and there's no way I'm parting with my memories, or telling Lui about Niya's sash.

So, I spin a story in which I was traveling downriver when I lost my boat in an accident. As I was walking the road, I saw Fastu thrown overboard from a ship—almost true—and managed to rescue him. We followed the road south, and Fastu told me about his family and home while we walked, rather than in the belly of the slave ship.

"How long did you walk?" Lui asks, forehead creased.

"Most of the morning."

"But that's—" the helper boy says and stops.

I twist to look from him to the Speaker. "That's—?"

Lui sighs. "There's another town north of here. You would not have been so far from it."

I squeeze my eyes shut. So many mistakes. Any number of small choices made differently, and Fastu would still be all right. It isn't my fault—I didn't send the Darkness after him. I didn't even involve him in what I'm doing as I did my friend Kirrana, who helped me investigate the snatchers and was violently abducted just before I was. Sweet sorrow, I wish I could find Kirrana and help her, but there's no way to do that now.

"Daughter," Lui says with unexpected kindness. He reaches out to lay a thin hand over my uninjured one where it rests on the table, his skin papery thin and surprisingly cool against mine. He pauses, looking down at my hand, then finally he says, "You did your best."

"It isn't enough," I say flatly.

"It is all we have," Lui says. "Sometimes, you do your best, and you fail. It will hurt. There is nothing I can tell you that will soothe it, but to remember that you are not alone."

I want more than to not be alone. I want Fastu whole again, and Kirrana returned, and the slavers stopped. At least one of those I can do something about. First, though, I need to make sure Fastu is cared for. "Can you return him to his family?"

"We have his parents' names, his own, their occupation, and their town. That should be more than enough to locate them. If they can't come to retrieve him themselves, the couriers will let us know and we'll put together a collection to send him home. People will usually give."

There's a relief in knowing that. I try not to think about how his parents will feel, to have their son back in body but not in mind. I hope they are like the shopkeeper I met in the king's city, who still loved her son and cared for him with a deep and steady gentleness.

"I need to continue south," I tell Lui.

"To your family?"

I think of Cari, whom I promised I would not leave. "I'll find them in Lirelei," I say. "We were separated, but I promised to follow them there."

It's not completely unheard of for young women to travel alone. Normally, though, such women wouldn't turn up at a temple hungry and disheveled, with an infected hand and in the company of a child rescued from the snatchers.

Lui purses his lips. "I think it's best if you stay here. We can send for your family." I open my mouth to object, but he *tsks* and goes on, "I understand you think you can travel safely, but look at you. You can barely walk, your hand is infected, and you likely haven't a coin to your name. You had better stay with Kelari Jerana, who brought you to me. I'm sure if you help around the house, she won't mind your company until your parents can come fetch you. If necessary, the temple can even reimburse her your board."

"I'm afraid I can't stay. I have an important matter to see to," I say coolly.

He chuckles. "Child! You can't expect me to believe such nonsense. No one would send a girl like you downriver alone in a boat on an *important matter* and expect any level of success. You won't make it to the end of the street in the state you're in, let alone to Lirelei. If this matter is so important, you can tell it to me and I'll see to it for you."

I grit my teeth, seething. There is no way this man can possibly *see to it* for me. I can walk as well as I've always been able to, and I've the money Niya hid within her stitches in my sash. I'll grant Lui the need to get my hand seen to before I travel farther, but that's all. I'm certainly not going to stay with some kindly townswoman, waiting to be rescued from the dangers of travel while the children still need my help.

"You had better take a bath while you're here," Lui suggests at my silence. "I've sent my boy on an errand. You'll have enough time to clean up while I compose a letter to your family. You can give me the directions for it once you've finished washing, and then my boy can walk you to Kelari Jerana's home. You'll be able to rest there."

I consider him. If I want to buy passage downriver with a reputable captain or fisherman, I had better not show up looking—and smelling—like a drowned rat. It's much better to just play along, and save what money I have for traveling. So, I say only, "Thank you. Perhaps I might write a letter to my uncle in Tarinon as well? He may also be in touch with my family, and might be more easily able to come after me."

"Oh, of course, that is no trouble at all," Lui says, all magnanimous generosity now that I appear to have acquiesced to his wishes.

"Thank you," I tell him, barely able to get the words out, and go to take a bath.

CHAPTER

6

Lui provides me with a kettle of hot water and two buckets of cold—plenty to mix together to scrub myself down a few times. There is also a goat-hair mitt and a square of brown soap. It is a heart-aching thing to find myself with my morning's wish granted. If only Fastu was still whole of mind and able to share in such simple pleasures.

I drop my clothes just outside the door to be given a quick wash while I take care of myself, keeping only my bone knife and my sash with me. I scrub as hard as I can with the mitt, as if I could scrub away my days in the slave ship, the fear and uncertainty, the reality of what's happened to Fastu and the choices I can't unmake.

It makes no difference, of course.

My hair is so matted around my braids that eventually I despair of working it free. My wounded hand hurts too much to be of use in combing through the knots with Lui's long-toothed comb, and I cannot manage it well with just one hand. I sit for a long moment, hair falling over my shoulders in clumps. Then I pull it together into a long, matted tail and gingerly tie it back. I don't have to solve everything right now.

I change into the spare set of men's clothes Lui has lent me and wrap a shawl over my chest for modesty's sake. After all, the tunic is designed for a slim man, and I am neither. My knife stays hidden in its calf sheath, and Niya's sash, still wet from my washing it, is wrapped beneath my borrowed tunic to keep it from view. Now I just need to send that letter and find a way to follow after Morrel's ship. I take a deep breath and open the door.

A man in dark purple mage's robes looks up from his conversation with Speaker Lui, both men seated at the table. The mage is solidly built, filling out his robes, his hair still full black and only the faintest of smile lines bracketing his mouth. He looks to be no more than a dozen years older than my own eighteen. And he's here, for me, because the Speaker sent for him after I specifically said I wouldn't see him. But then it's not as if Lui listened to anything else I said. I should have known.

"Daughter," Lui says, "this is Mage Ehelar. He has come to see to your hand."

The mage unfolds himself as I stand frozen, my thoughts racing. There's so much I don't know—about the Darkness and how often it falls, about how easily this mage might recognize the unorthodox form of the wards sewn through my sash if they are activated. But one thing is certain: mages are not to be trusted.

"It will only take a few minutes, I expect," Ehelar says, his gaze seeking out my hand. I've already hidden it behind my back.

"I'm fine," I say brightly. I transfer my gaze to Lui, where it transforms into a glower. "I told you I don't need a healer mage."

Ehelar shakes his head. "I've base training in healing, kelari. Let me see to it."

"There's no need." I cross the room to check my clothes where they hang on a drying rack by the fire.

"You'll lose your hand, child," Lui says reasonably. "You're burning up with fever."

I hesitate, remembering how he paused when he touched my hand—how cool his skin was against mine. I knew it before now as well, on the galley, but I lost track of myself. Lui is right, I do need help. But how can I accept it if that means endangering Niya? There's no way to know how often the Darkness falls, or if it will do so while the mage is here. If it does, he'll sense Niya's wards at work, and demand an explanation. By rights, he could force one from me. I could not live with myself if I betrayed her to the Circle.

"I don't require your services," I tell the mage, and reach out to check my clothes. They are still wet through. They need a brisk wind to dry, not the slow warmth of the small fire. "I can pay a healer just fine."

He looks almost relieved, as if my words have explained everything to him. "You don't have to pay me if you can't."

"Of course not, child," Lui says. "We have an agreement for the care of those who come to the temple."

Oh, blithering prairie dogs! I don't want their charity; I want away from this mage. I lift the clothes and turn, heading back to the washroom.

"Kelari," Ehelar says, his fingers brushing my elbow.

I jerk away, my heart hammering. "Don't touch me!"

"Child," Lui exclaims, sounding aggrieved. "That is no way to speak to your betters. You're acting like a feral stray rather than a well-raised girl."

"Easy, kelari," Ehelar says, standing perfectly still.

I edge away from them both, trying to tamp down on the panic roaring through me. He's not the same as the guards who snuck up on me in the palace hallways and abducted me. He's not here to hurt me.

"I mean you no harm. Let me help you with your clothes."

"I don't need help," I tell him hoarsely. What's he going to do, dry them?

"I can dry them."

I blink. "You can?"

He nods and lifts the clothes from my arms. His gaze drops to my hand and his eyes widen. For a long moment, we both remain still. Then, he gathers himself and turns away, nodding to Lui. "Could you give us a moment?"

The old man helpfully disappears into the sanctum, because *of course* he would leave a wounded girl alone with another man. Though not quite alone—Fastu still sits on his cushion, his gaze distant—but he needs help as much as I do.

Ehelar moves to the fire and spreads the tunic and skirt over the rack once more, then brushes his fingers over the fabric. Water streams out of them, puddling on the floor below.

In a matter of moments, my clothes are dry. I really ought to tell Niya about this trick.

Ehelar says carefully, "Your clothes are a cut above, aren't they? Or they were, before they became your only set. Speaker Lui called you a feral stray, but I think you're scared, not feral. You're running from someone."

I stiffen before I can catch myself. Light and shadow! I'm too tired and off-kilter to manage this conversation well. And Ehelar is far, far too perceptive.

"It's all right," he says softly.

My gaze snaps to him, and I'm stunned to see compassion in his eyes. Not pity, which I would recognize anywhere, but a mix of sorrow and care and fellow-feeling. It shocks me into silence.

"Whatever you're running from, I won't put you in danger. But please, let me help you. Just your hand. You cannot expect me to let you go, knowing you'll lose your arm, or your life, when I could have helped you."

It's something Niya would have said. It's the sort of approach my youngest sister, Bean, takes with every hurt stray she adopts.

But . . . he's a mage. It could have been *him* that brought the Darkness down on Fastu. Someone of magical talent had to send it out somehow.

"Is it a mage?" he asks, watching me keenly. "The one you're running from?"

I hesitate. I need to keep away from Garrin, from the Circle of Mages and Berenworth, but none of them know where I am. Garrin thinks I'm still being held captive, on my way to a short, painful life of slavery. I can't be certain how much the Circle or Berenworth know about me, but it will all be funneled through Garrin. The only one who could gainsay him is the captain who threw me overboard to a watery grave. No one's technically chasing me.

That doesn't mean I'm not running, or that I can afford for the mages—or anyone—to know I'm alive and free.

"No," I say finally, my voice coming out slightly hoarse. "Not a mage."

"Then you can trust me."

I can't. And yet, in the face of his palpable care, I want to believe I can.

"What can I tell you—what can I do—so you will trust me enough for this?"

I lick dry lips and ask, "Do you keep a record of whom you treat?"

"I do, but I can leave you off of it."

"Are there . . . other mages here?"

"No," he says at once. "I'm only here because my wife is from this town. It's close enough to a node that the Circle allowed me to take up residence here, seeing to the needs of the area. But what I mean is—there aren't mages traveling through here. It's too small a town."

"What's a node?"

He shrugs. "It's not something you would know." I wait, watching him, and finally he says, "It relates to the protective spells laid over the land. There are particular places—nodes—where they must be refreshed. It is my duty to see to the one here. It's nothing to do with you."

The protective spells? I grasp onto the phrase tightly. I've heard of them before, but I never wondered what exactly they entailed. They're meant to protect against curses and magical attacks. And I am relatively certain that applying them would make the perfect cover for casting the Darkness.

"Let me at least see your hand," Ehelar coaxes gently.

"If you tell me about these protections," I say, meeting his gaze evenly.

His brow furrows. "Why?"

I glance toward Fastu, then away. "Magic makes me nervous," I say finally.

"Ah." Ehelar rocks back on his heels, expression thoughtful. "I see. I can guarantee that my magic will not harm you. What else do you wish to know?"

"These protections. What do they actually protect against?"

"Foreign magics in the form of attacks, or attempts to influence our land. They're old, kelari, and hardly necessary anymore; a product of concerns over our land's sovereignty decades past."

And yet, why continue with something unless there were some benefit? Ehelar might only be following the orders he's been given, but somewhere up the line, someone sees a value in continuing this.

"How often are they cast?"

He answers with some amusement. "Quite regularly, although the rhythm of the spells doesn't directly map to a regular time of day."

"You did it already today?"

"I did, a couple of hours ago now." He glances toward the rectangle of light falling through the doorway, mapping the movement of the sun. "Two and a half, more or less. How did you know?"

I shrug. I'm breathing a little too fast again. He cast the protections about two and a half hours ago, almost precisely when Fastu fell to the Darkness. It's too unlikely to be a coincidence. I don't have *evidence*, of course, but I can't believe that the Darkness isn't wrapped up in these so-called protections.

"I don't suppose they've ever been changed?" I ask abruptly. "These protections?"

"No—not in, oh, I think the last time was about thirty-five years ago. You see, they're nothing to worry about."

According to the research I did with Kirrana, thirty-five years ago was when Berenworth first began operations in Menaiya, and the first of our children were snatched. It's still all corollary and not causal. I need someone with magical knowledge whom I can trust to verify it, but it's more than I had to go on this morning. And I can't ask another question without raising Ehelar's suspicions—I've already pushed my luck far enough.

"Kelari," Ehelar says, shifting forward, his robes swaying around him. I jerk back instinctively, barely managing to catch myself before I bolt. He's not the Black Scholar, reaching for me with a dagger in his hands any more than he was a soldier sneaking up on me a few minutes ago. I'm tired and jumpy, and he's just a . . . a well-meaning mage who unknowingly robbed Fastu of his mind.

Ehelar grimaces. "Kelari, please. I mean you no harm. Let me see your hand."

I promised him that much. And he's just told me he's the one who sends out the Darkness, whether he understands it or not. Which means, in this moment, Niya's secret should be safe.

He waits, one hand extended toward me. I force myself to hold my hand out to him, though I don't put it in his. His expression grows palpably grimmer as he takes in the damage.

"This wasn't from a boating accident, was it?" he asks quietly. "Someone did this to you."

I don't answer.

He slides his hand beneath mine, turning it. I grit my teeth and allow his examination, pretending the ripples of pain aren't really there. Are no more than what I've experienced when I've neglected my foot, although the truth of the agony slumbering in my hand is worse. Much worse.

He lifts the hem of my sleeve a bit, enough to verify the angry red lines stretching up my arm, and then he lets go. I hide my hand behind my back again, which is as childish as it is foolish, but I can't help myself. It's a weakness and I'm still a little afraid of him. I don't want him to see it, no matter if I just showed it to him.

He clears his throat. "Will you come sit at the table? It will be easiest to work there."

I nod. I've already lost my finger. If I can save my hand and keep Niya safe at the same time, then I'd be a fool not to try.

I'm trying very hard not to be a fool anymore.

CHAPTER

7

Seated across from me at the table, my hand cradled in both of his, Ehelar sends a cool wash of magic through my hand and up my arm. At once, the pain eases. I can feel my jaw aching from how tight I've been clenching it, can feel the constant low throb of my ankle. I close my eyes and breathe slowly and let him work.

Magic can encourage the body; it can be used to seal wounds shut; it can help burn an infection away or remind flesh how to knit itself together. All of which I desperately need. It can only push the body so far, however. Some things still require time and slow healing. I've no doubt my hand will require both.

Ehelar's touch is gentle as he cleanses my wound first with water and then with magic. My flesh and muscle shift as he knits them together, then the skin above them as well. Exhaustion settles on my shoulders and I shift to rest my other elbow on the tabletop, drop my head into my good hand. Even with magic prickling at me, I am tired enough to sleep here. Not that I would dare.

Still, I keep my eyes closed until he sets my hand down gently. Then I force my head up. Ehelar sits back, his expression pinched, his eyes shadowed. He was the picture of health a half hour ago.

Did healing me really take that much out of him? Lui shifts on his cushion to get a better look at my hand. He must have come back in at some point.

I glance down finally to my hand. It's still inflamed, though not as badly as before, the red diminished to pink. The wound itself, while discolored, is no longer sickening to look at. The skin has been sealed shut over my knuckle. It is stretched and shiny looking, and the scar will be a ragged one. But . . . it will heal. I can tell, just from its colors, that the worst is somehow past. I suspect my fever has broken as well.

"Thank you," I murmur.

He nods. "You should rest. I'll be back to check on you tonight."

Tonight?

"She'll be with one of the town wives," Lui volunteers in time to keep me from blurting that I won't be here at all. "Perhaps if we know when you might arrive, she can come back to meet you."

"Of course," Ehelar says, watching me intently.

I nod stiffly, wishing he were rather more arrogant and less observant. Like Lui.

Addressing me, Ehelar says, "If for some reason we miss each other, you should know that the infection may not be completely gone. If it returns, you'll do best with a mage to see to it. Although," he allows grudgingly, "a healer may be able to aid you as well."

"I understand."

"She'll be here," Lui says frowning. "If you cannot return this evening, she can come and wait for you again in the morning. It will be a few days before her family can fetch her."

I drop my eyes, hating that it's a lie I'm bearing witness to, one I agreed to earlier.

"Ah," Ehelar says, amusement and gentle disbelief wrapped up in the sound. For a moment I think he's going to tell Lui that he's wrong, that a stray won't stay when commanded, but all he does is smile blandly and shrug. "Then we've nothing to worry about."

He gets to his feet and takes his leave of us. I watch him out the door, my hand cradled in my lap. He didn't warn Lui. Even though he could see right through me where the old Speaker couldn't. It's not a kindness I have any interest in questioning.

"I'd like to write that letter to my uncle now," I say to Lui. "If it's all right."

"Of course, of course," he says. The ink pot and quill sit at the end of the table beside him. He passes them down to me along with two sheets of paper, one of which is blank. The other sports writing on one side. "Here's the letter I've written your family," he says. "You might add a note on the back if you wish."

"Thank you," I say and wait until he steps away to look into the temple. Then I take the blank paper and write as quickly as I may. But this letter isn't to my fictional uncle in the king's city; it's to my thief-friend, Bren.

For just a moment, I let myself wonder how Bren felt when he saw the box Bardok Three-Fingers sent, the box with my pinky finger in it, my grandmother's ruby ring still around it. Red Hawk wouldn't know it, but Bren would, having stolen that same ring from me once and then returned it. But will he be able to see clearly that the Black Scholar wasn't the one who cut away my finger? Or will he be so upset that he won't question Bardok's strategy— upset enough to push Red Hawk into a street war with the Black Scholar that will be the undoing of both thieving rings and anyone who gets in their way?

If there's any chance I can prevent the bloodbath Bardok Three-Fingers was hoping for, this letter will be it. Bren will also be able to get word to the princess about me without the message being intercepted by Garrin. I can only hope Alyrra may mention my safety to my cousin Melly, or send a direct note to my parents. Between assuaging my parents' fears and preventing blood in the streets, there is little choice for me now in whom I write to.

I pause, my quill hovering over the paper. Should I attempt to use some sort of code? There is a risk my letter might be intercepted by Garrin or Bardok. The thought is more than a little terrifying. But the risk is small, and I'm far enough away from them that even if they know I'm alive, they'll have as much trouble finding me as the royal family, especially now that I'm on my own. No, it's far more important that my words be understood should they actually reach their destination.

Bren. I need you to know that it was not the Black Scholar who took my finger, but someone else who is vested in both thieving rings' downfalls. They seemed to think their act would be enough to push Red Hawk to begin a street war, so I will only say this: don't allow it.

As for me, I am alive and safe and well enough to write to you. I need you to send a message to Princess Alyrra. It's vital she know that the man who betrayed me and delivered me to the snatchers was Garrin of Cenatil.

I will return to Tarinon as I am able. As for trusting that I am who I say, I will remind you of the chicken tasties we shared on a palace rooftop, and that you really ought to meet Kelari Freshna.

However embarrassing it might be to remember that, under the influence of the draught Bren's healer gave me, I suggested he marry the village shoplifter, it's a reference no one else can possibly know about. Just as only a few people in his circles—and none in mine—know that he brought the best chicken tasties in the city as a peace offering for me, arranging a predawn rooftop picnic after I punched him.

I can feel my cheeks burning at the memory. After mentioning such a moment, how do I sign off? Giving my thanks seems too cold, and the more heartfelt farewells I often use with my family seem a bit too intimate. Quickly, I scrawl, *Be safe, Rae,* and blow on the ink to dry it.

Lui's voice drifts in from the sanctum as he chats with a worshipper, the conversation low but steady. Hopefully, he'll remain busy there, though I can't trust I have very much time.

I may not have an envelope, but I know how to create a letterlock. I just need to be quick about it. I fold the letter, pressing the creases, and unfold it again. Using my knife, I cut a slit from the top of the center crease to the middle of the page, creating a long slice of attached paper, and then refold the letter once again. Then I cut a second fine slit through the pages and wrap the slice of paper left behind from the center fold around the folded missive and through the hole I made, tightening and twisting it until I've made a snug letterlock. It can't be opened without tearing the lock—Bren will know if the letter has been tampered with before it reaches him.

Finished, I address the letter to Artemian, Bren's friend, via the Tattered Crow Inn. It's the only way I can think of to get it to him safely.

Lui pauses in the connecting doorway, still looking out into the sanctum. I flip over the letter he thinks he is sending to my family and scrawl a quick message that will, no doubt, never be read by anyone related to me. I haven't even given Lui my family name, not that it would matter. He's sending the letter to Lirelei, thanks to the story I gave him, and that's nowhere near my hometown of Sheltershorn.

"All done?" Lui asks as I fold up the letter.

"Yes, thank you."

"Excellent. I'll take them to the couriers' after I've had my own lunch."

I tilt my head to hide my grimace. There's no rush for him: he knows when the couriers will depart, and that's his only concern.

But every hour I remain here, the galley continues farther down-river. I need to get to the docks as soon as possible.

"I'm feeling tired," I announce, rubbing my eyes for effect.

"I can have my boy take you to Kelari Jerana's home now, if you'd like. Or if you're too tired, you can lie down here first."

"No, no," I insist, gathering my now-dry clothes together. "I've caused you enough trouble. I'll be ready to go in a moment."

I close the washroom door and change quickly, then sit in the only relatively dry corner of the room. I run my hands over my story sash, lay it carefully over my crossed legs. There are a series of four small, embroidered circles worked into the design. When I flip the sash over, the knots for those circles are pulled through the double layer of cloth. I bite the first knot with the tips of my teeth and yank it out, thread and all. Four coppers and a silver coin clink into my lap, sliding over the fabric of my skirt.

Bless Niya and her magical stitching.

I leave the rest of the knots as they are, binding the sash around my waist once more. I was there when she sewed the coins into my sash. There will be a second silver, and enough coppers to make up most of a third. Best to leave them safely hidden till I know how much my passage downriver will cost. I don't even know how far I am from Lirelei right now.

I slip my newly freed coins into my pocket and step out again, my gaze landing on Fastu. He has barely moved, his gaze lost in the middle distance. I swallow hard.

"You'll take care of him?" I ask.

Lui looks up from the table, where he's bent over another sheet of paper, quill in hand. His expression softens. "Of course, daughter. I'm writing to his family now. I'll have my boy watch him while I take the letters to the courier office. I'll make sure he's washed and comfortable before I go. All will be well."

No, it won't, because Fastu is *gone*. But I dip my head, because Lui is also right: this is the best he can do for what is left of the boy from the hold. I will see Morrel destroyed for this, and Bardok, and Garrin too. More than that, I will see their work stopped, so no other child must suffer this fate.

Lui gestures to his helper, who returned while I was changing. The boy jumps up from where he was sitting in a corner—playing with what must be a prized set of marbles. He listens carefully to the instructions on where to take me, and then gestures me after him with a gap-toothed smile.

"Go in peace, daughter," Lui says.

"And you," I say. After all, he will take care of Fastu. I have no doubt of that. Even if he can't see me as capable—well, I did show up dirty and injured and hungry on his doorstep. But I can still fault him for assuming that my concerns didn't bear consideration, and that my current state of need is easily explained by my turned foot. As if my foot somehow makes me incapable not only of safe travel but also of being entrusted with any matter of import.

The boy leads me past the square and down one of the main streets of the town, the buildings to either side rising up in two and three floors of adobe and plaster construction, wooden ceiling beams protruding to cast familiar shadows along the walls. The walk does me good, allowing me to work through my anger and set it aside in favor of thinking of what I will do next. By the time I follow the boy through the entry of a three-story building and up a flight of stairs to a pair of doors, I have the beginnings of a plan.

"It's that one," he says, gesturing to the one on the left.

"Thank you," I say. "You can go now."

He hesitates, bobs his head, and patters off while I stand quietly before the door.

I wait until I'm sure he's gone, and then I turn and follow him down, on my way to the docks.

CHAPTER

8

Outside, a steady breeze has started up, tugging at laundry lines and bringing in the scent of fresh green things from the plains. Lui really needs to get a washing line, not that that's my concern.

I ask directions of an elderly shopkeeper, and am sent one street over, through a bustling market center that opens up to the river with its stone docks. They're relatively compact, beginning a little way upriver and continuing only a little past me. For a moment, I freeze, brought up short by the sight of the three great merchant galleys moored here, pennants flapping in the wind, and a quad of river wardens in familiar uniforms walking the docks before them. They wear the same uniforms as the wardens who attacked us on board the galley in Tarinon, just as two of the galleys fly the green and white pennants that are Berenworth's colors.

I'm shaking, my hands trembling, even though nothing's happened. *Stop imagining enemies at every step.* Perhaps they *are* enemies of a sort, but they don't know me from any other girl in this town. My focus needs to be on getting to Lirelei, not letting unspoken fears sink their claws into me.

I hold on to that thought as I start down the docks once more. With two of the galleys flying Berenworth's colors, I dare only ask about the third. Even then, as a woman alone, it would be far too easy for me to board a ship here and never be seen again. I need some surety before I board, though how I'm going to get that, I don't know.

At any rate, the deck of the galley lies relatively quiet, hardly a sailor in sight. I walk slowly along the dock trying to plan my next step. If only Lui had been willing to support my trip downriver—with the local Speaker as a guardian, of sorts, there would have been a much higher likelihood I could safely book passage, or find a trustworthy family to take me downriver in their own boat. Unfortunately, the docks end just a little farther down, without any sign of local fishing boats.

"Need any help, kelari?" a voice asks. I glance over in surprise to find a boy watching me from a few paces away. He's no more than ten years of age, all scruffy hair and grimy face and gleaming happy smile.

I find myself grinning back at him. "Do you happen to know if a galley's come through here? It's captained by a man named Morrel."

"You mean the *Blue Heron*?" The boy nods sagely. "It was here this morning. Just left an hour or two ago. Were you trying to catch it?"

"It docked here for the night, you mean?" I ask blankly. How close we had been to the opportunity for escape I'd wanted!

"That's right, kelari. Stopped to offload some cargo. Morrel never pays us boys well." The boy looks at me meaningfully.

I fish a copper from my pocket and hold it up, forcing a smile. I can't think about what's past now—it won't do me any good. The boy snatches it with smudged fingers, crowing with delight.

"Now," I say, fixing him with a stern look. "You have your coin, and welcome to it. But tell me truly, did it really only just leave?"

"Not two hours ago," he says earnestly, stuffing the coin in his pocket. "I don't think it's the boat you want, though. They don't take passengers."

"It's called the *Blue Heron*?" I watch my informant closely.

"Sure as sure it is. There isn't any other captain with a name like that coming through here. Look." He holds up his left hand, runs a finger across his knuckles. "Morrel's got a scar here, see?"

"That's him," I say, a shiver running up my skin. "I need to catch up with the *Heron*."

The boy's brow wrinkles. "You'll have to book passage with one of these ships, then," he says, waving at the galleys. "If you've the coin."

"What about this last ship here—how's that captain?"

The boy shrugs. "He's all right, but they're getting some repairs done. I don't think you'll want that one."

Which leaves me with the Berenworth galleys, which is no choice at all. "Are there any fisherfolk you would recommend I speak with?" I ask, well aware I'm grasping at straws.

"No real fisherfolk here. Sorry, kelari." His gaze flickers past me. "Ware!" he mutters and scampers away.

I glance over my shoulder just as a familiar voice says, "I should have guessed you'd befriend an actual stray."

"That," I tell Ehelar, as if I'm not at all unhappy to see him, "was a perfectly nice young boy. If you gave him odd jobs to do, he'd probably even take a liking to you."

The mage turns a thoughtful look toward the boy's disappearing form. "As you say." Then he tilts his head toward me, a faint smile touching his lips. "I wondered how long it would take you to give Lui the slip. I'm impressed, though. I didn't expect to see you for another half hour."

Indeed. "You wouldn't be the first to underestimate me."

"No. Lui certainly beat me to it."

I watch him steadily, taking note of the flash of humor in his eyes. "What are you going to do?"

"That depends on you. What are you trying to do?"

"I am traveling to Lirelei."

"Why?"

I hesitate. I'll have to go with the story I told Lui—

"Don't," Ehelar says shortly.

I raise my brows. "Don't?"

"Don't give me that nonsense you gave Lui. We've already established you're running from someone, which, I may point out, you didn't tell him at all. And that your injury was caused with intent. So, what's waiting for you in Lirelei? Or are you planning to buy passage from there and leave Menaiya altogether?"

I want to trust this man. It shocks me how much I want to be able to lean on him, tell him my truths and find an ally in him. But he's a mage, and I can't know how much he's under the Circle's control. He also won't be fobbed off with lies. That much is evident.

"Kelari?" he says, watching me keenly.

I close my eyes, take a slow breath, and then meet his gaze. "I made a promise, and I have to keep it. For that, I need to get to Lirelei as soon as possible. I cannot tell you what that promise is, only that . . . a handful of lives hang in the balance. I need to get there quickly."

He considers me steadily. "Lirelei is two or three days downriver, depending on the winds. Do you have any coin at all to book passage?"

I flush and nod. "I've a couple of silver, kel."

"One of these galleys might take you for that much. Will you have enough coin to keep you once you get there?"

I glance toward the pennants flapping in the wind. "I—is there any other option? Fisherfolk, perhaps?"

"Mostly farmers and traders here, though a few families keep boats to cross the river or go out for a little fishing along their lands."

I hesitate, but even though this man isn't my ally, that doesn't mean he can't be of aid. "I don't suppose you have any suggestions on whom I might speak with?"

He clasps his hands behind his back, considering me. "Why not book passage?"

Because the only galleys available belong to the company that arranges the flow of slaves out of the kingdom and brings in the gems the Circle of Mages requires for amulets.

"Ah," Ehelar says at my silence. "If you booked passage, you would be more easily traced."

I shrug and look away. It's a neat explanation, if untrue. "I'm also alone," I say, because I don't want everything I say to be a lie. "I'd trust a family more than I would a ship full of men."

His gaze flicks over me, pausing on what was once fine embroidery at my neck and the hems of my sleeves. Turning on his heel, he says, "Come along."

I follow after him, hope pushing me forward to catch up with him despite his longer stride. "Where are we going?"

"To find you a family with a boat. What else?"

"You're *helping* me?"

He slides me an amused look. "All I've done is help you, kelari. I don't know why it keeps coming as a shock."

"Calling me a feral stray was hardly helpful."

He casts me a reproachful look. "That was Lui, not me! I only called that boy a stray, and I've seen him enough to know."

"Manners," I say, struggling to keep up with him, "rarely go amiss."

He pauses and then shortens his stride, his gaze dropping to my feet. Satisfied I can now keep up, he says mildly, "Manners will win over that boy, you think?"

"Manners and kindness," I say, and decide an abrupt change of topic would serve me well. "Tell me about this family we're going to see."

He does, and by the time we follow the river road out of town and to the second farmhouse, I know that we're going to see a large family comprised of a grandmother, mother, father, and six children of varying ages, half of them pretty well grown, along with the eldest's wife and baby. The youngest child, though, had an accident two years ago, and Ehelar saw to his healing. The family was facing a difficult winter, and the mage refused payment. What he's doing now—bringing them a chance to earn silver while presenting it as an opportunity to repay his help—is generosity itself.

"How old were you?" I ask. "When you left your family?"

He tilts his head, brow furrowed. "I presented late, when I was twelve. My talent is not as great as many mages', though it suffices for all I've been called upon to do."

So he was raised by his own parents through his childhood. I wonder if that shaped him into the man that he is, far kinder than any mage I've heard of. Although perhaps that's untrue. The palace healer mage was brusque but vested in the patients she healed, and supported the princess's plan to open a house of healing for the poorer neighborhoods of the city.

Both of them seem innately different from the mages of the Circle, who knowingly back the enslavement of our children. And then there's the healer mage my parents sought out eighteen years ago, when I was born. They *begged* that mage to look at my foot, to use his magic to help straighten it, and he would not even see me. A few years later when my sister's talent surfaced, they knew at once they did not want her to grow into the sort of person he was.

But now, walking beside Ehelar, I wonder if maybe I've just never wanted to believe well of any mage, because then my parents' decision to hide Niya's talent would be harder to defend— even if I staunchly believe children shouldn't be taken from their families, ever, and especially not if their talent shows up when they're very young, as Niya's did when she was barely four. "Does it make a difference?" I ask. "I mean, if a talent presents earlier, is it more powerful?"

"Usually. May I ask why you're interested?"

"Oh, well." I look ahead to where the farmhouse awaits at the end of the dirt drive we've turned on to. "You're kinder than any mage I've met before."

"Talent doesn't make one unkind."

"No," I agree, and leave it at that.

The family is, as Ehelar expected, thrilled to see him, inviting us in and immediately setting food on the table and a kettle on the fire. The youngest races off to gather those working in the fields while we sit down with the mother and grandmother.

I let Ehelar do the talking. After asking about each member of the family, present and absent, he explains the reason for his visit.

"I know you've been planning a trip to Lirelei before your daughter's wedding," he says, tilting his head toward the eldest girl, Nesa by name. "I wondered if you might be able to move up your trip. Kelari Rae's errand is a matter of some urgency. I know it is still the planting season, though, and we can speak with a few other families if you cannot spare anyone to take her."

"There's no need to ask anyone else," the mother says firmly. "Nesa and I have been planning a trip, as you say. There's no harm in hurrying it along." She turns a thoughtful eye on her children, all of whom have congregated in the meantime. "With all the work we have, it had better just be you, Nesa, if that's all right? And one of your brothers to help with the boat."

"Of course," Nesa says with a quick smile for me. She's of average height, which makes her half a head shorter than me. Her thick arms and callused hands suggest she's probably as strong and capable as any of her brothers.

"I can go too," the second eldest of the boys says, a strapping young man who has *farmer* written all over his sturdy, muscled frame. The eldest sits in the corner with his baby cradled in his arms, his wife at his side.

Their mother hesitates. It will be hard for them to give up their best workers for my trip. "What about Gair?" she suggests, glancing toward the stocky young man who stands by the door, watching us quietly.

"What?" he says, darting a glance toward his mother. "Me?"

"Nesa would be with you."

His brow furrows.

"He won't even enjoy it," the second eldest mutters, loud enough for his mother to hear. "I can't believe you'd choose him."

"Gair gets along very well with Nesa," his mother says. "Which is more than can be said for you. If Gair would like to go, I think he would be the best one for it."

Her husband, quiet until now, just nods his agreement.

"Do come, Gair," Nesa wheedles. "I'd like your company in Lirelei."

"It will be loud and busy," he says, unimpressed. "You know I don't like that."

His brother rolls his eyes, earning a sharp rap on his head from his mother.

"It will," Nesa agrees. "But the trip will be lovely. We'll be on the river for *three days* each way. Surely that's worth a day in the city. And I could use your help—you're a much better judge of fabric than *him*."

Her other brother stiffens, comically affronted, but a glance from his mother keeps him quiet. Gair ponders Nesa's request and then nods stoically. "If you'd like me to come, I will."

His mother immediately begins assigning responsibilities to help get us underway as soon as possible. While Ehelar, Gair, and the father go out to inspect the boat and get it into the water, the mother oversees the packing for the trip, sending children running for what supplies we'll need. Nesa sits with quill and ink, writing down the shopping list her mother dictates.

"Kelari," I say hesitantly, as the mother bustles back into the room with a pair of empty packs. "If it isn't too much trouble, might I purchase some supplies from you?"

"Of course, dear," she says. "What do you need?"

I hesitate.

"What have you brought with—ah," she says, pausing as she realizes I have no bag at all.

"I don't have much coin past the two silvers," I say humbly. "Just a few coppers. I would like a cloak—or even an old blanket that could serve as one. And an extra pair of socks if you could spare them."

"We can certainly spare you both, and more as well," she says. "Not another word about payment. The silvers will cover it just fine."

"I don't mean to take advantage," I say, flushing. "I can pay at least a little."

She sighs. "It's not charity, child. I'm taking care of you same as I'd want another mother to take care of my own. Now, let's see what we can find in the way of clothes for you. Nesa, don't forget, you'll want cloth for a new set of sheets. A new cloak too—and *don't* let it be green again."

I follow after her gratefully, smiling as Nesa complains that green really is a *lovely* color for cloaks.

In addition to an old gray cloak and a pair of knitted socks, Nesa's mother provides me with a roomy beige tunic and a well-mended green skirt that is only a little short, as well as an old cloth satchel to store them in. Back in the main room, Nesa's mother hands me a pouch of dried fruits and nuts to keep "for later." I hold the pouch in my hand and wonder why I want to cry.

"Come along," she says and leads me over to sit by the banked fire, careful not to look at me until I've gathered my emotions once more.

An hour later, the family is ready for our departure. Their boat is a small affair with a single set of oars as well as a small, angled sail—the oars to be used when the sail is stowed away, one would assume. I'm sure there's a name for such a vessel, but I grew up on a horse farm and *boat* is good enough for me. I'm grateful, though, that the sail will allow us to move even if no one is rowing.

Ehelar comes to stand beside me as the family packs a few more supplies onto the boat. "I've been thinking," he says quietly, and pauses.

That doesn't bode well.

"You turned up here with an injury and a child who escaped the snatchers—who was, Lui said, thrown overboard."

I make a noncommittal sound.

"Now you're racing downriver as fast as you can because, as you said, you made a promise and a handful of lives hang in the balance."

This is why lies should, apparently, have nothing to do with the truth. It's also why I should maybe not tell the truth at all.

"Have you ever studied the Blessing?" I ask abruptly.

Ehelar's eyes flash with amusement. "A moment, kelari. Tell me this: do you know what ship the boy was thrown from? Are you following it now?"

My jaw hardens. "What makes you think I could possibly do anything, even if I caught up with it?"

"You've an edge to you. I think you would try. I hope you will not get yourself killed, kelari. At least go to the Port Authority in Lirelei, if you find the ship."

Only if I want to go to my funeral next. I learned that much the last time I went on board a slave galley, in company with Captain Matsin, and the river guard turned on us. But I nod in acknowledgement.

He laughs grimly. "You won't, of course, because you're still running from something as well."

He really does care, and I have a flash of empathy for him. Keeping my little sister Bean out of trouble was challenging enough; I would have had palpitations if Bean were attempting what I am now. "I'll do what I can to stay safe," I offer.

"And take care of that hand."

"That too."

He rubs his chin, then answers the question I asked to distract him. "I can't say I've studied the Blessing."

"Hmm. I wonder, how does the Darkness find the children?"

He frowns. "It's in their blood, isn't it?"

I keep my eyes on the small boat bobbing on the water, Gair opening the sail and strapping it in place. "Is it?"

"Why would you think it isn't? Better minds than mine have studied it. That's what they've found."

Greedier minds, perhaps, but I sincerely doubt they were *better*. Still, I'll be leaving in a handful of minutes, and this man isn't my ally in fighting the snatchers, nor am I going to make him such before I depart. "I'm sure you're right," I say finally. "Thank you for all your help. Truly."

"Of course, kelari. I hope . . ." He pauses, purses his lips. "Well, if you find yourself in trouble and can return here, I will do what I can to aid you."

I give him a heartfelt smile, my voice full as I repeat, "Thank you."

A few minutes later, I'm ushered onto the boat alongside Gair and Nesa, and we push off from the riverbank, heading toward Lirelei.

CHAPTER

9

B y afternoon, Nesa notes my attempts not to fall asleep while sitting on the bench and arranges a nest of blankets at the front for me, or the prow, as she calls it. I sleep through most of the day, as well as all of the night in our little camp on the riverbank.

The following morning, while Gair minds the sail, Nesa sits down behind me with comb in hand and says, "Let me see what I can do with your hair."

"It's bad," I admit.

"I can see that," she says, not unkindly. "But I like a challenge." She leans in and whispers, "I don't want you to have to cut it. Men like long hair, you know."

Not just men. My cheeks warm as I remember Bren sitting at my bedside, his long hair unbound, and my hand reaching out to play with it. Some things I should probably not think about. I ask quickly, "You're getting married soon, aren't you?"

"This fall." She tugs at a mat, working her way through it slowly, a little jar of oil beside her to help with the worst bits. "After the harvest. He's building a house for us out behind his parents' home."

"That sounds just about perfect."

"It will be. What about you? Do you have a sweetheart waiting for you?"

I stare out over the water and find myself thinking of watching the dawn come in with Bren on a palace rooftop. Which is foolishness, through and through. He only came to apologize and bid me goodbye—though he didn't quite manage to be rid of me then, either. "No one back home," I say finally, and immediately think of Niya, and Bean, and my parents. "But I miss my family very much."

"I'm sure," she says gently and doesn't press me for details.

In the afternoon I fall asleep at the prow once again, though Nesa nudges me awake to spend our final hour or so on the river working on my hair once more. We stop to make camp on the riverbank again. Between the good food my companions share with me, and the sunlight and warmth, one would think I would be perking up. I'm not.

"It's your hand," Nesa tells me when I apologize for sleeping through most of the second day. "Healing takes a lot of energy. You should rest up as much as you can."

I don't argue with her. She has wrestled the last of the mats out of my hair—having sacrificed only a very few tight knots to her knife—and braided it into a tidy plait down my back. Even my hand looks and feels much better, still healing, but no longer half as painful.

We pass through the remnants of a storm our final day, the wind whipping around and the water choppy. Gair straps away the sails, takes out the oars, and rows us easily enough, for the currents are still with us. He and Nesa switch off regularly, both of them aware of how anxious I am to reach Lirelei. Rain pelts us a few times, but it never stays long enough to make stopping necessary.

"We're lucky," Nesa tells me. "Gair thinks the storm blew itself out over Lirelei, and this is just the tail end of it."

The city reaches out to welcome us in the late afternoon. Built at the mouth of the river where it meets the sea, it curls around the sheltering bay and spreads its wealth of humanity over the plains, buildings growing up on either side of the river for a full hour before Gair guides our boat to a public dock.

Tarinon staggered me with its enormous population closed within its walls. Lirelei, unbound and spilling across the plains, is like the king's city let loose upon the earth. Far on the south side of the river, I can make out a higher structure built on the slight rise there—the old city, Nesa tells me, with its high walls and watchtowers. It looks like no more than a small patch surrounded by a sea of buildings. I cannot quite comprehend the number of people that must live here.

As Nesa finishes paying the dockworker for a night's mooring, Gair methodically tidies the boat. The docks here are busy with travelers and sellers of all sorts, including a few boats selling fried fish to passersby. Everything smells unpleasantly of fish and salt.

I settle my satchel's strap over my shoulder.

"You know where you're going from here?" Nesa asks, turning to me.

"To the main docks along the bay." Per her description, both the river galleys and the seafaring ships will be moored there.

She clears her throat, glances from her brother to me. "If you need to come back up with us, you can, no charge. We'll do our shopping today and tomorrow morning, and leave by afternoon."

"Thank you," I say, and mean it. Not that I plan to need her help, but I'm grateful for the offer. I hand her the rest of the promised payment, which leaves me with only a handful of coppers and a plan that is more hope than anything: find out where the *Blue Heron* is, and then decide just how I'm getting to the children.

Gair helps me out of the boat, steadying me as I step up onto the wooden dock with my good foot.

Nesa hops up beside me and embraces me lightly. "Be safe, all right?"

"I'll try," I tell her. "You both take care."

"You take care too," Gair says gruffly. He keeps his gaze focused downward on the boat, away from the rush and bustle of the docks.

I traverse the weathered boards to the road running alongside the river. A great bridge soars over the flowing waters where the river pours into the bay, allowing passage to the galleys below and an easy connection between both sides of the city. Brightly decorated wagons offer pedestrians a quick ride across at an affordable price. There are passenger ferries as well, steadily making the crossing.

The young woman I stop for directions tells me the northern docks across the bridge are where the passenger boats are moored. What I'm looking for is straight before me: the southern docks are reserved for the merchant galleys—first the river galleys, and then, past them, the seafaring galleys.

I doubt I would recognize the *Blue Heron* on sight—I spent most of my time in the hold and never saw it from the front. So, as I walk the dock inspecting each galley for a heron on the prow, I also look for people to ask. There's an old woman selling fried flatbreads stuffed with spiced potato, but she knows nothing of the *Heron* and waves me away when she realizes I'm not a paying customer.

A pair of sailors squat with their backs against a low dividing wall, separating the docks proper from the wide avenue that runs alongside it. I try them next.

"Haven't seen the *Heron*," says the first, glancing toward his mate, a lanky man whose hair falls in rattails down his back.

"It's out in the bay," the man says, pointing, "waiting to dock."

Hope flashes through me as I crane my head to catch a glimpse of the three or four galleys bobbing farther out in the bay. "Has it been delayed?"

He jerks his chin upward in affirmation. "More than a few galleys decided to stay docked until that storm passed through. Everything got slowed down, including the loading. The Port Authority's stretched thin trying to review everything and approve departures. There should be space for the *Heron* by tomorrow, if not tonight. You waiting for a delivery?"

"Something like that."

"The sailors'll be coming ashore by rowboat in shifts, since they don't need a full crew just sitting out there. If it's urgent, you can ask for your delivery to be sent with the next shift."

"Thank you," I tell the sailor. He bobs his head in return. They expect me to move on now, and really I should. But I hesitate. I need all the information I can get. "I—I don't mean to pry, but do you know if the captain of the *Heron* is . . . the reliable sort?"

The sailors eye me askance. "Well, he *is* the captain of a ship," the first points out.

"I know," I say, keeping my gaze on the lanky man with the rattails. "I just mean, I'm a woman alone. I don't know the captain or the crew. Would you send your sister alone onto the *Heron?*"

He laughs. "I would send my sister alone with a dragon grown; she'd cut up anyone who looked at her the wrong way."

I grin. "I wish I had your sister with me." Or my own sisters, truth be told.

The rattailed sailor tilts his head in agreement. "I've heard nothing right nor wrong about Morrel other than that he came into his first galley a bit sideways. He's been steady since, and bought the *Heron* honest-like. I don't see any reason to warn you off."

"What do you mean sideways?"

He shrugs. "Not sure how much truth there is to that story."

His companion grimaces. "Quite a bit. Had a friend who was second mate on that galley before Morrel came on."

"What's the story?" I press.

"There was a small galley by the name of the *Siren*," the first sailor tells me. "She's been retired now, but at the time, her captain took an injury, so he entrusted the *Siren* to his good friend Morrel while he was recovering. When he came back for her, Morrel had changed out most of the crew and wouldn't give it up."

He stole the *galley itself?* "Surely the courts would have sided with the true captain?"

The sailor shrugs. "I heard the judge ruled in favor of Morrel and two weeks later had himself a nice new carriage. Could just be a coincidence, but all of us out here know who the *Siren* really belonged to. But I'll tell you what, kelari, that was seven years ago. Since then, I haven't seen anything concerning about Morrel. So, if all you're worried about is sending a package with him or getting something delivered to you, I wouldn't be concerned."

"Just don't you go out to the *Heron* yourself," the rattailed sailor cautions me. "No need to court trouble. Send word with a sailor for a copper or two, or wait till the *Heron* docks and send an errand boy up to fetch the captain."

"Thank you." I dip them a slight curtsy, bringing grins to their faces, and continue down the docks. It's helpful but not all that useful to know that Morrel has always been untrustworthy. There's nothing that I can build on to get the Port Authority to help me. They won't want to search his hold if I just burst in talking about children being snatched. More likely, I'll end up dead, the fate that nearly befell Captain Matsin's quad and myself when we boarded a galley in Tarinon searching for Kirrana.

I take a slow breath, thinking of her. She could be here, somewhere among these ships, and I would never know it. She could be already gone, sent across the seas. There's no way for me to trace her on my own, no way to help her. But I can help the children on the *Heron*. That's what I must focus on now.

Toward the last of the galleys, I ask another sailor the same set of questions. He hasn't seen the *Heron* out in the bay, and so knows nothing of its arrival, but he assures me that whatever Morrel's history, the captain runs a tight ship and he doesn't know of any complaints.

As I'm turning away from him, he says, "You aren't that girl, are you?"

I look back at him, bewildered.

"The one on all the flyers," he clarifies, pointing toward a post upon which myriad papers are affixed. "Got put up this morning."

I walk over to the post, the sailor trailing me, and find myself staring at a relatively good likeness of my own face stamped onto each of three *MISSING* notices scattered over the post, overlaying other papers. Beneath my likeness is a quick description of me, including the half-healed scar on my left arm and my turned foot. And an offer of fifty gold coins for my safe return to the palace. Stamped at the bottom is Verin Melkior's official seal as lord high marshal of the realm.

I stare at the notice, hope stuttering in my heart. I could turn myself in, get safely back to the palace—and by then the children will be lost. I already know that. But surely there's *some* way I can use this?

"Is it you?" the sailor asks. "You've the foot and everything."

"She looks like she could be my sister," I say, since there's not really any arguing it. "But I'm a country girl, not some palace lady. I bet she has all ten of her fingers too. What do you think happened to her?"

He shakes his head. "I don't know, but fifty gold pieces for her return is quite a bounty, don't you think?"

"She must be important." I shift, offer the sailor a smile. "I'm sorry to disappoint you, but if I tried for it, I'm pretty sure we'd both land in trouble right quick."

He laughs. "That's fine, then. Knew it was too good to be true."

My whole body tingles with nerves. How quickly Alyrra must have had to move to have those signs made and posted all the way down the river. I scan the post again and pause, reaching up to lift the edge of a different flyer from the half-covered paper beneath. *REWARD*, the paper reads. *Wanted Dead or Alive.*

"Oh, that's that thief Red Hawk," the sailor says. "They always use the same stamp for him, since no one knows what he looks like."

I stare at the image of a cloaked figure with a hawk drawn over its hood, all stamped in red ink.

"See that," the sailor goes on with some amusement, pointing at the description with one stubby finger. "Medium height, long hair, may or may not wear an earring. If that isn't half the men *and* women in this kingdom!"

It's a bit absurd as descriptions go, but what my eyes have caught on is the list of his crimes.

The repeated robbing of noble lords and their households.
The torture and killing of fifteen men in the last year.
The disappearance and suspected death of ten more men.
The flaunting of the king's law in the king's own city.
The ongoing robbing and destruction of private properties.

I know Red Hawk robbed a good number of noble households over the princess's wedding—Bren told me of those plans beforehand, and I heard the reports after. But the murder of *fifteen men*? Their torture? And nearly that many more disappeared and most likely killed, as the Black Scholar intended to do with me?

"Did he really do all those things?" I ask faintly.

"Oh, I expect he's done a sight more," the sailor says. "They just can't prove it—or he hasn't claimed it."

"Oh." I clear my throat. "Well, thank you for all your help."

He nods and I make myself continue on my way, walking back toward the river. I always knew Red Hawk would be just as cutthroat as the Black Scholar or Bardok. He'd have to be, to become a thief lord. Worse, Bren would surely have been involved in some of those murders and disappearances, not to mention the thefts. He's Red Hawk's second-in-command, as he's told me repeatedly. It's a thought that leaves me slightly dizzy. I can't afford this kind of distraction.

At the next signpost, I tug free one of the flyers with my face and tuck it into my satchel. I came here with hardly a plan, hoping I could find some information to use against Morrel. Something unrelated to the snatchers that I could twist to my own purposes to have the boat searched or impounded—just long enough to bring the royal family's attention to it. All I've found is seven years of quiet since Morrel stole his first ship from its true owner—and nothing I can do about that.

By tomorrow, the *Heron* will be docked. I'll have to either act today, or as soon as the galley docks tomorrow. Once the *Heron* begins unloading, there's too high a chance the children will be moved without my knowledge. For even a hope of success, I need allies and a plan. I touch a hand to my satchel, thinking hard. Between my travel companions and the flyer, it might be possible.

I start back toward the public docks, working through my options as I walk. I will be no good to the children if I get taken prisoner, nor can I end the snatchers themselves if I'm dead. If I make this attempt, knowing the Port Authority could turn on me as easily as the river guard did in Tarinon, then I'd better be wise about it.

After all, this time I don't have a thief waiting in the background to jump to my aid.

CHAPTER

10

T he Port Authority is housed in a three-story building, the adobe walls painted a bright white with wide blue stripes at eye level. The engraved, iron-bound wooden double doors stand open to the beautiful spring weather, as do the shutters to all the windows. There are no balconies here, but the shutters are carved and the building as a whole is both utilitarian and lovely.

"You're really the woman on the flyer?" Nesa asks for the fourth time. Beside her, Gair stands with his big shoulders hunched. He holds a short length of silky ribbon, running it steadily between his pointer and middle finger. It seems to keep him focused.

"I'm her," I assure Nesa. "You know what to do when we go in—and after, right?"

She nods. "Mage Ehelar told us you were dealing with some trouble and you might need help. You can depend on us."

He also told me to go the Port Authority if I needed help, which is assuredly the most dangerous thing I've done yet. So I suppose it evens out.

I grip my skirts with my good hand, already missing the strap of my satchel. I've left it behind at the boat along with my change of clothes and spare socks—everything except for my bone knife strapped to my calf, and my cloak. I needed the hood to help hide my face around town.

I take a steadying breath. My stomach feels queasy, and I almost wish I hadn't eaten with Nesa and Gair as we discussed my plan. But I need to keep up my energy, and I can't know how this will play out. It's already getting late—it took nearly two hours to find Nesa and Gair on the busy market streets, and a little time after that to explain what I could of my situation and solicit their aid. I can't just stand here dithering as the day slips away.

"Let's go, then." I limp through the open gate in the low wall that bounds the building. Nesa and Gair fall into step on either side of me. Gair slips his hand into his pocket, hiding his ribbon.

The front courtyard is tiled in a spreading geometric design that brings to mind the waves of the sea. Benches line the space, though most are empty now. We continue through the wooden doors. The front room takes up the full width of the building. There are cushions on the floor lining the walls and even a few small tables, some of which hold tea trays. There are no rugs here, probably because sailors tend to track in dirt and mud. The floors are sparkling clean, though. An older woman scrubs one corner of the room, the cushions moved away for her to work.

We cross to stand in line behind an elderly gentleman who's arguing with one of the clerks at the front counter. There are three other clerks, but they're all busy, and this line is the shortest. We wait patiently until the man before us concludes his business. Then Nesa steps forward, pulls the folded flier from her pocket, and spreads it open for the clerk. "We're here about the missing woman," she says, and nods toward me with a grin.

The clerk looks from the flier to me and back again, his eyes widening. "That's—"

"Yes," I agree. "That's me. I need to speak to your superior at once, and these good folk have earned the proffered reward."

"Ah," the clerk says, still staring. He pushes himself from his stool. "If you'll just wait a moment, I'll speak with Kel Efrun. I'm sure he'll see you."

Grasping the flier, he hurries along the back of the counter to the hallway. Nesa and Gair exchange a bright look; I expect this feels like an adventure to them.

The clerk returns barely two minutes later in company with a middle-aged man—no doubt Kel Efrun, the head of the Port Authority. He is only slightly taller than me, sturdily built, with wide jowls and a trimmed, graying beard. He wears a formal-looking vest over his tunic, the buttons done up and a small gold pin over his breast—his mark of rank.

He glances down to the creased flier in his hand, and then back up at me. "Kelari Amraeya?"

"I would be grateful for an opportunity to speak with you, kel," I say steadily.

"Of course." Efrun tries to peer over the counter at my feet, hidden by the fall of my skirts. I wait as he pulls his gaze back up. "Why don't you all come to my office with me?"

We follow him through the back hallway to a wide stairway to the second floor, Efrun positively beaming as he notices my gait.

"Oh," I say, coming to a stop at the first step. "I'm afraid I cannot do the stairs just now, kel. My foot, you understand."

Efrun pauses three steps up and turns back. "Of course, kelari. Forgive me, I should have asked."

Considering how pleased he looked at the sight of my limp, he really should have. Even if I am using my foot as an excuse.

In truth, it's so rare my foot presents an advantage, I'm hard pressed not to grin as Efrun leads us back down the hallway to a room spread with worn carpets and old cushions: a gathering place for the Port Authority workers who don't have their own offices, if I'm not mistaken. There are a few small wooden crates set out as makeshift tables for tea or—on one—a half-finished game of anek, a strategy game I played incessantly with Niya growing up. Best of all, there's a window opening into a side alley.

"Please," Efrun says, gesturing us to the cushions. We sit together, Nesa to my right, Gair on the other side of her.

Efrun settles opposite us, shifting uncomfortably on the lumpy cushions.

He lays the flier down beside him and says, somewhat awkwardly, "I don't mean to question your identity, kelari, but it says here you have a scar on your arm."

He glances at my hands, his eyes bulging slightly as he spots my missing finger, which is distinctly not mentioned on the flier.

"Yes," I assure him and lift the hem of that sleeve, tugging it up to reveal the shiny new scar I got from the Black Scholar roughly two weeks ago. It curves its way from the inside of my arm up past the hem of my sleeve, almost to my elbow. The only reason it doesn't hurt as it should is because the palace healer mage was able to help speed my recovery along.

"Ah, yes, I see," he says. "Forgive me for asking, it's just that I must verify your identity."

"I understand."

"There are also a pair of questions that were provided. I'm sure you won't mind answering them?"

"Of course not."

He fishes a small envelope from his pocket and pulls forth from it a fold of paper. "Your cousin's name in the palace, kelari?"

"Veria Ramella, though I call her Melly," I say.

"Yes, quite," he says, nodding. "The horse you rode in the king's city?"

Really? I suppose that is a small enough detail it wouldn't be widely known. "Moonflower," I say, naming the ornery, bad-tempered horse I'd had the honor to keep company with thanks in large part to Melly's husband, Filadon.

Efrun looks pleased indeed. "Thank you, kelari! I am glad you've come to us. We'll see you safely returned to the palace."

"That is excellent news," I allow. "But first, will you see to my companions' reward? They have helped me immensely, and I wish them properly repaid for their kindness."

Efrun hesitates. "Ah, that I expect we'll have to send on to the young people." He nods toward Gair. "It will be disbursed directly by the crown."

There is *no way* I am telling Efrun how to find Nesa and her family. If things go sideways, they need to be able to disappear as easily as I intend to. "Oh no," I say as Gair hesitates. "They will not admit it, kel, but they lost their boat in aiding me. They'll be stranded here until they receive at least some part of the reward. I'm sure the Port Authority has the ability to pay out at least a portion of it?"

I turn to Nesa. "Perhaps if you accepted thirty gold coins in lieu of the full fifty? That would allow you to get back to your family."

"Oh yes, kel," Nesa says, clasping her hands together. "If there is a way—my mother is ill and we need to get back to her as soon as possible. We could come back again for the rest, in a month or so."

"I'm sorry to hear that. I might be able to advance you the thirty gold, given the circumstances. I do hope your mother is able to recover," he says, his bearing almost fatherly. I'm not sure what it says about my time working with thieves and courtiers that I know he's planning to line his own pocket with the remaining twenty coins, no matter how concerned and sympathetic he seems.

Gair nods, his gaze focused steadily on Efrun's chest. "Thank you, kel."

"Excellent," Efrun says. "I'll be back shortly with your reward."

Once the door is closed, Nesa lets out a great sigh. "That went well, didn't it?"

I nod, though relief seems a bit premature. "You'll stay close?" I ask.

Her eyes flick to the window. "We'll settle down at the end of the alleyway, just around the corner. We have your letter as well."

"Thank you. I know this is a lot to ask."

"We girls have to stick together," Nesa says. "Mama always says that."

"My mama would agree," I say with a grin.

I'm also glad for at least a part of the reward to go to them. Thirty gold will be enough to cover the costs of Nesa's wedding as well as buy them some additional livestock. It will certainly assure that they don't have another hard year like they did two years back, when Ehelar offered his aid. At least not for the foreseeable future.

Efrun returns a few minutes later with a sturdy leather pouch. "I'm afraid we've only twenty-five gold available, kel," he says with a nod to Gair. "Will it suffice?"

I grit my teeth. Given the import duties collected by the Port Authority on a daily basis, I sincerely doubt his claim.

Gair reaches forward and takes the purse, his movements slightly jerky. "Yes," he says, slipping it into his pocket. "Thank you."

Nesa nods. "We should be able to commission a new boat with that, and get home as well. It is much appreciated, kel."

She turns to me. "We've that letter you wrote," she says while Efrun listens. "We'll deliver it to the couriers as you asked."

"Thank you, for everything." I clasp her hands and kiss the air by her cheeks in the way of old friends.

Gair takes his leave with a bob of his head.

"Now," Efrun says once my companions have disappeared down the hall, "I will arrange with the couriers for your passage back to the palace as quickly as possible. I suspect you'll need to spend the night in Lirelei, though. Perhaps you would consider becoming the guest of my wife and me?"

He must count it just payment for the twenty-five gold he intends to pocket. "I would be honored, kel. However, first I need to speak with you about another matter. As you know, I was abducted from the palace. I believe that the royal family would reward you generously if you were able to hand over my attackers. Even if they do not, I know my family will." He already knows from his questions that I have a noblewoman as a cousin; that should convince him of the wealth that might come his way.

His iron gray brows shoot up. "They can still be caught?"

"I believe so."

"If it can be done, it will," he says readily. "I only have authority over the port itself, but I can easily arrange the cooperation of the city guard if needed."

"I believe it will fall under your purview," I say, and he smiles. I can almost see him counting the gold that will come to him for performing this service—and he won't even have to lift a hand, just give the order.

"Tell me what you can of them, kelari, and I will see to it."

I almost believe him, and he certainly seems focused and concerned as I describe being delivered blindfolded to a merchant galley, and being held in a tiny, dark room in its hold. I don't mention the other children being held with me, only my interview with the ship's captain. But when I finally say Morrel's name, Efrun's eyes flicker, his shoulders stiffening. It's not much of a change, barely visible, but I've grown better at reading people since I first went to the palace, and I don't miss the slight tension that creeps into him.

So, he knows or suspects Morrel is involved with the snatchers, and that I might have been abducted for deeper reasons than some unsavory political intrigue.

"The *Heron* is still anchored in the bay," I tell him, because I can't help myself. I've told him so much already; I might as well make the final argument. "It will be easy work to arrest and detain the crew. If you search the hold, you will find the room where I was held prisoner. I will be happy to help you locate it. Perhaps you'll even find evidence of Morrel's duplicity in his log."

Efrun clasps his hands over his vest, his expression distant as he considers his options. It's a far cry from the immediate interest with which he asked me how to locate my abductors. Then he nods once, decisively. "I thank you for putting your trust in us, kelari. The *Heron* is, as you say, at anchor in the bay. It should be easy enough to locate Captain Morrel and take him into custody this evening. I will bring him here for questioning, and so that you can identify him for us."

I want to believe him so much. I want to believe that the flicker in his eyes was just a realization he was going to have to do something he didn't want to, and not a harbinger of betrayal. But I've seen enough duplicity not to let myself be tricked.

"Thank you," I say with false sincerity.

Efrun rises, assuring me he'll have refreshments sent in, and begs me to remain safe and quiet. "It is best if you stay here until we sort this matter out. I'll post a young man at the door. If you need any help, just tell him what you require."

"Of course," I say. This means that only a couple of people will know I'm here at all—if that many. Perhaps only the front desk clerk will remember me, and he will be heading home for the night shortly.

Still, I chose this risk. As long as there's a hope of it working out, I can't walk away from it.

As soon as Efrun departs, I unstrap my calf sheath and slip it into my pocket instead. A wave of dizziness passes over me as I remember struggling to reach the knife at my calf while Bardok pinned my arm against a bench and sliced my finger from my hand. I won't be caught like that again. I wrap my good hand around the hilt in my pocket, the onyx and mother-of-pearl inlay cool against my fingers. I can reach the knife easily enough in my pocket, and a quick test proves how smoothly it can slip free of its sheath.

At a light tap on the door, I look up, giving my knife a quick shove so that it doesn't peek out of my pocket. The fabric around it bulges slightly, but it doesn't show.

A young guard in an armored leather vest steps in bearing a tea tray complete with a steaming pot and a plate of biscuits, none of which I trust enough to taste. He sets the tray on one of the crates by the cushions, dips his head to me, and departs. I pause, listening carefully, but can detect no sound of his boots continuing down the hall. He is my guard, then, as well.

I rise and cross to the window. It looks out into a relatively wide alley, paved and clean, and not particularly busy now, as the day winds down. I lean my elbows on the windowsill and glance casually to the left, to where it opens onto the waterfront. Then I glance to the right, where the alley continues past the building into a warren of tighter streets. Nesa and Gair wait at the end. As I sight them, Nesa waves and then they move on, disappearing around the corner where they'll wait for me.

It's a risk to have involved them, but if I am to survive at all, I need an ally in this. I've done my best to protect them in turn, but if they come to any harm trying to help me, it will still be my fault. I can only hope that I won't end up repaying their kindness with violence.

CHAPTER

11

Some time later, I rise and tap lightly on the door.

"Kelari?" the guard on the other side asks, opening the door himself. I'm glad to note it wasn't locked. The window is probably still my best escape route, should things go sideways, which would be the main reason I refused to attempt the stairs.

"It's starting to get dark. May I have a lamp?" I ask.

"Of course, kelari." He's tall and slim, and while he's young, his eyes have a certain coldness to them that I don't like at all. He swings the door shut and hurries away. From the sound of it, he goes no more than a doorway or two down the hall before pausing and returning. Another moment passes in which I imagine him lighting the lamp before he taps at the door and hands it through to me.

He's taking his job very seriously, and I'm not sure that's a good thing. It feels more like Efrun has chosen the perfect guard to keep me prisoner rather than assure my safety.

I carry the lamp to my crate beside the window and settle myself once more, taking the time to massage my foot and then stretch my whole body. The longer it takes Efrun, the more certain I am that he's listening to Morrel and coming up with his own plan. They'd have to be incredibly bold—or stupid—to cause me harm, knowing Nesa and Gair are witnesses. But Morrel might just be dangerous enough to try it. Still, as long as there's a chance I can help the children, I won't leave.

As the evening dusk deepens, I hear the faint sound of footsteps from the hallway. I rise to face the door, pressing my hips against the windowsill. There's the faint murmur of voices outside the door. I take a moment to smooth my hand over my braid, check my knife in my pocket.

A quick knock sounds on the door and then it swings open to allow Efrun entry. His gaze fastens on me at once, and he dips his head in greeting, but there's nothing friendly in his face. Rather, there's a tightness about his eyes that doesn't bode well.

He steps aside, allowing Captain Morrel to enter behind him. My heart skips a beat as I meet his startled gaze. At least I knew he might come; I was prepared for him. He didn't truly believe it might be me.

"You—" he snarls and catches himself.

"Captain." I risk a glance at Efrun. *Please don't let this play out this way.* I don't want it to—I want so much for things to go differently— but I knew there was every chance this would happen. Now, Efrun only moves to shut the door.

Morrel takes a step forward, eyes running over me, taking in my new clothing, pausing on my hand with its much-improved wound, dropping to my turned foot, before flicking back up to fix on my face. "How are you here?"

I force a smile. "Did you really think I would be that easy to kill?"

"Everybody drowns."

"I didn't."

Efrun clears his throat and asks, "Is this the man who aided in your abduction, kelari?"

Surely that much is obvious?

"Yes, kel," I say. "That's him. He took me onto his ship knowing full well what he was doing, and kept me imprisoned in a secret room in his hold. As you heard him confess just now, he also attempted to kill me."

"The girl is clearly unhinged," Morrel says blandly. "I've met her before. There's no possibility she is who she claims to be."

"My identity has already been verified. Though I'm sure the royal family will be very interested to hear your protestations. Kel Efrun, there is no question that this is indeed the man who called himself Captain Morrel and imprisoned me on his ship. Will you arrest him?"

Efrun leans against the edge of the desk, arms crossed and brow furrowed in thought. I can almost see his mind whirring through his options, trying to find the one that will enrich him the most. "Neither of your stories make much sense to me."

"What do you not understand?" I ask.

"You claim that Captain Morrel attempted to drown you—why would he go through the trouble of imprisoning you only to decide to kill you later?"

"I was a troublesome prisoner. Kel, if you are not going to detain him and turn him over to the royal family, then I will remove myself and make my own way to them."

Morrel chuckles. The sound raises the fine hairs on my arms. I slip my hand into my pocket, holding tight to the hilt of my knife.

"Oh no, no," he says, as if I've said something endearingly silly. "I don't think you'll find a way past us to the door, birdie." And then, louder. "Take her."

Movement flashes in my peripheral vision. I turn just as the guard from this afternoon hops over the windowsill from the alley and launches himself at me. I stumble away from him, pulling my knife free.

He grabs my left arm, wrenching me around. Pain shrieks through my wounded hand, echoed faintly by the still-healing cut running up my arm. A cry catches in my throat, and I flail at him with the knife, but I'm off balance and he's armored. The knife glances off his chest. He grunts and twists my arm.

My breath rips out of me in an exhale that is half-scream, my vision contracting. My knees slam into the ground, my arm behind me. I gasp for breath as the world slows again. The guard braces himself behind me, the pressure on my arm and the attendant pain keeping me on my knees. I've still got my knife, but the guard is holding me from a full arm's length away— I can't reach him, certainly not with enough force to cut through his armor.

The other two men have not moved. Morrel watches with amusement, while Efrun glances toward the door as if worried some late-night worker might hear us.

Betrayal leaves a bitter note on my tongue, mixed with the sour taste of my own foolishness. I *knew* this was a risk. I should have gone out the window the moment Morrel started asking me about my survival and Efrun did nothing. I clench my hand around the hilt of my knife. If one of them tries to take it from me, that will be another chance to use it.

Morrel opens the door and leans down to pick something up: a bucket. He turns to me. "The funny thing about drowning is that you don't need very much water at all. A man can drown in a hand's breadth of water, given the right circumstances."

My breath comes in sharp, painful pants as I watch him. *Think.* The soldier is wearing light armor, but his arms are unprotected, as is his neck. The window is no more than two paces behind us. There are more than a few ways this can go; I just have to find the one that will work for me.

Morrel places the bucket in front of me and steps back again. It is only half-filled, but it will be enough to spell my death.

"I'll have that payment you promised," Efrun says as Morrel goes to lean against the door. "Before we go any further."

"Certainly." Morrel takes a pouch from his pocket and tosses it to Efrun, who fumbles for it, barely catching it. "I'm sure her body will be worth some portion of the reward. That will cover the rest and more."

"Efrun, don't make this mistake," I say, keeping my voice firm, unafraid, even as I'm trembling in the guard's hold. "You know I was delivered here by two helpers. You know they have a letter of mine that will be sent to the royal palace. That letter has your name in it. You won't get away with this."

"Drown her," Morrel says coldly.

"*Hold,*" Efrun cries as the guard places his other hand on my back. The guard hesitates.

"It's a bluff," Morrel says impatiently.

"It isn't," Efrun snaps. "They mentioned the letter in front of me. If it names me—"

"Then find the fools that have it and kill them as well," Morrel says. "You do know where to find them, don't you?"

"I—no." Efrun grimaces. He really isn't cut out for a life of crime. "They left here an hour or more ago."

Morrel swears softly. "Then we find them. Tell your man to drown the girl, and then we'll figure out how to intercept that letter. It's being sent by courier, isn't it?"

Efrun nods. "Yes, that's right."

"Good. Finish the girl and go meet with the head of the couriers."

"But—he won't just *give* it to me."

"Do I have to do everything for you?" Morrel snarls. He gestures toward me. "Drown her. I will see to the rest. Or do you think you can betray us and not pay a price?"

I meet Efrun's gaze. "The royal family will come for you."

He swallows hard, glances toward Morrel, who might just come for him right now, and says, "Do it."

The guard shoves me down. The water closes over my face. I jerk, trying to get my head back above the water. My left arm screams in agony as the soldier bears down on it, and I lose the air in my lungs in a stream of bubbles.

Deep within my mind, an ember brightens into a spark and begins to burn, scorching my thoughts. The sorceress's name. No, no, *no*, I don't need that now. I don't need to be indebted to her yet again for my life. I will do this myself.

I push up *hard*, using all the strength I've built over a lifetime of working on a horse farm, powered further by pure panic. My head clears the bucket and I take a gasping breath as the soldier stumbles. Then he leans onto my back, bending his arms and using his whole body to shove my head back down.

Water splashes my face. I bring my knife up, bending my elbow and stabbing it backward over my shoulder. The knife sinks into something thick.

The guard gives an agonized scream, falling back. The knife jerks in my hand as it pulls free. I whip my head up, out of the bucket.

My breath burns back into my lungs. I shove the bucket hard with my newly free arm, sending a wash of water across the floor to darken the carpets. Try to drown me in *that*.

The guard falls back, his hands pressed over a gaping cut at the base of his neck, blood pulsing from the wound to coat his arms, the leather of his armor.

Efrun hurries toward me, panic on his wide, whiskered face. "No," he cries, just as Morrel snaps, "Get her!"

I don't have time to think. I stagger to my feet, still gasping for air, and throw myself past the fallen guard toward the window.

I reach the windowsill just as Efrun's hand catches the back of my tunic, fisting into it. Outside, Nesa and Gair pound into sight, but they're still too far. I twist, trying to break Efrun's hold. His other hand reaches for my wrist. I can't let him take the knife from me. I pivot, fabric tearing as I piston my hand out in a punch, my fingers fisted around the knife. I catch Efrun in the chest. He grunts, grabbing my arm instead, and I turn my hand. The blade slices through his vest as it slides over his ribs—and then plunges in, as if drawn to the space between.

He screams. I rip the knife free from between his ribs, but he's still holding me. I slam the knife back, this time into his stomach, where there are no bones to stop me. It comes out again with a terrible sort of sucking sound. Efrun lets go of me to stumble backward into Morrel, who has charged in behind him, a dagger in his hands and fury in his eyes.

I throw myself at the windowsill, one hand still fisted around the knife hilt. Nesa grabs me by my injured arm, yanking me over and out. I slam to the dirt on my knees, a pained scream lodged in my throat.

Morrel shouts, lunging forward, and then Gair steps over me, his arms moving. A cracked wooden oar swings through the air, catching Morrel in the chest. It slams him backward into the room, the pole splintering with the impact.

Gair drops it and turns to us, his eyes wide.

"Run," Nesa says, steadying me as I clamber to my feet. "Gair, come on!"

Overhead, something white wings by, skimming along the rooftops. We pound down the alley after it and turn the corner onto a slightly wider, paved street that is, thankfully, deserted. Gair pushes ahead, but Nesa slows her steps to match mine. I stare past her, at the great white owl soaring ahead.

"What happened?" Nesa demands. She's wide-eyed and terrified, her gaze flicking again and again to my right hand, still wrapped tight around the hilt of my bloodied knife. "Did you kill someone?"

"He was trying to kill me," I gasp out, tracking the owl as it turns onto an intersecting street. "I thought they would—I thought I could get away."

"But *why?*"

"The captain—he's a snatcher," I manage, fighting the roiling acid in my stomach. "He paid Efrun to kill me."

"Dear God," Nesa gasps between breaths.

"Turn right," I call ahead to Gair, and he does, swerving into the connecting street after the owl, and then slowing to let us catch up.

I can hear distant shouts carrying through the alleyways. I've no doubt they'll gain on us. Efrun may have waited until the workers went home for the day, but either he or Morrel made sure there were fighting men available nearby. I would put every last copper I own on it being Morrel.

The owl has alighted on a balcony railing. As I turn my gaze to it, it drops down and swoops low along the street, guiding us on. I follow after it, thinking hard. Nesa and Gair didn't choose this, not knowingly. I can't let them get caught with me. Nor do I want them to owe the sorceress any favors. For them to have a hope of escape, we'll need to part ways.

I keep a watch on the alleys we pass. Down the second, I spot a barrel standing beside a low building. Perfect.

"Here," I order my friends, and they twist to follow me, leaving the owl to fly on. "Up," I gasp out as we reach the barrel. Gair boosts Nesa onto the barrel, and she scrambles onto the roof.

"Lie down," I call, voice soft, as Gair follows her up. He turns around, offering his hand to help me up. But my hands are slick with blood and there are soldiers on my trail. Already, the shouts are drawing closer. I can't let Nesa and Gair be caught in my company.

"I'm going to keep running," I tell them as the owl sweeps by overhead. "Get back to your boat. If I haven't joined you in the next hour, leave. If you're worried about getting caught, leave anyhow."

Gair stares down at me, arm still outstretched. Nesa scrambles over to the edge. "They'll kill you."

"They'll kill you too," I say. "Stay hidden till they're past, then go back to the docks like nothing's wrong. Keep that letter till you get somewhere safe. Don't send it from here. You understand me?"

"But—"

At the back of my mind, the ember flares to life. "Do you understand me?" I grit out.

Nesa blanches. "Yes."

I turn tail and race as fast as I can down the alley, following after the owl. A shout goes up behind me, but it isn't Gair. I don't dare risk a glance back. Instead, I put everything into running after the owl, my heart pounding and head throbbing.

I skid around the corner and race along a thin road that skirts the back of a series of houses. I try to focus past the ember in my mind. My lungs burn, I've a stitch in my side, and my turned foot and ankle hurt with each step. I can't keep running much longer. I'll need to hide somewhere—wherever the owl is taking me—and then I can make my way through the quiet streets to the docks where Nesa and Gair's boat is moored to reclaim my satchel. A spare set of clothes and clean socks may not be a lot, but I can't assume I can replace them either.

And then? What will I do for the children on board the *Heron* then?

I follow the owl around a corner and stumble to a stop, gasping for breath. Tears leak out of my eyes. Nothing. I can do nothing. I have no way to stop Morrel, no way to board his ship and remove the children safely, and approaching the Port Authority has made a killer of me. I have no allies here beyond Nesa and Gair, no way to bring any power to bear on this situation.

The owl hoots once. I look up, blinking the tears and sweat from my eyes. It perches on the corner of a wall where the alley opens onto a wider street.

Somewhere beyond my view lies the bay, and the boats at anchor. *I'm sorry*, I tell the children. I can still feel Cari's small form clinging to me when the sailors first came for me. *I'm so sorry.*

I start forward again, pushing myself on as the owl flutters its wings. The intersecting street is quiet this late in the evening. The sounds of pursuit are further behind me now. Not because I'm faster, but because they must have missed where I turned. I don't want to know whether that's because the sorceress hid me from view, or if I was just quick enough to escape their notice.

I continue down the street, staying close to the buildings on my left. Suddenly, three figures burst from the alley just ahead of me. I press myself into the doorway beside me, watching as the one in the lead pauses, glancing down at something small in his hand that glints silver in the moonlight. He comes to a stop, and I know him, know the easy confidence and perfect balance of his stance, know the exact lines of his profile, his deep-set eyes and the grim line of his mouth, the long hair tied back in a smooth tail.

I stare at him, stunned, as the taller, broad-shouldered man behind him says, "Where next?"

I know this man too, older though he is. If he turns, I'll be able to see the scar that curves from the corner of his mouth to his chin. Just as I know that the first man bears a scar on his arm none too different from my own.

I step forward as the group casts around the street. The closest—a young woman I've never seen before—twists to look straight at me as I take another step forward, and then so does the older man.

"Hello, Artemian," I say.

Behind me, a shout goes up as my pursuers spot me once more.

CHAPTER

12

Artemian stares at me, and then Bren whips past him to catch me by the shoulders, the silver piece he held falling to dangle from a chain wrapped thrice around his wrist. "Rae! Sweet child of a—"

"I'm being hunted," I interrupt, jerking my chin toward the street behind me. My breath still comes in pained gasps. "Those men."

His hands tighten on my shoulders, as if he dare not let me go. He cuts a quick glance at his companions. "Artemian? A distraction. Lirika, stay with us."

His companions are already in front of us, blocking the approaching men's view.

"Quickly now," Bren says, sliding his arm around me and hustling me alongside him. I do my best to keep up with him.

We take the corner just as one of the men calls out. Artemian responds, sounding irritated.

"He'll slow them down, tell them I was meeting my sweetheart or the like," Bren says. "You want me to walk on your other side?"

I glance at him and realize what he's offering. "That'll help," I say, and he slips around me.

This time, his arm takes more of my weight and I put my own arm up around his shoulder, though I have to be careful of my hand. He isn't quite a walking stick, but as he matches my step I'm able to move just a little bit faster. The young woman, Lirika, remains behind us.

"Rae, you're on the run." Bren grins at me, his eyes dancing in the faint light of the alley. "Please tell me you've turned yourself into a river pirate."

"I've hardly . . . had time for that," I pant, fighting an absurd sense of amusement. I forgot how he delights in danger, the way he smiles with a knife in his hand. Just like that, I'm back at the Port Authority, my hand slick with blood. "I . . . killed someone, I think. Two people, probably."

Bren's arm tightens around me, but he doesn't speak. The owl wings past above our heads, no more than a ghost slipping by. It turns into the next alley. "Turn there," I gasp out.

Bren nods, and then a whistle sounds behind us and he swears softly. "They're past Artemian. He'll come up behind them if it comes to a fight. Turn."

I turn with him, and we plunge into the alley. It's so narrow, if I stretch out my arms I could touch either side. As it is, we barely slip past the shutters protruding from the walls as we race along side by side.

"They're gaining," Lirika calls from behind us. "Take cover; I'll lead them on."

"Those stairs?" I ask, looking ahead. They won't be easy for me, but at least—

"No. See that open window?" Bren says, gesturing as we run, only I can't properly see what he did with his hand.

"Where—"

"To the left."

I do; its shutters glow palely in the dark, swinging slightly in a wind that doesn't touch us at all. "Uh—"

"We're going in."

"*In?*" I echo. It's someone's home—

"Trust me," Bren says, his breath light with laughter. "Windows work both directions."

I grunt and then we're at the window. It's higher than I would like. As I grasp the sill and jump, my left hand convulses in pain. I start to slip back down, and then Bren's hands close around my waist, boosting me up. I tumble over the sill in a heap, trying not to scream. The next moment Bren flies over the sill to land beside me —except I'm sprawled out in a mess of limbs. He trips over my legs and thumps down half on top of me. That rips a short, gasping cry from me, his weight pressing on my left arm.

He rolls off me at once, coming up to a crouch balanced on his toes. "*Rae.*"

I sit up, curling my hand around in front of me, trying to breathe. His hands grasp my face, long fingers pushing stray locks of still-wet hair out of my eyes. I inhale on a gasp and hold it, waiting for the pain to pass.

"Rae," he whispers. "Tell me you're all right."

"It's just . . . my hand."

He leans forward, closing his eyes and resting his forehead against mine. I squeeze my eyes shut. I can feel his breath ghosting against my skin, the tension in his body mirroring mine. My left hand *throbs* from all the trauma I've put it through, and my body is trembling again—perhaps it never stopped. I know he can feel me shaking.

"I'm fine," I say softly, even though I'm not.

"Shh."

I quiet, letting myself rest against him, as if, in the calm of this moment, I am safe again. However impossible that may be. Outside, three sets of boots pound past. They pause at the end of the alley and then continue on, echoing into silence. They're gone—

The sorceress's voice whispers through my mind, like the hiss of steel sweeping through shadows. *Should I aid you again, you will owe me more than you do already. I suggest you work to fulfill your debt to me before going to the aid of others.*

I shudder uncontrollably. But the sorceress doesn't control me, and I'm not going to turn my back on the children because she considers her debt more important than my promise to them. As long as she doesn't collect on that debt too soon. I inhale hard to keep from whimpering.

Bren stays with me, holding me steady, until my breath starts to slow and the terror of the sorceress's words—and the chase—fade. Finally, I nod, my forehead brushing his, and he sits back, letting me go. I can't help wishing he was still holding me, just a little bit longer.

The room we're in appears to be a sitting room of sorts, cushions against the walls and a rug underfoot. There are a pair of doors, one on the wall to the right, and the other opposite the window. Both are closed. There's no sound from farther in the apartment.

Bren shifts, still studying me intently, as if he can see right through the dark.

"I thought you were dead," he says, his voice strangely vulnerable. "When I saw what was in that box—" He cuts himself off, shakes his head.

"It wasn't the Scholar," I say quickly.

"I know. I guessed as much, had a chat with him to confirm. He doesn't know who did it either."

It's as if a great weight has rolled off my shoulders. "I was so afraid." I exhale with a half-laugh. "I even wrote to you when I first got free to tell you it wasn't him."

"I didn't think you cared for the Scholar," Bren murmurs, eyes dancing.

My cheeks burn, and I'm suddenly grateful for the dark. "You're being absurd and you know it. I'm glad you had the sense not to kill anyone over—that box."

Bren sobers. In the shadows of the room, his eyes are dark as onyx, and as sharp. "I almost didn't. Artemian had to slam me against a wall and shout some sense into me. He was right, though. Sending fingers in pretty boxes isn't the Scholar's style. Who did it, Rae?"

I hesitate. I will tell him, but right now I need a few minutes to gather my emotions. I can still feel the memory of his hands on my face, still hear the echoes of the sorceress's words. I lick my lips, glance toward the window. "We're in someone's house, Bren. Shouldn't we get out of here? Talk later?"

He shifts, cocking his head, but the rest of the apartment remains quiet. I'm grateful when he says, "Later, then."

I lean back against the wall, waiting for him to give the word to climb out. He remains still, his face upturned toward the window.

I take stock of my body once more. I'm exhausted from my run. My left hand still throbs, though the pain has receded. I likely have a couple of new scrapes or bruises, though nothing terrible, as I assured Bren earlier. My foot is holding up all right. I pat it with my good hand, and sense Bren tilting his head to watch me. Maybe he just hasn't learned to thank his limbs for the work they do for him.

A short, multi-note whistle sounds from somewhere down the alley. He rises and peeks out the window. "We're clear. Let's get you back to our inn. I want to hear everything there."

I nod, pushing myself to my feet beside him.

"Everything, Rae," he repeats.

"All right," I agree, because he needs to know about Bardok and Morrel. If I can't bring them to the king's justice, then Bren's version will have to do.

CHAPTER

13

Artemian stands sentinel at the far end of the alley. Lirika is nowhere to be seen; I can only hope she's managed to give her pursuers the slip.

As soon as we emerge, Artemian starts toward us. As he passes, he murmurs a faint word to Bren that I don't quite catch. From then, he stays ahead of us, checking each alley before we turn into it and looking back to Bren only once for directions. Somehow, we avoid all the larger streets and pass only a few people still out this late at night. Bren and his fellow thieves may be relatively new to Lirelei, but their instincts for navigating the backstreets are impeccable.

Their inn is a modest but well-kept establishment, set back from the main thoroughfares. Artemian waits until we've reached him before stepping in, keeping the focus of those who look upon him. A lone serving girl waves to us as we enter the common room. Thick, flat cushions lie along the wall and here and there on the carpets that are spread to either side of the center throughway, though only one corner of the room is occupied: a small party drinking tea, their attention on each other.

Artemian breaks away to approach the serving girl while Bren and I continue across the room. He guides me to stay a half-step behind him, shielded from view. We follow the connecting hall to a flight of stairs that I take one slow, aching step at a time, my breath huffing out in an audible counterpoint. Bren paces me without a sound.

When we finally reach their room, Bren pushes the door open for me, his eyes crinkling with a smile that just barely touches his lips. "Well, that was infinitely easier than I thought it would be."

"I have questions about that," I say, having had a little time to wonder how Bren went from thinking me dead to getting to Lirelei about as quickly as I did. And how he ended up running through the streets at exactly the same time as me.

"So do I," Bren agrees.

I glance about the room. It's small but clean. There are cushions near a little fireplace to the right, shelves along the wall to the left containing a few rolled mats, a set of folded blankets, and a pair of packs. Across from me, a low table has been placed below the open window. There's nothing much else to remark on. At night, the mats will be unrolled to fill the room. During the day, with them put away, there's space enough for comfort. I glance at the packs again, guessing I'm in Artemian and Bren's room.

"Sit," Bren urges me. "I'll get a fire burning for you."

I ease myself down on a cushion and take the blanket Bren hands me, wrapping it around my shoulders because I *am* cold, have been cold for a while now.

He kneels before the small hearth, sets a few logs onto the bricks, and uses flint and steel to light the tinder. As the fire catches, a quick pattering knock sounds on the door. Artemian steps in, carrying a tray laden with food, the spicy scent of it enough to make my stomach grumble. He sets the tray on the table and starts portioning out food onto a plate.

Wordlessly, Bren fetches a pitcher of water and a wide basin for me to wash my hands over. I hold my hands out, and then begin to tremble again as I stare at the blood dried to them, caking my right hand and spattered across my left. Bren begins pouring and I force myself to scrub at my skin. He pauses, passes me a lump of soap. I can feel him staring at my hands, at my left with its missing digit, but I can't look up at him. Can't look away as I scrub at the death clinging to my fingers. And still the blood breaks free from my hands, dark red turning brown, staining the water in the basin. So much blood.

The guard's eyes stare back at me through my memory, terrified, scarlet gushing from his throat. I can feel the easy way the knife sank between Efrun's ribs, tore through his stomach.

Bile burns at the back of my throat. I look away from my hands, gagging, and then dive for the basin, lose the contents of my stomach. Even when I am done, my whole body trembles uncontrollably. My hands, gripping the basin's edge, are covered in pink-tinged soap.

"Easy," Bren says softly. "Easy."

He's beside me, a hand on my back. Steadying me, lending me a comfort I desperately need. Except it wasn't easy—or maybe it was. Too easy, to kill a man like that. Two men.

My breath comes in a strange, gasping sob. *I had to.* There was no other way out of that room alive. They were, each and every one of them, murderers. I was only defending myself. I would do it again—I know I would. Yet that doesn't take away the sight of the blood, the feel of muscle and tendon and skin parting beneath the force of the knife I wielded.

"Stop thinking about it," Bren says, rubbing my back. "Give yourself a minute."

I close my eyes and push all those thoughts away, shut them behind a door in my mind. There's only Bren crouched beside me, his hand resting lightly on my back. Not judging, or horrified, or anything else. Just waiting quietly, lending me his strength.

I take a slow breath, straighten. I don't know what to do with my hands, still sticky with soap and the last remnants of blood.

At least Bren understands. Wordlessly, he pours a little more water over the basin, and I rinse my hands in the clear stream, trying not to look at the mess I've left in the basin. Or anywhere else.

"What happened to the blade you used?"

I fumble it out of my pocket, sheath and all. My gaze catches on my hands again. There is still dried blood caught beneath my fingernails, in the creases of my palm. At least my left hand is cleaner, the healing wound unmarked by anyone else's blood.

Bren tugs the knife from my hands and passes it to Artemian, who already holds the basin.

"Wait—" I say, even though I trust these men. Completely.

"Let me clean it for you," Artemian says.

I swallow down the lingering taste of acid in my mouth, nod.

"Anything I should be careful about with it?" he asks.

It's bone. Water won't hurt it. Except . . . "It's sharper than it looks," I say. "Don't let it cut you."

He nods. "I'll be back shortly."

He steps out of the room, taking the basin with him as well, and then Bren is beside me again, placing a small bowl on the floor. "You'll want to wash your face," he says. He watches me steadily, only a hint of sorrow in his eyes. There's blood on my face too. There must be—and it won't only be there. I pull away the edge of the blanket to stare at the dried blood spattered across my tunic.

"We'll wash your clothes later," Bren says, as if that will fix everything. "Your face for now, Rae."

I swallow hard and do his bidding, then cup my hands and rinse out my mouth as well. By the time I'm done, Artemian has returned, bearing a clean basin and in company with Lirika. She's older than I realized, perhaps around twenty, with deep-brown shoulder-length hair braided back, a petite figure, and nimble fingers.

"Got away just fine," she says in answer to Bren's unspoken question.

"Your knife," Artemian says, offering it back to me.

The hilt gleams in the lamplight, every last trace of blood gone. I force myself to reach out, but Bren lifts it from his fingers first and sets it on the table. "We'll clean your sheath as well, first. For now, let it be."

I nod.

Artemian shifts his weight, watching me. "Can you eat?"

I curl my hands around the edges of my blanket, shake my head. I'm hungry, but I don't think my stomach will settle right now. "Not yet. You go ahead."

"We're fine," Bren says, making me wonder if they've already eaten—if they only intended to eat a little now to keep me company. Between Artemian's steady presence and Bren's gentle care, I feel as if I have finally landed somewhere safe, somewhere I'll be able to gather my strength and get back up again when I'm ready. Even the young woman, Lirika, sitting quietly on a cushion at the table, asks nothing of me I cannot give.

Time is precious, though; I can't waste it. I need to ask Bren's help against Morrel, and for that, I need to understand the nuances of his presence here.

"Does the princess know you're here?" I ask.

"Oh yes." He grins, leaning back against the wall and resting an arm on his bent knee. "Captain Matsin did, apparently, head up a search for you. But"—Bren lifts a shoulder in a half-shrug that conveys an affectionate contempt—"even he knew there was only so much they could do. After all, they never found your tax clerk friend, did they?"

He means Kirrana. I shake my head.

"I got a message from the princess asking me to meet her and Matsin at the Tattered Crow. It's rather unusual for a princess to show up in disguise at a rundown inn, with only the captain of her husband's bodyguard to protect her. So of course, I went. They both seemed to think I was your best hope."

"Matsin did too?" I ask, taken aback. To say he and Bren have a strained relationship would not be an exaggeration, and that was without Matsin knowing Bren is Red Hawk's right-hand man.

"He did," Bren says, smug as a cat that's gotten into the cream. "If the situation hadn't been so dire, I would have enjoyed it immensely. As it was, I was planning to come for you anyway."

"Because of my finger," I say hesitantly. It would make sense for Red Hawk to send his second-in-command after me, especially given Bardok's attempt to frame the Black Scholar. And the fact that Bren knows me. "That's what you mean?"

Artemian and Lirika make no move where they've settled by the small table.

Bren takes a slow deep breath, his expression hardening. "Partly. Who did it, Rae? The Black Scholar swore it wasn't him; you cleared him of guilt yourself. So, who?"

"Bardok Three-Fingers," I admit.

Bren's eyes narrow, his expression pulling tight. Lirika swears softly.

Taking my finger was Bardok's gambit to begin a street war between Red Hawk and the Black Scholar. It may still lead to a street war—only this one with Bardok's men. I don't want that either, because that's how innocents get killed.

I say quickly, "He's working hand-in-hand with the snatchers. Garrin had me delivered to him—"

Bren startles. "*Garrin?* As in Verin Garrin, the thrice-cursed lord of Cenatil?"

"That one," I agree.

Bren sits back, his gaze going to the fire. A lock of hair has escaped his tie and rests against his cheek, softening an otherwise dangerously sharp aspect.

"The royal family's involved then," Artemian says, watching me shrewdly.

"I think it's just Garrin."

"Do you?" Bren asks. "Do you not know?"

I gather the details I pondered while imprisoned in the hold. "Kestrin wouldn't have encouraged Alyrra to investigate the snatchers if he thought his father was involved. He wouldn't have trusted Garrin to—"

"To protect their interests? If Kestrin knew he couldn't distract the princess—"

"He *helped* her," I cut back in, determined to say my piece. "At the least, Kestrin can't be aware of Garrin's actions or he would have encouraged Alyrra to turn her attention elsewhere. He didn't make the attempt, he only warned her that the royal family can't oppose the Circle of Mages."

"He may have tried to redirect in private, for all any of us knows. You cannot be sure of this."

"I can't be sure," I agree, frustrated. "But based on every interaction I've had with them, I can't believe Kestrin is involved with the snatchers, or the Circle's support of them."

"Did you believe Garrin was?"

I wince. Garrin rubbed me the wrong way repeatedly, but I didn't suspect him until I found his family's portrait, asphodel carved into the frame and painted into the couch his family sat upon—the same star-shaped flower that characterizes Berenworth's seal. If that hadn't been enough, Garrin collecting me after I'd been bound and gagged in a storage room and sealing me in a crate himself to be delivered to Bardok would have done it.

"So," Bren says. "You don't know. It *could* be the royal family as a whole."

"Not Alyrra," I say doggedly.

"No, not her." He sighs. "I suppose you intend to try to take Garrin down then. I should no doubt be grateful you haven't set your sights on the Circle as well."

I have, but saying so will only infuriate Bren more. So I only make the argument he expects. "Garrin can't be allowed to continue."

"I think you'll find the royal family will disagree. At least, the king and Kestrin. They won't turn on their own, no matter what they've done. As long as it's not treason."

"How can it not be treason?" I demand. "He's stealing the king's subjects, selling them into slavery—"

"And perhaps the king approves."

That shuts me down. I stare at the rough weave of the carpet at my feet. The sorceress, though . . . she implied it was only Garrin who was guilty. Or perhaps it is just Garrin she wants. At the thought of her, I can once again feel her spells slumbering within my mind, a banked coal glowing in the dark. The touch of it is faintly painful and wholly disturbing.

"So, Garrin attacked you and had you delivered to Bardok. I wouldn't have believed Bardok would take orders from a royal, but he's already surprised me once. What then? How did you get free?"

I describe Fastu's ill-considered attempt to escape from the ship, and the execution Morrel had planned. But I dare not attempt to mention the sorceress who came to my rescue, or her demands.

"Morrel threw us overboard," I go on. "But he kicked my knife in after me." I nod to where it lies on the table. It's a truth, just not the whole truth.

Bren laughs, shakes his head in disbelief. "It's spelled, isn't it? It must be, though how it could have come to your hand *underwater . . .*"

"It's Fae-made. It won't cut me, and I suspect it will always come readily to my hand."

Bren nods thoughtfully. It's unsettling how easily he's accepted this half-truth from me, as if he knows there's more and yet doesn't question it, because he doesn't believe I would deceive him. It makes me feel slightly ill. But I don't have a choice—I haven't forgotten the sorceress's binding, or the smoke I breathed when she laid it on me.

"I'm glad you have it," Bren says of my knife. "What happened to the boy who was thrown overboard with you?"

"We made it out of the river together. The next morning, we followed a nearby road, hoping to find a town. We went—we went in the wrong direction. If we'd gone the other way, we might have made it in time . . ."

"The Darkness took him," Artemian says softly.

I nod. Bren and Artemian already know about my sash's wards, if not the truth of its provenance. "I knew my sash was a protection, but I didn't tell him at first. He was scared. He ran ahead to get help. I couldn't catch up, couldn't get to him in time." I take a shuddering breath and hold it, as if that might suppress all the horror of those few irrevocable minutes. The sickening truth that, as much as I love my body, had my foot not been turned, I might have been able to catch up to him in time. Or he may not have felt the need to run ahead of me at all.

"Your sash protects against the *Darkness*?" Lirika asks, leaning forward.

Bren says, "It's also Fae-made, and not something we want anyone knowing about just yet."

"Understood."

I nod my thanks, even though Bren knows that Niya's sash isn't Fae-made. He doesn't know where I got it from, but he's letting me keep my secrets. I won't argue with that.

"What then? How did you get here?" Bren asks.

I tell him how I left Fastu with the Speaker, and how the local mage had a look at my hand and then arranged my transport downriver.

"You got here this afternoon and there's a manhunt for you now. What happened?"

"I tried to report the captain whose ship I was imprisoned on."

Bren lets out his breath with a sigh. "Rae."

"*I know*. I knew the Port Authority might turn on me, but there are still children on that ship, Bren. I had to try. I had allies who took me there and played the part of witnesses for me, and then they waited outside."

"You have *allies*? God, Rae, you're—"

"What?" I say defensively.

"Pirate queen material," Bren says, his grin flashing again. "So, your witnesses should have convinced the Port Authority to keep you alive, because otherwise the Authority would be charged with your murder."

"Right."

"Didn't work."

I shake my head. "I had my knife with me. I made sure I stayed on the ground floor. I really thought I'd be able to climb out and run before anything happened."

"They still took you by surprise." It's an observation, not a judgement, but I feel it in my gut, sharp as the blade of my knife. Perhaps if I'd been trained as a soldier, or grown up a thief on the streets, I would have known to keep an eye out for the guard coming down the alley as well, to not let myself be distracted by Morrel and Efrun. I hadn't.

"Yes," I say tiredly. "They figured they could intercept the letter my allies were taking to the courier office—at least, Morrel thought he could. A guard caught me, and Morrel brought in a bucket with water, and they were going to drown me in it. That way, they'd have an unmarked body to turn in or dispose of, as they wished."

Bren doesn't move, his body both relaxed and ready to fight. "Go on."

"I managed to stab the guard in the throat. Then Efrun—the head of the Port Authority—came at me. He wasn't even armed, but he grabbed me, going after my knife, so I stabbed him too. In between the ribs, and his stomach. I jumped out the window before Morrel could get to me. Gair—one of my allies—hit him with a wooden oar through the window, and we ran."

I clench my jaw shut, make myself breathe through my nose.

"You did well," Bren says. He shifts, thinking. "Do we need to find your allies?"

"I don't know. We split up. They're the people who came downriver with me. I'm hoping they've made it to the public dock where their boat is. It's a small one. They're just country folk like me."

He scoffs. "*Just.*"

Artemian and Lirika exchange an amused glance.

"How did you get here so quickly?" I ask Bren. "You were in Tarinon long enough to get that package from Bardok, and meet with the Scholar. The princess, as well."

"She's very worried about you," Bren says. "She arranged for us to ride on an express courier boat straight to Lirelei. We skipped everything in between. There were men at the oars almost the whole way."

"How did you know that I would make it all the way here?"

Bren hesitates, then slips a silver chain from his pocket. With a flick of his fingers, he pulls it free of the thick, round, silver locket I remember him holding in his hand when I first saw him on the street. "Alyrra had this made," he says and passes me the locket, pocketing the chain once more. I flip open the jeweled clasp to find I'm looking at a compass, the needle twirling around before settling to point steadily at my chest.

"It points to you," Bren says. "The Fae ambassador had it made to help Alyrra track you down."

Genno Stonemane? He knows what I was investigating. He helped me understand the magical aspects of what I was dealing with more than once. When Kirrana disappeared, he asked the Fae mage, Adept Midael, the Cormorant, to find a way to track her. The Cormorant was able to pinpoint her location as the city docks, but even with that information, we still couldn't find her past the powerful wards protecting her. The compass in my hand is simply a more lasting form of the same spell, no doubt also fashioned by the Cormorant. Now that I'm no longer on the *Heron* with the ward provided by the Circle to deflect it, the compass clearly has no difficulty pointing to me. It's precisely what I hoped Alyrra would send with Captain Matsin to track me down.

"You were using this when we crossed paths," I say slowly.

"We got into Lirelei not three hours ago, Rae. At that point, you were holding still, so we dropped our things here and started hunting for you. In a city this size, with no ability to walk precisely where the needle points, it was somewhat more complicated than I would have liked. Then you started moving. Quickly. I didn't know if you were on a horse or in a carriage, or if we were close enough to you that your running would seem like something faster just from the movement of the needle. So." He shrugs. "We ran too."

The sorceress made sure we crossed paths. I'm glad of it, even as I worry over just what she'll do when I reach Tarinon. I close the compass with a snap, run a thumb over the royal seal engraved in its lid. It's both a tool to find me, and a way for Bren to legitimize his actions, should he need it.

"She must be very worried to have given you something with the royal seal."

Bren smiles slyly. "You don't really think the royal family would give a thief their official seal, do you?"

"But—but this is it! I've seen it before."

"Alyrra gave me the compass," Bren allows. "I had the seal engraved by an expert forger while we were making the rest of our preparations. I thought it might come in handy."

I give a disbelieving laugh. How utterly like the clever thief he is. "Have you needed it?"

"Not yet," he admits as I return the compass.

I watch him slip it back into his pocket. Alyrra asked Bren to find me because she needed an inconspicuous thief rather than guards. Just as I do. Bren may have no overt reason to try to rescue a handful of children he's never met, except that he cares. He's been there, where these children are now, and it will rub him the wrong way to turn his back.

I clear my throat and say, lightly, "I don't suppose you know any river pirates."

"Just you," Bren says, the corner of his mouth quirking. He leans toward me, and I could swear he knows exactly what I'm asking. Then he says, "What happened to that pendant I gave you, Rae?"

"Morrel took it. He let me keep it at first. It actually saved me from his crew." I can't quite bring myself to say what I mean, but the hardening of Bren's features, and the stillness of Artemian and Lirika, tell me they understand perfectly. "Once he decided to throw me overboard, he saw no reason to let the gold go to waste. He kept it."

Bren casts a sharp look at Artemian. "I don't think we can let that stand, do you?"

"I doubt it matters what I think," Artemian says. "I'll support you as always."

"Artemian," Bren says, rather as if he were chastising an errant child.

The older man grins crookedly, the scar that tracks from the corner of his lip to the bottom of his chin pulled tight. "He was far out of the city by then. It's no surprise he didn't truly fear Red Hawk's reprisal, don't you think?"

Lirika snorts. "More fool he. Do we cut him down in the streets, then? Or find out where he spends his time?"

I glance from her to Bren, my stomach twisting. Thieves' justice, I suppose. It will stop Morrel, which can only be a good thing, but that still leaves the children on board.

Bren glances toward me, a hint of a challenge in his eyes. "Rae wants his ship searched as well, though, don't you? That's why you went to the Port Authority."

"The children are still there. The ship hasn't docked yet, though it will tomorrow at the latest. Once it docks, the children could easily be moved without our knowing. I want to rescue them first."

"So, we take the children and kill the captain," Lirika says, nodding her approval.

"He needs to be questioned," I say sharply. "I want to stop more than just him. For that, I need to know the details of how he works. We can raid the ship, take him prisoner." I can almost see it playing out, quick and brutal: board the ship, grab the children, take Morrel, and escape.

Bren shakes his head. "No, not a raid. We'll take the ship."

I choke on my own breath.

He lifts a brow, as if he hadn't just proposed stealing a fully crewed galley at harbor in clear sight of the Port Authority.

"Take the ship! But his whole crew—you've only three people and—what would we do with a *ship?*"

"We need a ride upriver, since it sounds like the local courier office is in league with your friends at the Port Authority. A river galley will come in very handy. Morrel's men need to answer for what they've done as much as he does. You had Red Hawk's protection, and they knew it. They'll have to pay the price now." Bren's smile has the flash of swords in it. "I'll see what support Red Hawk has in Lirelei. We'll plan from there."

"Do you know the name of the ship?" Artemian asks me.

"It's the *Blue Heron.*"

"Excellent." Bren pushes himself to his feet. "You should eat a bit, if you can, and rest. Artemian and I will see what we can find out about Morrel. Lirika will stay with you—though you both might want to shift to her room." He pauses. "If you can tell us where to find your allies, one of us can carry a message to them from you. With the guards searching for you, it will be best if you don't leave your room for more than the necessary washing up."

I nod and describe the dock where Nesa and Gair moored their boat. "I asked around about Morrel when I got here," I tell Bren as he starts for the door.

He turns back to me. "Yes?"

"I couldn't find out much, other than that he stole ownership of his first galley from his friend."

Bren's smile curves dangerously over his mouth. "Did he? You're a gem, Rae."

I shake my head. "The sailors spoke of it as a clear thing, but they said the courts sided with Morrel. One of them said that the judge got a new carriage out of it, but that could have been a coincidence. And this was all years ago, Bren, before he ever got the *Heron.* No one had a word to say about snatchers or smuggling or anything of the sort since then."

"Perhaps a liberal application of drink will change that. His own sailors will know him well and might be convinced to speak. Either way, I'm glad for that tidbit. Artemian?"

Artemian nods, rising to his feet. "Ready."

"You'll tell me what you find out?" I ask quickly as Bren steps out. I am so unutterably grateful for this—for his support, for how quickly he's able to move. For being able to rely on him.

"Of course," he says, and flashes me a knowing look. "You're our river pirate, after all."

He's still grinning as Artemian closes the door behind them.

CHAPTER

14

I doze on the mat rolled out by the banked fire in Lirika's room across the hall. My dreams flow from Bardok's cruelly smiling visage as he towered over me in the underground cell, my bloodied finger in his hand, to the guard with his wide, terrified gaze and his life flowing out between his fingers, to the way my knife sliced through Efrun's gut.

"Wake *up*." Lirika's voice breaks through my consciousness.

I rouse with a half-swallowed cry, my vision full of blood— dribbling from my empty knuckle, streaming from the guard, drenching my hands. I gasp a breath, aware she's got me by the shoulders, that she must have given me a shake. "Sorry."

"Lirika!" Bren calls urgently through the door.

"All's well," she says, moving at once to let him in. I pull the sheet up around my shoulders. I'm wearing a spare nightshirt loaned to us by the innkeeper's wife over my skirt, my own tunic drying by the fire.

Bren peers in at me from the doorway, then turns away, murmuring indistinctly—probably telling Artemian I'm fine. I have a sudden memory of the night I woke in his house and tried to get up, still woozy from the healer's brew as well as losing blood to the Scholar's blade. That night, my companion was the one to scream, but it was still Bren who showed up at the door, rumpled and shirtless as he is now.

"You all right, Rae?"

I nod, glancing away, but I'm not really. My dream is still there, clawing at the back of my mind, and I can't quite get enough breath. "Just a dream," I say when he remains silent, watching me.

"She's been restless all night," Lirika says with unnecessary helpfulness. I shoot her a dark look.

"Want to get some air?" Bren asks. "I can take you up to the roof."

"That would be good." Maybe under the stars, my memories will feel less like they're going to smother me.

While Bren slips back to his room, I pull on my boots and then reclaim my bone knife in its now-clean sheath from the nearby table, strapping it to my calf. I rearrange the sheet around my shoulders. It's not quite a cloak, but it's close enough.

Lirika watches me silently, leaning against the wall by the door.

"Sorry," I tell her again.

She just shakes her head. Bren returns, wearing his tunic once more, though still barefoot, his hair falling loose past his shoulders. I follow him out the door and up the stairs at the end of the hall to an open rooftop. There are cushions set out around wooden tables, with carpets underfoot. A small storage room stands to one side where they must put everything when storms are expected.

I cross the rooftop to the far wall to gaze out at the city streets below, the lower rooftops here and there, the surrounding buildings mostly dark.

A few moments later, Bren joins me, setting a small lit lamp on the parapet between us. He must have found it on the rooftop somewhere, perhaps by the storage room. This high up and with the streets so quiet, there's no worry that anyone will recognize me.

"I believe this is yours," he says and slips a bag off his shoulder. I hadn't even noticed it on the way up.

"You found them!" I say with delight, catching the strap. It's the old satchel Nesa's mother gave me. I am unutterably thankful for this proof that Nesa and Gair made it back to their boat.

Bren nods. "They were relieved to hear you're well and left as soon as I suggested it. I watched them off the docks."

"Thank you." I don't know what I would have done if the guards had managed to catch and identify them. Thankfully, Morrel would barely have gotten a glance at them last night before Gair knocked him over. If they've set sail, there's little chance Morrel or the Port Authority guards will know where to track them down.

A smile flickers across Bren's mouth. "I thought you'd want to know they made it out."

"I did," I agree, beaming. I set the bag by my feet. "Did you learn anything about the *Heron*?"

He leans back against the parapet, resting his weight on his elbows. The lamp casts one side of his face in sharp relief. "They won't dock until tomorrow at the earliest, so we've plenty of time to arrange matters. I know you want details but...." He shakes his head. "That's better kept for morning."

I hesitate. "Why?"

He grimaces. "What did you dream about?"

Killing people. Nearly being killed. Surviving.

I can't find a way to say the words, the violence still too raw. I don't regret killing Efrun or his guard now any more than I did earlier tonight, when I lost the contents of my stomach thinking about what I'd done. I had no other option. I also can't stop the horror of it from haunting me. Just as I can't seem to escape the horror of the things that have been done to me.

I shrug as the silence draws out too long.

He says, gently, "You've been through a lot, Rae. Let's keep those other conversations for when you're not hoping to sleep again."

Fair point.

He looks down to the street and starts pointing things out: the broken shutters on the ground-floor apartment in the building across the way—a sign of poverty or that it's abandoned; the alley farther down where a stray dog was roaming earlier. He tells me how the streets connect, how to find my way to the harbor docks from here, or the river—the few directions he's walked.

It's calming talk. He's orienting me to the city, not because I need to know, but because it helps push away all the fears I can't deal with. Here is something I can understand and focus on. I lean on my good arm, both hands resting on the wall. It's good to just look out, listen to Bren's voice, steady and reassuring. It's good to be here with him.

The thought settles into me.

I knew I was glad to see him earlier tonight—deeply, truly happy to see Bren, and not in the way I was glad to also see Artemian. I didn't pause to think about it, didn't pause to think about any of it—the way I let him hold my face and steady me in the darkness of the room we hid in. The way it was his comfort I needed when I couldn't stand the sight of the blood on my hands.

Oh, this is all *wrong*.

I shift, trying to gather my calm. It's an impossible situation; there's no need for me to make it worse. I'll just go on enjoying his company for as long as we're traveling together, and it will be all right.

My movement draws his attention. His gaze flickers from the city to me, to where my hands rest on the wall, the one whole, and the other missing a digit. I straighten, dropping my hands.

"May I see?" he asks, gesturing to my left hand, hidden now beneath the fold of the sheet. He's dangerously handsome in the lamplight, his skin burnished gold and his hair falling past his shoulders in silken waves.

"If it's all right?" he presses. He holds out a hand, his fingers curled slightly, as if I might drop some small object into his palm.

"It's healing," I say, in case that's what he's worried about. He saw it already, when I washed the blood away. I'm not sure why he wants to look again.

He nods, but still he waits. It's not as if letting him look more closely will change anything, will it? I slip my hand out from under the sheet and offer it to him.

He slides his hand beneath mine, palm to palm, sending a shiver up my skin. In the lamplight, the wound is garishly dark, uneven and still swollen. My ring finger is puffy and faintly pink, as is the skin around the empty knuckle, but otherwise, it doesn't look half bad.

I raise my gaze to find Bren's expression so closed it's as if I'm gazing at a statue. He looks up slowly, and in the blackness of his gaze is a whole world of fury of which I have no concept.

"Bren?" I manage through stiff lips.

He closes his eyes, and when he opens them again, his wrath is shuttered away somewhere I can no longer see it. "He did that to hurt me," he says of Bardok.

Wait. "You said you're not Red Hawk," I say sharply.

"I did," he agrees, releasing my hand.

"Then—"

"Always with the same question, Rae." He spreads his palms in laughing exasperation. "How many times do I have to tell you I'm just Bren?"

Half a dozen, it seems. I flush, wrap my arms across my chest, snugging the sheet tight, unable to look at him. "Right."

"Do you want me to be Red Hawk?"

"God, no!" I exclaim. "That's not what I meant. Red Hawk has a pretty bloody reputation. I'm glad you're not him. It's just sometimes you say things, or you do things in such a way—it would explain a lot."

Bren doesn't answer, his expression inscrutable.

I look out at the streets, wishing I hadn't asked. "Thank you for bringing me up here, talking to me. It helped."

"Do you want to stay longer?"

"Do you know more of the streets?" I ask, curious.

"No, but I could make something up for you."

I huff a laugh. "What if I believed you and got lost?"

"I don't think you've ever gotten lost," he says meditatively. "You just find a new way."

"No," I tell him, amused, "I've definitely been lost before. But we should probably rest. We've been up here a while."

Bren leans over and blows out the lamp. "As you wish," he says and walks me back to my room.

CHAPTER

15

Dawn finally arrives in a lackluster easing of the darkness, the skies outside carpeted in clouds. A steady wind blows from the sea, carrying the inescapable scent of salt and fish with it, the sound of gulls calling overhead. I sit at the room's little table and listen to the rumble and clatter of the city waking up, the shutters cracked open, until Lirika rouses herself once more.

Just as she did last night, she watches the hall while I use the washroom. By the time we return to our room, I'm aware of all the various stiff muscles in my back and legs. I sink down on the cushion, glancing surreptitiously toward Lirika as she tidies away her sleeping mat.

My foot aches, the muscles too tight. I spend a moment wishing Lirika were somewhere else so I could massage it—or that I had thought to do at least a little while she was sleeping—and then catch myself with a grimace. I need to stop worrying what others might think, whether they'll be disgusted by the rough skin and calluses and darkened scars. My body needs my care.

I fold my left leg over my right, baring my foot. Gently, I massage it, grateful to find that I don't have any new blisters starting. I keep focused on my foot as Lirika looks over, though I'm aware of the time she takes to study me. I can't use my left hand very well—it still hurts to apply pressure with it, but I can use it to turn my foot and hold it as long as I keep pressure off my last two knuckles. I work with my right hand over the scarred, twisted shape of my foot.

"Question for you," I say, intent on breaking the silence.

"Aye?" she says, coming to sit across the little table from me.

"You're a thief, right? I've been wanting to learn how to defend myself, and how to pick a lock. Can you teach me?"

"Seems to me you're pretty good at defending yourself."

I grimace. "They didn't expect me to have a knife. If they'd planned for it, I wouldn't have survived."

Her eyes narrow. "You don't know how to use it properly?"

I shake my head. "I'm tired of being attacked—or locked up—without the ability to do something about it."

Lirika considers me for a long moment. "If you learn how to defend yourself with a knife, you're really learning how to kill. You sure you want that?"

My stomach tightens into a knot. "Isn't there something in between? I just want to be able to get away."

"There might have been if people weren't actively interested in killing you. But if you've got one or more men coming at you, you can't be trying to disarm them. They aren't going to let you go. You've got to do the most damage you can and run. That means fighting with a willingness to kill."

I look away from her, my breath coming a little too fast. "Is that what you do?"

"I haven't needed to kill yet, but no one's come after me in particular. I've never been outnumbered, and I've had time to train. If I'm teaching you right now, it's going to be how to stab your opponent as quickly and cleanly as possible, as much as possible, to make sure they go down. That's all you'll have time for before we get back to Tarinon."

I shake my head. I know I should probably learn, but I can still feel the way the knife cut into Efrun, can hear the nauseating sucking sound it made as I pulled it out.

"Don't go retching all over me now," Lirika says, patting my arm. "You probably need a few days before you think about knives. How's your hand?"

"I can use my thumb and first two fingers well enough," I tell her.

"I'll teach you a bit of lockpicking."

Lirika is a good teacher, her explanations brief but her patience making up the difference. She carries a lockpick set with her at all times in a slim fold of fabric she keeps in her boot. She opens it to reveal a miniature torque wrench and three picks of varying sizes, and talks me through each of their uses.

From there, we start with picking the door's lock, Lirika demonstrating on it twice and then walking me through the process twice more.

I have just managed to pick the lock on my own for the first time, and am starting on a second attempt, when a knock sounds in a vaguely familiar pattern. I grasp my wrench and picks and move back from the door.

"Come in," Lirika says easily, and Bren opens the door. He's dressed in clean but simple clothes: a moss green tunic and earth-tone pants, brown sash wrapped tight over his waist. Artemian waits behind him in the hallway.

Bren glances from Lirika, to me, to the tools in my hand, and his lips curve in a delighted smile. "Rae! Are you planning on joining our ranks?"

"No," I say, my cheeks burning. I turn and stump over to the table to lay the tools down on Lirika's fabric wrap, reminding myself to act normally. "I've just found myself locked in a room one too many times. I asked Lirika to teach me how to get out."

"You seem to have gotten better at windows," he says.

I throw him an irritated glance. I only jumped out of the first window because that's how Bren planned his rescue attempt to play out. The Black Scholar would have killed me otherwise. If anyone's to blame regarding windows, it's Bren.

"Breakfast," Artemian says. The word has the sound of a mild reproof to it. He sets his tray on the table beside the lockpick set. "Have you eaten at all yet, Rae?"

"I had a bite or two last night, after you left." Lirika brought up a slice of toast with butter for me. I managed to keep it down, which I considered a great success.

Artemian nods. "I'm glad to hear it."

He pushes up his sleeves and turns his attention to portioning out the platter of spiced eggs fried with greens, and a round flat-bread to go with each plate. It's rather a lovely thing, to think of him as the motherly type. That he moves like a consummate swordsman, that his arms show more than a few darker lines from fights long past, makes his care somehow all the more wonderful.

"What time will the *Heron* dock?" I ask as Bren seats himself across from me.

He meets my gaze. "Word is the Port Authority won't open at all today. All business at the docks is on a moratorium, so the *Heron* won't be able to come in until tomorrow."

He pauses, then says, "It's an emergency closure due to a pair of deaths last night."

I nod woodenly. "That's . . . good, then. I guess."

"It gives us more time to plan," he agrees.

"Do they have any leads?" Lirika asks, leaning forward.

Bren glances at her. "That's the interesting part. They don't, not officially, but"—his gaze slides back to me, darkly amused—"in other news, the bounty for finding you has gone up another twenty-five gold if you're brought in directly to the Port Authority."

"That's, what, fifty gold from the palace and twenty-five from the Port Authority?" Lirika whistles softly. "That's a pretty price on your head, kelari. I am impressed."

"Almost as good as Red Hawk's," Bren says, positively glowing.

I frown, trying to understand this. "So, am I still missing, or am I a wanted criminal?"

Bren waves a hand. "Oh, you're officially just missing. The Port Authority wants you brought to them first so they can keep you that way."

Artemian sets our plates out before us, his mouth quirked in a crooked smile. "They'll pay the full reward from their own pocket, without going to the palace. They've some slavers to appease, after all."

How can he say that with a smile?

Bren looks almost dreamy as he says, "And that's *before* you sail out of here on a stolen galley. I bet you'll be worth a full hundred before we reach Tarinon."

I look toward Lirika as the only possibly sensible thief in the room. She grimaces and takes a bite of her food, her gaze bent on her plate. Hmm. I turn back to Bren. "You've a plan, then? For taking the *Heron*?"

"We do." Bren takes a quick bite, chews, swallows. I'm not fooled—he's deciding how much to tell me. He goes on, "None of us know the first thing about manning galleys, so we've found ourselves a trustworthy captain. He's bringing a crew together now. We'll move at dusk, when there's enough light to see by, but not so much that folks will take note of what we're doing. We've a bit more work to do today, so"—he bends a level look to me—"it's best if you lie low here."

"I can't help at all?"

"There's a very good likeness of yours all over town with a *very* good reward attached," Bren says. "Please just stay here. Artemian and I can manage this."

I nod. I've no interest in being caught by the Port Authority, nor am I sure I would actually be able to help if I did go out.

The men finish quickly and Bren makes their excuses as soon as they are done. "We'll collect you an hour before sundown. Make sure you're ready."

"Understood," Lirika says, and then the men slip out and it is just the two of us again.

Lirika turns her gaze on me. "Better finish up, and then work on that lock. I'll try to find another one while you're at it."

I scoop up the last of my eggs with my final bite of bread, my thoughts on Bren's words. "What happens if someone recognizes me from the fliers tonight?"

Her mouth twists. "I expect we'll have a cart or the like for you to ride in."

"Will it be enough?" I ask.

She shrugs. "If it isn't, I'm sure we'll get you out alive regardless."

Ah. They are all risking their lives for me, and she's not convinced I deserve it. I can't fault her there. "Lirika, why did you decide to come along on this rescue attempt?"

She glances at me, disbelief evident in the quirk of her brows. "You think I would have refused just because you're not one of us? I'm here because Bren asked me. Now, do you want to learn to pick a lock or not?"

I sigh and set my bowl down on the tray. "Yes, but first we need to figure out how I'm going to walk out of this inn without risking anyone's life." My likeness on the flier is a good one. It has nothing to do with my clothes and everything to do with my face. I can't change that.

"Your hair's long on the fliers," Lirika observes. "We could cut it short. Real short."

I raise a hand to my braid, thinking inanely of the hours Nesa spent working out the knots. Of men liking long hair. "Cut it?"

Lirika's lips press together in disapproval. "Never mind."

I drop my fingers from my hair and clear my throat, embarrassed that I even hesitated. This isn't worth my friends' safety. "You think I can pull off looking like a boy?"

She shrugs. "At least enough to fool folk for a few minutes, stop people from looking too carefully."

"Do we have the clothes for it?"

Lirika eyes me speculatively, and I don't miss the sudden gleam of amusement in her eyes. "We can put you in Bren's clothes. He's not much taller than you, and your builds are close enough. We cut your hair short, add a little swagger to your walk . . ."

It's a good plan, though there's one thing I can't hide. "I'm always going to limp."

"We could lean into that. I could get you a cane."

I pause. I used a walking stick back home when I went for longer wanders through the plains. A cane would be no different, except for one issue. "I need my left hand for a cane. I don't think I'd be able to do it, not with my wound still so new."

"Never mind," Lirika says. This time her tone is kinder. "We'll just make you as convincing a boy as possible." She extracts a small pair of scissors from her pack. She is a literal treasure trove of tools, it seems. "Let's get started."

CHAPTER

16

Bren comes to fetch us an hour before sundown, as promised. He steps through the door after his signature knock and stops in his tracks, staring at me.

Lirika and I are seated on the cushions before the table, sharing a pot of mint tea. We've packed everything up, returned the padlock I practiced on to its home, and are only passing the time now, waiting for him to arrive.

Bren's jaw drops in shock, his gaze roving over my hair—barely finger length up top, cut even closer along the sides of my face and in back—and then drops to the rest of me.

"Are you—are you wearing my *clothes?*" he asks, voice strangely hoarse.

Lirika leans back. "They suit her, don't you think?" she asks cheekily.

The tunic fits surprisingly well, especially with the cloth binder Lirika improvised for me. The soft grey-blue is adorned only by a touch of embroidery around the neck and cuffs—no more than a simple line tracing the cuts. A small V gives the curved neckline a little definition at its lowest point. The fabric is soft, the cuffs slightly frayed from use, from all the times Bren must have quite literally hidden something up his sleeve.

The charcoal grey pants are a bit snug around my waist and hips—who knew Bren was so trim?—and the slight amount of extra length tucks easily into my boots. They're very much his, from the faint smell of him to the simple fact that both of the pockets have false seams—allowing my hand through to reach my knife, now strapped to my thigh. It explains how Bren always seems to draw his weapons from nowhere. I feel slightly shivery knowing that.

Bren's eyes darken as he looks at me, an emotion staring out at me that I don't recognize at all. He turns sharply and picks up his pack and Artemian's from where they rest against the wall. "There's a cart waiting downstairs. You have your packs?"

"Yes." I push myself to my feet, slip the strap of my satchel over my head, and swing my cloak over my shoulders.

There was no way to hide my turned foot, so we decided not to try. Instead, with my pants tucked in, the shape of my left boot curved around my turned foot is startlingly clear. It says, according to Lirika, that I don't believe I have anything to hide, even as I use the cloak to disguise my shape.

Lirika gathers the two remaining packs and slides me a look rich with amusement as we follow an uncharacteristically silent Bren out the door. I'm not sure why she finds Bren's reaction so entertaining. He hardly seems to approve of our actions. But then he hasn't said he doesn't, so maybe he does. Or he doesn't care either way.

I take the stairs down a little more slowly than usual, still favoring my ankle. Bren matches his pace to mine, keeping two steps ahead, and Lirika follows behind. As soon as I reach the bottom, Bren heads off again, leading us out the back door, past a stable boy who has his hands full with an ornery old nag, to a neat little cart harnessed to a sturdy pony.

Bren leaps up and deposits the packs at the back, atop a scattering of straw, before offering his hand to help me climb up, his grip surprisingly warm through my glove. I glance at him uncertainly.

He offers me a tight smile. The evening light burnishes the planes of his face and shines on his own long locks, tied back in a tail, as ever. "All right?"

"You . . . don't mind, do you?" I ask, my voice low. "About the clothes?"

His smile deepens and darkens. "You can wear my clothes anytime you like, Rae."

Mortified, I clamp my mouth shut and clamber the rest of the way into the cart without looking at him. He moves to sit on the bench beside the driver, his shoulders shaking with repressed laughter. Which is a good thing, I tell myself firmly. It means he's just teasing me, and that's a clear sign that he really doesn't mind. I settle in the straw across from Lirika, ignoring the thoughtful look she turns on me.

The city seems no different from yesterday. It's a little surreal, knowing that I killed two men, that whoever is heading the Port Authority now wants me caught for their own purposes. Whether that means a quick execution or being turned over to Morrel, it certainly doesn't involve being returned alive to Tarinon. Whatever those realities might be, the city around me bustles on with its own life.

The pony sets a quick pace through the streets, its driver keeping to quieter neighborhoods. Eventually, we come out from the back alleys along the river road and follow it a short distance upriver to a crowded public dock.

Bren pays the driver while Lirika and I clamber out the back. I keep my left hand with its missing finger clearly visible over the folds of my cloak and brace my feet against the stones underfoot in a decidedly masculine manner that would have had the ladies of the court looking at me askance.

"This way," Bren says, leading us to the dock. We pass a signpost, and there, flapping in the stiff wind, is my own face staring back at me. I grit my teeth and keep walking. Surely someone will notice? But the short length of my hair ruffles in the wind, utterly unlike the braid I'm supposed to have, and no one even looks at me twice.

Halfway down the dock, a roughly dressed sailor waits by a rowboat. Bren stops to speak with him and then swings his packs in. "This is your ride. You'll stay in the shadow of the main docks until we signal you, then come aboard."

"What if you don't?" I ask, my palms suddenly sweaty. Because this is real: Bren has brought together a motley group of sailors and fighters to take control of the *Heron*, take its captain and crew prisoner, and sail it away, all in full view of the harbor.

"Then find another way upriver," he says grimly. "Lirika?"

"Aye."

"You'll see Rae through for me."

"I will."

Bren hesitates, glancing toward me, then dips his head and departs without another word.

"Bren," I call after him. He turns, brows raised. I feel my cheeks warm, but I can't help myself as I say, "Just be careful, all right? You and Artemian."

He inclines his head, his expression gentling. "We will, Rae."

"You need any help?" the sailor asks as I turn back to the boat.

He's a rough-hewn sort, with a short, scraggly beard over a broad face, bulging muscles, and a missing foot, the appendage replaced with a wooden peg.

"Nah," Lirika tells him, hopping easily into the rowboat.

It's a good step down onto a moving surface, though. While I generally prefer to do things for myself, I don't want to turn an ankle over misplaced pride. My body deserves better than that. "Yes," I say, and reach out to take his hand.

We seat ourselves opposite the sailor's bench while he unties the boat from its mooring. A few minutes later he has us maneuvered out onto the water and turned downriver, back toward the harbor. He rows steadily and skillfully, each massive stroke with his arms pushing us forward across the water much faster than Gair ever rowed.

I slip my hand through the false seam in Bren's pocket to check my knife as the sailor brings us around the river mouth, angling past a series of smaller docks for the end of a large stone one. I can still remember my panicked attempts to reach my knife beneath the hem of my skirt while Bardok pinned me down and cut away my finger. I'm beyond grateful that Lirika helped me adjust the straps of my sheath to go around my thigh.

We gain the stone dock, and the sailor uses the mooring rope to tie us to a ring attached to the wall. There's a galley docked to the side of us. Thankfully, it lies relatively quiet. From here, we can see out to the galleys still waiting in the bay. The *Heron* is now the first in line.

We wait in silence nearly a quarter hour, listening to the slap of water against the hull, the low but constant rumble of movement and life drifting over the docks, the shrieking call of the gulls as they wheel and settle and wheel again, congregating in the open waters for the night.

"There," Lirika murmurs.

I squint and make out a trim rowboat disappearing behind the *Heron*, followed by a second one. How many men has Bren gathered? Does he know how many sailors are still aboard the *Heron*? Some of them must surely be on land for the night.

Beside me, Lirika mutters a curse.

"What?" I ask, and then see for myself: a handful of men are descending a rope ladder from the *Heron* to a rowboat that has been brought up to the front. "That's not one of ours, is it?" I ask, unable to help myself.

"No."

"At least they don't seem to have noticed nothing," the sailor says, proving once and for all he knows exactly what's meant to be happening on board the *Heron*.

We watch in tense silence as the rowboat leaves the side of the *Heron*. Darkness is gathering now, the sun fully set and the world growing dimmer. One of the passengers keeps a lantern held up, providing them with plenty of light to navigate the crowded waters. They disappear behind a galley, then reappear as they pull around to the next dock over.

I squint, studying the partially lit faces of the passengers, and my breath catches in my throat.

"What is it?" Lirika asks sharply.

"That's Morrel. The captain. He's left the *Heron*."

"Are you sure?"

I would know him anywhere, from his long, lean body, to the glint of silver in his ear, to his wide cheeks and sharp nose and the cruel line of his mouth.

"Yes," I say, my voice rasping.

Lirika swears again. "We'll have to wait till he comes back, then. We can't weigh anchor till we have him."

"But the longer we wait ..."

"You think I don't know?" Lirika snaps. "He's the one we want, though, and he's the one who will raise hell if left behind. No one will take note of a few sailors abandoned by their captain, but a captain deserted by his ship?" She shakes her head.

I stare across the waters to Morrel. One of the men is tying up the boat, the other passengers shifting about. There's a ladder of metal rungs attached to the wall, leading up to the top of the dock, just as there is next to us. In a few moments, Morrel will climb those rungs and disappear into the city. We'll either let him go, or, as Lirika thinks, we'll lie in wait for him, risking discovery for as many hours as it takes for him to return—and hoping he won't note anything amiss as he boards a galley no longer controlled by his own sailors. It's too much of a risk.

"We have to trick him back." I glance toward the sailor. "If you have a head start, do you think you can you row us to the *Heron* faster than a man with an empty rowboat?"

The sailor studies the far boat, taking stock. "I can do it."

"What are you thinking?" Lirika asks me.

"You go up there and tell Morrel your mistress wants to speak with him, that it will be well worth his time. Make sure he comes alone."

Lirika glances to where Morrel stands, reaching for the ladder up to the dock.

"He'll know it's a trick the moment he recognizes you."

"He won't want to let me escape. He'll follow." Able-bodied, male arrogance can be very handy sometimes. "You'd better run if we want this to work."

"I told Bren I'd stay by you," Lirika says, even as she reaches for the ladder attached to the dock beside us.

I grimace. It's the sailor who says, pointing, "We'll pick you up on our way out."

Lirika glances over to the smaller, wooden dock behind us, clearly no longer in use. "Got it."

She clambers up the ladder so fast it's like watching a lizard scale a wall. Not two breaths later, she's gone. Morrel has already disappeared along with his men, his rowboat bobbing silently beside the dock.

The sailor unties us from the mooring ring and moves us out into the water, keeping the nose of the boat pointed toward the old wooden dock.

"You a thief, by any chance?" I ask, keeping my eyes on the top of the dock.

"Nah. I'm clean now," he says wryly.

I guess that makes us both river pirates.

The thought brings me up short. I don't know what I look like —river pirate or something else—but Morrell will need to know me at a glance. My hair won't help with that, but my knife will. I slip it from its sheath.

I can't hear anything from the top of the dock; we're too low, the slosh of water lapping against stone too loud to allow me to catch the sound of oncoming footsteps. So, I tilt my head and pretend to trim my fingernails with my knife.

This is the picture I want: a girl who should be dead twice over sitting unconcerned in a boat, the knife she used to kill two men in her hands. My hand clenches around the hilt.

"You!" Morrel's voice cracks through the air, sharp with shock.

I look up and offer him a slow, cat-smug smile. "How good to see you, Captain Morrel. I was just thinking of you. You've something I want on board your galley. I'm surprised you left it at all."

He half turns, his gaze going across the docks to where his men must be disappearing in their chosen directions.

"You're all alone, Morrel," I sing out. "Not like last time. Shall we see who is faster?"

"What are you talking about, girl?"

"You are *very* slow today, Captain. I told you: I'm going to your galley to fetch the children you've stolen away."

He laughs. "You think you can sneak on board and steal them from me? I've a third of my crew on board to secure my ship." He pauses as the strength of his position dawns on him.

"Keep talking," the sailor murmurs. "Your friend isn't here yet."

I tilt my head back and smile at Morrel, gesturing with my knife. "I've a Fae blade and shadows to hide me. Your crew won't even notice I've come. They'll be ever so busy getting drunk with you gone."

I glance to the side and spot Lirika halfway down the wooden dock, stepping carefully. There must be rotted-out planks for her to navigate. Damn it.

"You're telling me all this because . . . ?" Morrel asks, his gaze gliding over me. He suspects it's a trap, but he hasn't worked out how it could be—not when he clearly has the upper hand by the numbers.

"Because I want you to know it's happening, of course! It's not like you can stop me. Unless you're going to swim after me?"

"I'll raise the alarm here."

I flash him a fierce grin. "Oh, please do, Captain. With that many witnesses that I've been taken alive, there'll be no opportunity to kill me before I tell my story to the royals. You *do* understand who I am by now, don't you?"

The sailor shifts and murmurs, "She's almost down. We're good."

"I'm going to your galley now, Morrel," I say, bright and cheery. "I'll be waving to you at your execution next."

I turn my gaze on the sailor and order, in the same loud voice, "Take us out."

He starts rowing at once.

Morrel swears and turns on his heel. I hear the faint thud of his boots as he starts running, lost almost at once beneath the sound of the oars cutting through the water.

"You know the royal family?" the sailor asks as he brings the oars around again.

"Yes. A little to the left—Lirika, can you jump?"

I stretch my good hand out, and Lirika leaps from her hold on the wooden pile, grabbing my arm and thumping down into the boat. My left hand twinges as my muscles pull tight, but it's an easy enough pain to ignore.

"Is he coming?" she asks, scrambling over to sit beside me. The sailor curses as the boat rocks, upsetting his rowing.

I glance behind me to see Morrel racing along the top of the far stone dock toward his own rowboat. At least he's alone, his crew too far away for him to call back. "Yes," I say. "Stay down. He doesn't need to know you're here."

She grimaces but shifts to crouch at the bottom of the boat. "I didn't think you'd manage it," she says, sounding faintly impressed.

I shrug, keeping an eye on Morrel as he reaches the rowboat. "Haven't managed it till we've taken the *Heron* and he's our prisoner. Kel, will you be able to keep ahead of him?"

"I'm working on it," the sailor says, his muscles bulging against his sleeves as he rows.

"Morrel's slow," Lirika says with satisfaction, peering past me. "He's not used to rowing his own boat."

We cut around an anchored galley, losing sight of Morrel, and head straight out into the bay.

"Lirika, we need a plan."

She tilts her head. "Don't you have one?"

"Not for on the *Heron*."

"He won't want to fight all three of us," she says slowly, staring out at the waiting galley. "If we want him to follow you up, you'll have to go alone. We can go around back and climb up from there."

"All right."

She casts me a thoughtful look. "He's dangerous, Rae. You'll need to keep yourself alive till we can get to you. If Bren's done, he'll be able to help you. Otherwise, I'll have to get up to you first."

The sailor clears his throat. "Haven't seen any signal yet, so there could still be fighting on board."

Lirika clicks her tongue. "That's not good. You'll have to keep Morrel distracted. We don't want him raising an alarm. Those other galleys are close enough to help if they decide they ought to."

I look back to the harbor, to the dark shape of Morrel's rowboat coming after us. "I can distract him."

After all, it's not as if there's a choice now.

CHAPTER

17

The still form of the *Heron* looms over us. The closer we get to it, the more trapped I feel. The quiet creak of timbers and the slap of water against the hull shouldn't make it so hard to breathe.

"You all right?" Lirika whispers, still crouched at the bottom of the boat.

I nod, pushing down at the fears rising up in me. Of course this is terrifying. I know what happened to me on board that boat; I know what those sailors are capable of. That doesn't mean I'm going to let it stop me. I just hope I don't have to kill anyone.

The sailor pulls in his oars and grabs the rope ladder hanging down from the deck, the wooden rungs clattering against the hull. "Quickly," he says, casting a glance toward Morrel. He's not that far away.

"Keep this over you," I say, dropping my cloak on Lirika. I half stumble the three steps to the rope ladder. The sailor steadies me by the elbow as I reach him. I haul myself up onto the first rung. "You'd better go."

He nods and I've only just made it to the second rung as he pushes the boat away. He'll bring Lirika around to the other side, out of view of the neighboring galleys.

I keep climbing. This isn't my first time on a rope ladder, or even on this rope ladder. I managed to make it up when my wound was still fresh. I've got no excuses now. I grit my teeth and push myself up as quickly as I can.

I hear Morrel call out to the departing sailor, hear the man reply, "That woman's crazy. I'm leaving."

Morrell laughs. I don't dare look back, just push myself faster. Far too soon, I feel the ladder jerk below me.

"I'm right behind you, girl," he calls to me. "Your help has gone missing."

I scramble onto the deck on all fours. The deck appears empty. I push myself to my feet and swing around, cast around frantically. Surely Bren should have left a sentry on duty? There's no one on deck, though. Over the thud of my heart, I can hear the faint ring of steel accompanied by thuds and grunts from underfoot. Then a voice barks a command and the fighting breaks off. Have the sailors surrendered? Or is it Bren's crew that has failed?

No. I can't afford to think about failure. Everything depends on them succeeding. I start walking, slow and steady, toward Morrel's cabin. For all that I said I came for the children, if I head to the hold, Morrel will realize there's trouble on his ship. If he starts shouting on deck, all our stealth will be undone. There's also no way I can fight him. I'm going to have to play this wisely: throw him off balance and keep him that way.

"Where do you think you're going?" Morrel demands behind me.

I turn to watch him clamber up the last two rungs.

"I've an interest in finding that pendant you took from me," I say, pitching my voice to carry over the faint sound of movement from the hold. "I assume it's in your quarters. Surely you weren't so foolish as to sell it? No, you wouldn't do *that*."

He strides across the deck toward me, and even in the deepening gloom I can make out the gleam of his bared teeth. He's going to kill me, and enjoy it too.

"Come along," I say brightly. "We can chat inside. I'm sure you have questions you want answered. I know I do. It's far too exposed out here." I glance worriedly toward the neighboring galley. "Someone might see us."

He blinks as I pivot and head for his cabin. The door is locked. I turn to find him hardly two paces behind me, brow furrowed as he watches me. He knows there's a trick here, but he can't figure it out and it's bothering him.

"Do you mind?" I ask, gesturing toward the door. My hands are shaking, but only a little, as if I half believe my own nonchalant act. "We don't have all night. I'd like to check on the children next."

"What's your game?" he asks roughly, unmoving. "I saw you last night. I saw you scared and half-drowned with blood on your hands. What the *hell* are you playing at now?"

"I want my hawk pendant back. I want the children. I want a look at your log, to find out your contacts. I'm happy to play whatever game you want in exchange for that." I gesture toward the door again. "Shall we?"

He pulls the keys from his pocket and unlocks the door, swinging it open for me. His gaze rakes the darkened interior, but there's no one here. I sweep inside and cross to the table, throwing myself into the chair at its head.

Morrel steps in and closes the door, but he doesn't lock it. I repress a smile—who knew I could get under his skin so much that he'd risk my getting away to allow himself an avenue of escape? Lirika won't even have to pick the lock to get in now.

He lights a lantern hanging from a rafter, bringing the contents of the room into sharp relief. There is his bunk, immaculately made, and a small writing desk, the compartments all closed and the surface clear. A chest sits at the foot of the bunk, and a few hooks on the wall above it hold a change of clothes and a sheathed sword hanging from a belt.

He turns to me just as a thud sounds faintly underfoot, followed by a sharp snarl of sound. Morrel tilts his head, brow creasing as he listens.

"There's no owl here tonight, though it may yet come," I say in a half-panicked attempt to command his focus. "I don't recommend sandbags again, in case you're thinking of that. They didn't work at all last time."

His attention snaps back to me, his whole body stilling. "What?"

"You do remember the great white owl perched above us that night?"

"Owls portend death," Morrel says, but he's listening despite himself, and he's just a little scared. I shouldn't have survived and we both know it.

"Not if you know their name."

A look of perturbation crosses his features. His eyes narrow and he starts toward me, hand on the hilt of his dagger. "Lies."

"Truths," I counter, spinning him a knowing smile. I slip my own knife from its sheath and lay it on the table in clear view. It's not like I could fight him with it, anyhow. "The owl portends your death, not mine. The knife is Fae-made and has tasted your blood once already. It won't be sated until it's drunk deep."

He jerks to a stop, barely three paces away. "It's just an old kitchen knife, not even steel," he says without any certainty.

I smile. "I really think we ought to talk about the things you're willing to give me to make me leave. Like that hawk pendant."

Morrel shifts, and I know he's going to attack. "Red Hawk's reputation doesn't reach the sea. I'm not afraid of your silver tongue, girl."

"Silver tongues, bone knives, white owls," I chant in a singsong voice, wishing desperately for Lirika to get here. I hold my hands up, wrists together as he takes another step toward me. "Tie me up, let me go. Either way, I'll have you."

Morrel hesitates a long moment before drawing a cord from his pocket and stepping forward to lash my wrists together. He ties them tightly, the whites of his eyes a little too visible.

Behind him, the door he never locked whispers open.

I need to keep him distracted.

"Do you know, this is the third time you've tried to kill me. I would have thought you'd learn by now."

"I would have thought you'd learn," he returns, drawing his dagger from his belt. He touches the tip of it against my lips, as sharp and unforgiving as a thorn. "I'm going to bleed you dry. First, though, I would like to hear you sing."

"Silver tongues," I sing, my voice as sweet and steady as I can make it. "Bone knives—"

"Shut the hell up," he snarls, lifting the dagger and turning his hand in order to smack me with the hilt.

"I think not," a voice says behind him. A hand closes on Morrel's wrist, twisting his arm around hard and fast, the dagger falling from his fingers.

"What—?" Morrel heaves himself to the side, just managing to tear himself free before Bren's elbow slams into his temple. Morrel drops like a stone.

I almost choke on the relief rushing through me.

Bren shakes out his arm and looks across at me, his gaze angry enough to scorch. "Did he hurt you?"

"No," I say, even though I can still feel the cold, sharp point of Morrel's dagger against my lips. Is that why Bren's angry? "I kept him off-balance for the most part."

Bren grunts and drops down to a crouch, binding Morrel's wrists and ankles with brutal efficiency. The scabbard of his short sword drags against the floor as he moves; it's the first time I've seen him armed with anything more than a dagger. He has one of those too, in a smaller sheath at his opposite hip.

There's another flicker of movement by the door. I look up just as Lirika steps in, her gaze flying from me to Bren.

"About damn time," Bren snaps at her. "Keep a watch."

Lirika obeys without a word, stepping out and closing the door behind her.

As Bren empties out the captain's pockets, he says, "I assume there is *some* explanation for your being here."

I shift, but there's no way to look capable when my wrists are still bound before me. Not unless I'm chanting eccentric threats. I lift my chin and say, "There is."

He looks up, meeting me stare for stare. I don't care if he's angry; I did what needed to be done. It was my risk to take. Does he think he's the only one allowed to do stupidly dangerous things?

Bren swears softly and rises. He drops Morrel's belongings on the table: coins and a second key, a bit of wire. Moving to kneel before me, he carefully saws at the knot at my wrists with Morrel's dagger.

"You could have been killed, Rae," he says quietly. "You understand that, don't you?"

"Of course I do."

"Of course you do," he echoes with just a hint of rue.

"You could have been killed in the fighting just now," I observe. "But you don't see me lecturing you. Or growling at Artemian for not stopping you."

The knot gives and my hands slide free of the cord. I flex my fingers. They're slightly stiff, half-asleep.

"I didn't growl at Lirika," Bren says, still crouched before me.

"No, you barked at her. Like an angry dog."

He grimaces. "She shouldn't have let you come up here alone." He lifts my good hand and rubs my wrist briskly. It's hard not to stare at him kneeling before me, his hair caught up tight in a warrior's top knot, the lines of his cheekbones and nose sharp in the lantern light, his eyes deep-set and dark.

"We saw Morrel coming ashore," I tell him instead. "We knew you couldn't take the galley out of the harbor without him."

As if on cue, Morrel moans and shifts on the floor behind Bren. Ignoring him, Bren releases my right hand, setting it gently on my lap, and takes my left hand in his. For a long moment, he stares at my hand, the curl of my fingers, the jagged pucker of peeling scar and scab over my final knuckle.

He exhales with a harsh laugh, his breath puffing warm over the back of my hand, and gently rubs my wrist. "So, you brought him back to us. What if it had taken me longer to get to you, Rae?"

"Lirika was coming. There were risks either way. This was the least of them."

"Really."

"Yes, *really*. It could have been dawn before Morrel came back, possibly later. The other sailors on shore might have returned with him, or in the meantime. Waiting would have risked all of your lives; this only risked mine. One life to protect many is not a hard decision. If Lirika or Artemian had done it, you wouldn't have been angry, would you?"

I force myself to tug my hand from his grip, lay it on my lap. My wrist is fine, and it's better if he doesn't touch me so much. It feels far too nice.

He sits back. "You're right. It was well done, Rae."

I suppress a grin, but I'm pretty sure he can see it in my eyes. He stands up, his lips quirking.

"Is the fighting in the hold over?" I ask.

"They surrendered once they saw it was that or die. We had a sentry posted who came to tell me you were on your way up the side of the boat with Morrel right behind you. It's the only reason I knew to end the fighting and come up here for you."

"It was surprisingly quiet below," I agree.

Bren looks faintly pleased. "Artemian may have gambled away six bottles of drugged wine to one of the crew a little earlier this evening, just before the last shift came on board to switch out with the sailors here. It helped push the fight our way a little faster."

Apparently, I'd been wrong. Morrel's crew must have started drinking before he ever left the *Heron.*

"What about the children?" I ask.

"No sound from them. I'll send someone for you shortly so you can help us locate their room. Until then, I want you to stay on deck with Lirika."

He nudges Morrel in the stomach with a booted foot. Morrel grunts, eyes slit open. I wonder how long he's been listening.

The fury Bren was holding back simmers up again, deepening his voice and glimmering in his eye. "If you try anything now, I will take you apart, sinew by sinew."

Morrel's lip lifts in a snarl.

Bren leans down, his boot pressing into Morrel's belly until the man's snarl shifts into a pained grimace. "There's a price to pay for your actions. Don't drive it any higher."

Morrel remains silent on the floor.

"Good," Bren says. He snags the bottom of Morrel's tunic and slices it free with Morrel's own dagger. "I'll thank you to keep quiet as well," he says and shoves the makeshift gag into Morrel's mouth. The man's jaw moves, but he can't work the wad of fabric out.

"Rae," Bren says, gesturing to me.

I push myself to my feet, grab my knife, and follow him out.

CHAPTER

18

L irika perches on the railing to my left. It gives her an excellent view of most of the galley as well as any boats approaching the open side of the *Heron*. Across the deck, the sailor who
brought us is hauling our packs on board. Bren has disappeared
into the hold to make sure the prisoners are fully taken care of before we look for the children.

"I'm sorry," Lirika says abruptly. "I should have gotten to you
sooner."

"It worked out."

In the gentle glow of the rising moon I can just make out her
expression as she grimaces. "Bren said you might be hard to keep
up with. No offense intended, but with your foot, I thought he was
exaggerating."

"Thanks," I say dryly.

"He's mad at you too, is he?"

"He got over himself."

Lirika coughs on a laugh. "That's good."

Artemian climbs out of the hold and heads straight toward us. I
push off from the wall, steadying myself as the boat bobs. It's not

quite as steady as it was on the river, but the harbor is still protected from the larger swells of the sea.

As he nears, he says, "We're cleaning up down there, but it's probably best if you help us find the children quickly."

He's right; they'll have heard the fight through the air vents and be terrified by now. I start forward, forcing myself to go slow so I don't stumble and fall.

"Are you all right?" I ask as I reach Artemian, noting the way the top of his sleeve sticks to his right arm, dark with blood.

He falls into step with me. "It's fine. A small cut, nothing serious."

"And the others?"

"A few of the sailors we brought on board are wounded; one died. We've a good number of prisoners, though, and some of them are wounded. We got them bottled up and they surrendered."

"What will you do with them?"

Artemian slides me a look from the corner of his eye. "Best ask Bren that."

I force myself down the ladder. The hold is filled with crates just as I recall, lit by a lantern hung from a central beam. There's blood spattered on the floorboards by my feet. I keep my back to the main space of the hold, aware of figures moving at the other end, some standing and some dragging bodies to the side. There's also the faint sound of someone moaning in pain.

"The children can't see that," I tell Artemian. "Not the bodies, at least."

He nods. "We'll make sure the worst is out of sight. Where are they?"

I lead him to the back of the boat, to the thin aisle left open behind a line of wooden crates. Two more obstruct the low door of the cell I remember. I grasp the first, testing its weight with my good hand. It's empty but bulky.

"Here," Artemian says, stepping up beside me. With his help, it's a moment's work to lift them both aside.

"We'll need that plaque," I say, pointing at the wooden rectangle with the familiar shape of the ward painted on it. He nods, slips out his dagger, and with three quick flicks of his wrist pries the plaque off the wall.

I bend down and remove the bar from the door, pull it open. The room within reeks of excrement and fear. Not a sound comes from it.

I duck my head inside the darkness, my stomach tightening into a knot, and say, "Is anyone here? It's me, Rae."

Silence. I shift, trying to allow more light to fall in from behind me. *Please.* They have to be here. "Cari? Lina?"

"Rae?"

Relief floods through me. "Yes, it's me. I've come back, like I promised. You can come out now. You're safe."

"It's a ghost," a boyish voice says.

"No," I assure them. "I managed to get out of the river that night. So did Fastu—I left him with a Speaker to be sent home." There's no need to tell them more than that, at least not yet. If ever. Instead, I go on, "I followed after you, and these are my friends who have taken over the ship. We'll send you back to your families, or wherever you wish."

The children don't budge. "Come along," I cajole them. "We'll get you a meal, and you can wash up. I want you to meet my friends. They fought the sailors and Captain Morrel just for you."

"They did?" pipes up the other boy. He hustles forward to grasp my hand. "Is he dead?"

"He's all tied up in his cabin." I guide the boy out to Artemian, who hunkers down and smiles gently, like a kindly uncle. The second boy comes out next, and then Cari launches herself into my arms.

"You were *dead*," she wails into my ear. I wrap my arm around her, not caring how she smells.

"I'm sorry, love," I tell her. "I know it was terrifying to watch. But we got away, and I'm very much alive." Still holding Cari, I duck my head back down to see Lina crouched on the other side of the door. She's nine, and the wariest of all the children. "Will you come out?" I ask her.

She looks from me, Cari still holding tight to my neck, to where Artemian squats as he speaks with the boys. Then she slips out of the room and straightens to look out over the crates. I push myself to my feet, keeping Cari's head turned away as I check to make sure Lina won't be able to see the bodies. Thankfully, they seem to be hidden. The men are seeing to their smaller wounds, wrapping up arms and talking to each other quietly. Wherever the prisoners are, they can't be seen from here. For all I know, they're lying bound and gagged on the floor behind the crates, not unlike Morrel.

Lina tenses, thin shoulders stiffening beneath the stained fabric of her tunic. "Who are all those men?"

"They're our friends." I ease Cari down to stand beside me. She clings tightly to my good hand. "This is Artemian. He came all the way from Tarinon to help us."

Artemian smiles and rises to his feet. "Let's get up the ladder and we'll find you a clean room to rest in and bring you food to eat and water to wash."

The children stare up at him with big eyes. He is large and imposing, and the scar by his mouth and blood on his arm draw their attention more than the tears pooling in his eyes as he looks back at them.

"Come along," I urge them, and they finally start moving when I do. We follow Artemian to the ladder, and I send the children after him before hauling myself up, rung by rung. I hook my left arm around each rung in an effort to reduce the strain on my hand, but my whole arm hurts from the treatment it's received today, and my ankle is still sore from all the running I did. It takes a while to make it up.

The children wait for me in a small clump beside Artemian. Cari is the youngest, then Lina, and then the two boys around ten years of age. They are all thin and dirty, their hair unkempt and their skin smudged with grime, and they look absolutely wonderful standing together, alive and whole.

We cross the deck to the main cabin area. Lirika has disappeared from her railing. Artemian leads us into a thin corridor dividing Morrel's cabin on the right from the galley kitchen on the left. There's a second door on the left, tucked behind the kitchen, another opposite it, and a final door at the end of the corridor that's cracked open.

"What's down there?" Lina asks as Artemian opens the door on the left.

"It's where the sailors mostly slept," he says, shifting to block their view. "You don't want to go in there right now."

The children don't argue, filing into what must have been the first mate's cabin. It's a good-sized room for a ship, I suppose, with a bunk to one side, and some cushions thrown on top of a ratty old carpet beneath the single window. It will fit the five of us very well —it's certainly bigger than the prison in the hold, and the window gives it an even greater sense of space.

"Here's the ward," Artemian says, setting the wooden plaque on the ground, propped against the wall. "I'll be back with food shortly."

The children gather by the window, staring out at the nighttime vision spread before them, moonlight gilding the tops of the city's buildings, and the windows and doorways lit up with the golden glow of lamplight.

"Is that Lirelei? Will you tell us how you got here?" Lina asks.

"It is Lirelei," I tell her, and launch into an abridged version of my travels, omitting my visit to the Port Authority altogether. By the time I finish, the galley has begun to move, the faint rhythmic creak of oars suggesting that Bren was successful in gathering an experienced crew complete with rowers.

Artemian knocks on the door, bringing with him a basin, pitcher, and a small lump of brown soap. I pour for the children while they wash their hands and faces, and before I am done Artemian is back. He carries a tray of food gathered from the kitchen: cold flatbread with olives and cheeses and a plate of peeled carrots. However odd the assortment of items for this meal, the children fall on it ravenously.

"Slowly," I caution them. "You don't want to make yourselves sick."

Artemian departs once more, and I spend the next hour focused on the children, making sure they don't overeat, checking each of them for wounds or injuries, and then helping them get situated for the night. Beyond the expected sores and lesions, the children seem relatively well. The two boys will share the bunk, while the girls and I share a blanket on the carpet.

A soft knock sounds on the door. I open it to find Artemian and Lirika.

"Bren asked me to fetch you," Artemian tells me. I'm glad to see he's changed his shirt, a slight bulk around his arm suggesting he's bandaged his cut. "Lirika can stay here if you'd like."

Behind him, Lirika smiles awkwardly, patently unused to children. I can't imagine whatever Bren wants will take very long. It should be fine.

Bren waits on the wide stretch of deck past the end of the corridor. Morrel's cabin opens to the deck directly, just beyond him.

"Rae," he says as we reach him. "We're about to go in to question Morrel. Is there anything in particular you need us to ask?"

I hesitate, remembering Bren's threat to take Morrel apart sinew by sinew, the violence in his eye when he spoke. I take a shaky breath and say, "I'd like to find out if he has a ledger or the like, somewhere he's recorded his dealings for his superiors. The snatchers."

"We've learned that already."

"Can I see it? Are you sure it's not written in code?"

"We're about to get it from him," Bren assures me. "You can look at it later. Anything else?"

I shake my head, remembering the men Bardok had chained in an upper-story room, bruised and bleeding. How does Bren intend to question Morrel? I don't *care* about Morrel, but I can't be an accessory to torture either.

Bren waits, still watching me.

My throat feels dry as sandpaper as I ask, "What are you going to do?"

He sighs. "Go back to the children, Rae. There's no reason for you to worry about this."

I want to stay with the children, I do, but I don't want—I *can't* walk away from this. "No," I say resolutely. "I'll come with you."

He glances toward Artemian, then says tiredly, "Come and watch, then, if it will make you feel better."

He takes my arm and walks me into the cabin with him.

Morrel still lies bound and gagged where we left him on the ground. Bren escorts me to the other side of the table, pulling out a chair for me. I slide into it without thinking, my chest tight with panic. If I'm here, surely I can stop Bren from doing something terrible?

Artemian cuts Morrel's ankles free and marches him to the table, shoving him down hard into a second chair. Bending, he murmurs something in Morrel's ear before pulling out the gag. Whatever it is, the captain's features go a little grayer.

Bren moves around Morrel and sprawls into the remaining seat with a lethal sort of grace. There's a cut near his left shoulder, but only a faint line of blood shows on the fabric. There's also someone else's blood spattered on his tunic, already dry. He tosses Morrel's dagger onto the table, where the blade gleams in the lamplight.

"We'll keep it simple, Morrel," he says. "I'm here because you abducted a woman wearing Red Hawk's sign. That wasn't very smart of you. Now, I've got your first mate on one end of the ship, and a couple of your crew on the other. I'm going to ask you a few questions I've already asked them. If anyone says something different, I'll ask what's survived of your crew how you used to punish insubordination." Morrel blanches. "Perhaps a couple of them would be willing to help."

Morrel keeps his silence.

"Very good," Bren continues, as if they're having a conversation. "We'll start with some easy questions. Who are your points of contact in Tarinon for the children you receive?"

Morrel darts a glance at me from the corner of his eyes. "They're thieves. We don't share names."

I smile grimly. He thinks I know, and he's at least partly right.

"Ah, but you know how to contact them. So, how do you?" Bren asks agreeably, and Morrel gives this information with only a cajoling reminder that his first mate will answer as well. I've no doubt he answers because of me.

"Where else do you collect people to be sold?"

"That's all."

"Are you quite sure?"

At Morrel's nod, Bren turns to Artemian. "Take a look around for the ship's log, would you?"

"Where was it Adeyn told us to look?" Artemian muses aloud. I don't know the name, but Morrel does, his shoulders tensing further. Perhaps it's his first mate.

"Behind the bed, wasn't it? In a hidden compartment," Bren says with a wicked smile.

Morrel watches with wide, panicked eyes as Artemian taps the wall behind his bed, moving his hand down until his knock sounds hollow.

"Ah yes," he says. He presses his hand against a smaller plank running above the bunk. It slides back to reveal a long, thin compartment. He lifts out a book and brings it to the table, setting it down lightly before Bren. Then he takes up a stance behind Morrel, waiting.

Bren rests his hand on the leather cover. "You're sure you don't receive enslaved children anywhere else?"

Morrel squirms but doesn't speak.

I reach across the table, my heart thundering. "Perhaps I should take a look," I suggest.

Bren grins, pushing the book toward me. "See if you can find yourself, kelari. That should help us break whatever code this is in."

I flip the cover open and turn to the back, the final entries. It is in code. Still, I have a little insight into what happened to me and the children. I start nodding as I read, even though it doesn't quite make sense yet. "No bone knives," I say meditatively, to mess with Morrel's mind a little more. "But this is where the owl showed up, and Fastu and I were thrown overboard. And this is the entry for Tarinon, I'm sure." I'm lying through my teeth, but Morrel believes me, his eyes widening.

Bren looks at Morrel with some disappointment. "Still quiet? I suppose we can also do this the hard way if you prefer. After all, I need to confirm what your men told me one way or the other." He gestures toward Artemian.

Morrel glances from me to the dagger in Artemian's hand. "Wait!" he cries.

"Pray tell," Bren says, smiling, and Morrel does.

Bren leads him through a series of questions from cities and towns to contacts and payments. I pass the log back to Bren, and he punctuates his questions by occasionally flipping through the pages of the log. Morrel puts up little resistance, and I realize that Bren uses a fine balance of cunning, intuition, and Red Hawk's reputation to get his answers. Not once does he draw his dagger or use his fists.

At last, Bren flicks the log shut. "That should be plenty," he says. "There's one other thing I need from you, though."

"What's that?" Morrel asks. His face is streaked with sweat, his tunic damp.

"You stole a pendant from my friend here. I'll have it back."

Morrel nods his head toward the chest sitting at the foot of his bunk. "It's in there," he says hoarsely. "You should know I respected it."

"Did you? When you threw her in the river, tied to a bag of sand?"

"It's an easy death," Morrel argues. He has clearly never nearly drowned himself, or he's desperate enough to hope Bren won't argue it. "She attacked my men. I had to. I didn't let them touch her, though."

Bren dips his head down, bending to look Morrel straight in the eyes. "I know," he says softly. "There's a reason I haven't done much else to you, either. But, as you say, certain deeds must be punished, including what happened to all the girls you didn't protect." He straightens. "The key?"

Morrel looks distinctly ill.

Artemian reaches out to pick up a slim metal key from the small pile of items Bren took from Morrel's pockets. "Is this it?"

Morrel nods stiffly.

It's barely the work of a couple of minutes for Bren to open the chest and rifle through Morrel's belongings. Bren knows exactly where a valuable trinket might be stashed, and he has it in his hand while I would still be sticking my hands in corners and lifting out clothes.

He returns to the table, the hawk pendant gleaming in the lamplight as it swings from its chain.

"Here, Rae," he says, holding it out over the table toward me. "You'd better hold on to this." I reach out a hand as I look up at him, at the reflection of gold and restrained violence in Bren's eyes. He drops the pendant in my hand and turns back to Artemian. "We're done. Gag him."

"I've answered your questions," Morrel says. "I can still be useful to you. You'll need an experienced hand to guide this ship. I can—"

"No," Bren says. "You can't. Allow me to introduce who can."

He goes to the door and opens it, speaking to someone outside. He turns back with a smile, and I recognize the particular sharpness of his amusement.

"Captain Morrel, I would like you to meet the new captain of the *Blue Heron.* I understand he is an old friend of yours."

A small, slim man steps into the cabin wearing a long black coat and a weathered captain's hat. His face has the look of worn leather, his eyes glinting with fierce delight in the lamplight.

"Morrel," he says, dipping his head in an insolent approximation of a bow. "I'll be glad to take your ship in hand."

Morrel bares his teeth. "You!"

Artemian's hand clamps down on his shoulder, keeping him in his seat. Morrel spits a profanity, and the next moment his head snaps sideways as Artemian delivers an open-handed slap. I flinch even though it's nowhere near a punch, just something to bring

Morrel up short, which it does. He shakes his head and glances from Artemian back to Bren.

The newcomer turns to Bren. "It'll be my pleasure to serve you, young master. We're heading upriver; there's a good wind and I'll have the sails unfurled shortly. Have you any further direction for me?"

Bren nods to Morrel. "We just have a detail or two to take care of, and then we'll be clear. You brought the papers?"

"Aye. They're here." He offers Bren a set of folded documents from a long pocket on the inside of his coat.

Bren opens them up, scanning them quickly, and then sets them on the table before Morrel. "You're going to sign these papers. They give rightful ownership of the *Heron* to the good Captain Belayn here."

"I'll do no such thing."

Bren smiles and leans in, his voice quiet. "I am all about choices, Morrel. Here are yours: you were going to make Rae sing, were you not? If you refuse to do this, then I will make *you* sing. You will sing, and sing, and sing, until I have cut away all the pieces of you that are not required to hold a quill and sign. Do you understand?"

A shiver runs through me. Surely it's just a threat. A bluff of sorts. Except it doesn't sound like one. Nor is there any hint that Bren is anything but deadly serious.

Morrel raises his chin. "The *Heron* is mine. I've given you everything you asked."

"You will die one way or the other," Bren says. "Choose."

"I'm not signing those papers."

Bren's lips quirk down as if he were faintly bemused. "I see. Interesting choice, especially now. I would have thought, if you were going to choose pain, you would have gone ahead with that from the beginning. It's always fascinating what personal connections bring out in a man. Artemian?"

Artemian sets a quill and ink bottle on the table, relocated from the writing desk against the wall, and unties Morrel's hands. His gaze moves from Bren to me.

Bren follows his look to me. Something flickers in his gaze, but then he reaches out, grabs Morrel's left arm, and forces his hand onto the table. The man snarls a curse, but Artemian is behind him, twisting his right arm so that he can't move. Without a moment's hesitation, Bren draws his dagger and slams it point down through the center of Morrel's hand, embedding it into the table beneath.

A scream lodges in my throat as I leap backward, half tumbling from my chair. Whatever sound I make is lost beneath Morrel's own screams.

Bren ignores us both. Instead, he pauses to hand the papers back to Captain Belayn, who looks only slightly shaken. Then he draws his sword. Morrel, choking back his next scream, stares up at him. I press my back against the wall, my heart thundering. I don't want to see Bren do this. He's not Bardok, he's *not*, but Bardok cut off my finger almost precisely like this, and now—

"You stole your old galley from the good captain here, did you not, Morrel?" Bren asks. "Do you know the punishment for theft? I was only just positioning your hand. To exact justice, I will need to cut it off. I might slip, of course, and get your fingers first. I'm sure I'll eventually find your wrist. Are you ready?"

Morrel whimpers, his gaze ricocheting from the dagger impaling his hand, blood leaking out around the blade, to Bren standing ready and waiting, sword in hand. "I'll sign," he gasps out. "I'll sign!"

Bren sighs and sheathes his sword. "A pity, that."

I lean against the wall, my legs weak beneath me, and try to calm my breathing. Thieves' justice. I should have known. Still, I thought such justice would be cleaner somehow. Without this edge of brutality.

I watch silently as Bren forces Morrel to practice his signature twice on a scrap of paper before allowing him to sign the documents deeding the *Heron* over to Belayn. It was brilliant of Bren to find the old captain: there's no question the man will keep our confidence, especially if he's been without a ship and with revenge on his mind all these years.

Only once the papers are signed and returned to Belayn does Bren reach over and yank the dagger out of Morrel's hand. "You've an appointment on deck now," he says.

Morrel whimpers deep in his throat. Artemian binds his wrists behind him again, uncaring of his wounded hand. He forces Morrel out of the chair and across the room. Belayn pulls the door open for them, then glances toward Bren.

"Go ahead. I'm coming," Bren tells him, his back to me.

Belayn steps out after Artemian and Morrel, shutting the door behind him. I'm still standing against the wall, though I'm steady on my feet now.

Bren turns and leans his hip against the table. Taking a kerchief from his pocket, he carefully wipes the blood from his dagger. "You've seen a little of thieves' justice now, Rae. Is it what you feared?"

I slide my hands into my pockets, trying to order my thoughts. My right hand brushes the hawk pendant with its chain. I wrap my fingers around it, fisting them tight as I try to think. "No," I finally tell Bren. "I was afraid it would be worse—I saw some of what Bardok did." I shrug uncomfortably. "I should have trusted you more."

He looks up from his bloodied kerchief, his gaze searching. He looks almost hopeful, which makes no sense at all. "Did you not find it brutal?"

"Yes." The edges of the hawk pendant press painfully into my palm, but I don't let go.

Bren remains still, his dagger gleaming in the lamplight, the kerchief smeared with scarlet. "Will you see it through with me?"

"What do you mean?"

"It's time for Morrel's execution. Will you see it through with me?"

I wish I were still leaning against the wall behind me. "Isn't it better if we—if we turn him over to Kestrin and Alyrra?"

Bren shakes his head. "You don't keep a man like that alive longer than necessary. That's only courting trouble. He's confessed his crimes; we've gotten all we need from him. It's time to finish things."

Morrel will be trouble. I know that. He'll take whatever chance he can get to escape or bring others down on us. He doesn't deserve any reprieve.

I only wish there were a court of law here, a judge to pass his sentence. Instead, there's Bren, a quicksilver combination of cunning and cool reasoning and simmering violence. And thieves' justice. I can only prefer that to the corruption that has rotted all the way through from the Circle and Garrin, to the Port Authority that sided with Morrel to kill me.

I squeeze the pendant painfully tight in my hand and nod. "I'll come."

CHAPTER

19

A steady wind blows across the deck, filling the sails and sending us skimming upriver. The sea is already behind us, and even the buildings of Lirelei have fallen away, leaving only a moon-lit landscape of rolling plains stretching out on either side of the wide ribbon of river. If there are houses along the river, or farther out, the occupants have long since turned in. Not a flicker of light disturbs the rolling landscape. It fades into darkness before it meets the star-speckled horizon.

Belayn leans against the railing to the right. Before him stand a dozen or so prisoners spaced out along the rail, each with a sailor holding him in place from behind. I recognize the heavyset form of Bull halfway down the line, and there at the end, hunched in pain, waits Thornbush. The remaining sailors Belayn brought with him stand facing the captives, quiet and ready for trouble.

As we near, my eyes finally catch on the thick, bulky shapes laid out by each prisoner's feet: sandbags. "Bren," I say, my voice barely audible.

"Is it not just?" He slips his arm through mine, tugging my hand from my pocket. I'm still clutching the pendant, the gold chain dangling from between my fingers. He glances down, then slides his hand along my arm to wrap around my fist.

"It's a terrible way to die," I say tightly.

"I know." He turns to face me. Gently, he tugs at the chain. I force myself to peel back my fingers, let it go. He unclasps the chain, lets the hawk pendant fall to its center. "They chose this for themselves. You weren't the first they tried to kill that way, though I'm fairly certain you and Fastu were the only ones to survive. Thieves' justice is equal in weight to the transgression, Rae."

His fingers brush the nape of my neck as he clasps the chain around me, making my muscles shiver and tense though I'm not cold.

"All right?" he asks softly. He's close, his breath warm against my skin.

I make myself turn and he steps back, dropping his hands as I look toward Morrel. He's the first in line. Artemian has him pinned with a dagger against his neck, the blade weeping a steady trickle of blood. His hands remain bound, and now so are his feet, the rope already attached to a sandbag.

Staring at him, I remember that other night on deck, when I stood where he is now, Fastu beside me. Fastu, who would have died that night, and still lost the light of his mind to the Darkness. How many other children has Morrel drowned? How many more did he send on to painful, difficult lives, and deaths, as slaves? Certainly, he doesn't deserve a better fate than he granted them.

"I'm fine," I tell Bren.

He slips his arm through mine again. This time I can hold it properly. Together we cross the deck to the prisoners.

As we join Captain Belayn facing the line of prisoners, Bren says, "You each know your crimes. Slavers. Murderers. Mayhap more. We visit upon you just one of the fates you granted those in your power. May God deal with you justly, and offer you only as much mercy as you offered those below you."

Morrel lunges forward, a strained, muffled cry issuing from his gagged mouth. Artemian twists, shoving him against the rail, and then flips him over, his head slamming against the outside of the galley. The sandbag rises up, pulled by his weight. Artemian gives it an additional push, tipping it over the railing.

All along the railing, the remaining prisoners are thrown over — some with as little grace as Morrel, others tossed together with their sandbag, the watching sailors stepping forward to help. I can't distinguish the impact Morrel makes as he hits the water from the accompanying splashes of the other sailors.

Bren's hand rests on top of mine, steadying me as the splashes fade away to quiet. I stare at the empty space above the railing numbly. They were here, and now they're gone. Just like that. Bren moves forward. I walk with him in a daze to look over the railing. There's a bit of froth on the water, barely visible in the dark, and that is all.

They're drowning down there. Nearly a dozen men, swallowing water and thrashing for air. I remember the crushing pressure, the screaming pain of my lungs burning. Each and every one of them deserves it.

"Easy," Bren says, shifting to pull his arm free and slide it around my back instead. I'm shaking again. I grasp the railing tightly with both hands, the pain of my left hand steadying me as I watch the froth disappear behind us, lost in the darkness, or perhaps dissipated on its own.

This will haunt me. I know it will—tonight, or in a week, or a month. This night will come back and sink its claws into me, but right now as I stare down at the last few bubbles disappearing among the dark waters, I'm a strange combination of numb and relieved.

There's no sorceress to pull Morrel free. He is likely already dead. As simply and completely as that. And I'm glad of it.

I gather myself and take a step back from the railing, Bren turning with me.

Captain Belayn bows to Bren. "I am deeply in your debt, young master."

"No debt," Bren says. "I only hope we might help each other in the future as needed."

"It would be my honor."

He departs, nodding as he passes Artemian, who stands a few paces away watching us.

Artemian's gaze moves from Bren's arm still wrapped around my back, to the pendant gleaming on my breast. He does not look in the least amused as he meets Bren's gaze.

My cheeks heat, and I take a quick step away from the comforting warmth of Bren's arm. I shouldn't be in the arms of any man, least of all someone with whom I have no hope of a future.

"I should get back to the children." I duck my head and hurry across the deck.

As I reach the passageway to the children's room, I hear Artemian say, "—the *hell* do you think you're doing? If you haven't told her?"

I stop short, just within the darkness of the hallway. Told me what?

"—not your concern," Bren says, his voice barely audible.

I tilt my head, trying to make out what else he says, but all I catch is Artemian saying forcefully, "I'm not just talking about that pendant."

"That's enough," Bren says, his voice sharp and clear now.

Artemian mutters something, and then says, "Don't play games with her. Trust me when I say it isn't worth it."

"Whatever this is, it isn't a game."

Artemian mutters an oath followed by an inaudible response, and then I hear the faint sound of soft-soled boots passing over the deck planks. Shaking myself, I hurry forward, slipping into the children's room before anyone sees me. Still, I can't escape the question of what Artemian meant, the thing Bren should have told me. Bren's voice saying, *It isn't a game.*

"Oh, thank *God*," Lirika breathes as I close the door behind me.

She's up and beside me the next moment, the children shifting. Cari's voice says, "Rae?" and then all the children start clamoring together.

"Did no one fall asleep?" I ask Lirika.

"No," she says in an accent of deep despair. "I told them every miserable folk tale I know."

"They were *terrible*," one of the boys affirms. "Couldn't you have told us any *real* stories?"

"I bet you have a few of those," I say to Lirika as she tries to get around me to the door.

"Yeah," she says, squeezing past. "Too much blood, not enough happy endings. Have fun, Mama Rae."

"I'm really more auntie material," I say, but Lirika isn't sticking around to listen. She bolts out of the room as if there were guards on her heels.

The children all look at me expectantly, waiting. They need me. Whatever I've been through, seen, and chosen in the last hour or more, I need to set it aside, close it behind that door in my mind. Find something bright and beautiful to share with the children so that they can at least fall asleep, whatever nightmares might plague them after that.

I take a slow, deep breath and reach back for a moment in my life that will take these children away from the horrors they've lived through. It's no surprise that Bean comes to mind. "Would you like to hear the story of how my little sister Bean shouted a dragon out of the sky?"

"A real dragon?" Lina asks, almost breathless in awe.

"Very real, very big, and very angry." I seat myself on the floor. The boys leave their bunk and curl up together around me on the floor, listening as I weave a story that is mostly true, lacking only the touch of Niya's magic that protected Bean when she most needed it.

The story is full of Bean's dramatics—her deep love of all creatures, her tendency to rush off to play the hero, her brash courage. As I watch the children and try not to think about what I've done, I find myself remembering Niya, quiet and steady, using her magic to protect Bean despite the presence of a mage.

I think back to my conversation with Ehelar, when he told me that talents that present early are often stronger. Niya has certainly taught herself some fascinating tricks over the years. I've never thought too deeply about them, but perhaps it isn't a small talent at all that she harbors, if she can help mothers safely birth their babies—under the guise of assisting our own mother in her duties as the local midwife. Maybe it isn't a small talent that can hide not just inert objects but living, breathing creatures in her stitches, carried safely in their hidden space for as long as a day. Or can sew wards that keep the Darkness at bay, day after day.

As Niya has grown older, I've often wondered if she wishes she had presented herself to the mages for training. My parents last discussed it with her when she was eight, already four years into her talent. She adamantly refused the opportunity they gave her. And they hadn't truly wanted to let her go anyhow.

After that, she was too advanced to be able to mask her abilities as newly discovered, and all of us, including her, would have faced devastating punishments if she revealed herself. After all, the only way the Circle can ensure that Talents will be brought to them no matter how young is if the penalty for refusing to do so would make even the strongest parent despair.

But even then, we'd thought Niya's talent a small one: something to play games with, to make a light or steady the heat of the oven. Only now do I begin to wonder if we have sorely misjudged it, if Niya knows better than all of us just how capable she is.

The children drift off to sleep soon after I finish my story. Eventually, I disentangle myself from their curled bodies and reaching limbs, and lie down on the bunk—it's the only space that will fit me, given the crowd on the floor.

I lie there thinking of Niya and her talent, and then Bren and what secrets he might be harboring, and then of the interrogation and executions I've borne witness to. The justice I've sought, and made, and dealt out myself, if it can even be called justice.

I do not fall asleep until late in the night. Even then, my dreams leave me restless and anxious, rousing each time one of the children does. I whisper meaningless platitudes to them, listen as they fall asleep again, and wonder if the day will bring any clarity at all.

CHAPTER

20

The following morning, Artemian checks in with me about the town Captain Belayn hopes to put into.

"He wants a town with enough distance from Lirelei that no one will know to take notice of us, as well as big enough to allow him to recruit a few more sailors and pick up some supplies," Artemian explains. "He's asked to keep going upriver. It will take until tomorrow night, if not a bit longer. As long as you think the children will be safe, Bren will agree."

He means safe from the Darkness. Anxiety roils in my stomach. The ward will hold; after all, the snatchers have no use for children taken by the Darkness. Morrel would have gotten a new one if this one couldn't hold two more days. "They'll be fine," I say steadily. "Do me a favor, though: see if you can find anything set aside specifically for food or water for that room below—spoons or bowls or the like. I need to inspect them. They shouldn't be used in the meantime."

"I'll see what I can find," Artemian assures me and heads off down the passageway.

I return to the cabin, my gaze dropping to the plaque with its painted ward. On closer inspection, the paint sparkles faintly; I suspect it's tinted with powdered stone, something that will hold magic for longer than ordinary paint, like a host of tiny amulets. I know it will work just as well today as it has since the moment I set foot on the *Heron* . . . but I wish I did not have to trust in it. I wish desperately I understood more about the Darkness.

After breakfast, I set up the cabin as a bathing room. I leave the eldest boy to take the first bath, and the rest of us troop out to the sunshine. From my visit to a certain brickmaker's yard in Tarinon, I know the ward will have a decent range. As long as we stay on the deck near our room, there shouldn't be any risk at all.

I bring along with me an armful of clothing from the executed sailors to be made over for the children. They're just clothes, I remind myself as I set them down. For a moment, I'm staring across a darkened deck to a line of men with sandbags tied to their feet. The sound of bodies hitting the water in a quick succession of splashes echoes in my ears.

No. The children need clothes, and I will use what I have. I push these memories, these men, back behind the door in my mind where they belong, where I put them last night. Sitting down in a patch of sunlight, I spread out the first tunic before me, thinking of it as nothing more than an old shirt. With quick, efficient moves, I snip off the sleeves at half their length and hem the ends using long, even stitches.

The children scamper about the deck, staring out at the plains and chatting with the sailor who rowed Lirika and me to the *Heron*. He's seated on a crate, carefully inspecting a rope for weak spots, and seems more than happy to engage with the children.

"So," Lirika says, plopping down beside me. "I hear you got to watch all the fun last night."

I hesitate. "I wouldn't precisely call it that."

"No? Bren doesn't usually let anyone watch him work, not counting Artemian, of course."

Ah, she means the interrogation, specifically. "I might have made a nuisance of myself," I say dryly, bending over my sewing. "I expect he thought it would be easier if he let me stay."

Lirika snorts. "Bren doesn't do things because they're easier, I'll tell you that." She gestures to the tunics. "How many of those you got to sew?"

"Four. This is the second. Then there's the pants."

"I'll help you with the tunics. Forget the pants for now."

"And let the children run around without anything on?"

Lirika grins. "They'll be covered to their shins with these tunics! I can help you with the pants if you give me till afternoon."

I raise my head, brows furrowed. "You're being unusually friendly with me. Why?"

She unfolds one of the remaining tunics and lays it out, taking her time assessing the sleeves. "I was never rude to you."

"No," I agree. "You were always polite. Even kind. But not necessarily friendly."

Lirika shrugs. "First, you're not some spoiled palace girl, like I thought you might be. Or some bumbling country peasant."

I swallow a laugh. Lirika's compliments might just be worse than her insults.

"I figured we'd be risking our lives for you, and you'd take it as your due. Most rich folk would. Then we saw Morrel rowing to the docks, and you didn't hardly hesitate. We're all upriver now with this galley to call our own because you led him up on deck and nearly got your tongue cut out before Bren got to you."

She meets my gaze. "I was supposed to be the one who got to you first. I thought for sure you'd be angry. We came as fast as we could, but rowboats are slower to maneuver, and I had to make sure no one saw me climbing up from the other ships. So, I apologized, and you just stood there, looking like you might have collapsed if there wasn't a wall holding you up, and acted like it was of no consequence."

"I wasn't going to collapse," I grumble. "Anyway, I'm glad you've decided I'm not half-bad."

"Nah, you're not," she agrees. "Now I'm going to help you with these tunics, and then I'm taking you to the upper deck to do a bit of training with you. Teach you a couple of knife skills."

My hands still on the fabric. "Knife skills?"

She raises her brows. "I have this wild guess that when we get back to Tarinon, you're going to go racing into one sort of trouble or another. If I'm not mistaken, Bren will be by your side or right behind you. So," she says with a sort of helpless exasperation, "if I want to have a thieving ring to call my own next week, I'd better make sure you're not *completely* helpless when that happens."

"Strategic," I allow, my stomach twisting at the thought of learning to kill. "I can see why Bren brought you along."

"Yeah, I'm sure he was just thinking about himself," she says, eyes bright with mirth. "Men, you know."

I honestly have no idea. "I can't leave the children unattended," I say instead, nodding to where they've congregated around the sailor, peppering him with questions. "They're not much trouble, but someone needs to be responsible for them. I need to make sure they've all bathed."

"Artemian can keep an eye on them after their baths," Lirika says, more than happy to volunteer someone other than herself. "Don't you worry."

It's not worry about the children that's making me shaky. "Lirika, I . . . I don't want to train to kill."

"Think about it as training to survive," Lirika offers.

I wipe sweaty palms against my skirt. She's right, but it's a terrible sort of logic. The men who are coming after me are killers themselves, slavers and worse. To survive them, I have to learn to defend myself. Still . . . "When I was at the palace, I started by learning punches and blocks and the like."

She grimaces. "We can start with that, if it will make it easier. Spend today on ways to break out of holds, that sort of thing. Work up to knives."

I nod. At least that gives me a day to get used to the idea. "You're really worried, aren't you?"

Lirika rolls her eyes. "Let me see. You want to take on the royal family, Bardok Three-Fingers, and maybe even the Circle of Mages —if I'm reading you right—all in the next week." She nods thoughtfully. "Yeah, not a thing could possibly go wrong."

It sounds pretty absurd when she puts it that way. "I don't think I'll be able to do anything about the Circle of Mages. I want to, but they're . . ."

"A bit more powerful than you or me? Who would have guessed?" Lirika grins, taking the bite out of her words.

"And I really don't want to take on the royal family—"

"Yes, yes," Lirika says impatiently. "You're also the same woman who turned herself into bait for the captain of a slave ship because the opportunity presented itself."

"I didn't *want* to do it!" I protest, half-laughing.

"That," Lirika says with feeling, "is the whole problem."

An unsuspecting Artemian shows up in company with Bren not ten minutes later, while we're still working on the tunics. Bren sinks down on the other side of me while Artemian lays out a meager set of items on the deck: a small pile of wooden bowls, a water bucket, and the ladle that went with it. Lirika eyes them in bewilderment.

"I couldn't see anything else that was just for the children," he says. "The bucket and ladle were in that room, the bowls— that's just a guess. Everything in the galley kitchen is pretty well mixed together."

I set aside my sewing to lift up the ladle. Bren nods knowingly as I inspect it. Running up and down the length of the handle is an engraving so fine my fingers slide right over it without sensing it. No wonder I didn't catch it in the dark. At its center, a stone has been inset in the handle as if pressed into the metal itself, the join almost seamless. The stone is nothing overly precious, perhaps peridot or topaz, but there is no disputing the fact that it is a jewel. Which could make this ladle quite literally the key to the Darkness.

"You think that ladle's trouble?" Lirika asks.

"There's a spell laid here." I trace the lines, tap the stone. "I'll need a mage to tell me exactly what it does, but my guess is it's related to the Darkness."

Lirika frowns. "Who are you going to ask? You got a mage you trust?"

I purse my lips, shake my head. The only mage I truly trust is Niya, but she's hardly accessible to me. There's Ehelar, but I'm unlikely to see him again, and I'm not sure I want to answer the questions he'll have if I do show up with the ladle in hand.

I could ask Prince Kestrin, I suppose, though his talent is as much a secret as Niya's. It's also much more likely to get me killed.

"Guess we'll have to go steal ourselves a mage next," Lirika says.

Artemian coughs on a laugh.

"Oh, I doubt that will be necessary," Bren says, leaning to the side to catch my eye. "Rae has connections to the Fae mages at court, don't you?"

"I do," I admit. It was Genno Stonemane who, at my request, assessed the items used for the Blessing and explained the enchantment on the cup provided by the Circle. "Except they've been getting less and less willing to help me, the more they know the Circle is involved. This"—I lift the ladle—"would probably constitute dangerously incriminating evidence against the Circle."

"Didn't one of them make that compass Bren has?" Lirika asks.

"The Cormorant," he confirms. "Which would suggest they're rather vested in Rae."

"Just because they're willing to help the princess track me doesn't mean they're vested in me. They probably bargained for something useful for themselves."

Bren considers this and nods. "The princess was quite desperate. It would have been good politics."

"Which means we need a mage," Artemian says. "Unless you want to trade in favors with the Fae."

"*No*," I say. I've got more than enough debts to the Fae already. Kestrin will be my best bet, if I can see him and Alyrra in private. "If we get to Tarinon without coming up with anything else, there might still be someone I can ask."

Bren grins. "More of your hidden allies, Rae?"

"Something like that."

"I would very much like to know whom you mean," he presses, still patently amused.

"I'm sure you would." I pass him a spare needle and the spool of thread. "You may work on Lina's tunic. I hope the two of you know how to sew?"

Artemian gives his crooked smile, and Bren bobs his head, his eyes sparkling. "We're to be tailors now, are we? As punishment for asking too many questions?"

"You might as well make yourselves useful," I say, grinning back at them.

I pass Bren the tunic I'm working on and lay out the next one to trim down. We settle in the sunshine with our sewing. It's a homey moment, all of us quietly at work on the fabric before us. It's simple work. With everyone's help, each child should have clean clothes to change into right after their baths. Mama would be proud of me.

The thought brings me up short. Would Mama be proud of me? I don't think she would blame me for Efrun and the guard's deaths, but what would she think of me now? I look down at the worn fabric I'm cutting apart, clothes from sailors whose deaths I witnessed without any objection, any sympathy or remorse. I've taken part in an interrogation that ended in violence, and I excused it almost at once. Brushed it aside, put it, with Morrel, behind the door in my head where all the darkness dwells.

Would Mama even recognize me now?

CHAPTER

21

My afternoon training with Lirika ends up expanding to include Bren, in large part because my turned foot means that I need to compensate for certain moves, or only do them with one hand but not the other. While Lirika excels at lockpicking, she is only what she terms a "moderately capable" fighter.

Unsurprisingly, Bren is able to provide that additional edge of expert advice, walking me through variations on each move and helping me adjust my technique so I don't slip or turn my ankle. Thankfully, the motion of the boat on the calm currents of the river is slight enough as to have only minimal impact on my balance. Still, by the end of an hour and a half, I am shaky with fatigue and more than grateful to return to the children.

I gather them around me on deck, ink and paper at hand, and write down the stories of their lives, their memories from the last three months or so, including the details of their snatchings. This way, they will not lose everything to the Blessing.

"Can you write about how you saved us too?" Cari presses as I work on her account.

"Not a word—we can't even tell about how Morrel threw me overboard, only Fastu."

"Will you get in trouble for helping us?" one of the boys asks.

"I don't know," I admit. I didn't pause to consider what Alyrra would think of our stealing a slave galley, or even of our execution of the captain and crew. Given that she sent Bren after me, though, I have hopes she will look the other way. Or simply not ask.

But I don't know what she can do if we're apprehended as criminals. Would she be able to protect not just me, but our whole group? I don't doubt she would try, I just don't know how successful she'd be.

"Better not to chance it," I tell the children.

They consider this grimly.

"I don't want to forget you," Cari says, her voice small.

I pull her into a hug. "I know. I'm afraid the Blessing gives us no choice."

Come evening, we snuggle up together in our cabin, the boys on the bunk, and the girls and I on mats on the floor. Like every night since I escaped, I lie awake staring into the dark until sleep takes me, and then fight nightmares until the restless cycle of sleeping and waking is no longer worth the effort.

"We're making excellent time," Artemian tells me when I bring the children outside after breakfast the following morning. "We should reach the town where Belayn plans to stop this evening."

I frown, glancing toward the riverbank. We can't be far from the town where Fastu and I ended up. If I'd bothered to ask its name, I could inquire about our destination now, but I was too focused on chasing the *Heron* to care about such details. Still, the trip downriver took Nesa and Gair and me three days; it will only have been two on the galley coming back up from Lirelei. We passed a few larger towns on our way down; it could be any one of those that Belayn has chosen.

"You'll miss the children, won't you?" Artemian asks, watching as Lina sits down behind Cari to brush her hair. The boys, meanwhile, are practicing their handstands. Cari jiggles where she sits, impatient to join them. I am so grateful to see their brightness, how resilient they are in the face of what they've survived. I can't help wishing I could find that same innocent joy myself.

"I will," I admit. "But I'm mostly grateful they'll be able to go back to their families. And that they all want to."

Artemian nods. "It would have been harder to manage if not."

Lirika walks up beside us. "Morning session?" she asks me. "Bren should be along in a minute or two—he's just speaking with Belayn."

I glance toward Artemian, grinning crookedly. "You'll miss the children too, won't you?"

He laughs and waves us away. "I'll watch them. Don't worry."

I follow Lirika to the upper deck, which once again lies quiet. She starts with a few warm-ups, then has me practice the punches, blocks, and defensive maneuvers I learned yesterday.

"These take advantage of natural weak spots," she says, showing me how to grab my opponent's wrist and pivot to shove my hand through their extended elbow. "No matter how strong your opponent is, an elbow is just an elbow. A knee is just a knee. Now try again."

I'm starting to get the hang of the move when Bren comes upstairs. He watches me through the sequence four more times before saying, "Looks good. Ready to learn a couple of knife-fighting techniques now?"

I glance from him to Lirika. "You think it's necessary."

"I think it could save your life," Bren says. "But here's the trick, Rae. Only draw your blade if you're prepared to use it, and by that,

I mean kill. It's your last resort. Once your blade is out, you will have only a few seconds to make your move, especially if your opponent is armed or knows how to fight. Knife fights finish fast. And sometimes, everyone dies. Winners just die later."

This is sounding worse and worse. "Bren . . ."

He takes a step toward me, regret in his eyes. "I will do everything I can to keep you safe, Rae. But you need to learn how to defend yourself too."

I look away, my breath unsteady. I know he's right. My knife saved my life in Lirelei, but it was a close thing—I almost didn't manage to stab the guard who held me. I need to know how to use it, and then do my best not to ever need such knowledge. I nod grimly. "I'll try."

While we go easy on anything that might involve my left hand, there's still plenty for me to learn with my right. Bren provides me with a piece of wood roughly the size of my knife and has me practice slashing and stabbing. I do all right until Lirika picks up her own piece of wood and steps in to give me someone to practice on. The movements are all slow, our focus on technique, and yet the first time I set the tip of my false knife against her side, I freeze up, my breath caught in my lungs. Then I whirl away, heaving and trying not to lose my breakfast all over the floorboards.

"You'll have to get past that memory," Lirika says.

"I know." I wipe the sudden sweat from my brow, trying to hide how my hands tremble.

Bren rests a hand on my back, waiting until I'm steady again, and then he says, "Try again."

I do, until I can simulate stabbing her without gagging. No matter that I'm shaky and bathed in sweat by the time I manage it.

"I think that's enough for today," Bren says, offering me a cup. I happily trade him my improvised knife for the water. My hands tingle strangely—nerves perhaps. The water helps a little, but mostly I want to go somewhere that I can curl up for a few minutes and not think, and wait for the shaking to stop.

"I need the washroom," I say, passing the cup back to Bren.

He nods, and I head across the deck to the stairs, the water in my belly swishing dangerously. Maybe I shouldn't have drunk the whole thing. It would be the height of ridiculousness to throw up *now*.

I wave to Artemian and the children from the bottom of the stairs and continue on quickly. Thankfully, they're halfway across the deck and busy with some sort of game. I make my way to the washroom, though really, I want my room. I want a blanket and an hour of dreamless sleep. I may as well wish for Mama to tuck me in while I'm at it.

By the time I'm done in the washroom, I'm a little steadier. I dry my hands and turn to the door, then pause. I can hear a pair of sailors in the passageway, voices carrying as they walk. It's a tight enough space I'd rather not have to shoulder past them, so I wait in the hopes they're headed toward the crew's cabin.

"What do you mean, so what? I know what the captain told us to expect when we came on board, but that's a thief lord up there teaching some girl to fight."

I go still, one hand pressed against the smooth grain of the door. *Thief lord?*

"Not some girl," the other sailor responds, voice gruff. "He put his sign on her for all of us to see, right before he ordered that execution. She's his, and you damn well better not look at her funny."

"You think I'm stupid? I'm not going to look at her at all. Still, I wish Belayn had said who was going to get him back his ship. That man has a reputation."

"We all know it. Now shut up before someone hears you. We've orders to keep quiet."

"It's only the children who don't know, isn't it?" the first sailor says, his voice fading as they enter the crew's quarters. A moment later, the door shuts behind them, muffling the rest of their conversation.

I reach for the latch with shaking fingers, my body cold through. The hallway lies quiet. I stand a long moment, my breath shuddering through me. How many times have I asked Bren who he really is? I've always known he wasn't telling me the whole truth. I've always known he isn't just Bren. But is Red Hawk just a part he's playing for the sailors, and the truth something else, or—or what? That's the only story that makes sense. Numbly, I recall Lirika saying *if I want to have a thieving ring to call my own next week*—because it is Bren's ring. Bren who is Red Hawk.

That man has a reputation.

I swallow hard. It's bad enough I've been hiding a growing attraction to Bren, an affection I don't know what to do with. If Bren isn't even what he told me—if he's what he explicitly told me he wasn't—

"Rae?" I look up. Bren stands at the mouth of the passageway, the water pitcher and cup from the upper deck in his hands. "You all right?"

I stare at him, the light at his back limning his silhouette, his face lost in shadow. I want very much to pretend everything is all right. But it isn't. "We need to talk," I say, my voice rasping.

"Of course." He moves quickly to the kitchen, reaching through the door to slide the pitcher and cup onto a counter, then turns back to me. "Your cabin?"

I force myself forward, push open the door. He follows behind me. "Are you feeling ill? Maybe we should have taken it easier today."

I turn to him, one hand out to press against the wall—it's the only support I'm going to find here—and say, "You're Red Hawk, aren't you?"

His eyes narrow. He gives the door a light push, shutting it all the way. "Rae—"

"Don't *Rae* me. Every sailor on board thinks it. Artemian and Lirika accept your decisions without question. You conducted an interrogation and an execution without blinking two nights ago. You put your sign on me like I'm something you own."

His brows jump. "That's not what that pendant means. It's a *protection*."

That's the only thing he's arguing?

"You were fine with me twenty minutes ago," he continues, a line forming between his brows. "What happened since then?"

He's changing the subject, subtly shifting the conversation, giving himself time to decide how to handle this.

I don't want to be handled.

I meet his gaze, chin raised. "I don't like to keep asking you the same question any more than you like answering it. So, this time you need to swear it to me."

He doesn't answer. He stands with his back to the door, his shoulders straight and his stance loose and ready, as if he's expecting a fight. His hair is caught back with a leather tie, the light from the window bringing out warm hints of brown among the black. It's his expression that carves out a hollow within me. Still. Closed. Assessing.

The silence draws out, and I find myself saying, "I know you lie, and I know you have your reasons. God knows, I've lied plenty in the last month or two. But if you swear you aren't Red Hawk, I will believe you."

He studies my face as if searching for something, and then he says, "No."

"No," I echo, as if the word will somehow change on my lips. Dread settles in my belly like a lead weight. "No, you won't swear it?"

"No," he repeats, as if he's only just now sure of the word. "I won't."

It's so simple, that admission, so quiet. I don't even feel it land at first. I stare at his chest, at the slight bump beneath his tunic that must be his own hawk pendant, my mind curiously blank. What did I think I was going to do, when I found out he was the thief lord himself, known for his brutality?

In my mind's eye I see a red-stamped image of a cloaked figure, see line after line of crimes listed out. Is that Bren too? Is all of that true? Surely, not all of it?

"Rae," Bren-who-isn't-Bren says, his voice suddenly sharp, and I realize I'm listing to the side as if my legs can't hold me anymore. I turn with a jerk, limp the four steps across the cabin to the bunk, and sit down hard. I'm breathing a little too fast, and this feeling in my gut—it isn't dread. It's cut too deeply, the edges too sharp for that.

I curl my fingers around the edge of the bunk, my left hand aching, and hold myself up by pure force of will. Numbly, I say, "I saw the flyers for you right next to mine."

He lets his breath out in a harsh rush that has the bitter ring of a laugh to it.

"It said you killed fifteen men in the last year."

He makes a sharp gesture. "There were seventeen men on this galley when we took it two nights ago. You brought the eighteenth. They're all dead now."

His words punch a hole through my lungs. He's right, and I approved of every one of those deaths. I also killed two more men on my own. Those are the only ones I'm being hunted for.

Whatever Red Hawk has done, the information on the flyer barely scratches the surface. *Torture. Killings. Disappearances. Robberies.*

He's done them all . . . and so have I.

He painted the streets with his own brother's blood, Morrel said. I don't know. Maybe he did. Maybe he had a reason, maybe that was justice, or vengeance. I wouldn't have believed it of Bren, but I don't know Bren at all, do I? Whomever I thought I cared for, he was probably just a figment of my imagination.

"Was he real?" I ask abruptly. "Or was Bren just a game you were playing?"

"He—*I* am real," the man before me says. He takes a step forward, spreads his hands as if imploring me, which makes no sense at all. "Bren is a name I use within my circles; it's what Artemian and Lirika normally call me. Red Hawk is just a title, nothing more. A mantle I wear, if you will."

"You expect me to believe that?" I demand, suddenly irate at how casually he's playing his deception, at how stupidly I let my heart get involved. "You may have played me as seven kinds of fool, but I've *met* your counterparts. I know what they're like, and there's nothing pretend about the power they wield or the violence required to maintain it. Red Hawk—you—are no different from that. The Scholar would hardly respect you if you were."

I inhale and click my jaw shut. But it's the truth. Our being here at all, on the *Heron*, is proof of it.

His hands curl into fists at his side. "I've never lied about *what* I am, Rae. I told you from the beginning I'm a thief. I told you I've killed. You were fine with it this morning. What does it matter if I'm a step above what I said?"

Was I fine with it? I believed Bren didn't kill unnecessarily—that when he did, it was for his version of justice, or simple self-defense. Which is what he told me weeks ago when I stayed the night in his home, after the Black Scholar took me hostage. But is there really such a thing as a just thief—an honorable killer? Or have I only been deceiving myself all this time, so that I wouldn't feel the horror of what I've chosen to do at his side?

I wrap my arms across my chest. "Fine," I say, since he's still watching me. "You're Red Hawk. Now I know."

Except I know nothing. I feel like I've lost my grasp on the man I thought I knew, the Bren who was always there for me, who met me on a palace rooftop for a predawn picnic, who talked me through the horrors I experienced by describing the streets of Lirelei until I was steady again. How can that Bren be the same man who masterminds the robbing of noble households, who executes whomever he sees fit, who—who has killed far, far more than I have any idea of?

"I'm still Bren," he says, his voice low and fierce. "That wasn't a lie, Rae."

"Fine," I repeat. I can't even find the line between fiction and reality at this point. It's all smudging together. Maybe there is no line, just a gray area that I've been walking for weeks. "You're Bren, and Red Hawk, and you've done terrible things but always for good reason, and there's no reason at all for me to be upset, is there?" My voice cracks on the final words, but there's nothing I can do about that.

He flinches. "Damn it, Rae. I've done terrible things for bad reasons as well. I'm in no way perfect."

I never expected him to be. But I still didn't expect this. Which just goes to show what a fool I can be.

He says, roughly, "I need—I'd like to still be Bren to you."

I stare at him in disbelief. "I can pretend a lot of things, but I can't live a lie like that. I can't pretend I don't know who you are."

"That's not—" He breaks off, shakes his head. "Can you trust me still?"

I don't even know where to look, can't understand what he means by such a question. Trust him in what ways? Of course I trust him to have my back. Do I trust him to always tell the truth, though? To not deceive me again? I thought I'd learned not to trust too easily after Garrin betrayed me and Bardok took my finger. But here I am again, having swallowed a deception whole, and Bren wants me to act as if it doesn't matter.

I rub my hands over my face, run them up through my hair, not caring how my left hand aches, how strange my hair feels feathering over the scab where my finger used to be. Everything hurts: my hand, my heart, the breath in my lungs. "I need to think," I tell him. "Can you—can you go? Please?"

"Go," he echoes. He looks away, out the window at the bright afternoon light reflecting off the river, then back at me. "We'll talk again tonight."

It isn't a question, so I don't answer it. He lets himself out. I listen as he stands for a long moment outside the door and then strides off toward the deck, his footfalls heavier and faster than usual.

I should never have asked him. Why did he have to come into the corridor at just that moment? What would it have hurt to keep my feelings hidden for the next week, and then parted ways in Tarinon, never knowing for sure? Now I have a mess of emotions there's nothing I can do with, and the knowledge that Bren lied to me in Lirelei, has been lying to me every day, and would have lied to me again this afternoon if I hadn't asked him to swear it. Why would he have let a whole galley-worth of sailors know the truth about him, but not me?

I stand up, but there's nowhere to go, nowhere to take this anguish and frustration, because outside that door is Bren. I turn and drive my right fist into the pile of blankets on the bunk. Once, twice, knocking them off the bunk in a jumble. I grab the folded edge of one and raise it up and smack it down against the bunk again and again. It only helps so much. I bend over the blanket, my vision blurring, and then I go down to my knees, bury my face in its folds, and let out my pain in a storm of tears.

CHAPTER

22

"Red Hawk is in a *mood*," Lirika announces, bustling into the cabin. I lie wrapped in a blanket on the floor, staring at the wall before me, and wonder if she will go away if I don't move.

"Are you sulking too? Oi, get up now! I can't deal with two of you grumping about."

She gives my back a nudge with the tip of her boot.

I jerk around to glare at her. "I haven't been sulking, I've been thinking."

She grins down at me, a tray in her hands. "I've brought a snack, grumpy. Get up and eat. We've work to do." She sets the tray on the floor and starts folding blankets with a vengeance.

I grimace and force myself to sit up. The quiet has given me a little space to try to understand what Bren's admission actually means. In terms of practical considerations, there seems to be very little difference between the thief lord's second-in-command lending his aid, and the thief lord himself. Except that Bren—as Red Hawk—has the whole of his networks available to him and doesn't need to ask permission for his actions or decisions.

That's all well and good, but it doesn't touch on the emotions knotted up inside of me. Those, I don't know what to do with.

I glance toward the tray. It bears a pot of mint tea as well as a plate with rye bread and white cheese.

I'm reminded unexpectedly of my cousin Melly, comforting me after I wept on her shoulder, offering me tea and a biscuit. Who would have guessed she and Lirika had so much in common? Although that's not all the tray has to offer. Taking up a third of the space is a small wooden box with a built-in lock; beside it lie two additional locks.

"Is that from Morrel's chest?" I ask of the familiar-looking padlock.

"Had to take what I could find. There aren't that many locks on board a galley."

"I'm surprised you found three."

"The box was in the chest, so the two of them came together." Lirika stacks the folded blankets on the bunk. "Let's have a look at your hand. Is it swollen at all?"

I hold out my left. "Seems fine." At least, it's no more visibly swollen than it was this morning.

She inspects my wound, tutting over it. "You're going to have a sweet scar, all that twisted line along there."

I look down at the uneven line closed over my knuckle, still thick with scabs. I force a smile. "Not enough to strike fear in the hearts of those who attack me."

She grins back at me. "No, but you've got Red Hawk's reputation for that."

I grimace. "I know he's Red Hawk. You don't need to keep repeating it."

She shrugs. "I figure you ought to try to get used to it."

Does she? How very thoughtful of her. "I see," I say flatly, pouring us each a cup of tea. "I'll get used to knowing Bren's real identity regardless. It's not as if there's much of a choice."

She makes a slight sound of disagreement as she takes her cup. A series of irregular thumps sounds overhead, followed by a faint cheer.

"What's going on up there?" I ask abruptly, gesturing to the ceiling—which is also the floor of the upper deck.

"Bren went up to train a bit. He was standing around like a thundercloud, so Artemian shooed him away and then sent a pair of off-duty sailors to spar with him. Now they're all up there matching their skills against him and taking bets on who can beat him."

I don't even know what to make of that.

Lirika snorts, reading my expression easily enough. "He needed to punch something. Men are allowed to do that, while we women are supposed to just hold it all inside us. But I'm game to hold a cushion for you to punch, or even spar with you, if you like."

"I already punched the blankets," I admit.

Lirika beams. "I *knew* I liked you."

I glance at her dubiously. "You decided that after I brought Morrel in."

"No, I decided I approved of you then. You've been growing on me the whole time, like a fungus. Can't say exactly when I started liking you."

Fabulous. I've always wanted to be taken for a mushroom.

"Eat up. I'd like us to have a go at all three of these locks before Artemian wants your help with the children again."

"He's had them a while already," I say, glancing toward the window. It's afternoon. Between our training session, Bren's revelations, and my . . . thinking, Artemian's already had the children nearly three hours.

"He'll be fine. He told me we could take our time, which is good because those locks will be a challenge."

"Then let's start."

She talks me through the technicalities of the simplest of the locks as she demonstrates by picking it herself, then passes me her tools. I work at the first lock, but my attention isn't what it should be, and I can't get the last pin to bind. I look up with a glare for the ceiling as another cheer goes up, this one louder than the first.

Lirika smirks.

I find myself saying waspishly, "I hope one of them beats him to a pulp."

"You don't, not really," she says, practically beaming. "He's also too good for that to happen."

"No one's too good for that."

"Given the capabilities of these sailors, he is."

My hand slips, and I lose two more pins. I throw the picks down in frustration. "So, he's Red Hawk. I get it, Lirika. But tell me this, how real was Bren? He said it's a name he uses, but is the person he pretended to be—" Well, no, that's an unfair assumption. Damn it. "Is the person he was as Bren actually real?"

Lirika's brow furrows. "Of course Bren is real. Didn't he tell you that's what most of us call him?"

He did, but that's not what I'm asking either.

"Right." I gather up the picks and hand them back to her. "I can't do this right now. Let's try again tomorrow. Artemian's had the children long enough."

She doesn't argue, though I get the feeling she's still trying to figure out my words. I follow behind her as she returns the tray to the kitchen, and then we continue on to the main deck.

The children are gathered at the prow, the wooden plaque with its ward on a nearby crate. They're playing some sort of game involving a great deal of shrieking and jumping. We can hear them clear across the galley, their voices breaking through the deeper rumble and occasional cheer from the fights still playing out on the upper deck at our back.

"I'm sorry I haven't been much help with the children," Lirika says abruptly. "I've never really been around little ones."

"It's fine," I assure her. "Artemian's got a way about him."

She tilts her head to eye me, her gaze measuring. "He had a family once, you know. His wife died in childbirth along with his second son. His first son is grown and gone now. Doesn't care to hear from Artemian, even though they're in the same city."

So much sorrow in so few sentences. "That's a lot to bear."

"Family is hard," Lirika says as we pass the steps to the lower deck where the rowers are currently at the oars. "My father sold me into a brothel. I was really lucky it was on the west side. Bren had been keeping a watch, and he raided it while they were auctioning my first night to the highest bidder. Got all us girls out as well as the two boys who were with us, and strung up the owners in front of the building."

I come to a stop alongside the railing, staring at her. It takes me a moment to gather myself, remember that Lirika won't want my pity. I ask instead, "What happened to the rest of them?"

She scuffs her boot along the worn wooden planks. "Most of them wanted work of some sort. It took a while, but Bren found them all places. I wanted to stay on with him, though. Help other girls, rob the men that would've paid to use me. So, he trained me up, and here I am."

I hesitate. This tells me a lot about her, but Lirika has also shown no inclination to spill her life story before now. "Why are you telling me all this?"

She jerks her chin toward the upper deck. "I figured you should know we're all a little broken in our way."

"That's an interesting way to defend him."

She rolls out her shoulders, as if this conversation were as dangerous as facing a fight. "You're probably a bit broken yourself, or you wouldn't—well, anyhow. He's more himself around you than he is with other people. I think it's good for him."

"What do you mean?"

"He was balancing on an edge. Bren was becoming the mask, and Red Hawk the reality. Then you came along, and I'd swear it's the other way now."

So she did figure out what I was asking. Her words ease my uncertainties a little, but realizing that maybe I do still know Bren brings other issues into focus. Other kinds of hurts.

Lirika goes on, "Almost no one knows him as Bren unless they're one of us. I think that says something."

I shake my head. "Only that he kept the other side a secret. Anyway, I'm not a thief."

"Oh, I wouldn't say that," she says with a sly grin. "I'd say you're in the thick of it with us now. Or did you already forget about luring Morrel on board so we could steal his galley?"

I grimace. "That was once. I'm not making a habit of it."

"That's a shame. You keep things interesting."

I start forward again, but she arrests me with a hand on my arm. "You're not just angry with him, are you?" she asks. "You're hurt. Your eyes are all puffy."

I shoot her an irritated look. "I'm upset with him," I say coolly, "because I believed him when he lied to me. He laughed off my questions, and I took his mockery to heart and ignored my own instincts."

"So . . . you're actually angry at yourself?"

Blithering prairie dogs! "It would be truly lovely if you would just let me be angry without having to think about it very carefully." Doesn't she understand that anger is so much easier to manage than hurt?

"I dunno," she says, tilting her head to study me. "But I've only seen Bren this out of sorts once before, and that was a bit different. Maybe he knows he shouldn't have made you doubt yourself. But maybe he also didn't think he had a choice. Which"—she rolls her eyes—"makes both of you angry with yourselves. Beautiful, really."

"If you laugh at me," I say with firm conviction, "I will put you in charge of the children for the rest of the day."

"Not laughing!" she exclaims, her lips quivering. "Definitely not laughing."

"Lirika," I say warningly, trying not to notice just how much she reminds me of Bean in this moment. How much I want to laugh with her despite everything.

"It looks like Artemian's waiting for us," she says brightly, starting forward once more.

I follow after her silently. But she's right, I'm not just angry with Bren—or myself—I'm also hurt. That he could have chosen to deceive me for so long. That he used laughter to play my insecurities against my better reasoning.

There is the truth of it: the hurt I'm struggling with is wrapped up in his laughter. In all the ways he's used it—to charm me into losing track of what I should have paid attention to, and worse, to make me actively dismiss my own instincts as laughable, that I might believe the lies he told me instead. I don't even know how much of his friendship—his teasing smiles and soft laughter— is real, and how much it's the character of *Bren* he's been playing for me.

Not that it really matters, I suppose. There was never much future past this journey open to us, and now there's even less. Red Hawk is *certainly* not interested in wedding a country girl and settling down to a quiet life. And I—well, I was only deceiving myself if I thought Bren cared for me in a way that would warrant a more lasting relationship. Either way, marriage was never going to happen, however attractive I let myself think him. Nor do I want anything less. Anything less would just end in sorrow, in my heart breaking in ways I wouldn't know how to mend, and I won't do that to myself. No momentary pleasure is worth that.

I take a slow, deep breath, let my grief sink deep down inside of me, and summon a smile for the children racing toward me.

CHAPTER

23

Dinner that evening with the children is a quiet affair. They're tired out from a day in the sun and half-asleep at their meal. Once we finish, I shoo them out to the washroom to clean their teeth while I deliver the tray of dirty dishes to the galley kitchen. For all their quiet, there will still be nightmares and tears to soothe tonight. It's best to turn in early.

"Rae," Bren says as I step out of the kitchen. I look up, startled. In the half-light of the passageway, he's more shadow than man, leaning against the wall at the entry. Beyond him, the deck lies bathed in the dimming colors of sunset.

"Yes?" I ask, and then curse myself for being a fool and standing there, waiting for him to go on. I should have just returned his greeting and kept going, but I didn't.

"I should—" I begin, just as he says, "We need to talk."

I hesitate.

"There are things I need to tell you."

More things? Now, after I had to extract the truth from him as painfully as a buried splinter? *Now* he has more to tell me?

"What things?" I ask, my voice sharp.

He runs a hand over his hair and I have a moment to regret my tone.

"You were right," he says, his voice soft. "I haven't been telling the whole truth."

I wrap my arms over my chest, as if I could physically hold myself together. "There's more? About who you are?"

"No, it's not that."

"What is it, then?"

His gaze skims over me, comes back to my face. In the twilit darkness, his expression is strangely grim, his lips a slash across his face, his eyes deep set and unknowable. "Let's go out on deck," he says. "It'll be easier to talk there."

He's right, of course. The passageway is no place for a conversation like this. "I need a few minutes to get the children in bed," I tell him. He nods and steps back, and I hurry away to round up the children. It takes at least a quarter of an hour to make sure they're all ready and tucked in. I sing a short lullaby and leave them drowsing in the half-light from the window. We never close the shutters, no matter how bright it is; every one of us needs to know we're not shut in, suffocating in the dark.

Bren waits for me at the mouth of the passageway. "The prow is quiet," he says as I reach him.

He falls into step with me. The main deck has only a few of the night crew out. They note our progress and by the time we reach the prow, they've all moved closer to the cabins. Just before me, a blanket is spread, with a pot of tea and a plate beside it with some sort of food. The sight takes me back to a palace rooftop, to the quiet and peace and hope of that morning, and to Bren assuring me he wasn't Red Hawk.

"I'm not interested in a picnic," I say abruptly. I turn and step to the rail. I'm being rude. I know it, but already the hurt is clawing at my insides. Better to just address the issue at hand and leave as soon as I can.

Bren's footstep sounds faintly behind me. "Rae—"

"You asked me if I can trust you," I say, glaring out at the darkening plains. The sunset is behind me; whatever colors it has left paint the sky at my back. "You must know you are the best ally I have left, whatever your name or title. I trust you as such."

He pauses not quite at the railing, his gaze trained on me. He looks unexpectedly desolate.

Well, good. I know that feeling as well.

"You asked me about the crimes I've been charged with," he says suddenly. "They're all true. I have killed, I have conducted interrogations that ended in blood, but I have tried to ensure they were in the interest of justice. Thieves' justice, of course, but I don't kill for the sake of it, or because it's convenient. I don't torture unless I'm visiting a punishment upon a man who has already proven his guilt—Morrel was a thief. By rights I could have taken his hand first. I . . . I know it's bloody. But I would not have you think me a monster."

What does it matter what I think? Still, I nod. I'm glad for this, for an assurance that even as Red Hawk, he leans toward justice of some sort, flawed as it is.

"I've made mistakes," he goes on. "Especially when I was building my hold as Red Hawk. I wanted safety and protection for my people; I wanted justice on the streets. Seeing you reminds me of who I was at the very beginning, believing I could right the wrongs around me. I lost my way for a time, and then when I came back to it, I didn't believe I could change anything beyond my own streets, with the rules I laid down. When I first met you, it was like meeting a part of me I left behind a long time ago. A part of me I don't want to have lost."

I was naively idealistic when I first came to Tarinon, but I'm not sure how true that is now. I grip the railing, staring down at the darkening waters below. Somewhere, far downriver, a dozen bodies bob at the ends of their ropes, hair floating around open eyes, fish darting in and out of gaping mouths.

No.

I take the nightmare image I've concocted and shove it behind the door in my mind, back among the shadows where it belongs, where Morrel and his crew have lived their lives. They were murderers and slavers, all. That's going to have to be enough for me. It's not as if I can undo what's already been done any more than Bren can.

But I can't deny this: I'm following Bren's path into a justice I make myself, bloody and ungoverned. I've convinced myself it's the only path I can walk. The truth is, it's not a path I'm sure I want to walk. While it might have been my only option to save the children, I have other choices ahead of me now. Choices I shouldn't assume are closed to me.

"I understand," I tell Bren quietly. "I know how easy it is to get lost, and how easy it is to turn to force as the simplest solution. I don't think you're a monster. I—I've been glad of your friendship these last weeks." Though, perhaps, if I had known who he was, I would have protected my heart more.

"I couldn't tell you who I was before. I'm sorry for that. When we first met, I couldn't trust you'd keep my secret."

"I know." He would have been trusting his life to someone he had only just met; I cannot blame him for his secrecy. But how many times has he spoken of himself in the third person since?

"I *couldn't* tell you, Rae," he repeats, and the deepening twilight lets me hear the agonized edge to his voice. "The help I offered was never meant to get this involved. It was best if you didn't know who you were dealing with. There were too many risks."

"Risks like the Black Scholar taking us prisoner, but not daring to hold you?" I ask dryly, the words a peace offering of sorts.

His eyes crinkle at the corners. "Risks like your Captain Matsin finding out exactly who he'd been chatting with."

"He's not my captain," I grouse to hide my answering flicker of amusement. Bren's delight in needling Matsin suddenly takes on a whole new light. "Why are you telling me now?"

"You asked me for my word," Bren says.

I am so glad that it meant something to him, that he didn't just swear to a lie to keep me in the dark. And yet I don't quite believe it. Not after he held on to his secret so long, so tightly. "Is that all?" I press.

He shifts toward me, drawing a half-step closer. "You saw me, Rae. You watched me work. You flinched, but you didn't look away."

No, I didn't. But Bren is talking about more than just Morrel— this is how he works. Vigilante justice, because everything else has failed in his eyes.

"That was quintessential Red Hawk. You stood by me for it."

I wrap my arms across my chest, nod.

"I should have told you back in Lirelei. It was easier not to— easier to pretend that I could keep on being only Bren with you."

I make a sharp gesture, my heart aching. "I understand: you kept your secret. You had to. I wish you had just said that there were things you couldn't tell me, instead of laughing at me, making me doubt my own reasoning. I wish you'd trusted me that much."

He opens his mouth to answer but I hold up a hand, force myself to go on. "It's the laughter that hurts the most. It's why I punched you before too. I know I'm not easy to get along with. I know I'm prickly, as you call it. That's how I keep myself safe. I'm so used to contempt or derision or disgust, people thinking my mind is as useless as they believe my foot is. I started thinking of you as a friend and . . ." I shake my head, my throat closing up. I'm not going to cry in front of him. I'm not.

Bren closes his eyes, head bent.

"It's me I'm angry with," I say, my voice rasping. "I should have trusted myself more."

"I'm sorry I made you doubt yourself," he says, his voice gentle as velvet. "I'm so sorry I laughed. You're absurdly clever, Rae. I couldn't think of another way to protect my secrets that was as elegant and simple. I never considered the cruelty of it."

"Every time I reasoned my way to the truth, you turned it on me with a laugh," I say tightly. "You should be sorry. It's hard to trust you when I've already been betrayed by someone else, and you—whom I thought of as a friend—do the same to me with a *smile*. I am trying not to be a fool, Bren. I am trying not to be some simple peasant from the country, but if all the city is good for is cruelty, I'll keep my country ways. How could you let every sailor on this galley know who you are, and yet not trust me with the truth?"

He flinches, reaches a hand toward me.

I step away, turning to face him. "Why, Bren?"

He lets his hand drop. "The sailors knew because Belayn insisted. It was a trading of secrets, because they were as involved in the taking of this galley as we were. If they attempt to report what we did, they'll only end up condemning themselves. This way, we're known allies."

"That's no argument," I say, feeling sick. "I did the same."

He rakes a hand through his hair. "Rae, if I only cared for you as an ally, or a friend, I would have told you the truth in Lirelei."

"What?" I say, unable to make sense of this.

"I keep trying to pull away from you, Rae. It never works. It's as if I'm caught in your orbit; I can only get so far before I come back again. I thought in Tarinon I'd be able to walk away, that I'd say farewell, and you'd go your way and I'd go mine." He laughs softly. "You're in no way predictable, Rae. I love that about you so much. I kept getting pulled back in, circling around you. And then when you disappeared, when your *finger* arrived on my doorstep, I would have taken the city apart to find you."

"Y-you would have done what?" My voice is shaking. *I'm* shaking. I care for Bren, I know that, but I never really believed he would feel the same way about me.

"You see?" he says, as if he hasn't just upended my world. "All you knew of me was Bren. I was terrified that you'd find out I was really Red Hawk, and wouldn't want anything more to do with me. You were right: it was cowardly not to tell you. I just didn't want to lose you."

I press my hands hard against my face. I don't know what to think, how to understand any of this. I liked Bren, impossible as it was. I don't know what to do with liking Red Hawk, and now to find out this? What does a thief lord do when he falls in love? I can't even tell what Bren is asking for. I drop my hands and ask, "What does it mean to you that you care for me?"

"I don't know."

I stare at him, and all the little hopes that I didn't even realize were growing in me curl in on themselves, small and helpless within my breast. "Bren, no. You can't say that. You can't tell me you care for me and then say you don't know what that means. What am I supposed to do with that?"

He stares at me through the deepening shadows, dark eyes so intent I can barely breathe. He's heard my words, the timbre of my voice, far too clearly. I didn't tell him he couldn't care for me; I didn't even mention my own feelings. I asked him what he would do with his. He's clever enough to know that means I care in return.

"Well?" I say sharply before he can question me, make me say it aloud. I need to know what he intends, need to think about all this, before I admit anything more. "You always know what you're going to do. So what are your intentions?"

He laughs again, and this time I hear the sorrow in it. Is that how laughter works for him? When he can't bear what he's doing, or saying, he lets himself laugh?

"There's no winning this time, Rae. I'm only telling you this so you understand why I hid the truth from you. I know you're a country girl from a good family. I know that where you come from, if a man tells a woman he cares for her, it means he intends to court her. That's not something I can do."

I hold my breath so he doesn't hear the sob caught in my chest. It's not fair. I've never let myself hope for someone who would love me as I am. It's the worst of ironies that I've finally found someone, a boy I already care for, and I still can't have that future.

I shift to lean against the railing, as if a little more space between us, something to lend me support, will somehow ease this. *Niya*, I remind myself. I've promised my life to my sister, and that's always been enough. It doesn't matter what Bren intends; I know where my path lies. Somehow, though, my heart still feels like it's shattering.

"You'll be targeted because of me," Bren goes on, his voice aching. "You already have been. I've lived with a great many regrets; this is one I don't know how I would survive. I don't want to be the death of you."

I have to swallow twice before I can answer. "I understand," I say, and stop there. Because I can't say aloud that I have started caring for him too—let alone that I might love him. It will only hurt him more, or make him feel he has to do something he can't.

"You know that I'm not looking for anything less," I say, my voice cracking. "I need someone who can promise me a lifetime, not just"—I wave my hand helplessly—"a few stolen moments."

"I know."

"So then, nothing changes."

"Except now you know."

"Now I know," I agree. I straighten, push away from the railing. I wish, oh how I wish, he hadn't told me. "Good night, Bren. Thank you for . . . being honest with me." However much it will hurt to carry this through the years to come.

"Will you have some tea?" he asks, gesturing toward the forlorn shape of the pot, no longer steaming. "We don't have to talk."

I shake my head. I can't. Not now, not after what he's told me. "Maybe tomorrow, with the others." I cross the deck back to the cabins, one slow step at a time, as if Bren isn't standing still and silent behind me. As if my whole world hasn't just been irrevocably changed.

CHAPTER

24

We reach Belayn's chosen town shortly before dawn. I lie in the dark listening to the elevated voices of the sailors as they maneuver the galley alongside the dock. My sleep was broken as usual, only this time it was Bren's revelations that have left me miserable and ridiculously prone to tears. Neither of which does anyone any good.

One of the boys shuffles off the bunk and goes to look out the window. Our cabin faces the bank opposite the town; there are only silvered plains and a farmhouse or two visible.

"We'll see it soon," I promise as the others sit up.

"Will we have the Blessing here?" Cari asks, slipping her little hand into mine.

"Yes," I say, grateful for this distraction. I describe the Blessing again, though I've done so before. It seems best to ease their fears as much as possible.

As dawn lightens the sky, I slip out of the room to fetch breakfast. Artemian is already in the kitchen, chatting with the cook. He helps me load up a tray with the last of the food originally set aside for Morrel's personal use: a canister of almonds and a half-dozen tangerines. The cook ladles out a large bowl of oats.

"I don't know how much of that we'll eat," I tell him apologetically. "It's all we were given when we were in the hold."

He pauses, sets the bowl down. "There's roast potatoes left from last night? And a bit of fish stew."

"That would be good." The children all but devoured the stew last night, even if the smell put me off altogether. The potatoes, on the other hand, were delicious.

"Wish I had more eggs for the little ones today," he says, filling a pair of serving bowls. "There you go."

Artemian lifts the tray and follows me out. "If the children are all up, I'll fetch the town's Speaker," he says. "Belayn has offered his cabin for the Blessing. You can take them over there when you're ready."

A larger cabin will definitely be more comfortable for the Blessing. The children clamor around Artemian, as happy to see him as they are to have their meal. He laughs and pats heads and only just manages to peel himself away.

By the time the children have eaten and washed, the sun is fully up, sparkling on the river. We troop over to Belayn's cabin. They immediately crowd the window to have a look at the town. I follow after them.

It's a vaguely familiar waterfront, not unlike the handful of towns Nesa and Gair and I passed. I frown, studying it. Surely it isn't their hometown? Could we have made the trip upriver that quickly, despite fighting the current? Belayn has had the sailors at the oars a few times, and has kept us sailing through each night.

I lean forward over Cari's shoulder, studying the visible buildings. I only spent a short while at the docks, and most of that time I was focused on the galleys, not the buildings behind me. Would I even recognize the town? I scan the docks and my eyes light on a familiar young face, slightly grimy. The boy whom I bribed for information races by with two other urchins.

Darkness take it! That means Artemian has gone to fetch Lui. Between my foot and my hand, he will recognize me easily, regardless of what I've done with my hair. He'll want an explanation of my presence; how I've shown up again with even more children saved from the snatchers, after running away from the accommodations he arranged for me.

"I'll be right back," I tell the children. I skirt around the table and am halfway to the door when it swings open. I come to an abrupt stop as Artemian ushers Speaker Lui inside. Bren follows on their heels.

Lui glances about the room, his first interest the children behind me. I'm wearing the skirt and tunic Nesa's mother gave me, wonderfully worn and nondescript. My shorn hair gives my face a sharper, cleaner aspect now which means there's a roughly one in ten chance Lui won't recognize me. Until I take a step or he sees my hand.

And then Cari, sweet child that she is, resolves it all by saying, "Rae, is that the Speaker?"

"Yes, it is," I say at the same time that Lui blinks owlishly at me and says, in accents of deep surprise, "Kelari Rae?"

Bren pauses, his gaze moving from me to Lui. He throws me a displeased look and very deliberately closes the door and leans against it, hands in his pockets. As if I planned this!

There's no choice but to brazen it out now. "Kel," I say to Lui, dipping my head. "I am pleased to see you again."

"Ah, you . . ." He glances toward Artemian with sudden understanding. "Of course! This is your Uncle Artemian. I did not make the connection at first."

Artemian's brows shoot up before he can catch himself. Bren blinks and then presses his lips together to seal in a laugh. At least he's back to his usual mode of enjoying trouble, though I've no doubt he'll have questions for me after.

"Yes," I tell Lui, "that's him."

"Ohh," Cari murmurs, all the children watching with interest.

Artemian gestures Lui toward the table. "I didn't realize you knew each other."

I back out of the way as Lui sets his bag down on the polished top. My eyes catch on the deep gouge in the grain, but there's no evidence of blood. I pull my eyes away and gather up the children, leading them over to sit in an orderly line on Belayn's bunk.

Lui tells Artemian, "Your niece came to me for help after she found that poor child, Fastu."

"Yes," I say, hoping he won't mention Fastu's fate before the children. "Speaker Lui gave me the paper to write you a letter— one you would have received if you hadn't already left Tarinon to follow after me."

"I see," Artemian says warmly. "Then we are in your debt, Speaker Lui."

"Nothing of the sort," Lui says, clearly flattered. "I'm only sorry Kelari Rae saw the need to continue on when I had already arranged a safe place for her to stay. I was worried for her."

"She had to," Lina pipes up from her seat on the bunk. "She was coming to help us."

I stiffen.

"Whatever do you mean, child?" Lui says. "Did Kelari Rae know you had been snatched? *All* of you?"

"She did," Bren says firmly, drawing Lui's attention to himself. "You may have the whole of the story, but not before these children are Blessed. We do not know when the Darkness might strike, kel."

The children frown, glancing as one to the wooden plaque with its painted ward, propped against the wall where I left it.

Thankfully, they all seem to remember my request not to speak of it, and Lui is as helpfully unobservant as ever.

"Of course, the children must come first," he says. He returns to unpacking his bag. "It's a lovely morning, is it not? All the more lovely that you are all free and safe. Now, let me tell you a bit about the Blessing."

He keeps up a gentle patter of explanation as he lays out what he needs. Bren waits by the door, and while I feel his gaze resting on me, I keep my focus on the children. I wonder what story Artemian gave Lui to explain the presence of so many children rescued from the snatchers, and how we are possibly going to match that story with an explanation of my involvement. With Artemian as my uncle.

Lina surprises me by stoically volunteering to receive the Blessing first. She sits before Lui, head held high and shoulders stiff. The other children hold their breath as Lui presses the opal to her forehead and then offers her the cup.

A slight shudder runs through her as she drinks. She looks around in confusion. "Where am I?" she asks, a hint of fear in her voice.

"Be easy, daughter," Lui says gently. "You have been on a journey, and we will see you home safely."

"Rae wrote everything down," Cari assures her. "She'll read it to you, all your memories you lost, and then it will make sense."

Lina nods, shoulders hunched as she studies us.

"I should like to hear those stories as well," Lui says slowly.

"Of course," I say, thanking God I was wise enough not to record anything about the children's rescue. "The children each have their own copy to take with them. But they need the Blessing first."

Lui nods and gestures to the boys. "Who's next?"

"I'll go," Cari says stoutly. She hops off the bunk and marches forward to prove her courage. The boys don't argue.

As Lui finishes, a soft knock comes at the door.

"Ah," Lui says. "That will be Ehelar."

"What?" I say before I can help myself.

Lui shoots me an amused glance just as Cari says, "Who are you all? What is this place?"

"It's all right, daughter," Lui says, using the same gentle tone as before. "You've received the Blessing, and we'll be sending you home to your family now."

At least that's better than some rubbish about being on a journey.

Lui continues, "The young woman there has written down your story for you, so you'll know what's passed as well."

Cari nods and allows me to guide her to sit on the bunk once more.

Comfortable that Cari has been seen to, Bren steps away from the door, allowing Ehelar in. He is dressed in modest mage's robes over a well-made ensemble of tunic, pants, and boots. His clothes are beige and green with a darker violet embroidery that meshes with the deep plum tones of his robes.

"I thank you for allowing me here," he says as he surveys the room.

"I'm not sure why you'd like to see the Blessing," Bren says mildly, "but we would hardly refuse a mage."

Ehelar dips his head and then pauses, staring at me.

"That would be Kelari Rae," Lui says. "You will remember her from a week or so ago."

Bren remains still by the door, but I recognize that loose, ready stance of his. What, does he think he's going to have to fight a Speaker and a mage over me? It's not as if I require saving from *every* situation I end up in.

"It has only been a little while," I agree lightly. "I thank you for your help the last time we spoke."

"I presume," Ehelar says with a faint smile, "that your journey was successful, then?"

"Quite."

"We've still two children to bless," Lui says, nodding toward the boys. "I don't like to delay such things."

"Of course," Ehelar says. "Please, proceed."

He watches closely as each boy receives his blessing, and then inspects the items of the Blessing while the children crowd around me. I give each child their paper to hold and tell them that Lui will read them their stories when they reach the temple.

"Why not do it now?" Lui interrupts. "I'm curious to hear them. Ehelar can read with us, if one of you might also help?" He looks toward Artemian and Bren.

"Of course," Artemian says.

I sit with Cari on the bunk, Artemian and Lina take the floor by the door, while Lui remains in his chair beside one of the boys and Ehelar and his partner hunker down by the window.

I read quietly to Cari, trying to ignore the stories being recited around us. She listens intently to the tale of her abduction: how she was playing in her hometown's streets when a stranger asked her for directions, then asked if she could just show him the way; and how she was then whisked away in an empty alley, gagged and thrown into a waiting wagon. It is not that different a story from those I heard from the snatched in Tarinon, which makes it somehow that much more heartbreaking.

There isn't much beyond her arrival in the dark hold, but it's enough for Cari to understand how she got where she is—Blessed and waiting to go home.

"An interesting tale," Lui says, returning the younger boy's paper to him. He holds it tightly, pressed against his chest.

"Very," Ehelar agrees quietly, having finished his read.

Artemian says nothing, returning Lina's paper to her with a sad smile.

Lui says, "I am very curious, kelari, how you found your uncle, and further, why these children were expecting you. Really, I can't imagine how you even managed to leave town."

"I found a family to travel with," I say, deciding to grant Ehelar a reprieve. "My uncle followed after me. He caught up with me in Lirelei. These children—well, I . . ." I hesitate, but even the time I've had since Lui's entrance has not helped me come up with a plausible tale.

"Kelari Amraeya knew where they were because she was with them for a short time," Bren says, shocking me into silence by this bald statement of the truth. "You will, perhaps, recognize this seal."

He slips the jeweled compass from his pocket, passing it to Ehelar first. The mage inspects the seal on the cover, his brows raised, then flicks it open. He frowns, and I remember with some relief that the ward leaning against the wall behind him will be misdirecting the needle. He won't be able to tell it's meant to point to me. Not unless there's some magical way for him to discern the target of a spell he's looking at—I've no idea if that's possible.

He studies it a moment longer before shutting it with a click and passing it to Lui, his expression pensive. Does Ehelar recognize the seal as a forgery? He likely spent a part of his youth at the mage's complex within the palace walls. He'll be familiar with the royal seal. I tamp down my unease. There's nothing I can do about any of this except hope he'll let any oddities slide. Which he's done before, but now, knowing I'm both safe and dealing in questionable matters, he might try to demand answers I'm not willing to give.

"You are on the *king's* business?" Lui asks, in accents of absolute disbelief as he stares at the compass.

I grin. *That* will teach him to make assumptions.

"The royal family's," Bren concurs, unfazed. "You will also have seen the fliers by now, asking for Kelari Amraeya ni Ansarim's return? We were sent specifically to find her and deal with those who abducted her. I've a letter with the royal seal explaining as much as well, if you need to see it."

He does? That seems as unlikely as the forgery proving to be real. If Lui and Ehelar demand to see it . . . I take a slow breath and discreetly straighten my posture. A great deal is riding on Bren's story. The least I can do is act like the royal attendant I am.

Lui raises his gaze to stare at me. "I *thought* the face on the fliers looked like yours once I saw them, but there was no mention of your injured hand, and . . . you wished to go to Lirelei, not Tarinon."

"I wished to see to the safety of these children first," I explain coolly. "It was my abductors who cut off my finger. The royal family would not have known of that." Or they might only have found out from Bren after they'd already commissioned the flyers.

"And then your uncle . . ." Lui glances toward Artemian, brow furrowed.

"You cannot be surprised I wished to aid the royal family in finding my niece," Artemian says, unperturbed. "I am sure you understand, however, why we did not share this information with you at first."

"Of course. I am glad we could help you, kelari," Lui says to me.

"I thank you both," I say on cue.

His gaze drops to the compass he holds, but he doesn't ask for additional proof. Ehelar merely dips his head. It's a little unnerving that he hasn't said anything; he's far too observant not to have questions.

"We would appreciate your discretion in this matter, of course," Bren says to the men, his manner mild, but there's an underlying strength to it. A reminder that he is on royal business, and a refusal to honor his request is tantamount to treason. I'm not quite sure how he does it, but it's brilliant.

"As you wish," Lui says, handing back the compass.

"I'd like to see your hand again, kelari," Ehelar says. "You did promise you'd have another healer look at it. Have you?"

"I said only if necessary," I argue, my cheeks heating as Bren flicks me a sharp glance.

"As you say," Ehelar says. "Since I am here, I may as well check on it."

"A good idea," Bren agrees.

I shoot him an irritated look, but nod. I trust Ehelar to check it, and I would have agreed myself if Bren hadn't beaten me to it.

Lui rises and begins packing his bag. "The children can come to the temple for now. I'll find them families to stay with by this evening, and have letters sent to their own families as well."

"What of Fastu?" I ask, since the children only know him by name now, and not memory.

"His family sent a letter; his cousin is on his way to collect him."

That's a relief, at least.

Ehelar shifts. "If the rest of you would excuse us, I'll see to Kelari Amraeya's hand now."

I can't imagine an audience would bother him. His magic was subtle before, in no way frightening. Nor did Lui's presence bother him. Which means he wants words with me, the magic just an excuse.

"Of course," Lui says. "Come, children, say your farewells."

The children take their leave of me quietly. There are no hugs, for they no longer know me, and have only heard that they trust me. They allow me to clasp each of their hands before they go. Lina even proffers me a brave little smile and whispers, "Don't worry. I'll look out for everyone."

I smile back, my heart hurting that Lina should be the one to comfort me, rather than the other way around. The children file out with Lui, followed by Bren and Artemian, the door not quite latching behind them.

The crack does little to assuage my nerves as I turn to Ehelar and the questions he will no doubt ask.

CHAPTER

25

E helar seats himself on the chair Lui vacated, watching me as if he thinks me the feral stray the Speaker once called me.

Then he says, "Lui hasn't thought to ask how you've been safe from the Darkness, given that you were held prisoner the same as Fastu, but someone ought to. I'd like to see to your hand, and perhaps when we're done, you might tell me."

I consider him and appreciate that he is seated where he is, that I don't feel closed in with him before me, my back against the wall with nowhere to go. I suppose I *am* a bit feral. Or I've just had enough things done to me that being backed into a corner would bring out my claws.

I cross the room to sit before him and hold out my hand in silence. I'm not agreeing to answer, not until I've figured out why he wants to know. The wooden plaque with the ward sits against the wall by the door, the perfect explanation that will also protect Niya, as long as I claim to have kept a smaller, similar one with myself. But I'd rather not explain at all.

He inspects my hand, his touch light. The cool wash of his magic flows through his fingertips and up my arm, easing tension and numbing the pains I've grown used to. I let myself rest in the quiet it brings. My wound doesn't hurt as it did the last time I saw him, but it still aches with every movement. To suddenly be free of that pain, however mild, makes me realize how much it's been wearing on me.

"You're healing up," Ehelar says as his magic fades. "I would counsel you to try to rest it a little more, if at all possible." He releases my hand and sits back, though the surcease of pain remains.

I stay where I am, seated before him. "I am curious why you're here at all, kel."

He raises his brows. "You asked me about the Blessing before you left, questioned the provenance of the Darkness. I took a few days to consider your questions and thought I would investigate it myself. Lui agreed to send for me the next time he gave a child the Blessing."

"I see." He cares, whether he needs to or not, and there's something wonderful about that.

"Good," he says with a flash of humor. "Now I hope you'll help me understand the answer to my own question. No slaver would take a grown woman captive and not mark her the same way they do the children. The Darkness is their protection. How have you been safe?"

I hesitate. As much as I trust Ehelar, the ward points to the involvement of the Circle—to his mentors and all he's sworn his life to. He might hear my words and turn on the Circle, or he might decide to protect them. I can't know which without knowing him better.

"It's curious," Ehelar says into the quiet. "That compass your companion carries is imbued with one of the strongest tracking spells I've ever encountered. Yet it couldn't find you while you sat a half-dozen paces away. Nor could the Darkness find you, though it took Fastu in your company."

"Not in my company," I say roughly. "He ran ahead. I couldn't get to him in time."

"But if you had, the ward you must carry would have protected him, am I not correct? The same way these children were safe with you while you traveled upriver—I sincerely doubt you only just recovered them an hour or two ago and managed to dash off their stories while waiting for Lui to arrive."

It takes all my presence of mind not to wrap my arm over my waist and hide Niya's sash from his sight. I've worn it every day since before I was abducted, but until we took the *Heron*, I didn't wear it openly. On the *Heron*, I felt safe and didn't bother layering its bulk beneath my tunic, with another sash on top. I didn't even consider that a mage might show up when I tied it over my tunic this morning.

But now Ehelar is sitting in front of me, asking me about wards.

If I don't answer, he'll look with his mage sight, and there's a good chance he'll find his answer. Nor is it one I can explain. There are some risks I'm willing to take. Niya's safety is not one of them.

"Your answer is there," I say, pointing toward the wooden plaque with its ward.

He turns, brow furrowed, and blinks in surprise. "What is that doing there?"

I stiffen. "You recognize it?"

"It's a second-level ward. Every apprentice makes four or five score of them over the course of our training. I understood they were always destroyed afterward."

Four or five score? That would explain the Circle's ability to easily supply such wards to the snatchers. "Clearly not," I say in answer. "That one was above the door to the cell where the children were imprisoned."

"That makes no sense," he says, brow furrowed. "Those are inherently flawed wards, and anyhow, there's no known ward against the Darkness—"

"Because it comes from inside the snatched?" I ask, echoing his argument from the riverbank. "Are you sure about that, kel?"

He keeps his face turned toward the ward, but he's watching me from the corner of his eye. "Did you travel with another of these? When you were thrown from the ship?"

"We guessed about the wards." I tilt my head toward the door, indicating my companions. "I managed to get hold of a smaller one before I was abducted."

"You didn't tell Fastu?"

"Not at first," I agree, my voice breaking. I clear my throat. "By the time I did, he didn't believe me. He ran ahead, and I couldn't reach him in time. I know I should have told him at once," I say wearily. "At the time it seemed too dangerous."

"How so?"

Ehelar's no fool. He'll put it together himself after only a little reflection. I may as well help him along. "To admit to the average person that there's a protection against the Darkness? A *magical* protection the snatchers have access to? One you just told me you learned how to make as an apprentice, and yet which no one—not even you—thought possible? Consider the implications."

He stares at me, the truth of my words falling into place. "That can't be."

"I wish it weren't," I agree. "You reasoned it out yourself a moment ago."

He stands up abruptly, turns to the window, then pivots and crosses to the plaque, picking it up to examine it. I rise to my feet, watching him.

"Is it any different from what you made?" I ask as the silence drags out.

"Yes," he says finally. "Ours were a step below this. But only a step." He traces one of the circles, studying the magic there that remains hidden to my eye. "Someone has adjusted it here, added one—no, two—small changes, and now it is both stronger and . . ."

"And?"

"More specific. This won't just stop any magical attack; it stops a particular one."

I wait, watching Ehelar, and he doesn't disappoint.

"I've never heard of the Darkness being a magical attack, yet if this guards against the Darkness, then . . ." He rubs a hand across his mouth, but that doesn't mask the dawning horror in his eyes.

"You understand, then."

He takes a slow breath, exhales. "If a faction of mages has gone into league with the slavers—"

"Only a faction?" I interrupt, unable to help myself. If I'm going to tell him the truth, I may as well trust him with all of it and get what I can from him. At best, he may actually be able to answer the questions I have. At worst, he'll tell the Circle of Mages what they already suspect about me—that I'm a danger and need to be dealt with. Permanently.

Which is a worry for another day.

"There's no reason to believe that it's more than a faction," he argues, but even as he speaks, I can see him thinking it through and coming to a different conclusion. Thinking of all those wards he made that should have been destroyed instead showing up among the snatchers. Someone made sure that every apprentice would make dozens of them. Ehelar is clever enough to reason that out very quickly. Even if it's not what he wants to believe.

"It seems—" He breaks off, shaking his head. "I don't know, kelari."

"You told me yourself the Darkness is a magical attack. Who is capable of sending out a magical attack in this land?" I ask.

He runs a hand over his hair. "I would have noticed such a thing."

"You've done it yourself," I say mercilessly. "Do you remember when we first met? You told me you renew the protections on the land; that's why you're here."

"If you're suggesting—"

"You renewed them two hours before you met me, which was precisely when Fastu fell to the Darkness."

The plaque slips from his fingers, hitting the floor with the crack of wood. "No," he says hoarsely. "That's not—that can't be."

He pivots, striding away from me. He makes it to the door, then swings back around and goes to the window instead. He stops there, his hands gripping the sill, and stares out. "You have proof?"

"Ancillary evidence only, kel, nothing conclusive. I am not a mage, nor have I been able to ask the help of any other mage sworn to the Circle. But every piece of evidence I've seen points toward it."

"Every child," he says in a ragged voice. "Every child who has fallen to the Darkness has fallen because of the protections we cast?"

He must have known a child somewhere, somehow, perhaps before his talent manifested. He's seen more since, bereft of the light of their minds.

"Yes," I say quietly.

"Tell me." He turns sharply toward me. "Tell me exactly what you are doing, and I will help as I can."

"No, kel." I meet his gaze, painfully grateful for his words, but he's still reeling under the implications of what he's learned. He may wake up tomorrow feeling differently. "I cannot tell you everything. It's too dangerous. But I do need your help."

"What do you ask?"

"First, tell no one—no one *at all*—what we have discussed today. It will put you in danger and risk everything I am working on."

"Then you are planning something?"

"Yes, but my focus is the snatchers. I have been ordered to leave the magical aspects alone." Not that I intend to obey that order, but there's no reason to tell Ehelar that, not when he might still try to protect the Circle, or at least his mentors in it.

"What's the second thing?" He seems steadier already, as if knowing what's being done makes the horror of it easier to bear.

"Assess the protections you cast. See if you can discover what part of them involves the Darkness."

"Even though you don't intend to do anything about them?"

"Knowledge is still important, kel. If we know what part of the protections is actually an attack, we might be able to find a way to, ah, gain the Circle's approval in removing them." I know perfectly well they would only do so if there were no longer any gain in aiding the snatchers, but I'll gather what information I can in the meantime.

Ehelar smiles painfully. "I would have done so regardless. I am not casting the protections again until I know what to leave out. But I am glad you hope to address it if you are able. How will I contact you?"

That's a trick—connecting him directly to Red Hawk could endanger them both. Nor can I trust that anything sent to the palace won't get intercepted. Slowly, I say, "There's a hostler in the royal stables named Sage. She knows nothing about this, but if I'm at the palace, she'll be able to reach me."

"Hostler Sage. Very well."

"The third thing is this." I cross to where I set my satchel by the bunk and pull out the ladle with its inset stone. "I need to know if there is any magic attached to it, and if so, what it does."

Ehelar walks over to me, leaving the plaque on the floor, as if he cannot bear to touch it again. He takes the ladle warily.

"The stone is a common one," he says slowly. "It can hold a spell like the one woven here for a couple of years before fading."

"You've seen such stones before?"

"Of course." He raises his gaze to me and says steadily, "As apprentices, we were trained in how to create our own amulets. We practiced on semiprecious stones such as these until we perfected our technique. Each of us made dozens of these, easily."

"You returned the stones to your teachers, I presume, because they could not hold very much power anyhow."

He nods, well aware of what he's saying. "We did."

"What of the spell it powers in the ladle? What is that?"

"Any liquid this ladle holds will take on certain magical properties."

I remember my conversation regarding the Darkness with Genno Stonemane what feels like a lifetime ago. "Let me guess: it creates a marker that is carried in the blood if consumed?"

Ehelar winces. "Yes."

I pause. "What if the ladle only touches the water, but isn't used to drink it?"

"I doubt it would matter. The properties are transferred to liquids that come into contact with it."

I consider this silently.

"Kelari, this ladle . . ."

"It was in the holding room," I say, gesturing downward. "I presume its marker is the one the Darkness seeks."

He holds the ladle in his hands, his expression sickened. "This is . . . not what I expected from you."

"It's a great deal to take in."

He laughs, but there's no humor in the sound. "When I first met you, I thought you were escaping an abusive husband or the like. Instead, you've uncovered a magical conspiracy that I've unknowingly supported." He looks at me curiously. "Why did you trust me enough to tell me all this?"

I didn't. I was only protecting my sister. Still, there's another truth here too, one I can admit: "You were kind to me. You helped those who could not afford your aid, and provided them with a way to repay you that allowed them their dignity."

"You mean the family who helped you travel to Lirelei."

"They trusted you too. That means a lot."

"Nesa and Gair returned late last night, you know. I was planning to stop by to see them when Lui's boy came to find me."

My breath escapes me in a sigh of relief. "I'm glad to hear it. Please tell them I'm safe as well."

"I will." Ehelar hands the ladle back to me. "It's still a risk to take, telling me all this."

I set the ladle down on the table beside me. "It was more of a risk that you'd figure out half of it on your own, ask questions in the wrong places, and make yourself some enemies. Anyhow, you told me if I came back upriver and needed help, you would do what you could to aid me. I'm taking you at your word."

He laughs softly. "I had no concept of what I was offering."

"You did insist on asking me questions today."

"I did," he agrees. "You have my confidence, and I can think of no better use of my time than to assess the protections. Is there anything else you need of me?"

I pause, thinking back over our conversation, over the fact that it was the protections Ehelar cast that stole the light of Fastu's mind. I've now seen the Darkness attack twice, and only once was it in the morning. I remember Ehelar saying something about the timing, but I can't recall what. "Are the protections ever cast at night?"

"Yes. The need to refresh them doesn't align perfectly with a full day. The timing shifts back about twenty hours every day. It makes for a couple of broken nights of sleep a week."

I nod, his explanation fitting together with what I already know. "That explains the Darkness taking children at all different times."

He grimaces but doesn't argue. Instead he says, "What of your companions? They are who they claim to be?"

I raise my brows.

"You were running from someone when we first met. I suspect now it was the snatchers, and not your so-called uncle, or the other young man. I want to be sure you are in good hands."

I feel an unexpected warmth in my breast for just how kind Ehelar is. "I am. You need not worry about me anymore."

He huffs. "No. You are only taking on slavers and skirting around a conspiracy of dangerous proportions. What should I worry about?"

"Keeping yourself and your wife safe," I say firmly. "If you cannot do anything more than you have today, you've already done enough. The only thing I truly ask of you now is your silence."

"I've already promised it, kelari. I give you my word again. And I wish you all success in this. I do not know much of the slavers, but I've seen the Darkness. It took my closest friend when we were children. I do not want any part of bringing it down on others. I'll study the protections and send you word of what I find."

"Thank you, kel," I say, and mean it with all my heart.

CHAPTER

26

I 'm still sitting in my chair, the ladle beside me, when Bren steps in and shuts the door behind him.

He leans against the doorjamb. "Tell me I don't need to go after that mage."

I snort. "God, no, Bren. He's an ally." I rise and lift my satchel.

He looks away with a disbelieving smile. "Of course he is. What was I thinking?" His gaze comes back to me, measuring. "Is that why you didn't tell us you'd been here before? That it was this town, this Speaker who helped you on your way to Lirelei?"

"No! I would have told you. I don't even know the name of this town; I thought it was farther upriver. I didn't recognize where we were till I looked out the window. I was coming to find one of you when Lui walked in."

His shoulders sag. "Then you'll tell me, next time, if something isn't right?"

His words, his patent relief, make me want to reach out to him —not that I would dare. "I'll tell you."

"I lied to you, played you against yourself," he says, an edge to his voice. "I can't imagine you've forgiven that already."

"I haven't," I admit, gripping the strap of my satchel. "I don't think I'll be able to forgive you until I know you won't lie to me again. I understand if you can't tell me something—I have things I can't tell you. But I need to know you won't knowingly deceive me."

He crosses the room in long, swift strides, coming to a stop so close he's all I see, broad shoulders and unwavering gaze. "I won't deceive you again," he says, his voice low and fierce. "I swear it." Catching my good hand, he lifts it and brushes a kiss across my knuckles.

His touch, the intensity of his voice, his *words* root me to the spot. I can't quite breathe, my chest suddenly tight. His expression shifts as he watches me, his gaze darkening as his lips quirk, and he brushes another kiss over my skin, slow and searing.

He's *teasing* me. I jerk back a step, my legs knocking into the chair. My hand is still caught in his, my cheeks on fire. I can barely think. "Y-you're not allowed to act like that if you're not courting me."

The words sound strangely like a plea.

He releases my hand gently. "No, of course not," he says with just a hint of rue. "But you believe me? I won't deceive you again."

"I believe you," I say, still a little shaky.

He nods and moves away, taking a seat in the chair facing mine. He's giving me a moment to gather myself. I sink down into my chair, pulling my satchel onto my lap. I can still feel the touch of his lips burning against my skin. I should brush it off, clear my mind, but I don't want him to know how much he's affected me.

He doesn't speak, his gaze resting on the table. The quiet draws out. Then he looks up, a quick flick of a glance, amusement crinkling the corners of his eyes.

I flail about for something to say and recall our first topic. "You were expecting to have to explain some of what happened to the Speaker, weren't you? You brought the compass with you."

He leans back in his chair. "I always have that with me."

Oh. I don't want to think about that either. "Do you really have a letter explaining what you're doing—or excusing you?"

"That was a bluff," he admits with a sly smile. "If you present someone with one piece of evidence, and offer to fetch another, there's a good chance they won't insist. I wouldn't have mentioned it if they seemed like the sort to demand it. I knew the Speaker wouldn't, and the mage defers to him, at least on the surface."

"I thought as much," I say, feeling somewhat vindicated.

"What do you intend once we return to Tarinon?" he asks. "You only talked about freeing the children. We've done that; I gave the Speaker a purse filled with Morrel's money to guarantee their safe passage. I've no doubt you've something dire planned next."

"You're the thief," I observe. "What are you intending?"

"I was thinking I'd let the princess know you're alive and safe, and see you returned to your family."

It sounds so simple. And not at all what needs to be done—or at least, there's a great deal more too. "Then you're leaving Bardok to me? Excellent. I'll have Captain Matsin take care of him."

Bren's eyes widen rather endearingly before he manages to sputter, "You know better than that! Bardok is my business."

"Why? Because he tried to manipulate you? He's been stealing children for years, if not decades. Whatever his problems with you, he needs to face the king's justice. The people need to see that slavers will be punished by the king, and not believe this is just thieves fighting over territory."

"The king's justice won't ever reach him," Bren argues. "Try to involve the king's soldiers and you'll lose Bardok altogether."

"But—"

"*Rae.* Think about it. Bardok has ruled his territory for nearly twenty years. You can't imagine that he doesn't have his own men in the guards, not to mention moles in the palace."

"Like you do?" When I was still at the palace, Bren sent me messages through a young page who knew precisely whom he served. It's not a stretch to imagine he would have men among the guards as well, now that I know he's Red Hawk.

He shrugs. "Precisely. Bardok will know if we involve the guards. Things will get messy fast. He won't just sit and wait for us to attack; he'll have his own plans in place, somewhere he can hunker down and direct his men from. You can't imagine he'll let his territory go without a fight. We'll end up with that street war he was aiming for, only on his territory instead of mine."

"No," I say tightly. Street wars are brutal, and bystanders often get killed. I don't want innocents dying because of me.

"No," Bren agrees. "I intend to take out Bardok and his closest associates in one blow. For that, I need allies, not palace guards."

"What allies?"

"The Scholar won't be amused to find he's been made Bardok's pawn—that's half of the information I sent up from Lirelei. If my people handle it right, he'll join his men with ours. That should be plenty to take out Bardok."

"So, you'll kill him in a street battle."

"No, a planned attack with minimal other casualties." Bren meets my gaze. "Bardok's a thief. Leave him to our justice."

He made essentially the same argument about Morrel—that it was too dangerous to wait for guards to be involved, that thieves' justice was the only real option we had. I believed him then, and I don't know how to argue it now. Because everything he says, all his arguments, seem perfectly reasonable. The farther I walk this path, the more impossible it seems to leave it.

I'm afraid of what it will mean for me, for who I am, if I agree to every murder ahead of us. I don't want to kill so easily, whether it's my hand at the blade or not. Whether it's Bardok, who deserves to have all his fingers cut off, or not. Maybe especially because it *is* Bardok.

"I don't think your thieves' justice is the final answer," I tell Bren. "Maybe it's all we have right now, but to actually stop the slavers? To make a difference in what we're trying to do? We need rule of law. Every time you choose a different path, you undermine that a little more."

"I've never worried much about the king's law, except insofar as it threatens us," Bren says. "It has never actually helped us."

I try not to roll my eyes, but it's a close thing. "The fact that it exists at all means we still have some level of prosperity and safety. We haven't descended into chaos or anarchy—or a dozen little thiefdoms. No one wins if there is no overarching law to guarantee basic rights and rules."

Bren smirks. "So you've said before, and yet here we are, a pack of thieves protecting the basic right of children not to be stolen from their families, and every guard in Lirelei looking to kill you."

I flush. "I know exactly where we are. I know certain aspects of the law have been corrupted, that there are deep things wrong. But the only way to start over is to have a revolution. Not only will that not happen, but too many innocent people would die that way. So, we fix the law we have, we drive out the corruption."

"That's your work, not mine," Bren says. "Whatever our philosophical differences, or agreements, we risk too much trying to involve the princess with Bardok. She would have to bring in Verin Melkior, as the lord high marshal of the realm, and by the time a few quads of soldiers from the city guard are assigned to raid Bardok's house, he would be long gone. We must maintain the element of surprise. It's the only way we'll catch Bardok without carnage in the streets."

That's the argument I can't refute: philosophy or no, I don't want innocent people dying because of Bardok's crimes.

"I understand," I say finally, wishing that our systems weren't so corrupt. That there really was another option.

"So now we're clear on what I intend," Bren says, watching me steadily, "we're back to the question of what you're planning."

To stop the Circle, though I don't know how. I can imagine what Bren will say about that. Instead, I say, "I aim to bring Garrin to justice as well."

"Ah, yes, Verin Garrin, the only heir past Kestrin himself. His trusted and beloved cousin." Bren shakes his head. "You can't, Rae. You must know that."

I lift my chin. "If the royal family won't deal with him, then I will."

He tilts his head back, eyes closed. "Rae. Sweet, prickly Rae. No."

My cheeks burn at the endearment. He's going to be impossible with those, isn't he? "What do you mean 'no'?" I demand.

He opens his eyes again to regard me wearily. "You are not cut out for murder. If you need someone to kill him, I'll see to it. Don't you dare get his blood on your hands."

"I'm not getting it on *your* hands." I press my fingers against my temple, my thoughts catching on the coal that still slumbers in my mind. "I don't intend to kill him myself either. Anyhow, I've—I killed those men at the Port Authority."

"Self-defense is a far cry from murder. What do you intend to do to Garrin, if not kill him?"

If I'm expecting Bren to be more honest with me, I need to do the same with him. However much I can. "There's something else," I admit. "I don't think I can actually tell you what it is, though."

His brow furrows. "Why not?"

Because the sorceress laid a binding on me. Not that I really know how it works. Perhaps I can skirt around it, if I'm clever enough. If I act like I am telling a story, the spell might not catch what I'm doing. "I'm going to try to tell you a story. We'll see how far I get."

Bren nods, still confused but willing to hear me out.

"Once there was a country girl who fell into a river. She had a nice little knife, and she cut herself free of the weeds that held her, but she didn't have enough breath to make it to the surface."

Bren has gone utterly still watching me.

I look away from him, drop my hand to the pendant hidden beneath my tunic. "A bird pulled her from the waters, and her friend as well, who had fallen in beside her."

In my mind, the ember begins to burn a little brighter, flickering and catching at the edges of my thoughts. "The girl struck a deal—"

Flames slide through my veins, searing the air in my lungs, licking at my fingertips, burning *burning*—

Each breath is a battle, a fight against ravenous flames. I force myself to think nothing thoughts, as if I might deprive the fire of fuel: water, ice, safety, Bren, *water*. Slowly, the burning recedes, leaving me shuddering, huddled on the ground, Bren's arms around me keeping me upright. I gasp for breath through lungs that feel parched. Scorched.

"Rae," he pleads, "tell me you're all right. Please."

"Mmm," I manage. His hand presses my head to his neck. Is he shaking, or is that me?

"There's smoke on your breath."

"I told you," I rasp, my tongue tasting of ash, "there was something else."

He laughs helplessly. "Rae, I swear. If you burn yourself to a cinder, I will kill Bardok myself just to spite you."

I pull back slowly and poke his chest. "No Bardok for you."

He shakes his head. Now that I can see his face, the worry in his eyes is startlingly clear. "What just happened?" he asks. "No—don't try to tell me. You're under a spell of some sort. A curse?"

I shrug. Maybe it is one. I don't know magic well enough to know how it retains its power. I point to my lips, though, reminding him of how it silenced me.

"Or a binding of some sort? To keep you silent?"

I nod.

"Given what we were talking about before, this mage"—he pauses as I shake my head—"or rogue magic user has a bone to pick with Garrin."

"Knew you were clever," I say, patting his knee.

"Do you know *why* they want Garrin?"

I nod slowly. At least, I have what the sorceress claimed: that she would offer him a justice the royals could not. But that's not a *why*, is it? I don't really know anything about her motivations.

"Then you're comfortable that they don't pose a danger to the princess or anyone else you might care about in Tarinon?"

I grimace. I'm not comfortable with the danger the sorceress poses at all. The only reason she really needs me is to breach the magical protections around the palace. Once she's been summoned there, I doubt anyone could stop her. If my suspicions about her are true, she's the face of the so-called curse that has plagued our royal family for generations—a curse that has slowly whittled our once expansive royal family down to almost nothing. Or at least, that's what the rumors say, and Stonemane's warning never to speak her name aloud lends some credence to my fears. What I'll do if she is bent on a wider vengeance than just Garrin, I don't know.

I bite my lip, staring at the floor. I don't know, and I cannot pretend I'll be able to fight off the ember's compulsion should it force itself upon me. Without understanding what the sorceress intends beyond Garrin, I have no way of knowing if I will betray Alyrra or the rest of the royal family with him. Not unless I speak to the sorceress again.

Bren swears softly.

"I'm sorry," I whisper.

"Don't be; this isn't your fault. We'll figure it out." He rises and holds out his hand. "Come on, I'll walk you to your room."

I stand with his help, and am pathetically grateful when he offers me his arm. I need something to lean on, my strength not quite returned. My lungs ache, and my whole body feels uncomfortably weak. At least the taste of ashes has faded from my mouth.

Bren lifts my satchel from the table. "I actually do want to hear what happened with your mage ally. Perhaps after you've rested?"

"I'll tell you while we walk," I say.

Bren doesn't argue, proving just how worried he is.

CHAPTER

27

I doze for what's left of the morning, my bed the sleeping mat I shared with the girls, every blanket we had heaped on top of me to make a warm little nest. I surface at one point to the shouts of the sailors as they help push the galley away from the docks, but I drift off again soon after.

Eventually I jolt awake from a deeper sleep, shadows reaching for me from the edges of my dreams. I sit up, shedding blankets grown suddenly too warm, and make myself focus on the half-lucid thoughts that have slipped through my mind over the course of the morning.

Here is the truth I don't want to face: I've been carrying a spell in my mind that could destroy the royal family in a single breath, including Alyrra. She is precisely what our land needs— quietly focused on addressing the injustices she witnessed while living in the city, committed to aiding her new people. It would be better for me to bring down the sorceress's wrath on my own head than risk what good Alyrra will bring to pass as princess and future queen.

Working quickly, I pile the blankets on the bunk and roll up the sleeping mat. Then I move to the center of the room and take a deep breath to steady myself. I am about to do something monumentally foolish. I might as well be clear on that with myself. But I don't see any other way forward, nor can I involve Bren. Not only can I not explain this to him, but I've no guarantee the sorceress won't do something to him. No, this is the only way forward that I can live with.

Holding grimly to that thought, I reach for the ember nestled deep within my mind.

It blazes to life, searing my thoughts with a fierce, white-hot light. Dimly, I hear my voice shaping a name I already know: *Sarait Winterfrost.*

I drop to my knees, aware of the taste of ash on my tongue once more, the scent of smoke whispering past me. Then the ember dies down to a mere spark. I bend over, my good hand braced on the floor, and gasp for breath. That was nowhere *near* as painful as calling the binding itself down on me.

The room brightens, shifting strangely around me—a quick swirl and resettling—and the sorceress says, her voice whispering with fury, "You are alone, girl, and far from the palace. That was not well done."

I swallow hard, ash coating my throat, and force myself back to my feet. "Honored mage."

She's as beautiful as I remember, and as terrifying. "Why do you call me to you now, without having fulfilled your debt? Are you in such straits that you would indebt yourself again for my aid?"

"Not for aid," I say, sickeningly aware of my arrogance in thinking I could question someone as powerful and dangerous as the sorceress before me.

Her lips flatten in displeasure. "I did not mark you for a fool."

Shows how much she knows. At least I knew I was being foolish going into this.

"Explain yourself."

"You have said that I must repay my debt by calling you when I next face Garrin of Cenatil."

"It does not seem that difficult an order to comprehend," she agrees.

"I understand it, veria," I say, deciding to give her an honorary title of noblewoman. It can't hurt, at least. "But I am sworn to the protection of Princess Alyrra, her husband, and the king." Not entirely true: I never took an actual oath, but there's no need for her to know that when it might as well be true.

"I did not ask them of you," the sorceress says, irritation sliding through her voice like the flick and swish of a viper's tongue.

I press down on a ripple of terror. She needs me. She would not have set the coal in my mind if this was something she could do herself. "Can you swear it to me, veria? I have no compunction granting you Garrin if his family will not punish him. I cannot give up the rest of the family."

She eyes me as if I were no more intelligent than the dead wood beneath her slippers. "You have no choice, little servant of mine. You owe me a life debt."

"And yet," I say, my voice cracking with fear, "I would rather you claim that debt from me now, than risk those I am sworn to protect."

"Are you so forgetful? I will take the life of one you love, not yours."

I shake my head, as if I have the power to refuse her, or any power at all. But if I owe her a life, it is *my* life, not someone else's, that I will give her. There is a good chance that, with her Fae appreciation for the exact repayment of debts, she will allow it. "No. You may only have mine. It is precisely equal to my debt."

The sorceress crosses to me in a whisper of skirts, her hands cupping my cheeks in a frigid hold. I am unaccountably taller than her. She forces my head down with a jerk, looking straight into my eyes.

No—*no*. The eyes of the Fae, their gaze—

My vision expands, or perhaps it contracts, for suddenly there is nothing but her, deathless eyes and pale skin, and a flash of images: Bren in Lirelei, cradling my face in his hands as we hid from my pursuers; Efrun's expression as my knife plunged into his belly; a freewheeling burst of memories of faces and darkness; the king, smiling over a paper bearing my blood and a lock of my hair; Kestrin, squatting on the floor while a viper nestled around my ankles, saying, *I should like to rely on your confidence*; and then, even further back, the princess, walking toward the palace walls on the first day I met her, saying, *Horses are a great deal easier to get along with.*

Most horses, I hear my own voice responding.

And her voice, light with amusement, *Most days.*

The sorceress releases me, my vision splintering and then slowly reforming, showing me the room once more. I've sunk to my knees, her grip on my face the only thing keeping me from collapse.

"You have the loyalty of a dog," she says with some amusement and lets me go. I tip sideways, catching myself on my left hand. A faint, gasping cry escapes my lips as pain jolts through my hand and up my arm. I jerk my hand away, still unbalanced, and end sprawled on the floor, a mess of limbs and shaking muscle.

My hand throbs in time with my head. I lie there, letting the pain wash through me, and find myself on the verge of laughter. So, I'm a dog, now? I always thought of Lui's "feral stray" description as pertaining to a cat. If I had to choose, I'd prefer that. My breath wheezes in a faint laugh, because *really*. Of all the ludicrous things I should be thinking about in this moment, splitting hairs over the animals people take me for seems the least relevant of all.

"That should not have hurt you so much," the sorceress says, sounding faintly taken aback.

I squeeze my eyes shut and then force them open. She can't possibly be worried about causing pain, not with all her terrifying threats and utter lack of concern for anyone's life. She nearly let Fastu drown, for pity's sake—

She nudges me with the toe of one slipper. "Roll over, girl."

I don't. I start halfway up, my vision swaying, and scramble back only to run into the wall. I freeze there, like a cornered animal, a *dog*, my breath coming in gulps, my left hand pressed to my chest. She takes two steps forward and folds her legs beneath her, seating herself elegantly before me. Then she reaches out and takes my hand by the wrist, peeling it away from my chest.

Oh *God*—

Her magic flows into my hand in a wash of warmth, utterly unlike Ehelar's. "I see," she murmurs, as the warmth slides up my arm, pools in my breast, and then spreads through the rest of me, cradling every hurt I have carried, easing the ache in my head.

"I don't owe you . . . for this," I manage to breathe.

"No," she agrees. "One should reward loyal creatures, don't you think?"

She releases my hand, but her warmth still runs through my veins. "You *are* loyal to the princess, though not blindly so. And to her husband, and a little bit to the king. So, I will grant you this: the princess and her husband are safe from me."

"What of the king?"

"Perhaps."

I draw myself together, carefully straightening my stance so that I'm sitting properly, facing her. "I cannot betray the king to you. I don't—I don't know that he's involved with the slavers."

"Nor will you give him up without having passed your own sentence on him," she says, sending chills up my arms. It drives the last of her borrowed warmth from my body. Is that what I have become? Like a thief lord in my own right, passing judgement and carrying out sentences without regard for anything but my own understanding of morality?

The sorceress rises to her feet. I push myself up after her, dimly aware that my ankle hurts not at all, that my hand does not even throb, though it's still a little stiff.

"Go back to Tarinon," she tells me. "Ask your princess for justice against Garrin. When she cannot grant it, I will." She pauses. There's something strangely human in the way she regards me, her head tilted and the faintest of creases around her well-deep eyes. "So long as you call me as I bid you, I will leave the king be. For now."

I nod slowly.

"Good," she says, and steps forward to touch my forehead. "Do not call on me unless you have Garrin in hand."

The ember nestles into my mind once more, like a wild thing settling into its den.

"Safe travels, Amraeya ni Ansarim," Winterfrost says, and with a swirl of skirts, dissipates into a wash of sunlight.

CHAPTER

28

A shadow fills the window. I look up in mild confusion as Bren
crouches on the sill, filling it completely. He leaps down, his
gaze flying from me to every corner of the small, empty cabin.

I blink. He came in the *window?*

"Are you all right?" he demands, crossing to me in a heartbeat.
His hands grasp my forearms, his expression half-panicked. Someone rattles the door.

"I'm fine," I promise. "There's no danger here."

"Then what just happened? I came over the side of the boat and
couldn't see through an *open window.*"

I nod, not at all surprised the sorceress protected our conversation from being overheard, or overseen, at that.

The lock on the door clicks and Artemian comes bursting in,
dagger at the ready.

"Did you pick the lock?" I ask in confusion.

Lirika pokes her head in behind Artemian, her face lighting
with a relieved smile as she sees me. "I did. But the lock wouldn't
budge till a moment ago—neither would the door."

Bren drops his hands, his fingers sliding down my arms before he lets go. "What just happened here?"

"Mmm." I consider my options, feel the ember flicker in response, and tap my lips. "Can't say."

Lirika chokes on a laugh. Artemian shoots her a quieting glance. Bren, however, understands, his jaw tightening. "Can you tell me anything?"

I shrug. "Just thinking about what I need to do when we get to Tarinon."

"I'd like to tell Artemian and Lirika what you shared with me earlier, if that's all right?"

I nod. If Bren thinks they need to know, I'll trust him on that. "You'd better all sit," I say, grabbing cushions from the bunk and tossing them to my companions.

Lirika plops down a little to my left, shoving her cushion up against the wall as a backrest. Artemian folds his legs to sit across from me, and Bren takes a seat to my right so we form a sort of lopsided circle. He gives a quick, succinct description of what he's gleaned from me regarding the sorceress, though of course he doesn't know who or what she is, leaving Artemian and Lirika both looking utterly stunned.

Lirika recovers first. "Didn't I say you keep things interesting?" she says, her lips twitching into a grin.

Artemian shakes his head. "So this rogue magic user just showed up again? Why?"

I glance at Bren. I can't just explain things like that. I *might* be able to nod an answer, but I'm not about to attempt speaking one.

"Did you invite them?" Bren asks with appalling intuition.

I dip my chin.

Lirika snorts. "You're getting back at Bren for keeping secrets, aren't you?"

"Hardly," I say, but I can't quite keep my shoulders from shaking with laughter in response. There's a slight edge of hysteria to it which I can't quite swallow down. No doubt it's the relief of knowing the sorceress has promised the rest of the royals' safety, coupled with the absurdity of Lirika's suggestion.

Bren looks slightly affronted.

"Right," Lirika drawls. "So you've got this magical enemy to the royals hanging around, planning to murder Garrin or worse if you can give them an opening. I mean, isn't that a good thing?"

Her words dispel my laughter. I shake my head, sobering. "I am trying not to support murder. This can't even claim to be thieves' justice."

Bren studies me. "You called them in because of what we discussed, didn't you? That you can't be sure they won't attack the rest of the royal family."

I nod.

"Are you satisfied with the conversation you just had?"

I consider this, nod again. The royal family will be safe no matter what. If Alyrra fails to bring him to justice, Garrin will be destroyed. It's the best I could possibly hope for. I'm not risking my sisters or my parents or myself to Winterfrost in exchange for a man like that. Regardless, surely Alyrra will be able to see to Garrin herself?

Bren says, "From what you implied this morning, you seem to think you have a choice in calling in this magical enemy against Garrin. Do you?"

I shrug.

"It hinges on something?" Artemian asks shrewdly.

"I have . . . great respect for the princess," I say carefully, waiting to see if the ember will spark. It obligingly remains latent.

Bren grimaces. "Then we had best get you in to see her as quickly as possible."

I shake my head. "I don't think I should go to the palace."

"No," he agrees at once. "It was a manner of speaking. I'm not sending you into that nest of vipers. Alyrra can meet you in the city."

"She'd trust that?"

"She already has once, when she asked my help in finding you."

I forgot that.

"Looks like we've got everything settled then," Lirika says. It's almost a challenge, the way she says it. As if she knows there's other trouble brewing.

I grimace, thinking of my conversation with Ehelar earlier. "I want the snatchers stopped," I say to Bren. "The royal family already knows about Berenworth Trading Company's role in transporting the children and bringing in money and gems in payment. But it won't be enough, will it?"

I learned of Berenworth's involvement through my research with Kirrana; it was one of the few things I was able to convey to the royal family before I was abducted—even Bren knows of it. He was there when we raided a Berenworth galley in an attempt to recover Kirrana, and found a roomful of children instead.

"The Berenworth galleys docked at the town we just left had been impounded," Bren says. "The royal family may actually be doing a good job on that front."

"That's only one piece. The Circle is still casting the Darkness, protecting the snatchers, and benefiting from the slave trade."

He sighs. "I don't have moles in the Circle, but I can get some in, at least among the servants. With Berenworth out of the picture, the snatchers will break apart for a short time. But new operations will develop—especially with Berenworth still functioning outside of Menaiya. They'll make inroads under a different name, is my best guess, re-establish their networks. So, we keep a pulse on the

Circle, watch for the new actors, and use what we learn to help the children."

"That doesn't actually *stop* the slavers," I say tightly. "It just keeps rescuing children under a system that enables their enslavement."

"Sometimes justice is stopping oppression any way you can, rather than taking out the criminals at the top."

I see what he means. I understand. But I can't agree. "Justice needs to be both."

Artemian opens his mouth to answer, but Bren raises his hand, silencing him. Lirika watches us with avid interest as he says, "We don't live in a perfect world. You can't imagine that any of us could take on a dozen mages in one go. Finding a way to kill one mage at a time—*if* murder is your answer, Rae—even that will only end quickly and badly."

"I don't want murder to be the answer," I say roughly. "I wasn't looking to murder anyone when I went to the Port Authority. Even with the *Heron*, we were there to rescue the children."

"Indeed. A good intention carried out with blood on the end of a blade."

I flinch. I agreed with him on Morrel's execution; even now, I don't quite regret it. But in the end, I don't want to be what Winterfrost saw in me: deciding people's fates on my own—judge, jury, and executioner. Because one day, I will be wrong.

Bren shoots me a sharp look. "Oh come, Rae. What else is thieves' justice? Or any justice? It can't survive without a method to enforce it." He shakes his head in frustration.

I don't want to argue this right now. "Murder aside, the Circle is the real problem, isn't it? As long as they're sending out the Darkness, and providing their wards, the slavers will be impossible to stop."

"Not if we install moles to uncover their operations, find and monitor their contacts," Bren says, impatience edging at his tone. "Damn it, Rae. You cannot save the whole world. You can't fix every injustice."

I glare at him, and Artemian says, thoughtfully, "She can certainly try to fight the injustices she's chosen. That's her decision, not yours."

Bren throws him an irritated look.

"You calculate every risk, don't you?" I ask him. "Every single time something happens, everything you do, you're calculating risks and deciding your actions."

He spreads his hands, the movement short and frustrated. "How do you think I've survived this long? Become what I am? It's not by running into danger headfirst. This? It's beyond dangerous. I need you to trust me, Rae. I'll get you to Tarinon and you can meet with the princess, show her you're alive and well."

"What then?"

"We make sure you survive whoever it is that's after Garrin, and you leave the rest to me."

He's not going to hear me. "I'll talk to Alyrra, and figure things out from there," I say finally.

"You know what she'll say. She's already told you to leave the Circle out of it, hasn't she?"

"She doesn't know just how involved they are."

"It won't matter," Bren says, frustrated. "Rae, you can't do this."

"I haven't said I'm doing anything."

Lirika reaches out and pats my knee. "Pretty sure that doesn't mean a thing."

"Some friend you are," I complain, glancing toward Artemian for support. He offers me a slight nod, not of approval but of acknowledgement. He probably doesn't want me running after the Circle either.

Bren leans forward, catching my eye. "Promise me you'll tell me before you do whatever you decide," he says.

"I promise," I tell him. I'll probably need his help regardless.

"This," Lirika says with obvious relish, "is going to be good."

CHAPTER

29

O ver the next two days of travel, I fall into an easy rhythm with my companions. In the mornings, Lirika keeps me company on the upper deck while Bren continues my training. It's a lovely, sunlit time, the summer heat slowly starting to creep up on us, a gentle wind offering some relief.

Bren remains concentrated on the techniques he's teaching me; when he touches me to fix my stances it's the most professional of taps or turns. There's no judgement from him, or any undercurrent of attraction to upset my equilibrium. There's just understanding and a focused effort to find the techniques I can best use with the body that I have.

In the afternoons, Lirika and I continue to work on my lock-picking skills. The small wooden box proves to have the most complex lock of them all, and it takes hours of attempts, along with a significant amount of lecturing on the inner construction of what I'm working with, for me to finally learn to pick it.

We share our meals together on deck, Bren and Artemian and Lirika and I. We talk about all sorts of things, and it feels strangely like home, even if home itself feels more distant than a childhood memory. When Lirika demands to know how justice that fails to protect is any better than justice created to fill the gaps, it's a conversation I can imagine having had with my sisters—even if here and now the answers are very real and present. And, in truth, just as uncertain.

Artemian locates a pair of anek boards, and we take turns playing each other, the games running deep into the night. To my surprise, Bren is not half as good as I expected.

"It's these rules," he grouses as Artemian moves the final piece in what amounts to a total rout of their game.

"You do usually cheat," Artemian observes. "Maybe you should go back to that."

"It's not cheating," Bren says, very carefully not looking at me. "It's changing the rules."

"Yeah, well, you better do that or I'm going to bury you," Lirika says, returning from her foray to the kitchen. She takes Artemian's spot, while he switches over to sit across from me, my anek board already set for the next game.

Bren glowers. "I don't have to change the rules to beat you."

"Pretty sure you do," Lirika says, setting down her bowl. "I just learned a new trick from Rae, and you are going to *weep*."

"A new trick?" Artemian asks me.

I shrug. "Country strategy. You city folk really need to keep up."

Bren rolls out his shoulder, a glint coming into his eyes. "That's it. I'm not following anyone else's rules now."

Lirika grins slyly. "Have you met Rae? Doesn't matter whose rules you're following, country strategy's gonna knock you off your cushion there."

"I don't know if it's *quite* that good," I say, making the opening move on my own board. My cheeks are warm; at least I can count on the brown of my skin and the lantern light to hide my blush. "What did you bring from the kitchen?"

"Want some?" she asks, her eyes brightening even more.

I reach out to take a sliver from the proffered bowl. It's the size of a small twig, about as long as my pinkie and significantly more slender. "What is it?"

Artemian and Bren exchange a glance that tells me I'm in trouble.

"Won't know if you don't try it," Lirika says, grinning.

I'm going to regret this. I pop the thing in my mouth and crunch down. The most nauseating, salt-drenched flavor coated in oil explodes across my tongue. For a moment, I remain frozen in horror, the taste growing stronger the longer I hold still, then I leap to my feet and spit over the railing. Repeatedly.

Lirika shouts with laughter. I can hear Artemian's deeper rumble beneath her.

"What *is* that?" I demand, once I've spat out everything I can. "It's *awful*."

"Dried fish fried in oil," she says. "It's considered an acquired taste."

Pity the souls who are forced to acquire it. "Do you have anything to drink?"

"Just this," Lirika says, slipping a small silver flask from her pocket.

"Not that," Bren says firmly. "I'll get you some water." He slips off at once.

Artemian watches me, eyes gleaming with laughter. "It couldn't have been that bad."

"No," I agree. "It was worse."

Lirika shakes her head. "It's just fingerling fish!"

"I've never actually eaten fish before."

"I can see you avoiding Cook's fish stew, but surely you had fish at the palace?"

I shake my head. "I always went for what was familiar."

Artemian considers me thoughtfully. "You only ever take the necessary risks, is that it?"

What a curious thing to say. "It's just food. Not a lot rides on it." I shrug. "I didn't want to embarrass myself in front of the court."

Bren arrives a moment later with a cup of water for me and a pot of tea to share. I gargle and spit twice, then drink what's left, much to my companions' amusement.

Lirika renews her threats against Bren, keeping her bowl of fish by her side, and we start our games. A half hour later, when Bren just manages to wrest his victory from Lirika's outraged clutches, he points out, "The problem is you're not actually country yourself. You can't expect the same strategy to work for you."

"It's a *strategy game*. And you broke the rules."

"Redefined them."

Artemian shoots me an amused look and refills my cup of tea.

All too soon, the days we have come to an end. On the afternoon of our third day, we pack up our belongings, and one of the sailors rows our small party across the waters to the low banks of the river. We will travel by foot to Tarinon, leaving Captain Belayn and the *Blue Heron* to continue there on their own.

Belayn will see if he can intercept some "cargo" meant for Morrel in Tarinon. Beyond that, he'll have to register ownership of the *Heron*. It won't help him if we're sighted on board. Nor would it be wise for us to ride into the docks, which are square in Bardok's territory.

Instead, we scramble up the riverbank and set off for a nearby inn run by Bren's "friends." It's a lovely walk, the sun high but not too hot, the road we join well maintained.

Within an hour, we reach the inn, a sturdy two-story adobe affair facing the road, with a small wooden stable built out back, as well as a constellation of smaller structures—a goat byre, a large chicken coop, and something that might be a storage shed.

"They've only a donkey to spare," Artemian tells us as we set down our packs in the room he arranged for us while we waited outside.

"That's fine." Bren glances out the rear-facing window. "You and Lirika can take it into the city. You ought to be able to trade off riding it and make good time."

Lirika frowns. "I thought you wanted me to keep Rae company."

Her presence in the group finally clicks into place in my mind; she's here not just as a capable thief, but also as the only other woman of the group. Her presence is meant not so much to save my reputation—which is certainly unsalvageable by now—but to assure I have a female ally. And, truly, it worked. The fact that Bren considered that, arranged for that—it was wonderfully thoughtful of him.

"I'm fine," I say now. "You don't need to stay for me."

"We don't know what Bardok or the Scholar have been up to since we left," Bren observes. "It's better if you and Artemian can watch each other's backs."

Lirika makes no further argument, and the two depart a few minutes later. Bren sees them out, returning only after he completes his own quick assessment of the inn, thief-style, checking all the exits and entrances. "I'm going up to the roof to watch the road," he says. "You're welcome to come along."

"You thieves have a thing for roofs, don't you?" I grin, picking up my satchel once more.

"What?" Bren asks, bewildered.

"I really haven't spent *that* much time with you, but it seems like every time there's a rooftop available, you head for it."

"You're one to point fingers, what with your predilection for windows," he observes, eyes laughing. "Once you're a proper thief, you'll take to rooftops as well."

I snort. "Don't count on it. I like places I can get out of easily."

"We all do," he agrees. "But you can't beat a rooftop for a view."

Or a picnic, I almost add, barely catching myself in time. I swallow the words, my cheeks warming.

"What?" Bren asks, eyeing me curiously. I'm sure I look self-conscious.

"Nothing," I mutter, ducking my head and stepping past him into the hall. "Come on, or you might miss that view."

CHAPTER

30

The roof is wide and well kept, one corner playing host to lines of laundry, the rest relatively empty. The sturdy adobe walls rise up to form a waist-high parapet, perfect for leaning on.

"Oh," I say, crossing to the far side. "You can see the city from here!"

It wasn't visible from the road, but from this far up, I can see past the rolling green tops of the plains to a line of yellow—the city walls—and beyond it only a shadowed glimpse of the myriad buildings hidden from view, disappearing into the distance. The river lies lower down, invisible from here, and part of the city disappears behind a swell of grasses to the west.

"We're really not that far," Bren agrees. "We could have all just kept walking, but . . ."

I grimace. "I would have been all right."

Bren glances at me, a line appearing between his brows as he parses my response. "No," he says. "It wasn't because of you. I would have asked how you felt about the walk if I thought we should attempt it. I'm more concerned about what's waiting for us. That's the south gate up ahead. My territory lies on the west side.

It's better for Artemian and Lirika to take the donkey to West Road than risk an entry through the Black Scholar's territory."

I look out over the plains again, my gaze lingering on the distant city. He may have asked his people to negotiate an alliance with the Black Scholar against Bardok, but it makes sense to be careful until he knows the outcome of that.

"Tell me a story," Bren says, settling sideways on the wall, one knee propped up before him, the other dangling on this side. He can watch the road with a tilt of his head and still easily look back to talk to me.

"A story?" I echo. "What do you mean?"

He shrugs. "Something about you. When you were small, perhaps. Or something else."

"Why?"

Another shrug. "Pass the time."

"I'll trade you stories," I say on a whim.

He considers. "All right. Your turn first."

I lean against the parapet, gazing out as I think. The smell of baking bread wafts up to me from the kitchens below, and there are flashes of color among the grasses, wildflowers waving in the breeze. I reach up to my hair to check my braid before I remember I don't have one anymore. I rub the back of my head instead.

So many of my stories involve a touch of Niya's magic—Genno Stonemane's visit, or the one with the goat at the harvest fair. I can't mention her secret, though. Then there's all the scrapes Bean has gotten into, including that time with the dragon that I told the children about. But it feels unfair to give Bren a story that isn't fully true, not when we're both still working on not hiding truths from each other.

"You must have a few stories," Bren says, watching me. "You come from a loving family, don't you? All country wholesomeness and heartfelt care."

"More or less," I allow, my thoughts sliding sideways to something I haven't thought about in a long time.

"Less?" Bren echoes, one brow arched in disbelief.

"Well, there's my grandmother. Not," I say quickly, "the one whose ruby ring I inherited. My paternal grandmother. I haven't met her since I was a few months old."

"Why not?"

I shift uncomfortably. "Are you sure this is the story you want?"

"Are you willing to tell it?" The sunlight gleams on Bren's hair and burnishes the planes of his face, the deep brown of his eyes glinting with gold as he watches me. I'm reminded forcibly of how well he reads people, how important it must be to him to understand how the people around him work.

I exhale slowly. I'm sure it's only a small ugliness, compared to what he's seen in his life. "When I was born, my parents sought out a healer mage to help with my foot."

Bren nods.

"They found one, but he wasn't concerned with the needs of peasants. He refused to see them, even though they offered to pay for his services. So, they brought me home, and my grandmother came to visit. She made a couple of comments that my parents disregarded, and then one day, when I was being particularly crabby, she told my mother she should have left me at a temple on their way home. That I would always be a burden on my father, and little help around the house, and that if they were very lucky, I'd die young and they'd be rid of me."

His face hardens. "What happened?"

"My mother called my father in and asked my grandmother to repeat herself—which she did. Mama says Baba just looked at his mother for a long moment, and then he turned around without a word, went into the guest room, packed her trunk, and they started the trip back to her home an hour later. She's never been allowed to see us again."

I take a slow breath, my gaze on my hands. My father writes to her annually, sending her enough money for the coming year, and that's all. Each time, she writes back demanding to know if he's ready to apologize for his treatment of her. To her mind, she didn't do anything wrong.

I don't doubt that even now she'd feel the same way about me. More so, I suppose, since I've lost my finger and been abducted and made myself utterly and completely unmarriageable. Which I always was, I remind myself fiercely. It's not like Baba ever mentions me to her anyway—he doesn't mention any of his children when he writes.

"You still carry that with you, don't you?" Bren asks quietly.

"I don't even remember her."

"Doesn't mean she can't hurt you."

I clear my throat. "Well, I generally try to forget what I know of her. I'm afraid it doesn't make a particularly entertaining story. If you'd like, you can give me a miserable one in return, so we're even."

Bren huffs a laugh. "Is there something in particular you'd like to hear?"

I stare out over the wall, thinking about the Bren I know, and the things I've heard of Red Hawk. Like the men he executed earlier this year, and the story of what he purportedly did to his own brother, painting the streets with his blood. Do I really want to know the truth? Even if I did, do I have the right to ask?

I lean my hip against the wall, facing him. "I wonder about when you were younger," I finally say. "But I don't want to pry. You could tell me a story about stealing some ridiculous thing on a dare, and I'd be happy."

"I've stolen more than a few ridiculous things," Bren allows, his gaze tracing my features. He looks away sharply, toward the road. "But I'll tell you a story to match yours. It's only fair."

I hold back the instinct to tell him he doesn't have to—he knows that.

His smile is a painful thing. "I came from a loving family too, more or less. The more was my mother. She was a widow, and worked cleaning homes. I would go everywhere with her, helping as I could. The less was my older brother. When I was six or seven, he fell into bad company and racked up a debt he couldn't pay. One day he promised me a sweet if I came with him."

I swallow hard. "Bren . . ."

He turns his head to look at me, his eyes dark and so very tired. "He sold me. I'm lucky I never got transported out of Tarinon. I worked in a carpet-weaving workshop for years until, one night, someone knocked over a lamp and the whole place went up like a torch. About half the workers there died, perhaps four got out and stayed in the vicinity, and I got out and ran."

"That must have been terrifying."

He shrugs. "I don't remember it. That's how I first met Artemian, you know. He came across me covered in soot and sniveling in an alleyway, and brought me a blanket and food and water. He figured out very quickly what had happened and brought a Speaker to give me the Blessing. The Speaker was willing to help me find work, since I wouldn't say a word about my family, but I didn't trust him not to sell me into something similar. So Artemian promised he'd look out for me. He took me home, told me everything I'd told him about myself that the Blessing had stolen. The only thing I refused to share was my name. He gave me a new one—that's where the name Bren came from."

"It's not a particularly Menaiyan name," I observe.

Bren smirks. "No. Artemian lived on the coast for a few years. It's the name of a bird in one of the coastal dialects. I think he gave it to me in the hopes I'd admit my true name. I repaid him by escaping him."

I know that feeling of unreasoning distrust. Lui would have called Bren a feral stray as well. "What did you do after that?"

"I lived on the streets, started learning how to look out for myself. Gathered a small group of urchins around me who were just as desperate as I was. But I kept going back to Artemian. And he kept helping me, even when all I seemed to be was trouble."

"You grew into Red Hawk from there?" I ask, unable to help myself.

"In a way. I kept gathering my network, reeling in older kids who needed help, looking out for younger ones, doing men and women favors when they least expected it, letting them pay me back as they saw fit. People started paying us to keep their streets safe, to keep the gangs away from their neighborhoods or their businesses. We didn't steal from them, we just took payment—money, food, goods, whatever the agreement was—and kept our side of the deal. They didn't ask any questions in return." Bren sighs. "Then one day I saw my brother again."

I wait, watching him steadily.

He dips his head. "You're right, of course. I laid a trap for him and caught him. I had questions for him—about my mother, who I learned had died a year before, and about just how much he got for me. After I was done questioning him, I cut off his hand for stealing what wasn't his."

Thieves' justice, or a twist on it. Even the king's justice orders cutting off a thief's hand after a few infractions. Given what his brother did, I'm amazed at Bren's restraint.

"But I didn't just want him to suffer. I wanted people to know they couldn't do what he did and expect to never pay a price. I didn't know how to write yet, but I knew how to get a message across. So, I chained him to a wall and used his blood to draw a bird in flight over his head. I made sure everyone on that street knew his story, and not a one of them dared touch him until the city guard came for him." Bren's gaze is dark as midnight. "The name was born from that. I didn't argue it when I heard it."

He's watching me intently now, waiting for me to say something, only I don't know what to say. *I'm sorry* seems far too weak and irrelevant. He doesn't want my pity, so I dip my head, give him instead my understanding, the respect of acknowledgement.

"You don't fear me, Rae? Knowing I cut off my own brother's hand?"

I'm sorely tempted to give Garrin up to a vengeful sorceress, so who am I to judge? "That seems more merciful than not," I say, my voice barely more than a whisper.

"I would have liked to kill him."

"But you didn't. Even then, you were trying to make your own justice. It wasn't pure revenge. As for now? You're still you," I say. "Red Hawk is your mantle, as you said. It's your choice how you wear it."

He hesitates a long moment. "I'd like to think that. I've lost track of Bren before, when things got bad. But Bren is who I'd rather be, even if Red Hawk commands more respect." He glances toward me. "It's also easier to be Bren around you."

I snort. "That's because I didn't know who you were until a few days ago."

His lips twitch, but his eyes remain serious. "No, it isn't that."

I shrug my shoulders. I don't want him to start talking about how he feels about me again, not unless something's changed. Which it hasn't. I flail for something else to say and find myself asking, "So what kind of bird is a *bren*? A hawk?"

He grins ruefully. "Oh no, Artemian didn't think as well of me as all that. He named me after a particular kind of gull; it has a brown hood of feathers half the year, and is known for stealing worms from other birds."

A delighted laugh escapes me. "He knew you were a thief even then."

"That's not even the worst of it," Bren says. "These particular gulls have a reputation. Apparently, the local plovers will trade worms in return for an early warning of approaching predators."

I start laughing and find I can't stop. "Oh God, Bren, you're a thieving gull who takes *bribes*."

"It's very apt."

I wipe the tears from my cheeks. "Artemian is an absolute genius."

"He's a good man," Bren agrees, more seriously. "He watched out for me for a long time. He didn't start working for me until a few years back. He fell on hard times, got sick and couldn't work, lost his job and then his home. I found him and told him I'd give him whatever he wanted, he just had to name it. I would have bought him a house in the country and a brace of horses to go with it if he'd asked."

"He didn't," I say. Artemian wouldn't have wanted charity, even if it wasn't that at all. It takes a moment longer for the unspoken fact that Bren could have afforded to give so much so easily, years ago, when he was still building his reputation. I've never thought of him as wealthy before. But then of course Red Hawk would not be a pauper.

"He wanted work," Bren agrees. "So, he joined me, but he's getting old for this kind of profession. When this is all over, I'll make sure he gets out into something better."

"That's good." I wonder if Bren has ever thought about leaving his line of work. I suppose, at his level, it would be close to impossible to walk away. The thought aches, which is my own fault for letting my mind go down that track.

He looks back out to the road where a wagon approaches. It disappears behind a slight rise, then rolls back up as we watch in silence.

"Do you feel up to doing some more training?" he asks.

"Sure."

We spend the next hour drilling blocks and jabs, improving my footwork. Finally, I sink down to sit with my back against the wall, my tunic damp with perspiration. I'll have to change back into the clothes Lirika appropriated for me from Bren, though it's been good to practice my moves in a skirt. Knowing how to navigate that while staying alive is its own skill.

"I'll fetch something to drink," Bren says and heads for the stairs while I lean my head against the wall and try not to pant.

My turned foot aches—not blisters, thankfully, but muscles pulled too tight through the arch of my foot. Taking advantage of Bren's absence, I peel my boot and sock off and cross my left foot over my leg so I can massage it. It's slow going. I let my mind wander back over our conversation as I work.

Bren sets a water jug and cup down beside me.

I startle and quickly yank the hem of my skirt over my foot. "I didn't hear you—"

"It's all right," he says softly, sitting down before me. He pours me a cup of water and hands it to me. I take the distraction he offers gratefully, gulping down the contents, but when I lower the cup, he says, "Your foot hurts?"

I stiffen. "It just aches a bit. It's nothing unusual."

"Let me help." He leans forward to fold the edge of my skirt off my foot.

"Bren!"

He looks up, and there's nothing sly or mischievous in his face. "It's all right, Rae," he says again, gently, and waits.

I look from my foot to him and realize I do trust him. Still, it takes all my courage to nod.

Ever so gently, he slides his hand beneath my heel and moves my foot a little closer to him. "Where does it hurt?"

"Mostly along the arch," I say, my voice strangely thin.

He uses his thumbs to massage my arch, pressing firmly. It hurts, but it's a good kind of hurt. I close my eyes, resting in the moment, in how unexpectedly safe I feel with my foot cradled in his hands. In the comfort of being here, and the inexplicable sweetness of his touch, and the warmth of the sunlight falling on our shoulders. I could rest here forever, content in the moment.

Eventually, though, he finishes. As gently as he began, he sets my foot down.

"Better?" he asks.

I ease my eyes open, nod. I make myself shift to my knees and lift the jug. "I can pour water for you."

His mouth quirks. "The ever-practical Rae," he murmurs. He holds his hands out for water to wash with, then does the same for me.

I dry my hands on my skirt, aware of how he's watching me from the corner of his eye. I'm not sure what he expects of me. So, I put my sock back on, and then work on my boot.

He rises and walks away, following the wall a few steps, then pauses to look out, his hands beating a steady rhythm on the flat adobe surface.

I pour myself another cup of water, wondering at his behavior. He seems . . . I suppose fidgety isn't the right word, but something's bothering him. Weighing on him. Perhaps he's worried about Artemian and Lirika.

"You all right?" I ask, rising to lean against the parapet.

"Fine."

I sip my water, watching him.

He glances toward me, then back out over the plains. "If all goes well, you'll be going home to your family within a few days."

I stare out at the plains, considering his words. I don't think Bren's right: I can't imagine my family is all at home waiting for word of me. Alyrra will have told them about my abduction, and Mama will surely have come to Tarinon to try to help push forward the search for me. She's likely come alone: Bean is too young, too much of a handful, and Niya's secret is too dangerous to risk exposure at the palace. But Mama will be here, in Tarinon.

"Won't you?" Bren presses.

"Yes," I say, because that much is true: if I survive what's ahead of me, I will go back to our quiet life in the country. It's a good life. I've never found it lacking before, and yet the thought of returning weighs down my limbs. Still, Niya is at home. She will need me, and that is not a future I will ever walk away from.

"I doubt Alyrra will want me to stay on with her," I say into the quiet. "She'll consider it too dangerous given the enemies I've made, as will my cousin who invited me to Tarinon in the first place."

"You'll make a good life for yourself out in the country," he says, voice flat.

"I shall endeavor to not make a bad one," I say, my heart aching. I don't want this conversation, don't want to make either of us unhappy skirting around the edges of the things we can't have. "Although it seems rather far, right now. Perhaps we should just focus on surviving our return to Tarinon?"

Bren huffs softly. "I suppose that's wise," he says and lets the matter drop.

CHAPTER

31

I head downstairs sometime later to take a quick bucket bath in the ground floor washroom, aware that Artemian and Lirika—or the carriage they send for us—should arrive shortly. I bring along my satchel; with the painted ward by my side, I feel no apprehension in removing my story sash while I scrub myself. I inspect it carefully when I'm done, noting the frayed lines of embroidery that I found earlier. At least they don't seem any more worn than they did before. I'll just have to keep the wooden plaque with me as much as possible for now.

I dress quickly, wrapping the sash about my waist beneath Bren's tunic and adding his sash over the top. Then I make my way back to the room. The day is winding down, the sun slowly sinking in the sky. I set my satchel down and look out the window at the deepening shadows. Shouldn't we have heard from Artemian and Lirika by now?

The faint pad of footsteps outside precedes Bren's signature knock. I open the door to find him waiting with a tray of food. "Eat upstairs?" he asks. "I can leave your meal here if you prefer."

"I'll come," I say at once.

"If we haven't heard from Artemian and Lirika by the time we're done, I'm going after them," he tells me as we take the stairs.

"I thought it was getting late," I say worriedly. It's not quite evening, but it's also not that far to the city. Certainly not with a donkey to help them along, and with the ability to send us a carriage once they're safely there.

"Yes," Bren says.

We reach the roof in silence. Bren looks out at once, scanning for travelers before setting down the tray with its offerings of curried fish, rice with peas, and a side of spiced potatoes. "Fish?" he asks.

"No."

He smirks. "It's not all as bad as what Lirika gave you."

"I am a potatoes sort of girl," I tell him steadfastly.

"I rather thought so," Bren says smugly, scooping out potatoes for me. "That's why I asked for them."

Bren eats quickly, on his feet, watching the road as the sky lights up with the coming sunset. I set my plate on the parapet beside his and match his speed. "I'll leave my pack with the innkeeper," he says. "I want you to stay in the stables while I'm gone."

I consider this with some misgivings. "You're worried something will happen?"

"I'm worried something *has* happened. I don't want you to be easily found."

I swallow hard. "All right."

We return to our room to collect our belongings. While Bren has his conversation with the innkeeper, I polish off the last of the potatoes. By the time he returns, I'm ready and waiting, my satchel over my shoulder.

He closes the door behind him with a wry look. "There are folk in the hallways. May I suggest the window?"

"Always," I say dryly.

"Spoken like a proper thief."

I boost myself up onto the sill. It's a ground-floor window, easy enough to let myself down from on the other side. Bren follows me out with a graceful leap.

The yard lies quiet. He takes my hand and we cross the yard to the stables. The six roomy stalls all lie empty. We take the old wooden steps beside the door to the hayloft. Bren must have scouted this out earlier.

He settles me in the far corner, then lifts and stacks a few more bales to better hide me from view. "I'll be back as soon as I can," he says. "Don't move unless you have no choice."

"I won't, just—be careful, Bren." If he doesn't come back, I don't know how I'll sneak into the city unobserved, or reach his people to alert them that something's wrong. No, that's not true. I can join a group of travelers, perhaps, and then go to the Tattered Crow, connect to Bren's network from there. I just don't want it to come to that.

Bren drops down to a crouch before me. "I'll be fine, Rae. I'll figure out what happened to Artemian and Lirika, and then I'll come back for you, or send someone you can trust. I swear it."

"Don't," I say sharply, raising a hand. "Don't make promises you can't keep. Just promise me you'll be careful."

His eyes darken. He says, his voice so gentle it's almost sweet, "I'll be careful."

I nod. "Then go."

His gaze lingers on me a moment longer. Then he rises and turns away, his fingers brushing against the pendant hidden beneath his tunic. He'll be Red Hawk now, more than Bren. Touching the pendant must help remind him of that. I wait until I hear his foot on the stair before I touch the matching pendant beneath my own tunic.

Once the stable falls silent, I nestle into my cloak and try to nap. It's an impossible venture, but after the walk and training with Bren, I'm tired enough to have unfounded hopes. Not that they do me any good.

Instead, I lie there as the evening deepens into night, worrying about Lirika and Artemian, where they are, what could have happened to them. Eventually, I tear my thoughts away from panicked imaginings of them dead or wounded, and instead think of my own plans, of how I might convince Alyrra to deal with Garrin even if I cannot speak of the sorceress.

A woman screams.

I sit up with a jerk, my heart in my throat, listening intently for more. There—a man shouting something, loud and authoritative. The faint sound of sobs. I scrabble a little farther back behind the bales, hunker down. I have no idea what's happening out there, but I'm not about to go find out.

I'm wearing the pants and tunic I took from Bren, and my hair is short—perhaps if I'm found, I can pull off being a boy. Though I didn't bind my breasts, which means anyone looking carefully will see my profile and know the truth. I fasten on my cloak and remain crouched in my corner, listening for some clue as to what's happening.

Down below, someone shoves open the stable door, hinges squealing. Whoever's there is either angry or desperate.

"Search everywhere," an unfamiliar voice barks. "I want to know who they saw coming in here."

Oh no. My hiding place was meant to keep me safe from a casual glance, not protect me from a focused search. I look around helplessly, but I'm already in the farthest corner the loft has to offer. There's nowhere else to hide. I shove my satchel with the ladle and ward in it behind another bale, scattering some loose hay on top of it, for Bren to find when he comes to look for me. He knows I wouldn't leave it behind unless something was wrong.

Boots sound on the wooden stairs. I huddle lower, but I already know I'm in trouble. I listen in agonized silence as one set of boots walks toward me while the other moves away.

A stocky, broad-shouldered man steps around the piled bales and looks down at me, a dagger gleaming in his hands.

"Kel?" I ask, deepening my voice. I keep my boot hidden beneath a flap of my cloak, my left hand tucked under as well.

"Get up, boy." As I push myself to my feet, he calls out, "I found one."

I stand anxiously, hoping he won't see my foot. Even though I've learned a few tricks, I know very well I can't possibly pit my knife against his dagger and win. A second man appears, carrying a lantern. He is tall and lithe, with a savage smile and dark eyes.

"What have we here?" he murmurs. He passes the lantern to the first man and turns to inspect me. "We heard there were two of you who snuck into the stables. You're not the one we're looking for, though. I'd know him anywhere. Where is he?"

Bren must be safe, then—because who else could they be looking for?

"I asked you a question." The man takes a step forward.

I know better than to pretend, at least about this much. "I don't know, kel. I just happened to cross paths with him. He left a half hour ago." More like an hour, maybe more, but there's no reason to tell the complete truth.

"You're lying." In a single smooth move, he unsheathes his sword and flicks it out, the tip pressing into my throat. I flinch but don't dare step back.

I lift my hands, palms out, as if to convince him I am not dangerous when he's the one with murder in his eyes. He pauses, his gaze homing in on my left hand. I swallow a curse as he looks back at my face, his eyes stripping away the difference created by my short hair. Of all the moments to let someone see my hand with its shorn-away finger—

"You're Red Hawk's girl, aren't you?"

"What?" I say in a final, hopeless attempt to lose his interest. "I'm just passing through."

He shifts back, eyeing my custom boot. "Cripple," he says, the savage smile widening. Oh, how I'd like to cut that word out of his mouth with my bone knife. The very violence of the thought freezes me in place.

He gestures with his sword. "If you can take three steps without faltering, I'll let you go."

I raise my chin and say coldly, "I walk with a limp."

He laughs. "Don't I know it? Now tell me where he is."

I press down on the anger simmering beneath my skin. I can't afford to antagonize this man, however much I might want to. "He left. He didn't tell me where he was going."

He grimaces and sheathes his sword. "It'll be the city, then," he says to his companion, reaching out to grab my arm. He shoves me against the wall, my arm twisted behind me. His hands brush over my sides dispassionately as he searches me.

"Got a knife," he says. I try to jerk away, but there's nowhere to go, his hold on my arm unforgiving. He shoves his hand through the pocket's seam to grab the hilt of my bone knife.

He passes it to the man with the lantern. Then he leans in close, his voice in my ear and his breath sickeningly warm against my skin. "You even try to escape, and I will slit you open from your belly to your chin, you hear me, girl?"

I nod jerkily.

He drags me down the stairs, pausing momentarily to speak with the other searchers before marching me across the yard, through the kitchens, where the cook and her helpers cower against the back wall, and down the hall to the main room.

Bardok Three-Fingers stands at the center of the common room, sword in hand. He's a massive man, built tall and broad, with heavyset shoulders and a wide face. At his feet lies a crumpled body.

Panic roars through me, tightening around my heart like a fist. I shove down at my fears, trying to focus. If Bardok is here, that means he must have intercepted Lirika and Artemian, and learned from them where we were staying. He came here hoping to cut his rival down while he was at a disadvantage, with no one to fight by his side. Bren got away, and instead, Bardok has me.

I swallow hard. My captor shoves me to my knees before Bardok. I stare at the body sprawled at his feet, realizing belatedly who it must be: the innkeeper, an apron wrapped around his front, barely recognizable for the scarlet spread across it and puddling on the floor. A middle-aged woman huddles against the wall by the empty fireplace, weeping. The other occupants have gathered beside her, tense and silent, a ring of armed men keeping them in place.

"Well, I'll be damned," Bardok says softly, studying me.

"You probably will," I agree, my voice not quite steady. I'm shaking, but I can't fall apart right now. I've got to keep myself alive long enough for Bren to turn himself around. I don't think I can play Bardok the way I did Morrel, but I can at least fight for time.

Bardok's laughter booms out around me. I meet his gaze, chin raised.

"So Red Hawk likes his girls looking like boys, does he? Well, the hair improves your looks, I'll say that much. Though I still don't know what he ever saw in you."

It is somewhat mortifying to realize that Bardok knew exactly what Bren's interest was in me before I did.

The thief lord straightens and continues wiping away the scarlet from his sword with a stained kerchief. "You're a palace chit too," Bardok observes, his eyes gleaming with interest. "Is he selling out to the royals?"

"Not hardly." Bardok must not know it was Garrin who sent me to him—not with such a palpable display of disgust at the idea of taking orders from the royal family. I suppose if Garrin used a go-between, neither of them would be aware of who they were working with.

"I'm not sure which would be harder to believe—Red Hawk rolling over for the royals, or him falling for a plain-faced wench like you."

I raise my brows. "Guess you'll just have to ask him."

My knees ache from kneeling for so long, and I can't seem to control my shaking. Somehow, Bardok's much more terrifying than Morrel. Perhaps because he's already demonstrated he has no compunction when it comes to torture or dismemberment.

"Mmm. What shall I do with you?"

"You could try sending me downriver again."

"Because that worked so well the first time," he agrees, tilting his head. "How'd you get free?"

"He found me."

"Not possible."

"After I killed two men in Lirelei."

"Possible," Bardok amends. "How'd you manage that?"

"With a knife."

Bardok laughs. "The girl has claws." He pockets the kerchief and steps over the innkeeper, bringing his sword around in a lazy arc to rest at the base of my neck. "You were supposed to be long gone. So well gone, in fact, that Red Hawk would never find out who really sent him that finger of yours. You told him, didn't you?"

"Didn't have to," I say, lying with a smile. "He already knew, though he was glad to have my confirmation."

"Either way, you're bringing me back trouble when I let you go with your life. Not very wise of you."

I'm not about to apologize for surviving and fighting snatchers like him. "He crossed half a kingdom for me," I say instead. "Says something, doesn't it?"

"True," Bardok allows, letting his sword lie heavy against my shoulder.

I wait, watching him silently. Even the people by the fireplace remain still, everyone intent on Bardok.

He lifts his sword away and sheathes it. "I may as well use you to bait a trap. But make no mistake, you will die before I part with you."

CHAPTER

32

My return to Bardok's home is strangely similar to the first time I visited, only this time the man sitting across from me in the darkened carriage is far more terrifying than the Black Scholar.

The carriage pauses at the city gates, but the guards on duty wave it through after speaking to one of the accompanying riders. It's late night now, the streets mostly quiet, and no one takes much note of our passing. I press myself into the corner of my bench, keeping my gaze on the thief lord opposite me.

Bardok heaves himself to his feet as we clatter to a stop before his house. Standing, he takes up most of the central space of the carriage, his shoulders hunched and his head bent to keep from hitting the roof. He clambers down and says to the men waiting there, "Take her to the cells. I'll want her in the morning."

I step down from the carriage, and even though I'm on a city street, there's no escape here, nor do I expect it. I'm surrounded by armed men, the only way forward the door Bardok disappeared through. I follow him silently, one of the men taking my arm in a firm grip.

I don't actually know the way to the cells. The last time I was taken there, I was nailed into a wooden crate and could barely breathe. This time, I am guided down a side corridor and around a corner to a narrow stairwell. At the bottom lies the hallway with its bench where Bardok cut off my finger. A dark stain mars the wood, and I wonder in a detached, surreal way if it is my own blood I'm looking at.

"This one has a girl in it. Might as well put them together," one of the men says, pausing to look through the grate in the first door. "Might need that second cell soon, if we're lucky."

A sudden, unfounded hope blooms in my breast. I wait as the first man unlocks the door, and then I'm marched forward and shoved in. In the wash of lantern light before the door swings shut, I find myself facing a girl crouched at the back of the cell. Lirika.

I clench my jaw to keep from speaking her name, waiting as the sound of our captors' footsteps fade to silence. In the darkness, I can no longer see her.

"Is he dead?" she asks, her voice low and hoarse, barely there.

"No," I say quickly, moving toward her. "He came after you, but as far as I can tell, Bardok's men didn't cross paths with him."

A silence, and then she says, "Good."

"Are you—unharmed?" I ask uncertainly, coming to a stop.

"They tortured Artemian." She shifts, and I track her movement to the side of the cell. "I think he's dying."

I squeeze my eyes shut, listening. I can hear his breath, labored and heavy, but when I open my eyes I can't catch even the faintest shape of him. I start hesitantly across the darkness toward him. "What happened, Lirika?"

"They caught us before we ever made it home. They knew we were with Red Hawk. We wouldn't talk, so they tortured Artemian and made me watch. For every question I didn't answer, they hurt him more. I tried to—I didn't want to tell them." Her breath catches and she coughs, a dry, pained sound, her voice raw from screaming and crying and begging. "I couldn't just watch. He's—he's always been kind to me. He was screaming for me not to answer them. He was screaming, and I—I told them."

I am shaking again in the darkness, tears sliding down my cheeks. "I'm sorry," I say. "It's all right that you told them."

"They were torturing Artemian, and *he* didn't break. I did."

"You didn't have a choice," I say, sinking down beside her. "That's how interrogations work; they take away your choices."

She doesn't answer.

"If you must blame someone, blame Bardok," I tell her, reaching out blindly toward her. My hand touches something—her arm, I think. "You only did what you could."

She shifts away from me, and I let my hand drop.

"I can't even properly see Artemian to help him," she says, her voice small.

I stare down into the darkness. From his breath, I know we are crouched beside him, but the dark is nearly absolute. "Has he woken at all?"

"No."

I close my eyes, bending my head, and send up a prayer for the man before me. Together, we wait out the night, listening to Artemian breathe.

The thud of boots moving steadily down the stone stairs echoes into the room. With their approach comes a brightening of the darkness, light falling through the grate in the door. I take the moment before the door opens to turn my gaze on Artemian.

He lies curled on his side, his face tense with pain, his eyes closed. No, I realize with a sickening lurch, only one of his eyes is closed. The other has been burned away. His tunic is missing as well, baring a lean, muscled body covered now with lacerations and burns, some thin, others as thick across as my finger.

Oh God. I press a hand to my mouth, commanding myself not to be sick. Beside me, Lirika tenses, watching the door as it swings open.

Bardok stands outlined in the light of the lantern on the bench behind him. He gestures toward me with his knife. "Come along. We're going to see just how desperate Red Hawk is for you."

I rise to my feet. "What do you mean?"

"No questions," Bardok rumbles. "Move."

Lirika reaches out and squeezes my shoulder, the first time she's touched me of her own volition tonight. I glance toward her and she murmurs, "Don't betray him."

"I won't."

I step into the hallway, waiting as Bardok sheathes his knife and locks up the cell once more. I could try to run, but he would catch me in moments and be on his guard thereafter. It's not the right time for such an attempt.

His hand closes around my arm. He marches me upstairs, hauling me along with him when I can't take the stairs fast enough. Out on the street, a carriage waits. I climb up and take a seat facing backward while he confers with the driver.

"What time is it?" I ask hesitantly once he's settled himself on the opposite bench.

"An hour till dawn," he says. "Now be quiet."

The carriage rattles through the sleeping streets. I grip my knees. It's hard to think past the fear fogging my mind. I put a hand against my chest, where Bren's pendant rests beneath my tunic, thinking of Lirika's words. My promise to her.

Finally, the carriage rolls to a halt in a large, open space. A square, perhaps. Through the window, figures move in the flickering light cast by the torches they carry. After a moment, the driver opens the door and steps back, a lantern in his other hand.

"All secure, kel."

Bardok grunts and steps out, gesturing for me to follow. I clamber down as quickly as I can, not wanting him to grow impatient and yank me onto the hard cobbles. But he pays me no attention. Instead, he's scanning the square.

It's a small market square with a row of wooden stalls along one side, a single large tree growing in each corner, and a low platform at the center, the sort used by performers. The square is surrounded by two- and three-story buildings. We must still be on the southeast side of the city, in Bardok's territory, because these buildings are large and well maintained, the streets that open onto the square wide. Nothing like the crowded, poverty-stricken west side that Bren calls home.

The tall man with the savage smile steps forward to report in. He and Bardok converse in low tones. I sidle closer, keeping my gaze on the cobbles as I strain to hear them.

"We've men hidden in the entrance of each building," the tall man says. "We've kept all signs of them off the roads, so Red Hawk won't see them. If he comes."

"He'll come," Bardok murmurs. "His honor won't give him a choice. You've stationed men at the opening of each street?"

"All but the alley, as you said, kel. We'll leave that open for them to run into, then come out of the buildings there and cut them down. We've blocked off the end, so there'll be no way out once they go in there."

"Good."

I wrap my arms across my chest, my stomach churning.

"Will you let them take the girl?"

Bardok snorts. "I'll cut her to pieces first. She doesn't leave my presence alive."

Regardless of what happens to me, I'll have to warn Bren to fight his way out instead of taking the deathtrap disguised as an escape route. At least they haven't gagged me. In all likelihood, Bardok will leave me able to scream, the better to draw Bren's attention.

I force my focus back to the square as the tall man says, "There's been no sign of them yet."

"Excellent. Bring the girl."

The tall man prods me along behind Bardok, moving toward the platform. It's only about waist high, with a few sturdy wooden steps leading up to it. It isn't until the driver raises his lantern to light the steps that I realize what Bardok's men have cobbled together atop the platform: a makeshift wooden gallows. Swinging from the long arm of the gallows is a single noose.

A shock runs through me, and the next moment the tall man has my arm twisted behind me. "Keep walking," he says mildly and forces me stumbling up the steps.

A stool has been placed below the noose.

"Wait, please," I say, desperation in my voice.

"I would prefer not to gag you," Bardok says in a bored tone. "I suggest you shut up."

I bite my lip. I'm bait for Bren. I knew that, argued for it, only I didn't expect it to be quite like this. I don't know what I expected, but not this—being forced up onto a stool, my hands tied before me, a noose tightened around my neck, and a suggestion that I not lose my balance mockingly delivered.

The stool is unevenly balanced, one of the legs marginally shorter than the others. I brace my feet, my left foot thankfully steady beneath me. Still, I can't stop my breath shaking in my lungs, my body trembling. If I don't calm down, I'll slip and kill myself before anything even happens.

My mind flashes back to Lirika in the cell, telling me not to betray Bren. But surely she didn't mean I should purposely kill myself to save him? Only, is my life really worth his life, or the lives of his men, should they be lost trying to rescue me?

I swallow hard, and my left foot slides on the stool. I scrabble to keep my balance, my bound hands flailing, and then someone reaches up and grabs me by the back of my tunic, steadying me.

"Not yet, you fool girl," a voice I don't recognize says.

I whimper in relief, then hunch my shoulders, humiliated. I need to be strong, to at least *appear* unafraid. Except I don't know how to do that right now.

Just breathe. I force one slow breath, then another.

Bardok has put me where he wants me. This is how slavers think: that power is having absolute control over a person's body. Bardok has arranged me this way because, to him, I am no more than a thing to be used, a pawn in the games he plays. He will use me and toss me away as he has countless other bodies. In that way, he's the same as Garrin and the Circle, profiting from lives they consider disposable.

But I am not just my body. I've command over my own mind, and that's where my true strength lies. I can face the fate Bardok intends to mete out to me on my own terms, and do my best to warn Bren. I won't stop fighting until there's nothing left of me.

From the corner of my eye, I catch a flicker of movement. I blink, staring as a tiny grey hummingbird darts up to me, wings brushing my bound hands. The bird slips between my fingers into the cup of my hands—and *flattens.*

My fingers tighten around the small fold of paper it transforms into, my heart thundering in my breast. It's a spell bird, like what the Fae mage, Adept Midael, the Cormorant, sent me once before. Bren must have reached out to the palace for help.

I clutch the paper, taking stock of the men around me. Bardok has moved to the edge of the platform, still speaking with the tall man. The man who grabbed me from behind has drifted away to chat with the carriage driver with his lantern, both faced away from me. I tilt my chin down. I hold a single fold of paper, easy enough to open with a nudge of my thumb. In the lantern light, the words are simple and clear.

This paper contains a shield to protect you. Keep it close.

I clench my hands shut, try to breathe through my shock. I don't need to look at the words again to know who wrote this note: I would know my sister Niya's hand anywhere. It's there in every line and curve of the letters. I gaze across the still-dark square so that no one guesses what I hold in my hands.

I can't imagine how Niya could have dared to send a spell winging through the city in search of me. Or how she convinced the Cormorant to teach her this—it's not a spell used by human mages, so far as I know. I'd never even heard of such a trick before the Cormorant's bird found me. Or maybe he sent her note for her, and she hasn't exposed her magic. Regardless, what possessed Mama to risk bringing Niya to Tarinon? There's certainly no way Niya came here alone.

Bardok dismisses the carriage driver and within a few minutes the carriage is gone. The square lies ominously quiet, Bardok's men well hidden. Dawn filters into the sky overhead; with its dim light I can tell that the doors to the surrounding buildings are cracked open. How many thieves are waiting there, ready to set upon Bren and his allies? Enough to keep every resident of these buildings hiding within their apartments, that's for sure.

From somewhere down the road facing the gallows comes the faint sound of horse hooves, a steady *clop clop*.

I look up, searching the streets, but the light is still too dim. I can't make out any details. Bardok turns as well, focused on the sound. The hoofbeats come to a stop. A minute later a man hurries across the square toward Bardok.

"It's a girl on a horse, kel," he says. "She says she's here for her sister."

I stiffen. What is Bren thinking? He can't send *Niya* into this square full of murderers!

"What?" Bardok says, at a loss.

"The prisoner," the man says, gesturing toward me. "It's her sister. She says she has a message for you, kel."

Bardok turns an appraising glance on me, his lips curling as he takes in the look of horror on my face. "Is she armed?" he asks the man.

"Not that we can see. We haven't searched her."

"Let her through then. Keep four men around her. If she tries anything, cut down the horse and kill her."

"Kel," the man says and departs.

I watch, straining my eyes. Through the gloom I make out the form of a horse walking forward, its white coat pearlescent in the dawn, its hooves clopping against the pavers. Perched on its back, eyes intent on me, rides the diminutive form of my sister, Niya.

CHAPTER

33

I drink in the sight of my little sister, fierce and unflinching on her white horse. Niya is my opposite in so many ways, from her petite frame to her luminous gray eyes, to her flyaway hair, wisping out of her braid even now. The steel in her gaze, the intent focus of her whole being as she rides toward me, is new, but I recognize it regardless.

She intends to save me.

Her ears and neck and fingers glitter with gems, giving me a terrifying idea of what she plans: every one of those jewels has been fashioned into a tiny amulet. She isn't just a slip of a girl riding into a pack of bloodthirsty thieves; she's a mage with a single-minded goal, and anyone who steps in her way will feel her wrath.

Except that revealing her talent in public will brand her a greater outlaw than Bardok Three-Fingers will ever be.

"Niya," I croak. "You need to leave."

She offers me a tight smile, bringing her horse to a stop a few paces away from the platform. "Always the big sister, Rae. You know, someone has to look out for you too."

"You have a message," Bardok says, stepping to the edge of the platform. "Deliver it."

"Kel," she says, dipping her chin. "My name is Niyagara ni Ansarim. That is my sister behind you, royal attendant to Princess Alyrra. The princess wishes you to know that she will not forgive a direct attack on her personal household."

Bardok laughs. "The guards have been hunting me for years. You think I fear your little goose girl princess coming after me? She can no more find me than her guards can."

"She doesn't need to," Niya says. "I already have."

What is she *doing*? And how could Bren involve her?

"Kill her," Bardok says, nodding to the four men who surround her. He turns his back on Niya to regard me with disgust. "It seems you're not worth Red Hawk's interest after all."

"No!" I cry as the men draw their swords. One of them grabs the horse's reins just below her head—it's Lemon, I realize inanely, sour-tempered and liable to nip.

Niya shouts as the other plunges his sword into the soft flesh between Lemon's foreleg and chest—but the tip rebounds with enough force to tear itself from his grasp. I nearly lose my balance on the stool, scrabbling to stay upright, my breath sobbing in my breast. She's warded.

Bardok reaches out and grabs my arm, keeping me on the stool. The fight playing out behind him sounds like no more than a scuffle. He pays it no attention. "I think I had better send you back in pieces, don't you? Perhaps that will garner some attention."

"No," I say again, but I'm not listening to him. *Please let Niya get away.*

Lemon, angry and at least halfway spooked, tries to back up. When the man gripping her reins stays alongside her, she throws her head from one side to the other, clocking him in the face. He releases the reins with a muffled cry as he falls on his rear. Niya immediately turns Lemon, letting her shove past the men before coming back around to face us.

Bardok draws his sword and steps back, eyeing me thoughtfully. He touches the tip of his sword to my boots. "Perhaps I'll start at the bottom and work my way up."

My attention jerks to him. "I—I'm a thief," I say, raising my chin. I need to keep his attention until Niya escapes. "You should start with my hand. Really, considering you started with my fingers, perhaps you should finish those first, and *then* move on."

He frowns, considering me. Like Morrel before him, he knows I'm up to something, but he can't figure out what.

Behind him, Niya transfers the reins to one hand and holds her other hand up to her chin. Unfurling her fingers, she blows over a black stone resting on her palm. A cloud of midnight dust whirls forward. It wraps around her and then *whooshes* out, expanding and clinging to each man it touches.

They scream.

Bardok whirls around in time to see the dark cloud before it reaches him. He raises an arm as if to ward it off. I flinch back, holding my breath as it envelopes me—but it slides past without touching me, the ward in my hand protection enough. Or perhaps it's my sash's doing.

Bardok shrieks and flails at the air, fists swinging, his face ashen pale and his eyes wide and staring. "No," he shouts. "You're dead! You're *dead*!"

All around us, men cry out as they face their phantoms— illusions or memories, I can't tell. How is Niya doing this? Is it another spell from the Cormorant—or is this *her*?

I glance toward her only to see Lemon tied to a ring attached to the platform and Niya scrambling up. The darkness has spread through the square, thinning as it reaches the edges. A number of

Bardok's men have burst from the houses to lend him their aid, but they stumble and fall as they step into the spell.

Somehow, though, Bardok has managed to keep his feet. The others on the platform have all fallen, screaming and gibbering and begging for mercy.

"You," he gasps, his eyes fastening on me between one blink and the next. He roars, throwing himself forward, and slams into me, knocking me off the stool as he stumbles past. The paper spell flies from my fingers with the force of his impact.

My scream is cut off as the noose snaps tight around my neck, a line of fire at the top of my throat. My legs kick out helplessly, the ember in my mind flickering to life. I raise my bound hands to my neck, but I can't grasp the rope, my fingers unable to grip it.

Niya shouts my name, and then she's there, wrapping an arm around my waist. Something strange flies up my skin, or perhaps under my skin, and then the rope around my neck gives way.

I fall hard, Niya unable to hold me, and slam into the wooden platform on my side. Painfully, I drag in one breath, then another.

"Rae, oh God, Rae! Please!" Niya gasps, bending over me frantically.

Still trying to catch my breath, I blink the shadows from my eyes, only to be blinded by flashes of white streaking down from the sky.

"Rae, are you all right?" Niya begs.

I try to nod, but my neck *hurts*. My eyes are still seared by the crackling white magic. Except it's gone now, only its afterimage glowing in my vision. "What?" I manage to force out. "Light?"

"I think those were the protections the Circle maintains," Niya says, casting a nervous glance about. "They just destroyed the illusions I used. I—I didn't realize they could do that."

Oh. *Oh.* "Niya," I whisper, my voice ragged.

"Can you get up?" she asks, tugging at me.

I sit up and catch sight of Bardok closing in on us, looming over my sister's shoulder. She reads the terror in my eyes and twists to face him, but his sword is already slicing through the air.

I reach out to grab Niya, my bound hands knocking ineffectually at her—and the sword slams into the air before her with enough force to send her sprawling into me. I end up on my back, gasping for breath again.

Bardok snarls, raising his sword once more. Niya rolls off me, gaining her feet. She must have a bird-shield similar to the one I lost, but its power won't last forever. We need to stop Bardok before he batters his way through her protections. She raises her hand, her brow furrowed in concentration. Then she moves her hands toward him and pauses, as if waiting.

What is she *doing*? Niya doesn't know combat magic—

Bardok is expecting Niya's attack, even if I don't know what I'm seeing. As he closes again, he pivots and comes at us sideways. Niya yelps and twists to avoid his blade. It still smacks into the air beside her, shoving her farther away.

"You may have a shield," he says, bearing down on her, "but that doesn't mean I can't tie you up and take you with me to listen to your sister scream. You'll be begging me for mercy before I'm done with you."

I think of Artemian, broken and burned, of the desolation in Lirika's voice. Choking back a sob, I scrabble to the side, trying to stay clear of Niya's feet. Bardok takes another swing at her which she only just manages to avoid, stumbling slightly as the blade sparks against her magical shield. She needs help.

I may lie curled on the ground, my hands bound before me, but I'm not letting Niya face this man alone. Bardok's been focused on my sister, and that's brought him closer to me than he either notices or cares. Coiled on the platform, I gather my strength and then twist, lashing out. The heel of my good foot slams into Bardok's knee. It's a variation on a move Lirika taught me on the *Heron*, and as my boot connects, I can hear her saying, *No matter how strong your opponent is—a knee is just a knee.*

Bardok goes down hard, toppling over the leg I knocked out, toward me. I roll away. He takes the force of his fall on his side, one hand still curled tight around his sword. The blade smacks against the wood by my face, sending splinters flying.

I scramble back, my breath shuddering in my lungs. Niya swoops down to grasp my arm, pulling me to my feet and hustling me toward the stairs, out of Bardok's reach. "Quickly," she whispers.

We're not going to be nearly fast enough. Bardok heaves himself to his feet, favoring the knee I kicked, his expression murderous.

"Bardok, old friend," a familiar voice says. "You've been stealing from me, and I've come to collect."

Bardok snarls, turning to face the newcomer. I watch with unutterable relief as Bren boosts himself up onto the platform beside us. *Finally.*

He is dressed in his usual tunic and pants, only now he also wears an armored leather vest over the top, with leather bracers on his arms. His ebony hair is pulled tight into a warrior's topknot. He seems his own particular brand of nightmare, drops of scarlet on his cheek and his face as harsh and unyielding as a hawk diving for the kill.

He gains his feet and pauses beside us, his gaze running over me. "You all right, Rae?"

"*Why* is my sister here?" I demand.

Niya snorts a laugh.

"I'll answer that," he promises. "Just not right now."

He moves past us, unsheathing his sword. A half-dozen other thieves clamber up behind him, red armbands wrapped around their forearms. They stay with him, all of them armed and ready to fight. A glance shows me the square is awash in fighters—including at least a dozen soldiers in palace armor. Bardok's plan to bottle-neck Red Hawk's men seems laughable now, thieves and soldiers working together to flush out men from the buildings, chasing them into the streets. There's fighting everywhere.

God, I hope the people inside are safe.

Bardok's men scramble forward to stand at his side, the tall man who captured me at his right, the remaining two to his other side. They're outnumbered, but not terribly so.

"I've a mind to kill you now," Bren says, moving forward with lethal grace. "Only I've made a promise to deliver you up alive for someone else to enjoy. So long as my sword doesn't slip. What do you think of that?"

"Sold your honor to the highest bidder," Bardok mocks. "Then again, you're just a boy. What do you know of honor?"

"Strange words for a slaver," Bren says lightly, balancing on the balls of his feet. "It's a pity I've agreed to only take your hand for your crimes."

"If you think—" Bardok begins, stepping forward, and then a wind screams over the tops of the buildings behind us, fierce and strangely focused. It curves around to slam straight into Bardok, sending him flying back several paces to skid across the wooden platform to the very edge. The men beside him are thrown side-ways, like pieces knocked aside on a game board.

"*There* it is," Niya says triumphantly.

"You did that?" I demand.

Bren casts us a sharp look and then crosses to the prone thief lord, ordering his men forward. There's movement in the dark around the platform—more of Bren's men, closing in on Bardok's men who are still getting up from the cobblestones.

"Well," Niya tells me, her voice low, "you remember that mage who used a wind against Bean, back during that whole business with the dragon? I couldn't think of anything else that wouldn't bring down the protections, so I tried to do the same thing. I suppose there must be a trick to it I don't know, to get the wind to come so quickly."

That's what she'd been trying to do with her hands.

"You had fine timing," I rasp. My throat aches fiercely, throbbing with each heartbeat.

"You want his hand?" a voice asks. I look back sharply to the gathering of thieves. Bren's men have pinned Bardok to the platform. They're watching Bren now, waiting.

For a long moment, Bren stands facing his enemy, his sword at the ready. Then he shakes his head. "I've no use for it. Bind him."

"Your hands, kelari," a man says from beside me, holding up a dagger. I start, not having heard him approach. He's around thirty years of age, with a sparse beard and thin lips. Gathering myself, I offer him my bound wrists. He saws through the ropes with a few quick strokes.

"We'll get you to safety," he promises and gestures us toward the end of the platform. Two more thieves have come up from behind to join him.

There's still fighting in the square, but it's in pockets now, groups of men hacking at each other, the moans of the wounded whispering on the wind.

"Go on," Bren calls to me from across the platform. "Edhren will guard you."

I raise a hand in acknowledgement, and Niya and I hurry after the sparsely bearded man, Edhren. His companions fall in behind us.

"Can't believe . . . you brought Lemon," I wheeze. The familiar, sour-natured mare with a yellow star on her forehead snorts as we near her, her ears still pinned.

"She missed you," Niya says, which is a patent lie. Lemon has never missed anyone with two legs. Not even Bean. "Also, she likes to bite."

Can't argue with that. The men wait nervously as Niya takes a moment to calm Lemon before we mount. I heave myself up, my whole body hurting. I start to slide back to allow Niya in front of me, but she says, "No, let me ride behind you. In case I need to concentrate."

I kick the stirrup free and she uses it to swing up, wrapping her arms around me. I lift the reins, then rearrange them—I'm used to threading them back out between my last two fingers on each hand, but I no longer have a pinkie on my left. I grip them loosely, without threading them at all, and glance toward Edhren.

"This way," he says, gesturing. "Stay close."

"Kel," I say, glancing toward Bren, too far away now. "Artemian and Lirika are being held at Bardok's house—"

Edhren beams at me. "We know, kelari. Red Hawk sent a half-dozen men to get them out while the rest of us came here. They should be safe by now."

Oh, thank *God*.

"Come." He moves off briskly, wending a path through the square that takes advantage of the spaces between the last few knots of fighters, and the fact that what fighting is left seems concentrated more on the other side of the square now. No one seems that interested in crossing paths with us. Rather, men scramble out of the way when they see Lemon, breaking away from their battles to avoid us.

Niya wraps her arms around my waist. A cool wash of magic slides into me, flowing up my torso and easing the pain around my neck.

"Niya," I whisper. "You need to stop."

"Too late for that."

"How did you do all that back there?" I ask, my voice rasping. "How are you even here?"

She huffs a laugh. "In case you didn't notice, you got abducted from the palace, Rae. We received an express from the princess, and a carriage arrived a few hours later to give us the option of coming to Tarinon. Mama was intent on going by herself, except I made the point that I might be able to do things she couldn't. It took some arguing, but here I am."

"There's *no* way Mama and Baba would risk your safety—"

"To find you? I insisted it was my decision. God, Rae. You were snatched. Did you really expect us to sit at home and hope for news?"

"What could you have done from here that you couldn't do from home?" I demand.

"Serve as a distraction so Red Hawk and Matsin could slip their men in while Bardok tried to figure me out," Niya points out. "Cut you down before you were well and truly hanged."

She's right. Of course she's right. But I don't want my sister to pay for my life with hers. "Niya—"

"Anyway, Genno Stonemane came to pay his respects at the palace and brought the Cormorant with him. Adept Midael has maybe been teaching me a bit in secret since."

"He's been *teaching* you?"

"Yes. Alyrra sent for Mama and me earlier tonight with word that she'd heard from Red Hawk about you, and that she was sending Captain Matsin and a few quads of her royal bodyguard to help get you back from Bardok. So of course Mama and I insisted on meeting with your thief friend."

Matsin is here? I shake my head, unable to worry about that right now. First things first. "Niya. Were those spells you used yours or the Cormorant's?"

"Doesn't matter. I promised him if I was caught, I'd take the fall. I won't blame him."

"I'm going to kill Stonemane," I say wrathfully.

"The Fae can't intervene in local politics," Niya says defensively. "If you must know, the shields were Midael's, as were the memory illusions. The wind was obviously mine."

"The protections responded to the illusions," I say tightly. "The Circle will have noticed. We have to get you out of here."

"I know," Niya says softly. "We can't get out of here any faster than we're going, though."

We cut around another group of skirmishers, and I catch sight of a figure on horseback moving to intercept us. The men with him all wear red armbands, but I know without a doubt they aren't Red Hawk's men. Because the man they're escorting is the Black Scholar.

He meets my gaze, and a shudder runs through me. He wears the long, flowing black scholar's robes he's known for, his clothing equally dark beneath them. He's a handsome man, in his late forties, his hair still fully black, cut short to frame his face. He wears a well-trimmed beard and mustache, adding a touch of sophistication to an otherwise austere look. He also tried to kill me the last time I saw him.

Our escort makes to pass around him, but he urges his horse forward. Niya tightens her hold on me, and I can feel her stretching to look over my shoulder. Damn it, *not now!*

I turn Lemon a few prancing steps sideways, knowing better than to try to run, however much I want to. Since he's here as an ally, I need to keep him as one, deal with him as quickly as I can, and get Niya out of here before the Circle comes looking for her.

"Kelari Amraeya," he says, with just a hint of emphasis on my name.

The escort Bren assigned glances between us, their expressions growing grim. The Scholar deftly guides his horse through their numbers, forcing one to stumble to the side, and brings his horse up alongside mine, head to tail so that we're facing each other.

"Kel," I say, holding Lemon still. She shifts uneasily but stays put. "I did not think to meet you here."

I knew Bren had planned to involve the Scholar in fighting Bardok, but I didn't consider that he could pull together both his alliance with the Scholar and support from the palace on such short notice. Alyrra apparently didn't go through Melkior, but instead sent her personal bodyguard, and it seems the Scholar had advance warning from Bren's express courier from Lirelei.

The Scholar's gaze goes from me to my sister. "It seems this is a night of surprises."

I shift, drawing his attention back to me. I don't want him looking at Niya—I've got to get her *away*. From his notice, from this place where she cast her spell. For that, I need to appease the Scholar so we can keep going. "I apologize," I say abruptly, thinking of how I humiliated him in front of Bardok.

There is a hard glint to his eyes as he looks back at me. "Do you?"

"Bardok has been playing a few games," I say with care. "One of those played out the last time we met."

"So it did. What have you done with Bardok now?"

"He's been taken captive, kel."

"Mmm. I would have preferred to mete out justice at once, but I suppose I will have to be patient."

I cast a quick glance across the square. The platform lies empty, Bardok already moved somewhere safer for holding. Between the red-banded thieves and the dozen or so soldiers present, his men have been forced toward the far side of the square. And time is slipping by.

"Is that why you're here?" I ask.

"I am here," the Scholar says slowly, "because Bardok made the mistake of attempting to set Red Hawk's men against mine. Why wouldn't I add my men to Bren's to bring Bardok to account?"

I realize a moment too late that he's watching for a reaction from me, because the last time we met I didn't know Bren *was* Red Hawk. I don't suppose it matters now, though. "I'm glad of it," I say. "I hope we might, ah, deal peacefully with each other going forward."

"Certainly," the Black Scholar says, his gaze measuring. "Though I believe you owe me a pretty ransom."

At least he hasn't realized I accidentally stole one of his books — the archer's journal with Winterfrost's name in it, at that. "Ah, but, kel, I gave up my finger so you could improve your relations with Red Hawk. Surely that was sacrifice enough?"

He huffs a laugh, his gaze flicking to my left hand, the empty knuckle there. "Indeed. I suppose blood for gold will serve." He draws his horse back a few controlled steps. "I believe you will do very well, kelari."

Has every thief in the city decided my future lies with Bren? "Thank you," I say, miffed.

His smile grows a little deeper as he dips his head and moves away.

I urge Lemon forward into a smooth-gaited running walk, pushing past Edhren in an effort to get to the edge of the square. He breaks into a run, staying at our side. It's relatively quiet here. We should have no trouble reaching the edge of the square, the street guarded by a contingent of red-banded thieves. We've taken far too long to get away—

Niya's hands tighten around my waist a bare heartbeat before walls of pure white magic blast up from the ground not five paces before us, enclosing the whole of the square. Lemon spooks, twisting away with a panicked neigh. Our escort lunges out of her way. Men's voices rise in a cacophony of shouting across the square.

A lifetime of training kicks in. I adjust the reins, pulling smoothly on the left rein, turning Lemon's head so she runs in a tight circle over the uneven pavers. It won't stop her—I don't have the strength to do that—but it brings her around enough times that she slows and becomes willing to finally stop of her own accord, nostrils flared and ears tipped forward stiffly. My left hand throbs in counterpoint to the fear pulsing through me. At least she didn't stumble and fall.

"Easy," I tell Lemon, trying to calm myself as well.

The shimmering white walls stand as high as the surrounding buildings, completely sealing us in. There isn't a crack visible any-where.

We're far, far too late.

CHAPTER

34

"Quick," I say, kicking my foot free of the stirrup. "Get down!" Niya dismounts at once. I slide down after her and pass the reins to Edhren, who takes them with some confusion. "Lead her away. I've got to hide my sister."

"I'll stay with you—"

"Not with the horse," I snap and turn to grab Niya's hand. "Come on!"

"Rae, there's no way—" she protests, but I'm not listening. I drag her behind me into the open door of the nearest building and jerk to a stop.

The white magic of the wall cuts right through the hallway before us.

"Rae," Niya says, her voice so very calm and resolute. "I can't run from this."

I turn on her. "You haven't even tried! Can you get through this wall? Is there a way you can study it?"

She walks up to it slowly, her gaze moving over it. "I don't have the training, Rae. This is far beyond me."

"It's taking a lot of power, isn't it?" I demand. "If we hide you long enough for it to falter—"

"No," Niya says, the white of the wall reflecting gray off her face. "It's likely powered by an amulet."

From outside, there's the distinct sound of boots. No—they can't have found us already!

Bren bursts through the half-open door and comes to a stop, chest heaving. "I take it," he says, glancing between us, "that it was your sister who made your sash."

"You have to help her."

"You can't," Niya says sharply. "You both know the punishment for hiding a Talent, and no one is getting out of this square until they have me."

She steps forward to glare up at Bren. "You have to keep Rae safe, do you hear me?"

"Captain Matsin," a voice says from outside.

Bren looks at both of us, his gaze lingering on Niya, and then he says, "Let him in."

I look over in a daze to see Captain Matsin step through the doorway, his helmet under his arm, blood spattered on his leather and bronze armor. Captain Matsin, who was the prince's personal bodyguard. He knows Kestrin's secret better than I do, and he's more than used to protecting Kestrin's hidden magical talent from discovery.

"Please," I beg him. "You can't let them take my sister."

"Of course," Matsin says. "It will be easy enough if you'll come with me, Kelari Niyagara. Mages can sense a Talent by touch; they'll know those spells were given to you . . ." He trails off as he takes in our faces. "Oh," he says, and squeezes his eyes shut. "I see."

From the square comes the sound of a voice raised in demand, echoing off the cobbles.

"There's no way out," Niya says, turning back to Bren. "Keep my sister in here. Don't you dare let them take her, you hear me?"

"I won't," he says.

I catch her sleeve. "Niya, you *can't.*"

"There's no help for it, Rae. This day was always coming."

Her words punch a hole through my lungs. Has she always expected this? To be caught and made a slave to the Circle? Because that's what amulet-bearers are, whatever euphemism the mages might use. Most older Talents are too volatile to be trained—or too old to be safely inculcated into the order the Circle has established. Someone who willfully trained herself separately from them? Such a Talent could never be trusted in their eyes. Perhaps it's just me who's naive; this day was *always* coming, and I just couldn't bear to believe it.

Niya turns to Matsin. "I'll come with you, but you have to give me your word you'll get our mother out of the palace."

He grimaces. "I don't want to take you out there," he admits.

"You don't have a choice either," Niya says, inexorable in her determination. "The longer you wait, the more you'll come under suspicion. Just promise you'll get my mother away."

He nods. "They'll still search for her."

"Send her to the Tattered Crow," Bren says. "We'll take care of her."

How are they planning this so calmly? My sister is about to walk into magical bondage. My *sister.*

"No," I snarl, grabbing Niya's arm. "You're not going out there alone."

She twists away. "You can't protect me. Just stay here, Rae."

"I'm not letting you—"

Bren steps between us, his back to Niya. "She's right, Rae. There's no time. You have to let her go before you're caught as well. Tell her goodbye now."

"No, I won't," I say, trying to push past him. He grabs my wrists, his grip like iron. Behind him, Niya inhales on a watery gasp, blurts, "I love you, Rae," and darts out the door, Matsin following in her wake.

I lunge after her, but Bren is there, transferring his grip to my arms and forcing me back against the wall. "Rae, stop! *Stop.*"

"No," I cry, shoving at him, using the tricks he taught me to try to wrench myself free of him, but it's no use because he knows everything I try. He's stronger, and quicker, and more experienced, and my sister has walked out of that door with Matsin and I will never see her again.

"How could you?" I scream at Bren. "How could you do that? She's my sister!"

"You can't save her."

"I could have tried," I cry, and the fight goes out of me. Because Niya is already gone. Even if I walk out that door now, I can't bring her back. I sag against the wall.

Bren eases his hold on me, then lets go. I sink down until I'm sitting hunched on the floor, grief dragging at me, tearing at my lungs. Each breath is a battle, my whole body shuddering, my face wet with tears I didn't know I was crying.

"Rae, I'm sorry," Bren says, crouching before me. I can finally hear the ache in his voice.

I stare past his shoulder to the empty doorway, the dawn so bright now it lights up the square beyond. Niya knew the mage who came to investigate wouldn't leave without her. That all of us— thieves and soldiers alike—would be held and checked before being released. There was no other way out, however much I railed against the truth. She was found out saving my life. It's all my fault.

I shake my head. No. This doesn't have to be the end of it.

"I'm not letting them have her," I whisper.

Bren leans toward me, brow furrowed. "What's that?"

I meet his gaze fiercely. "I'm going after her. Don't you dare try to stop me."

He tenses. "Rae, you can't go out there."

"I know that," I snap. "I'm not talking about now. I'm talking about later. Today, or tomorrow, or as soon as I can plan it. Don't tell me I can't. You might have helped save me this morning, but you made sure someone was there for Lirika and Artemian because they're *your* family. You would never have left them to Bardok. And I'm not leaving Niya to the Circle. That's what family does: we save each other every day of our lives."

Bren rises and holds out his hand to me. "All right."

I look up at him, at the hand he offers to help me up. "What?"

"You helped me steal a galley along with its captain from under the eyes of the Port Authority. I see no reason why we can't steal back your sister. I am a thief lord, after all. And you've the makings of a pirate queen."

I take his hand, haul myself up. "You're going to take on the Circle with me?"

"Your sister took down Bardok for me. I'm going to help get her back," he says carefully. "You know we can't stand against the whole blasted Circle."

"Right," I say, ignoring this. "I need to talk to the princess as soon as possible."

Still holding my hand, he turns toward the door. "Then let's go."

By the time we emerge from the building, the magical wall has dissipated and the mage has departed with my sister. Matsin is already on his way over to us, mounted on a great black horse.

"I'm leaving for the palace," he tells us tersely as he draws up. "My second in command is here. The prison carts are being loaded, and I've a healer seeing to your wounded in a side street."

"And your story?" Bren asks.

"As we discussed," Matsin says. "My men and I received word of a thieving dispute and didn't have time to call in the city guard, so we dealt with it ourselves. Bardok is already en route to the palace holding cells, along with those of his men well enough to be moved. You and your allies are free to go, considering you lent the guard your aid. Of course, I've no idea who you really are."

It's a tidy story, without too many loose ends. "You're giving him the glory?" I ask Bren.

He shrugs. "I've been promised the opportunity to question Bardok in return. We got you out alive. That will suffice."

"It's not my glory, actually," Matsin says with a hint of a smile. "I've heard a few men talking by now, and the story that is going about has nothing to do with either guards or thieves, and everything to do with your sister." He turns to Bren and says, "You need to get Kelari Rae to safety now. The Circle will use what they can to search out Kelari Niyagara's family—hair for now, blood once she's been tried and sentenced."

Bren nods. "We'll be quick. Her mother?"

"That's why I'm leaving," Matsin says.

I clear my throat. "I need an audience with the princess today. It's urgent—both about my sister and a traitor in the palace. You'll tell her?"

Matsin hesitates. "Where?"

Bren says, "At the princess's discretion, somewhere in the city."

"I'll send word," he promises, and with a dip of his head, departs.

The bearded thief, Edhren, brings over Lemon. I mount up, grateful to take the weight off my feet. It takes us a little longer to depart. I have the distinct feeling that Bren is walking me past his men as he confers with those he needs to, making sure they see me, know my face. I don't have any smiles left in me, but I nod to those who meet my gaze, grateful to each of them. They risked their lives for mine—this fight might have happened anyhow without me, but not now, not like this.

We turn down a side street and proceed to a small, waiting carriage. Bren will have Lemon brought after us by one of his men.

"How many men did you lose?" I ask as I dismount.

"Five, for now. We've more wounded, some of them seriously so."

"I'm sorry," I say softly. They all had families, loved ones, people with whom they thought they would still be this evening.

Bren studies me. "They died for me, Rae. Not you. They died to maintain our code. Don't blame yourself."

"The code Bardok violated?" I ask. "The thieves' justice he's happily ignored for decades?"

Bren grimaces. "I assure you, I'm aware of our shortcomings. Why do you think I turned him over to Matsin now?"

I stare at Bren, processing this. He means he *could* have taken Bardok without Matsin's help. He didn't. For Bren to make such a decision—to turn a fellow thief lord who specifically wronged him over to the king's men instead of seeing to his own justice—speaks to an unexpectedly deep shift.

"You're really all right with giving up Bardok?"

"I've gotten justice my own way before," he says. "There's never an end to it."

"Bren?" I ask, unsure what this all means.

"Oh, I'm still Red Hawk," he says, flashing me a grin that, for all its brightness, is edged with weariness. "I just want to see your version of justice for once."

"I'm glad," I say finally. "I didn't want to watch another clandestine execution. Not when there was another option."

"I know," he says. He opens the carriage door and offers me a hand up. "Neither did I."

CHAPTER

35

I wake from a troubled doze to the sound of soft voices outside my door.

I sit up with a jerk, my thoughts flying to Niya, to the feeling of Bren's hands around my wrists as he held me back, to the utter helplessness of watching my sister walk out of my life, out of her own, into a future no one should have to face.

I inhale hard and feel a faint line of pain across my neck, curving from ear to ear: the bruises left behind by the noose, eased by Niya's efforts to heal me this morning, but still very much there. We don't yet have a plan to rescue Niya. Bren counseled sleep once we set a few possibilities in motion—meeting Alyrra, as well as Bren sending out through his networks for anyone who might work within the mages' complex, because, as he put it, there are servants everywhere.

I push myself up off the bed and cross the room at a stiff, un-comfortable limp. I'm back in the same room I stayed in before in Bren's house, with its low bed and side table. Bright morning light leaks through the shutters, painting stripes across the carpet. When

I swing the door open, I find Bren consulting with a solidly built, graying older woman.

"Kelari Bakira?" I ask uncertainly, remembering the woman who watched over me the last time I was here.

Bren smiles at me. He's bathed and changed into regular clothes, damp hair falling against his shoulders. "Rae, I've gotten word your mother is at the Tattered Crow, in company with two more folk. Will you come see who they are with me?"

Bakira tuts. "The child ought to rest."

"I've rested," I assure her, as if an hour or two lying down were all I needed. My voice is still rough, my throat aching. But I need to make sure Mama is safe, and start laying plans to help Niya. I look back to Bren. "I'm ready when you are."

Bakira smacks his arm lightly. "You had better feed her at the least!"

He dips her a bow. "As you order, kelari, so it will be."

"Rascal," she mutters, a smile pulling at her lips. "Don't let him run you into the ground, child."

"I assure you," Bren says, "Rae doesn't need that warning. I'm the one who's having trouble keeping up."

"Oh hush," I say, annoyed. I glance into my room and find myself staring at my satchel—the same one I left behind in the stable's hayloft. Bless Bren and his attention to details. "I'll be ready in a few minutes."

"You'll want this," Bren says, starting forward to offer me a familiar onyx and mother of pearl hilt.

"My knife!" I say delightedly, taking it from him. I still have its sheath in my room.

He laughs softly. "I admit I was not quite so thrilled to see it when Bardok sent it to me."

"No," I agree. "Bren—are Lirika and Artemian all right? I know you sent men for them."

"We got them out," he assures me, his good humor falling away. "Lirika is resting. I sent Artemian to the princess's new house of healing in the hopes that the healer mage there will see him."

"You'll let me know if you hear anything more about him?"

"I will."

I hesitate. "I'd like to visit Lirika when she wakes up, if she'll see me."

"I'll make sure she knows. For now, though, you should get ready. The carriage will be around front in ten minutes."

I grab my satchel and the sheath from my room and hurry to the washroom. Working quickly, I peel off Bren's old clothes. I still wear his pendant. I stand a moment, my hand fisted around the circular disk with its hawk design, and then let it go and wipe myself down once with a wet rag, scrubbing at any dirt smudges. There are bruises along my leg and side where I hit the platform when I fell from the noose, and from touch I know I must have bruises ringing my neck from ear to ear. Other than that, there's only my tender ankle and my left hand, the scar showing pink-red through the flaking scabs.

Finished, I pull on the slightly sour-smelling but still significantly cleaner tunic and skirt from my satchel. I take a moment to inspect my travel-worn story sash with its treasure of sewn wards. There are a few more threads fraying now, along the lines of the wards. The story symbols themselves are largely undamaged.

I wrap the sash snugly around my waist, trying not to worry. I will just have to keep the wooden plaque with me. Thankfully, it's still in my satchel along with the ladle.

Bren waits in an upper sitting room with its soft but sturdy carpets and floor cushions, and only a thin line of mosaic banding the tops of the walls. It's striking to know this is actually Red Hawk's house. It's nowhere near as well appointed as the Black Scholar's, or as ostentatious as Bardok's. The furnishings are simple and comfortable, the decorations few but well made. Clearly Bren doesn't use the money he steals for luxuries.

I remember Kirrana telling me about the noble households that were robbed by Red Hawk over the royal wedding, about how both jewelry and food staples were taken. I was shocked at the need to steal food, at the reality of whole communities where everyone might be hungry and thus unable to feed their equally hungry neighbors. It's a reality Bren is well aware of, one he hasn't let himself forget. I suppose it's just another piece of what sets him apart from his rivals.

"There's food for us in the carriage," he says now. "I'd like to get to your mother as soon as possible."

I nod and regret the motion at once, my neck protesting.

"It's possible it's a trap for you," he continues. "More likely, her companions are trustworthy, but she'll eventually be followed by guards searching for both of you. Have you got that ward from the ship?"

I pat my satchel. "I figured they wouldn't think to work around their own slavers' ward when tracing her."

"I do like using my opponents' weapons against them," Bren says, mischief in his eyes, and starts for the door. I stare after him, my breath deserting me.

"Coming?" he says, and then glances back at me. "Rae? You all right?"

"Yes," I say, smiling slowly. "Yes, I am."

My mind is racing as I take the stairs down one at a time, my ankle aching even as the rest of my muscles loosen up. Bren slows his pace to keep me company. I don't look at him, don't do anything but think about his words and what I can do with them.

The carriage ride is short and taken up with eating the assortment of utterly delicious chicken and vegetable tasties Bren has arranged for, the spiced filling stuffed inside layers of flaky dough.

They're not the same as the ones he brought with him to our rooftop picnic a few weeks back—these were likely made by his own cook—but they're still worth all the attention I can spare. Even if each time I swallow, the muscles at the top of my neck throb with pain.

Bren eats quickly and efficiently, a slight smile touching his lips as he watches me. "They're not going anywhere, you know," he teases.

"But I am," I tell him and wash down my meal with a drink of water from the flask he's brought.

The driver pulls us around to the back of the Tattered Crow, alongside a second carriage. A young man steps forward to open our door, dipping his head and saying to Bren, "All's safe, kel. No one here we don't know except the two ladies and the lordling with them. They're in the upstairs room we keep for your meetings."

"Lordling?" Bren asks.

"He isn't dressed it, kel, but he holds himself a bit finely. He's got pretty features, long curls that would get in his eyes if he worked, and he's very used to being listened to."

Bren glances toward me, eyes crinkling at my wide smile. "Should be fine then."

Outside, Bren gestures two of his men ahead of us and leaves two behind with the carriage. As we cross the yard to the tall adobe building before us, he says, "I take it you recognized that description?"

"It's my cousin's husband, Verin Filadon."

"He's one of Kestrin's closest friends, is he not?"

"Yes."

"Handy," Bren murmurs and guides me through a narrow back hallway to another set of stairs.

"I never realized how very many stairs there are everywhere," Bren mutters, staying beside me as I make my way up.

"Tell me about it," I grumble. "Every time you go up, you still have to come back down."

"We could take a window."

I shoot him an aggravated look, ruined somewhat by the smile pulling at the corners of my mouth. "I don't usually have so much trouble with stairs," I tell him. "It's just if I have blisters or accidentally strain my ankle."

"I take it that palace life was harder on you than country life?"

"Palace shoes," I say with some disgust as we reach the top of the stairs. "I would sometimes use a walking stick back home," I admit. "Not inside, but out on the plains. It helped with the long walks."

Halfway down the hall, a door bursts open and my mother rushes out. "Rae!"

"Mama!" I cry, hurrying forward.

The two men who went ahead of us stand together just past the door, watching tensely, their hands on the hilts of their swords. Bren must wave them back, though, for they make no other move.

Mama reaches me a moment later, pulling me into a tight hug. I forgot she was slightly shorter than me, but I haven't forgotten the absolute comfort of her embrace. "Sweet child," she says, resting her head against my shoulder. "Oh, my sweet child."

"Mama, they took Niya," I say, my voice cracking.

"I know," she says, and I can hear the anguish in her voice. She holds me a moment longer, then steps back to take a good look at me. Her expression falters.

"It's not as bad as it looks," I say quickly.

Bren coughs discreetly. I do my best to ignore him, though Mama glances at him before returning her focus to me.

"Your hand?" she demands.

"It's healing," I assure her and hold it out for her to see.

She blanches.

Desperately, I wave at Bren and say, "This is my friend Bren. He's the one who found me in Lirelei."

He dips her a bow, his smile slightly strained. "Kelari," he says gruffly. "It's an honor to meet you."

Wait, is he *nervous?*

"I thank you for returning Rae to us," Mama says. "We are in your debt."

"Rae?" my cousin Melly asks, stepping into the hallway as well. Her eyes widen as she takes in the sight of me, short hair, scrapes, bruises, and all.

"We should get inside," Bren tells me. "The rooms here should all be empty, but it's best if we don't take chances."

I nod and hurry toward Melly, Mama beside me. My cousin is a little pale beneath the natural brown of her skin, and her eyes are badly shadowed, but otherwise she seems well. "How's the baby?" I whisper, pulling her into a hug, careful not to press her belly.

"Fine," she says, her grip tightening. "God, Rae—I've been so scared for you."

"I know."

She lets me go and tugs me into the room. Filadon waits just inside, slim and handsome and distinctly unsettled. He bows over my hand, freezing as he catches sight of my missing digit. Then his court training reasserts itself and he rises with a faint, empty smile and guides me into the rather strange assortment of chairs gathered in a circle. Mama and Melly sit on either side of me, leaving Filadon to sit down opposite us.

"We can't stay here long," Bren warns, moving to stand by the window, one eye on the outside. "Say what you need as quickly as you can. I'm afraid it won't be safe for you to meet again unless your family is cleared of any"—he gestures vaguely—"charges."

He means harboring Niya. I turn to Filadon. "You and Melly will be safe?"

"We're not of your personal household, and I'm well positioned at court; we can plead innocent. Kestrin, Alyrra, and Matsin were in discussions when I left—I went with Matsin to hear his report to Kestrin after he came to warn your mother to leave."

"Can they help us?"

Filadon shakes his head. "Not directly. If it appears the royal family is sheltering Talents from the Circle, that raises questions as to why they would want those Talents. It's a political quagmire."

"And indirectly?" Mama asks.

Filadon shrugs elegantly. "A great deal depends on what you intend to ask. Matsin relayed your request for an audience. Alyrra has cancelled her afternoon plans and will instead take tea with Veria Havila at her family's villa in the north of the city. Matsin will meet you at the side door and conduct you in." He glances toward where Bren stands. "You're to come alone, but I'm sure it's to be expected you'll have someone waiting in a carriage for you."

I sag into my chair in relief. *This afternoon.*

"If you tell us what you intend," Melly says, "we can prepare Kestrin and Alyrra to hear you."

I take a slow breath, organize my thoughts. "Do you know where Niya is now?"

Filadon grimaces. "The Circle has their own holding cells within the mages' complex behind the palace. She's most likely there. Based on what Kestrin was able to find out before I left, she should be put on trial tomorrow. The sentencing will follow shortly after."

Which means we don't have a great deal of time—as far as I understand, once her punishment is carried out, the Circle will set a number of spells on her that will allow them to always find her. She'll be their slave.

A fierce anger rises up inside me. Not only do they take hidden Talents as slaves, but they've consigned thousands of children to abduction and slavery over the last few decades. I may have despised them before, but now? Now I will stop at nothing to bring them to their knees.

"I'm taking down the Circle," I say quietly.

Bren exhales with a sigh.

"What?" Filadon asks uncertainly.

"The Circle. They're the ones behind the snatchers; they profit from every child sold into slavery. The Darkness is something they created, and the children that can't be found are only lost to us because of the wards the Circle gives the snatchers."

"You're sure of all of this? You have evidence?"

"I have, and I can show Alyrra when we meet. She already knows some of it."

Filadon frowns. "If she already knows, then—"

"I'm not letting them have Niya," I say tightly.

Filadon sits back, nods. "Now *that* the royal family may look the other way for." He glances toward Bren. "You'd have to have quite an accomplished thief on your side to help Niya escape. Even so, the Circle would still hunt you."

Which is why I need to deal with the Circle at the same time.

"We need to leave shortly, Rae," Bren reminds me. "Is there anything else you need to share?"

Right. I turn to Filadon. "Tell Alyrra that when I was abducted from the palace, I was set upon by a pair of guards. They left me in an empty storage room, and Verin Garrin came to me there."

"*What?*" Filadon starts to his feet, his expression murderous. "*Garrin?*"

I nod. "He took me through the secret passages of the palace and sealed me into a crate with his own hand, sent me on to Bardok Three-Fingers. He's protecting the snatchers, covering up for them, and profiting from them."

"No wonder he hasn't found any leads on what happened to you," Filadon snarls.

Melly says, with a quiet sort of vehemence, "I think I would like to see him die for that."

Mama looks to Filadon. "But he's a lord. Will they actually punish him?"

Filadon curses softly and paces away from the circle of chairs, then turns back to us. "He's the spare heir. He knows he's essentially untouchable. Still, none of us ever imagined—"

"Do you think the king knows?" I interrupt. "Alyrra doesn't."

"Nor does Kestrin," Filadon says. "Nor can I believe the king could know but not tell his own heir."

Bren clears his throat. At my look, he gestures toward the door.

"Tell Alyrra," I say, rising to my feet. "Tell her about Garrin, and the full complicity of the Circle, and that I intend to get my sister back." I need her to have had time to think about it before we discuss it together.

"Taking down the Circle—*how* do you propose to do such a thing?" Filadon asks.

My grip tightens on my satchel. "I've an idea about that. I'll need to speak with the princess first."

Melly steps forward to give me a hug. "We'll make sure she knows about all of this. Please take care, Rae. Stay safe. I . . ." She hesitates, and then pulls back to dash the tears from her face. "I will look forward to seeing you again," she says firmly.

"I love you, Melly," I say. "I hope you'll tell your baby lots of stories about their Auntie Rae."

"You had better tell them yourself," she says and bursts into tears. "Oh, I *hate* this part of being pregnant."

I laugh, my throat aching from more than just bruises, and give her another hug, then step back for Mama to do the same.

Filadon reaches out to clasp my hand and dips a bow over it. "Be careful, Rae."

I smile and nod, but I don't intend to be careful.

I intend to do what I must.

CHAPTER

36

Mama settles next to me on the padded carriage bench and says, "Tell me everything."

I do for the most part, starting from when I first agreed to investigate the snatched. I don't give her all the details—just a quick summary of what I learned and how. I move on quickly to my own abduction and give her the same story I first did Bren. I don't attempt to trick the sorceress's binding.

Finally, Mama sits back. We're nearly to Bren's house, the going a little slower now, the streets busier. "You really believe we can rescue Niya?"

"And take down the Circle," I say.

Bren, seated across from us, says, "Which raises the question of how exactly you intend to do such a thing. What is it you wouldn't tell Filadon?"

I shrug uncomfortably. "I need to speak with the princess first."

"What do you expect from her?" Bren presses. "Even she can't stand against them. Every time you've gone to an authority, it's only come back to haunt you."

"This time will be different. I know I can trust Alyrra and . . ."

"And what?" Mama asks.

I take a slow breath. "I do not want to be judge, jury, and executioner."

Bren grimaces. "So, you'll make her your judge. What difference does that make?"

"Her approval is as close to the king's justice as I can get," I admit. "Further, I need to know that what I'm doing will actually change things."

"How do you mean?" Mama asks.

"The Circle may be the topmost mages of our land, but they've controlled the training of the rest of our mages. I want to make sure that the Circle isn't replaced by more of the same."

Mama nods. "You want the royal family ready to push for a different sort of Circle, put the mages they trust most in power."

"They might not be able to help Niya directly, but they can affect what comes after. If the Circle were different, we wouldn't have had to hide Niya in the first place. If they raised different kinds of mages—imagine if they didn't take children away from their parents, Mama! Just that would change the types of people they grow into."

"You expect to accomplish all that?" Bren asks, disbelieving.

I don't blame him for that reaction at all. I'm dealing with it myself. "Considering how everything has gone up till now, I fully expect to fail. That doesn't mean I won't try."

"No," Bren agrees after a moment. "The thing about you, Rae, is you never do things by halves. If you're going to save one snatched child, you'll try to save them all. If you're going to rescue your sister, you'll try to aid every Talent out there like her. I'm not even surprised anymore."

"Yes, well, if you ask nicely, I'll let you help me again," I say, annoyed.

His eyes sparkle. "Is that how it works?"

My cheeks warm, and I become exceedingly aware of Mama watching us both far too shrewdly. I clear my throat. "You will come with me to this meeting with Alyrra, won't you?"

"Of course, though it sounds as though I will be expected to wait outside. I can find a way in, if you prefer."

"No, no, outside is fine," I say quickly. "Just so someone's there to make sure I come back out."

"But you trust Alyrra," Bren says, his gaze searching.

"I do. I've just learned to be careful of doing the same for those around her."

He nods and turns to Mama. "There's something I feel I ought to tell you, kelari."

"Yes?" Mama says.

"Rae and everyone you will meet among my people call me Bren." I look up sharply at this, but he is focused on Mama. In the dim confines of the carriage, the curtains pulled to keep us safe, Bren appears equal parts shadow and thief lord. "However, I am better known by the title of Red Hawk."

I stare at him, aware of how Mama's grip on my hand has tightened, how she's stiffened slightly. And of how carefully he's watching her. Why would he tell her so openly, so quickly? When he hid it from me for so long?

"I knew that your people were working to help Rae," Mama says. She glances from Bren to me. "I just did not realize you were . . . so closely involved."

"I hope you will keep my confidence," Bren says. He's lost that natural grace of his, even though he hasn't moved. He looks strangely stiff instead.

"I am grateful to you for aiding Rae, offering me shelter, and planning to help my second daughter," Mama says. "You can be sure that I will not betray you."

Bren dips his head, but I catch the flicker of a frown across his brow before his expression clears. Perhaps he doesn't like debts any more than I do. "I thank you, kelari."

"Mama," I say, abruptly. "What about Bean and Baba? We need to warn them before the Circle can send anyone after them."

"We stopped at the main city courier office on our way to meet you. Filadon sent a letter by express courier. It should reach them before any other riders."

"What will they do?" I ask.

Mama gives a sad, strained smile. "We've a cabin in the mountains. Baba will take Bean there."

"A cabin? How did I not know this?"

"We've always had a plan. We just hoped that Niya would be a part of it. I took her there every year when we went foraging in the mountains for herbs."

"That's why you were gone so long," I say, remembering those yearly trips. "I always wondered."

"The cabin is about four days' ride from our home. It's in an unsettled valley, two days from the nearest town. Baba and Bean will be safe there until..." Mama hesitates.

"Until we can join them," I supply, even though it sounds like some kind of fairytale ending. What are the chances, really, of freeing Niya? Of all three of us being able to safely journey to the mountains, and on from there? As if some wonderful future awaits us just past the sunset.

Although, considering the thief lord across from me, if anyone can smuggle us to safety, Bren can. It's just a question of getting Niya free. And putting an end to the Circle's corruption in support of the snatchers. And dealing with Garrin and the sorceress. That's all. I swallow a laugh.

The carriage pulls up behind Bren's home. Mama managed to bring along a single trunk of belongings, which Bren orders delivered to my room. "I can move you to a larger room if you wish to stay together," he says once we reach it, "or you can use the room next door, kelari."

"Oh no," Mama says, looking in at my little room, "we'll be perfectly comfortable here. Thank you."

Bren nods. "I'll send up extra blankets and pillows, then. Rae, you should try to rest while you can."

"You too," I say with some amusement. "Pretty sure you're as rested as I am."

"True," he agrees, though I have the distinct feeling he won't take his own advice. No doubt he needs to deal with the fallout from this morning's work. He dips us a slight bow and departs.

Mama closes the door behind him and turns to me. "Rae, just how well do you know that young man?"

My cheeks burn. "I—we've travelled together, Mama. He's probably saved my life a few times now."

"Hmm." She purses her lips. "Do you go around with him alone a great deal?"

"What? No—or not, I mean, not a *lot*. He made sure there was another woman traveling with us from Lirelei."

"He really is Red Hawk?"

I nod uncomfortably.

Mama studies me thoughtfully. "None of this is quite what I expected, but I am very grateful you're all right."

As am I. Now that I've got Mama alone, I have a few more questions for her. And a desperate wish to change the subject. "Niya told me she spent the last week or more studying with the Cormorant."

Mama rubs her temples and moves to sit on the low bed. "Yes. She loved it, Rae. I've never seen her so—so determined and happy at the same time." There's a mother's burden of regret in her voice.

"She never wanted the Circle," I tell Mama. "But I suspect she always wanted to study."

"We should have found her another way."

I sit down beside Mama. We should have, though *how* we could have done that short of moving to another land, I don't know. Perhaps we should have moved. Regardless, it's too late for such regrets. "Does Alyrra know? About Niya?"

"She will now," Mama says. "She didn't before. When Stonemane stepped forward with the spells for Niya to use last night, Alyrra ascribed it to his friendship with our family. The Cormorant kept his meetings with Niya discreet; I made sure of that."

"You were there?"

Mama raises her brows. "If you think I would allow any of my girls to be alone with another man, especially in secret, you have forgotten how I raised you."

I laugh despite myself. "I'm sorry, Mama. I suppose I have been alone with Bren a bit, but these have been extenuating circumstances."

"I know." She reaches out and pulls me into a hug. "I'm grateful to every ally and friend you might have. Especially given their willingness to help Niya. Just be aware . . ." She pauses, her arms tightening around me, and then murmurs, "No, never mind that."

"I love you, Mama," I say into her shoulder, deciding I don't want to press her on whatever she would have said about Bren.

"I love you too, sweet child." She leans back. "Now, let's take care of a few of these wild curls, and then you can rest as long as possible." She tweaks one of my short curls, and for a moment I feel like a child again before her, safe and loved.

It's a warm, lovely feeling, and I'm not at all sure why it makes me feel like crying.

CHAPTER

37

C ome afternoon, Bren and I take the carriage to my audience with Alyrra. Kelari Bakira sits in the corner of the bench, focused on her sewing, to all appearances a perfectly uninterested chaperone. It is only because of her, and Bren's insistence that the more we all went out together, the more risks we ran, that Mama agreed to stay home.

I haven't seen Lirika yet—she asked not to be disturbed—but Bren has gotten word that Artemian was seen by the healer mage as hoped, and will remain at the house of healing for a few days to receive treatment. I send up a prayer that they will be able to ease his pain.

"We'll be there shortly," Bren says as we swing past the wide plaza before the great arched entryway of the palace gates.

"I thought Veria Havila lived at the palace," I muse, gazing up at the familiar white stone walls with their intricate carvings.

"Oh, Havila lives at the palace," Bren assures me. "It's her son and his family who live at their family villa."

Beyond the window, the busy urban streets fall away, replaced by the wider, cleaner boulevards of the nobles' district to the north side of the city. Havila is *the* matriarch of the court, a fierce and capable older woman who makes playing at politics an art form. I'm glad that Alyrra's relationship with her has developed enough that she can lean on her now.

As we drive, Bren describes the layout of the house and grounds. By the time we roll to a stop at the villa's side entrance, I've an excellent idea of how to navigate the whole property. "How do you know so much?" I ask.

"I may have paid a visit a few weeks back."

"You—this is one of the houses you robbed during the wedding!"

"I'm a thief, Rae. You know that better than most."

I wish this part were different—the unapologetic thievery, rather than anything to do with justice or rights. Although perhaps I'm wrong there as well. There is something inherently unjust when a few people have an excess of wealth, while so very many are hungry and cold on the other side of the city. Doesn't the one have a responsibility to the other?

In the country, it would be a given—we all take care of each other. Here in the city, those bonds have been forgotten, have rotted away, and nowhere more so than among the nobles. Perhaps it isn't so shocking that Garrin, raised as a possible future heir to the crown, could sell into slavery the very children he should be protecting simply to add a little more to his already staggering wealth.

Bren glances out the window at the white-painted adobe walls that bound the villa. They are easily one and a half times the height of a man, topped with iron spikes all down their length.

"We'll be waiting at the corner," he says. "If you don't come out in an hour's time, I'll come in after you."

I nod and immediately grimace. I wish I could remember not to move my head so much.

I step down from the carriage with the driver's help. Between my aching legs and my turned foot, navigating the carriage's step is a greater challenge than I like to admit. Three hours of broken sleep may have refreshed my mind somewhat, but my body needs a great deal more than that to heal.

I knock on the carved wooden door set into the wall. It swings open to reveal a face I know well. Captain Matsin is dressed in the leather and velvet armor of the royal guard, his helmet polished to a high shine. He looks perfectly fine, as if he wasn't part of a blood-bath this morning.

"Kelari," he says, bowing to me.

I attempt a curtsy in return, but end up stopping before I really start, my legs and ankle hurting too much for the gesture to be either graceful or worth it. With unexpected clarity, I remember how the captain of the river guard—the one who betrayed us on board that slave galley—bowed instead of curtsying. At the time, I wanted very much to learn to do the same. I haven't spared it a thought since, though.

"If you'll follow me," Matsin says.

I step through to a small garden, rife with flowers. "Kel, do you have any news of my sister?" I ask, unable to wait.

"The hearing has been fixed for tomorrow at midmorning," Matsin says, as he bolts the door shut.

"Do you know where she's being held?"

"The mage's complex. Zayyida Alyrra will be able to tell you more."

I follow him through the garden and into the building. Bren's descriptions immediately fall into place around me, so I know that we pass the two main sitting rooms on the ground floor. The larger of the two is closed, and I hear the faint murmur of voices from within. They're too muffled for me to tell if one of them belongs to Alyrra.

Matsin continues up the stairs at the end of the hall. I take a steadying breath, reach out to grasp the railing, and start after him, one step at a time. I don't want to strain myself now, when I'll need all my body can give me to take on the Circle.

The landing is decorated by a wide glass mirror in an ornate metal frame. As I take the final few steps, my reflection comes into view. I haven't seen myself since I was abducted, and now I find myself staring harder with each step. I wear the fresh sky-blue tunic and cobalt skirt my mother brought with her from among my old court clothes. It's the rest of me that holds my attention.

My face is haggard, the lines of my bones pronounced. A scrape stands out in shades of pink and purple on my left cheek-bone, from when I hit the platform below the gallows. My eyes appear sunken, the shadows underneath so dark they are nearly bruises. A solid purple line mars my neck despite Niya's ministrations, rope-thick and curved slightly upward, disappearing only as it reaches the back of my neck. The loose curls of my short hair frame my forehead before smoothing away along the sides of my head, doing nothing to soften my aspect.

I look like a stranger. Yet, gazing at myself as I pause on the landing, I find I have never felt more comfortable in my body. Oh, it hurts, *everything* hurts, but it's mine. Every scar, every scrape, everything I have done, it's all mine. My body has gotten me through everything I have faced.

I offer my reflection a wry smile, a twist of the lips that makes me look hard-eyed and determined and surprisingly dangerous, and continue on. Matsin waits patiently for me to join him at the top. I count doorways as we walk, and know before he opens the penultimate door that he's ushering me into the family's private library.

"Wait here, kelari," he tells me briefly. "The princess will see you shortly."

I seat myself on one of a trio of plush armchairs beside the empty fireplace. He closes the door, leaving me alone.

I don't have long to wait.

Alyrra enters the room like the first, quiet drops of a thunderstorm. She seems barely there, moving in on soft feet, and yet there's a sense of weight about her. She crosses the room with a whisper, and while I'm still trying to lower myself into the deep, painful curtsy that is her due, she's suddenly there before me, tugging me up by my arms. "Rae!"

"Zayyida," I say, straightening.

She grips my hands and steps back to study me, her lips pressed together. She doesn't say anything—no apologies, no exclamations. She's seen the results of violence before, though, and I don't miss the darkening of her hazel eyes as she takes in the evidence of what I've been through.

I'd forgotten how pale her skin is, how her brown hair sets off the pink in her cheeks. She looks well, if worried, right now. Tired too, what with the faint shadows still visible through the cream applied below her eyes.

She gives herself a small shake and gestures to the chair behind me. "Please sit. How are you?"

I wait until she's seated herself and then sink into my own chair gratefully. "I'm well enough, zayyida. Did Filadon speak with you?"

"At length. I would like to ask Kestrin in to hear your story with me."

I hesitate, considering her. At a glance, Alyrra is just a young woman. I'm always surprised by her maturity, given her years, but for all her apparent privilege, she's led a difficult life and she's learned to hold her own. Still, I don't know much of Kestrin, and he might easily feel caught between his concern for his kingdom and his love for his cousin. "Are you sure, zayyida?" I ask. "You know about Garrin?"

"I've had a long conversation with my husband already; he is hoping you will speak with us both together." She meets my gaze steadily. "I would trust Kestrin with both my life and the lives of his people. *Our* people. Can you trust me in turn?"

There isn't much of a choice, but I'm grateful she asked. "Zayyida," I say, dipping my head and ignoring the accompanying twinge.

She rises and moves to the door. I hear the faint rumble of Matsin's voice, and a few minutes later, Kestrin lets himself in.

"Kelari," he says, crossing the room toward me. I rise, preparatory to curtsying. He stops in shock, his gaze fastened on me. At least I know exactly what picture I present.

"Don't curtsy," Alyrra says sharply. "Your foot is hurting you, is it not?"

"Yes, but . . ." I say uncertainly, because this is the prince after all. He's always struck me as much more difficult to know and more used to the formal trappings of power than Alyrra.

"Please," Kestrin says, his voice rasping slightly. He gestures to my chair. "Sit."

If I actually manage to survive all of this, I'm going to make *sure* to learn how to bow. I sit down, my hands clasped on my lap. Kestrin's gaze drops to them as he takes his own seat, only I've covered my left hand with my right. Grimacing, I flatten my hands against my knees and let them see exactly what's been done to me.

"I've asked Rae to tell us her story," Alyrra explains to Kestrin, and turns to me.

I launch into an abbreviated version of my abduction. I've had the telling of this story a few times now, and it comes easily to me, with just the turns of phrase that suit it. Alyrra listens with an appearance of growing horror that hardens into tightly reined fury. Kestrin, on the other hand, retains a cool expression that only sharpens as my story continues, until his eyes are as dark as black ice riming stone, and as perilous.

"The head official of the Lirelei Port Authority paid out half the reward to your helpers and then ordered your death?" he asks.

"Yes. After I escaped, whoever took power there offered an additional reward if I was brought straight to them."

"Corruption at every step," he murmurs, shaking his head. "Go on."

I do, touching only on the most important details, finishing finally with my rescue last night, and my sister's arrest. "The Circle has my sister, zayyida, zayyid. They will enslave her and profit from her none too differently than they have from the lives of thousands of children across our kingdom—only they will take her magic rather than sell her for gems."

Kestrin shakes his head slowly. "I would that we could help your sister, but we cannot oppose the Circle over her discovery, even for the good of our kingdom. They hold my family in their fist. It will be nothing for them to destroy us and install a new ruling family—one that will bow to their particular wishes."

I stare at the empty fireplace. There are so many things I don't want to do, and so many things I don't know how I will live with. I've come to Alyrra because I can't destroy the Circle by myself and call it justice. I cannot be another Red Hawk, creating my own law, or play at being Winterfrost, above all justice.

I know what lies behind the door in my mind, the things I have shoved there that I cannot bear to remember. I also know the kind of people who live in that darkness, without any moral or ethical bounds to guide them—they're Morrel and Garrin; they're Bardok and Efrun. Behind that door is where monsters lurk, and I will not let myself become one of them.

There is no court of law to rule against the Circle. There is no place to turn to for justice. But if the crown prince and princess—

our future king and queen—approve of my actions, it will be something. I will make it be enough.

"The Circle has put themselves above the reach of justice," I say quietly. "They flaunt the king's law, commit terrible crimes. If you could bring them to justice, would you?"

Kestrin glances down to the ward he holds, then to the ladle in Alyrra's hand. They look at each other a long moment, and then he dips his head. Alyrra says, "We would. But there is nothing we can do that would actually make change."

"What if I can?" I ask, a nervous sort of hope thrumming through me.

Kestrin considers me. "Then you would have my blessing, kelari. But I cannot imagine what you could possibly do."

I rub my left hand with my right, massaging my palm just below my empty knuckle. "I have an idea. It is not one I can share with you. If it works, the Circle's mages will fall. But, zayyid, there is no use in replacing one corrupt body with another."

"No," he agrees. "If you were to succeed, I can assure you that my father and I will work to put into place those mages we trust most—including those we believe truly care about our land."

I hesitate. "I met a mage, zayyid, while I was traveling downriver. He was kind and aided me not once but twice, though I had nothing to offer him."

"You think we should look into him?"

I shake my head. "I was thinking more of the fact that his talent presented late, and so he grew up with his family and community until he was twelve. His loyalty to the people and the crown, and the depth of his kindness are, I believe, due at least in part to that."

Kestrin nods. "I'm aware that the current method of removing Talents from their families assures their loyalty to the Circle and nothing else."

"My family—we hid Niya because we did not want her to grow into a mage who would disregard the needs of their people, as did the mages my parents asked for help. Zayyid, it is as dangerous to our land as it is cruel to the children and their families to take them away so young."

"A system of home study for the early years," Alyrra says, surprising me. "I don't see why not, Kestrin. If we are to replace the Circle, we must make sure the next generations are trained as something better."

"True." Kestrin weaves his fingers together and sits back. "Let us be clear, then, kelari. You will destroy the Circle through some unnamed method. In return, you wish us to look aside when you disappear with your sister."

I dip my head, suddenly nervous. "Or allow us a decent lead to escape, yes."

"You further wish us to promise to restructure not just the Circle but how Talents are recruited altogether."

That's dangerous wording. "I-I'm not asking for any promises."

Kestrin smiles faintly. "No?"

He is definitely testing me, but I don't know how to respond. I shake my head and keep my mouth shut.

"No," Alyrra agrees, eyeing him sharply. "What Rae needs is for us to use the time we have to assure she has won us more than a temporary victory."

Kestrin considers me a moment longer and then turns a tender smile on Alyrra, that harder side of him melting away. "I understand. What would you do, my love? I would give my blessing, but I'm a little afraid of your attendant."

Alyrra fairly glows with amusement and, perhaps, happiness. They really do suit each other. She says, "Rae has my blessing to do whatever she can to stop the snatchers. She has always known that." She turns to me. "Kestrin and I will work to assure that the new order of mages will be structured differently, and that they will join with us to destroy the slave trade. We'll do what we can to influence the training of Talents as well, though that may take time."

"I'll speak with my father," Kestrin agrees. "Mage Berrila ni Cairlin, the palace healer mage, may be my father's best choice to step in if you are successful. Can you give us no detail of what you intend?"

"No, zayyid. Only that if my sister's punishment is meted out and you still have had no word from me, then you can assume I have failed."

"Her hearing is tomorrow morning," Alyrra says, brow furrowed.

"I know." I bite my lip, thinking quickly over all I came to speak to them about. They have said nothing of Garrin as yet, though they listened carefully to my explanation of his role in my abduction, and how the asphodel that symbolizes his family is drawn into Berenworth's seal. I clear my throat and say now, "There is also the question of Verin Garrin."

Kestrin sighs. "We are aware."

I glance from him to Alyrra. If they don't see to Garrin, my debt to the sorceress will come due.

"Do you think he will be punished?" I ask. I'm overstepping my bounds, but I can't help myself.

Kestrin turns his gaze on me, regarding me coolly. "Kelari, have you considered the implications of how you were abducted?"

"I don't know what you mean."

"That a royal attendant should disappear after a private audience with the king is problematic enough. Your particular audience with my father was about my own secret talent. You walked out having agreed to provide a magical hold to my father, were stolen in a way that implicated him, and took my secret with you. My father was furious and—extremely worried."

Alyrra smiles faintly. "Melkior has been having a very bad day every day since."

"So he should," Kestrin says acidly. "This was all done on his watch. *Garrin* has been aiding Melkior in his investigation of your abduction. My father has involved himself as well, but he impressed upon Garrin the importance of seeking out the smallest details of your disappearance. Garrin swore to do all he could—in fact, he has been providing daily reports, which I can only assume were lies."

"You mean he . . ." I trail off, relatively certain I shouldn't say what I'm thinking out loud.

"Played traitor," Alyrra supplies, having no such compunction herself. "He arranged your disappearance and covered the trail, while swearing to do everything he could to find you. Now we learn that he has also been complicit with the snatchers for, what, decades?"

"It couldn't always have been him," Kestrin points out. "He's about my own age. This is thirty years or more of such work."

"His family, then," Alyrra says, coming to the same conclusion I did. "His father married into your family, did he not? He far outlived your aunt. It's quite likely Garrin was brought up to this."

Kestrin gives a pained nod. "It can be investigated now that we know whose records to seize. I just . . ." He closes his eyes, shakes his head. "We were raised together—at least as much as I was raised with anyone. I don't want this to be true." He looks up at me. "Not that I doubt you, kelari. Your story fills in gaps we could not explain. I just hate to believe my cousin would betray us, and our people, so deeply."

Alyrra reaches across the space between their chairs to set her hand on Kestrin's arm. "There's a little time to investigate it," she says. "We don't need to decide his fate today."

I would prefer if they did. Despite the binding, I need to tell them what I carry, because the only way out for me is if the royal family deals with Garrin themselves. "There is something else that happened to me," I say slowly.

"Involving Garrin?" Alyrra asks.

"Yes." I hesitate, trying to find a way to explain. "Verin Stonemane has a book I gave him—did he show it to you, by any chance?"

Alyrra nods. "The archer's journal. We've both read it." She pales, my meaning catching up with her. "Do you mean you've met the sorceress named at the end?"

I begin to nod in return and catch myself as the ember sparks to life. I raise a hand to my temple. They know Winterfrost—of course they do, given that she has a generational vendetta against the royal family. I'm only grateful that Stonemane shared the journal instead of keeping it to himself.

Kestrin frowns. "She intends to use you against him? That's . . . very unlike her."

"Perhaps she's changing," Alyrra says as they watch me. "She never let anyone go until you. Rae, are you all right?"

I nod, not trusting myself to speak. Hesitantly, I tap my finger against my temple and look toward Kestrin. He's studied magic, after all. Surely he will understand me?

He doesn't disappoint. "She's left behind a spell in you, hasn't she?" He leans forward, holding out his hand. "I would like to take a look, kelari. I swear you no harm."

I brace myself for the ember to flare and reach out to rest my right hand in his. He holds my hand lightly, his fingers surprisingly smooth and soft, quite unlike Bren's. Kestrin's magic feels like a whisper of smoke under my skin, curling and spreading. I shiver, and his hand tightens around mine. I know the exact moment his magic brushes against the ember—it brightens, flaring to life. I stiffen, holding myself tight as a fist.

Kestrin releases my hand with a jerk. I hunch back in my seat, my breath a little too fast, but the ember doesn't spread. It just smolders steadily, where it is, my head aching but not burning up from the inside.

"It's a compulsion of sorts," he tells Alyrra. "Layered beneath a binding. I could not study it without drawing her attention."

"So, we must keep Rae away from Garrin," Alyrra says readily.

I straighten, the ember already starting to die back down. "You must deal with him, zayyida. Zayyid. Please."

"It makes no sense," Kestrin says abruptly to Alyrra. "The way she works? She has pushed each of us to give ourselves up to her. But Garrin . . ." He stiffens, horror flitting through his gaze.

"Kestrin?" Alyrra asks softly.

"He wouldn't give himself up for anyone, would he?" He looks away, anguish written deep upon his features.

I focus on the carpet underfoot, careful not to raise my gaze. I have no idea what they're talking about, what Kestrin has just realized, but I do know that either they must deal with Garrin, or I must. There is no other choice.

Alyrra rests her hand on Kestrin's arm. "We can't know anything for certain except that the Lady has changed her approach." She turns to me, allowing Kestrin a moment to gather himself. "Rae, is this something you can explain? Why the Lady chose you in particular?"

My only option is to be oblique. "I have been investigating the snatchers," I say.

Kestrin nods, his anguish hidden once more. "Of course. The sorceress has been watching; she knows Garrin is involved."

Alyrra grimaces. "He certainly hasn't proven himself worthy of his station, or his life. Either we deal with him or"—she gestures toward me—"Rae will be forced to do so. Is that right?"

They both look at me.

I dip my head again, ignoring the pain from the bruises around my neck. At least the ember doesn't flare. "I am sorry, zayyid," I say carefully. After all, the last thing I want is to be labeled a traitor right now. Or a willing vessel for his enemies.

Kestrin rubs his mouth, and for a moment he is not a prince at all, just a young man not much older than me, faced with the burden of difficult decisions. Then he drops his hand, his expression settling into that particularly impenetrable look of his.

Alyrra says thoughtfully, "At least there is some choice: we may deal with Garrin directly, or leave him to the Lady."

I cast her a look ripe with horror. Leaving him to the sorceress means *I* will be forced to set the sorceress on him. She gives me a slight shake of her head.

"That is no choice," Kestrin says, to my relief. Alyrra must have known he would respond so. He continues, "My father would never leave any of his kin to the sorceress. But Garrin . . ." He shakes his head, returns his attention to me. "Kelari, I thank you for all you've done and shared with us. Is there anything further we need to discuss?"

"No, zayyid." I push myself to my feet and dip them a strained, wobbly curtsy. "I thank you both, truly, for this audience."

Alyrra takes my hand to help me out of my curtsy. "We are indebted to you, Rae. If you are successful against the Circle, we will owe you even more. I am only sorry that, after all you have been through, I can offer you so little right now."

"Well," I say brightly, walking with her to the door, "you put me in touch with Red Hawk. That has been a boon."

She laughs and steps back. "A good thief is worth a great deal. A friend is worth even more. I am grateful for your friendship, Rae."

"And I, yours, zayyida."

Matsin waits in the hallway to escort me back to the carriage. As I step out of the side gate and cross to the carriage where Bren waits, I find myself thinking of Alyrra's parting words.

Friendship is certainly worth more than a cunning ally. But Bren is both a cunning ally and a friend, for which I'm unutterably grateful. Perhaps that is what Mama meant to caution me about.

CHAPTER

38

B ren sits up as I enter the carriage, his eyes bleary and his hair mussed.

"Were you napping?" I ask, unaccountably amused. "I thought you were supposed to look out for me."

"Kelari Bakira was watching the villa," he says defensively. "I won't be much good without a little rest."

"Glad you're finally taking your own advice," I say with a grin and turn to Bakira. "Thank you for keeping watch, kelari."

"Of course, child. I thought you would be out in the next five minutes, else I would have woken the young master."

"How did it go?" Bren asks as the carriage starts forward.

I recount my interview with Alyrra and Kestrin in some detail.

"I could have told you they wouldn't actively help you," Bren says as I near the end.

"I already knew that."

"Did you get the blessing of our future king and queen to destroy the Circle, then?"

"Unequivocally."

"Rae, you *are* dangerous." Bren settles back against the bench, his mouth tilting into a wicked smile. "I'm going to bet you have an idea for taking down the Circle. Let's hear it."

"I might," I hedge. "It's . . . rather drastic."

"Everything you do is drastic, Rae."

"Unkind!" I protest. "I've done many things that aren't."

"Name three, since the time that I've known you."

I wrack my brain. "I've eaten biscuits, drunk tea, and—taken a bath!"

Bren chortles with laughter. "I love you, Rae."

I flush, startled. Even Bakira casts him a sharp glance. He can't mean it. He's teasing—of course he is—but he's not supposed to say such things! Worse, I'm not supposed to feel as if his words have stolen my breath.

He goes on, as if he hasn't said anything of import, "Allow me to point out that you've also stabbed two men, helped capture a slave galley, rescued a parcel or two of children, helped take down a thief lord—not to mention stolen a book from another thief lord—attacked a foreign prince—"

"He attacked first!"

"And jumped out a window not once but *three* times: the first, with your own blood on your hands and the second with someone else's blood on your hands."

That's not something I want to think about. "The third time was without anyone's blood on my hands," I say quickly. "So, you could say I'm improving."

He crosses his arms, watching me. "It's a good thing most country families stay where they start. I'm not sure the kingdom could handle too many more coming to town."

"You're just intimidated," I grouse. "I would have thought you had more courage than that."

Kelari Bakira gives a delicate cough into her fist and then goes back to her sewing, but there's a definite deepening of the smile lines around her mouth.

Bren shrugs, his eyes bright. "We can't all have your levels of courage, Rae."

I scoff. "It's not courage. I only do what has to be done."

"Yes," he agrees. "You do."

Mama, Bren, and I discuss our strategy for the next morning over an early dinner.

"You'll get no support from the princess or her husband if anything goes wrong," Mama cautions me once I've updated her on the outcome of my audience. "Are you sure about this? I understand what the Circle has done, but there's a difference between helping your sister escape and attempting to break the power of the Circle itself."

"I'll end up imprisoned or worse either way," I say, pushing my plate away. I've taken three bites of rice. I have no appetite for anything else. "What they're doing is unconscionable."

Mama pushes my plate back in front of me. "It is," she agrees. "I've always taught you to stand for your values. I just didn't expect" —she waves a hand—"this."

I make myself take a bite of chicken. I almost forget myself as the meat, spiced and grilled to tender perfection, nearly dissolves on my tongue. I look down at my plate with its chicken skewers served up with yellow rice and seasoned yogurt with new appreciation. Maybe I *can* eat.

"I know," I tell Mama. "But now that you know, do you think I should do this?"

Mama doesn't answer at once. When she does, her voice is soft and aching. "I deprived Niya of her right to be herself. I made her give up a part of who she is, hide it, instead of fighting for her.

Maybe it's too late now to fix what's past, maybe all I can do is support you, but if that's all that's left to me—I will do it with all my heart. Save your sister. Change this world so other mothers won't have to make the decisions I did. I will walk with you every step of the way."

Bren looks from Mama to me in awe, his next bite halted halfway to his lips. "Your whole family, Rae."

I steadfastly ignore him. "Then we need to plan. We have to get to Niya before her sentence is carried out, ideally before her hearing finishes. The only option I can see is if I walk in and demand an audience with Head Mage Hedhrawy. If I time it for right before the hearing, he'll likely leave me locked in his office or a temporary holding room and plan to come back and deal with me when it's over. I can act from there."

Hedhrawy is the same mage who sent the viper to sleep that was coiled around my ankles in the princess's suite, what feels like a lifetime ago. It's hard to reconcile that man, who seemed perfectly polite and caring, with a man who would condemn hundreds if not thousands of children to slavery each year. Except he isn't condemning anyone he ever met, so perhaps he just doesn't think about it very carefully. Or consider their humanity.

Mama frowns. "Wouldn't it be better if I went instead? I'll be able to demand a certain level of respect."

"No," I say sharply. "Bean needs you, Mama. You have to stay free for her. You're her mother as much as you are mine and Niya's. If anyone goes in there, it needs to be me."

Mama purses her lips unhappily, but I know she understands. She just doesn't want to agree.

"Then what?" Bren asks. "You'll be sentenced and punished, you realize. They won't let you go; at best you'll be imprisoned for life."

I'm rather getting used to such happenings. "I know," I say equably. "It's how slavers work. For them, power is about control over others' bodies. Whether the Circle realizes it or not, that's precisely how they operate. But just because I give myself up to them doesn't mean I can't stop them. I'll take a lockpick set with me and get out." I hesitate, glance at Bren. "Though I'd like someone else in there with me, in case things go wrong."

Bren regards me coolly. "If you think I'm going to let you walk in and present yourself for imprisonment without anyone to get you out again, you're sorely mistaken."

I flash him a grateful smile.

Mama looks between us, a line appearing between her brows. "You don't really need to speak to Hedhrawy, though, do you, Rae? Couldn't you both slip in through a servants' door or the like?"

"There are guards at all the entrances, including the servants' doors," Bren says. "Rae is right: the best way in is to sweep in the front doors demanding an audience." He turns to me. "I've had a discussion with my people. I'll help you with your sister, as I promised, but I would prefer not to put a target on my back. I do things sideways, Rae. Not up front."

I rub at my hair where my braid used to lie. "Yes, well, this won't be very sideways."

Bren leans back in his chair, but there's that glint in his eye that I recognize, the same gleam that comes out full force when he's wrapped up in something dangerous. "I thought not. What, then, are the drastic measures you're willing to take against them, Rae? If you can actually manage them once you've given yourself up and had your little chat with the head mage, and slipped out once more?"

He doesn't think I can. Perhaps he's right. I still have to try. Slowly, I push my plate away for the second time and lift my satchel from the floor. I slip out the ladle and lay it on the table before me. This is for Fastu, I remind myself. And every child like him.

"If the Circle is guilty, then the most just thing I can imagine is bringing them the same future they've assured every child who escaped and was taken by the Darkness." I meet Bren's gaze. "The Circle will drink something while they listen to the trial. I will just make sure it is very well stirred before it's served to them."

Mama closes her eyes. It's Bren who says, quietly, "You're a little bit terrifying, Rae."

I shrug, look back down to the ladle. "We don't know that it will be permanent. With the whole of the Circle fallen to the Darkness, perhaps those who replace them will finally be motivated to find a cure."

"Perhaps," Mama agrees. "Or perhaps you will rob these mages of their minds for the rest of their lives."

I shudder but make myself respond, "Better that than allowing them to continue to do the same to innocents."

"I agree, Rae. I just wish this didn't have to fall to you."

"It won't," Bren says, lifting the ladle from before me with quick, nimble fingers. "Rae will have enough on her hands dealing with Hedhrawy. It will fall to me."

I meet his gaze, my heart aching. I don't want him to protect me like this, not when it's my choice. "I can do it," I tell him.

"No," he says with infinite gentleness. "You will be the distraction that gets us in the door, and I will be the knife they won't see coming from the side. It's the only way this will work."

I want to argue, but I've always known that I draw attention easily. Bren will be able to slip in where I would only be noticed for my limp. "If you want a distraction," I say, my resolve hardening, "then I will give you one. Hedhrawy will never even notice you."

Bren's look is bright and bloodthirsty. "I'm depending on it."

CHAPTER

39

M ama and I eat a quiet breakfast together the following morning, the faint sound of voices carrying to us from somewhere below. Bren is no doubt receiving the intelligence he requested about the mages' complex—or perhaps he's navigating the political void left behind by Bardok's death. Regardless, he doesn't send for us.

Once we finish, I make my final preparations. I dress in the same clothes I wore yesterday to my audience with Alyrra, though I take the time to unpick the seam of the pocket first. I strap my bone knife to my thigh, tuck the lockpick set Bren has provided for me into the top of my boot, and make sure the ends of my story sash are hidden beneath my tunic.

My fingers linger a moment on the sewn wards, but I can't tell if they're any more frayed than before. I'll have to leave the painted ward behind today for our plan to work; otherwise it will protect the Circle as much as it will me. But my sash should still easily withstand one last brush with the Darkness.

Bren arrives at our door a few minutes later, dressed immaculately in a forest green tunic and cream pants, his sash cream with green accents. Over this ensemble, he wears a softer moss green wide-armed robe trimmed in gold. With his long hair tied back at the top with a silver clasp, the rest falling loose over his shoulders, and his boots polished to a shine, he looks every part the nobleman.

"Weren't you able to get the servants' clothing?" I ask uncertainly.

"Of course," he says, peeling back the hem of his sleeve to show a rougher brown fabric underneath. "On further thought, I decided it would be easier to enter the palace complex if I'm escorting my dear wife to visit her noblewoman friend."

"You are *not*." I exclaim at the same time that Mama says, "I thought you said you have a safe way in."

He hesitates, glancing from me to Mama. "I do, but I think it will be harder for Rae to navigate." He looks back at me, eyes gleaming. "I won't do anything untoward. We'll be very proper."

I gather my dignity about me, my cheeks burning. "Let me guess: your way in involves a number of windows."

"More climbing and crawling than windows, but yes. On the other hand, you're familiar with more than a few noblewomen in the palace, aren't you? Pick any one you like and say we're going to visit. If we've dressed the part, the guards should let us in easily enough. We'll walk to the mages' complex from the palace."

The guards don't tend to check on those entering unless something in particular attracts their attention. I raise a hand to my throat, my fingers brushing the bruises there. "They'll have questions."

Bren slips a small cosmetics pot from his pocket and offers it to me on the palm of his hand. "This should cover up what we don't want seen."

Mama plucks it from his hand and unscrews the top to reveal a soft brown liquid, almost a perfect match to my skin tone. "Clever," she allows. "Come, let's apply this."

I perch on the bed and Mama uses a corner of her kerchief to dab the liquid along the line of bruises and then blend it into my skin tone.

I've rarely worn makeup before. In the country, cosmetics are reserved for important gatherings and weddings. I suppose this means I've got a little more of the city in me now. The thought brings a wry smile to my mouth.

Mama sets aside the cosmetics just as Bren knocks at the open door again. In his hand, he carries a pair of—canes?

"You mentioned you've used a walking stick before," he says somewhat awkwardly. He leans the canes against the wall by the door. "If you'd like to use one of these, you're welcome."

I stare at the canes, trying to think. I'm aware of how Mama is watching me, how Bren leans against the doorframe, casual and yet not. He's nervous about his offering. I bite my lip. I don't use walking sticks in public; I never have. I've always done my best not to draw attention to my foot . . . but I'm changing, aren't I?

I force myself to get up and cross to them. They're both wood, the first with a darker handle carved in the shape of a bird, the other with a round knob at the top. I grasp the bird-handled cane and take a step with it, testing it. It fits my hand perfectly, my grasp feeling only slightly strange without my pinky to fill in the remaining space. It will make walking easier, and if there was ever a day I wanted to make sure my body had all the support it needed, this would be it.

"I'll use this one," I say, and give it a little toss, grasping it by the middle. I remember how Veria Havila would bear her cane like a weapon. "I can always beat Hedhrawy over the head with it, if necessary."

Mama laughs. "Let us hope you won't need to." She turns to Bren and says, "I am entrusting my daughter to you. I do not care what you must do, you will bring her back to me."

"Kelari," he says, bowing, at the same time that I say, "Mama!"

She smiles at me, the expression strained. "You'll understand when you have children. For now, just be careful and come home to me. I don't think I can bear to lose both you and Niya."

"You're not going to lose either of us," I say firmly.

It's a promise I hold close to myself as I follow Bren down to the carriage that will bear us to the palace.

Bren fills me in on all he's managed to learn about the mages' complex as the carriage rattles along toward the palace. In the space of a day, he's amassed an extensive description of its layout and the reinforced underground cells where magic-wielding prisoners are held. He makes me repeat everything back to him, from the location and access points for certain servants' corridors, to the order of the offices of each mage who has a seat on the Circle.

"You found out a lot," I observe.

"Not really," Bren says, and I can tell he means it. "We don't know the rhythms of the building. Without that, we don't know how or when things happen."

"How did you learn this much?"

"We identified three of ours who have friends or family who work there. I had another of my people interview them and report to me this morning. That way," he grins wryly, "I still got a few hours' sleep."

It hasn't escaped me how carefully Bren has kept me separate from his wider ring, although he made sure I was seen after the battle in the square. Since our return, I've really only interacted with him. Even Lirika has kept herself separate.

"Have you had any further news of Artemian?" I ask.

"He's improving, though there's no saving his eye." Bren shifts, looking out the window. "He should be back with us within a few days. I hope to see him settled and out of thieving once he returns."

"I'm glad. What about Lirika? What will you do with her?"

Bren sighs. "I doubt she will stay with us. I always offer my younger thieves a way out. She'll have her own choices to make."

"She blames herself—for Artemian, and for talking."

Bren runs a hand over his hair. "I'm aware. I doubt anything I say will make a difference. Some wounds can't be reached by words or bandages."

"I hope you'll still talk to her."

"I will, Rae. I always do, whenever one of my crew gets wrapped up in something more than they can manage."

I suppose it's his kindness that makes him such a different sort of thief lord. That he never forgets the humanity of his people, their needs and dreams.

I glance out the window, unhappy to see that we're already rolling through the wide plaza before the main palace gates. I reach up, my fingers brushing over the back of my head. There isn't a noblewoman in existence with short hair.

"Here," Bren says. He picks up a small package from beside his feet. "This is for getting past the guards."

I untie the cord and unwrap a lovely embroidered shawl wide enough to drape over my head. Such shawls are more common in the country but not unheard of in the palace, which makes it about perfect for me. Bren's gift is a pale blue with turquoise, indigo, and amethyst accents, a motif of flowers embroidered along the edges, with a scattering of smaller matching flowers across the central span of the fabric. "It's beautiful," I breathe. I look up at him, suddenly uncertain.

"Quickly, now," Bren says, the warmth of his tone at odds with his words. He nods toward the window.

Right. It's a disguise, nothing more. I shake it out and drape it over my head, throwing the long end over my shoulder. It will provide the perfect cover for my short hair—not necessarily disguising it so much as lending it, and me, an air of additional respectability.

"What surety do we have that the complex's guards won't just throw me in prison at once, even if these ones let us through?" I ask worriedly.

"There is no surety in anything we've planned."

"I thought you would have calculated all the risks," I say, trying to hide my nerves.

"I've found that with you, at a certain point, all calculations are moot."

My cheeks warm. "Is that supposed to be a compliment?"

He chuckles. "You can certainly take it as one." Then he shakes his head, sobering. "It's all one risk after another now, Rae. As for the guards, you played the part of a royal attendant for a little while, at least. Act like a noblewoman and they'll respond accordingly. Use their understanding of the world against them."

I think back to the attendants I served with, and Jasmine immediately comes to mind. Haughty, privileged, and utterly certain of her place in the world. She improved her manners in the end, once she decided Alyrra was worth her respect, but she'd shown her true colors before that. I can still remember her saying *our barnyard princess . . . has taken in a little lame mongrel.* But I'm no more a mongrel than she is.

"All right?" Bren says, watching me.

I straighten my spine. "All right."

The carriage comes to a stop, and a young guard steps up to the door. "Your business, please," he says, looking from Bren to me. He pauses momentarily, his eyes skimming over me.

"My husband and I are here to meet my good friend, Veria Dinari, and her husband for morning tea," I say, raising my chin haughtily, ignoring the twinge of the bruises ringing my neck. "Is there a problem?"

"Ah, no, of course not, veria," he says, clearly not taking any chances on affording me less respect than I might deserve. "Forgive me for delaying you."

He steps back and shuts the door. We continue on, turning right to follow the side road along the outside of the palace.

"Dinari? The lord high marshal's wife?" Bren asks with some amusement. "Really?"

"She never approved of me. It seems an appropriate way to repay her."

He snorts. "I've always wanted to meet her husband."

"Maybe I can arrange an introduction for you after all this."

Bren slides me a disbelieving look.

"You'll have done his job for him. The least Melkior can do is offer you proper thanks."

Bren laughs outright. "I should live to see the day!"

"You should," I agree.

The carriage pulls to a halt in a small, open-sided courtyard.

Bren strips off his robe as the driver dismounts to open the door. "We'll walk from here. Ready?"

No, but that doesn't really matter. I'm not leaving without Niya. "Of course," I lie, and follow him out of the carriage, cane in hand. He looks more like a wealthy merchant now than a noble-man. It's in the clothing, but also in how he carries himself.

We follow an arched gallery through to an open-air walk I know well. I resettle the shawl over my head and shoulders, looking around anxiously. It's the same path I used to take to the tax offices. The nobles will walk here, as well as the soldiers and servants I once knew—

"No one is going to recognize you. You've changed more than you realize," Bren murmurs, offering me his arm. "Walk with me."

I take his arm with a stiff smile. We leave the palace proper and follow the paths curving past the tax offices—I send up a silent prayer for Kirrana, may Garrin rot for what he did to her—and continue around to the mages' complex. The complex consists of a number of smaller outer buildings and a massive central building built in the rough shape of a circle, though the sides are many and angled, rather than single and smooth. A covered gallery extends along the sides, carved pillars rising to form exquisite arches, creating a gorgeous facade to the building. The main entrance is marked by a single wider arch, twice as large as the others.

"I'll stay with you until they separate us," Bren reminds me as we follow the path to the main entrance. Here, the path is paved with a soft brown tile, and I find it easier to carry my cane than use it. A band of green marble tile marks the beginning of the wide courtyard surrounding the complex. From there, we pass over a mosaic of colored marble, geometric patterns set against a background of white. For all I know, there are spells layered into the stones here. I'll just have to hope we don't get caught by them on our way out.

"You said you had the perfect excuse to be with me, and to leave me once we're within," I observe as we near the great arch. I slip my arm free of his and let my shawl drop to my shoulders.

He grins. "You're not going to like it."

I eye him narrowly. "You're *not* my husband again. They won't separate us if you say you are, and you need to stay back."

"I'm aware," he agrees affably. "You see, there are now multiple rewards out for your return."

"Multi—you!" I laugh and shake my head. "You're terrible."

"I don't see any reason why they should keep such money."

He has a point. I also used the same excuse for Nesa and Gair, so who am I to judge?

"Here we are," he murmurs, and we pass under the arches and across the gallery to the great wooden doors, carved and inlaid with bronze. A pair of guards wearing the emblem of the mages stand at the open doors. They are both tall and slim, with their hair cropped short and their expressions ungiving. They may as well be the same person, repeated. As we near, they step forward, partially blocking our path.

"I am here to see Head Mage Hedhrawy," I inform them coolly.

"You have an appointment?" one of them asks.

"My name is Kelari Amraeya ni Ansarim. You may ask him."

They exchange a look. "It may be better to return tomorrow, kelari," the first says. "Today is a busy day."

I raise my chin, channeling my inner Jasmine. "I think not. I have come about the hearing. You will allow us entry and carry my name to Mage Hedhrawy at once."

"He will be interested, I assure you," Bren says. "Perhaps you have not heard that Kelari Amraeya is Princess Alyrra's attendant? Or that she was abducted? Surely you will have at least heard that the young woman to be tried today is her sister?"

"Ah," the first says, as both men's eyebrows jump up to their hairlines. Perhaps they *are* the same person.

"I gave them my name," I say to Bren with a show of irritation. "It is not my concern if they fail to listen. I will see Hedhrawy regardless."

Bren dips his head. "Shall we go in, then?"

I step forward, passing between the guards, and they immediately scramble to stay with me.

"Kelari!" cries the first. "Of course we'll speak with Mage Hedhrawy on your behalf." He draws himself up in an attempt to recover his dignity. "If you will just follow me."

"If you would but lead the way."

He turns and strides forward at a pace I have no intention of matching. Bren offers me his arm once more, a mischievous smile on his lips. I grin back at him. Arm in arm, we stroll into the mages' complex.

CHAPTER

40

We await our audience seated on an ornate, cushioned bench to one side of a wide receiving hall, the floor tiled in colored marble, the walls banded with sections of fine floral mosaics separated by engraved white tile. Crystal chandeliers hang from the ceiling, dozens of luminae stones glowing gently even now, when the daylight is bright enough. It's a careless show of the sheer wealth of magic the Circle commands.

A fountain plays before us, the water rising up to dance in breathtaking arcs and shifting patterns. I consider the curtains Niya sewed for us, catching sunshine and summer breezes in her stitches, and know that what I'm looking at is nothing more than a magical parlor trick.

Bren reaches out and covers my hand with his own, his skin warm against mine. "You ready for this?" he asks softly.

"No," I admit, glancing down to our hands. "But that doesn't really matter."

"You'll do fine. You held off Morrel. You'll have no problem with this man."

It's entirely different. I had a history to call on with Morrel, one that fed his superstitions. I've got nothing against Hedhrawy except the truths I carry. If he's anything like Garrin, that won't faze him.

"It will be fine," I agree. I turn my hand to give his a squeeze, and then clasp my hands together primly on my lap. "You're not worried about your part?"

"No," he says comfortably.

A young mage with short-cropped hair and a round face hastens into the receiving hall, accompanied by the guard.

"Kelari Amraeya?" the mage asks, crossing to us, his robes flapping about his pant legs.

I incline my head. "I am here to meet Mage Hedhrawy."

"This way," he says.

"I'll wait here, honored mage," Bren says as I rise and brush out my skirts. "Perhaps you'll speak with me once you've taken Kelari Amraeya in."

"Head Mage Hedhrawy has invited you both in," the mage says firmly.

"I have no need to accompany Kelari Amraeya any further," Bren returns, as if he has no relation to me at all. "I will wait here for a word with you when you are able to return."

His brow furrows. "As you wish."

I follow him through the wide arched opening and then almost immediately through a door on the left. We enter a polished hallway which connects, as Bren told me, to a second long hallway at the end of which lies Mage Hedhrawy's office.

We step through the door into an ornate sitting room that reminds me of the evening rooms in the palace where the noble ladies often gathered: low brocade sofas in cobalt and gold, the ubiquitous octagonal tables with polished silver trays set upon them, ready to receive cups of tea and plates of refreshment. A thick, multi-hued carpet spreads across the floor, adding a splash of red to the blue and gold decor.

"Kelari," my guide says impatiently. I follow him across the carpet to a large office, the walls lined with shelves and a massive desk facing the door. A window looks out through the arched gallery toward the tree-lined path.

Hedhrawy sits behind the desk, perusing a paper which he sets down as we appear in the doorway. I remember him well from the incident with the snake. Then, his presence had signaled relief, that the viper nestled around my ankles would be safely removed. Now, looking at the tall, broad-shouldered man seated before me, his belly pressing lightly against the front of his tunic, I feel nothing but a crawling sort of nausea.

"Kelari Amraeya," my guide announces.

"Indeed," Hedhrawy says, staring at me—for a heartbeat, I see a simmering anger reflected back in his gaze, and then it is wiped away. He offers me a bland smile. "I recall you well, kelari. Please, be seated."

As I move to one of the brocade-cushioned chairs before the desk, my guide bows and departs, closing the door firmly behind him.

"To what do I owe this pleasure?" Hedhrawy asks.

I raise my chin and meet his gaze. It is time to start playing for the space Bren will need to get situated—and for my sister's freedom, more because that is what Hedhrawy expects than because I have any real hope of him granting it. "You will perhaps have heard that I was abducted some time ago."

"I had, yes. I had not realized you were returned to us."

Oh, but he must have, if Niya's already been questioned. He just didn't expect me to show up here. I settle back into my chair and say, "I am sure you've heard that my sister, Niyagara ni Ansarim, rode out to help rescue me only yesterday? I was being held by some disreputable criminals here in the city—Bardok Three-Fingers and his ilk. My sister was instrumental in his capture. She has since been charged with harboring a secret magical talent."

"So I am aware. She stands trial this morning." He regards me as a cat might a mouse. "I suppose you have come to plead for her release. Surely you're aware that harboring a magical talent in secret is a crime of the highest order?"

"Hers is only a small talent, as I'm sure you'll find."

"It is not at all."

I smile benignly. "I think you'll find you're mistaken."

Hedhrawy leans back in his chair, studying me coldly. "Why is that?"

"Such a crime hardly compares to other, greater crimes under your purview. One must keep perspective."

"I know of no other such crimes."

I furrow my brow as if perplexed. "But, honored mage, if you are not aware, then the rest of the Circle must surely be allied against you."

"Are you trying to play games with me, girl?"

"No," I assure him earnestly. "It is only—well, perhaps it is *they* who are not aware. Of the ladles."

"The what?" he asks, bewildered.

"The *ladles*, honored mage. The ones every slaver in this kingdom has access to? They are embedded with tiny amulets that your apprentices make in unceasing quantities, and are spelled to leave a marker in the blood. Though surely, if so many ladles are being made, the Circle cannot be unaware."

He eyes me with patent disbelief. If it weren't for the slight hardening of his jaw, I would believe he has no idea what I'm talking about. "I have never heard such nonsense before in my life."

"Then they weren't aware? I suppose it would have to be kept secret from at least a few of the Circle. They cannot all aspire to be slavers."

"You appear to have lost hold of your faculties," Hedhrawy says pityingly. "Your sister's arrest on the heels of your own experiences must have been a little too much for you."

Questioning my sanity is not going to save him. "I am in full possession of my senses. So much so, that I have written missives to each of the mages on the Circle, detailing what I've learned of the ladles. They will be delivered if you keep me here."

He stiffens at my lie, then catches himself. "Child, you have no idea of what you speak. What ladles? Can you produce them? How do you know they were made by the Circle?"

I swallow hard—not because of his questions, but because of what his initial reaction tells me. The whole Circle doesn't know. Of course not. What political body is always only of one mind?

I gather myself and answer coolly, "I have in my keeping one such ladle. It will be sent to your greatest opponent on the Circle. Further, an explanation will be delivered to each of the printing shops of the city. The Circle will not suffer—there is too much power here for that—but you will surely take the fall to appease the anger of the people. You are, after all, sworn to protect them, not profit off their pain."

Hedhrawy leans back in his chair, studying me. He's dropped his pretenses, which means he's very sure of himself. I am going to be in serious trouble if this doesn't go to plan. "That young fool Garrin was supposed to have dealt with you."

"I am not that easily gotten rid of," I agree, my palms clammy. Of *course* he and Garrin are in each other's pockets. "If I leave of my own accord, I assure you I will not return."

He turns in his seat to gather paper and ink. "I am not so easily fooled, girl."

I take a steadying breath, well aware that this is the outcome I expected. "Are you not concerned about the information I have?"

"Not at all," he says easily. "You forget that we are very capable of conducting our own interrogations here. I will have the names of all your allies from you by afternoon, and by evening they will have joined you here. Your plans will fail before they've begun."

A shudder runs through me. I ask quietly, "How do you do it? How do you trade the lives of our children for *stones*?"

Hedhrawy flicks me an irritated glance. "I have no compunction in exchanging the rubbish of our society for a steady supply of what we most need to maintain our supremacy. Now, be quiet."

The rubbish of our society? I will *destroy* him for that. I clench my jaw and watch as Hedhrawy pens his missive. I can't argue with his taking up more time, bringing us ever closer to the hearing.

As he signs it with a flourish, I ask, "What do you intend to do with me?"

Hedhrawy sets his paper aside to dry. "I will dispose of you as necessary."

"How?" I ask, panic edging my voice. I just need a little time, half a chance to escape him so I can rejoin Bren.

He smiles faintly. "Afraid, finally?"

"You can't intend to kill me. Someone would notice a body being moved through the grounds," I say, gesturing to the tree-lined path visible from the window.

He tsks softly. "Such a fool you are. I can't imagine how Garrin failed to deal with you, though I intend to get an explanation." He lifts the letter, now dry, and folds it with exact precision. It must be to Garrin. As he slides it into the envelope, he says with some disgust, "I do not deal in bodies, kelari. It is your mind I have no use for. You ought to know exactly what fate to expect—but only after I have questioned you thoroughly."

A knock sounds at the door as Hedhrawy finishes addressing the envelope. "Enter," he calls.

The mage who acted as my guide opens the door and bows to Hedhrawy. "I've dealt with the young woman's companion, master."

I stiffen. "What did you do?"

The mage smirks. "He didn't care for you at all, kelari. Did you think he did? He only wanted the reward for bringing in one of your family. I paid him off, and he's departed."

I drop my gaze, trying not to let my relief show.

"Well done," Hedhrawy says, handing the envelope to his lackey. "See that this is sent to the palace as addressed at once."

The mage takes it with a bow. "The trial is almost ready to begin, master. The prisoner has been escorted to the council chambers."

Hedhrawy nods, his gaze settling on me. "Excellent. How would you like to see your sister sentenced and punished, kelari? Perhaps we can come up with a sentence for you for harboring her. Before the Darkness touches you, that is."

My stomach tightens with dread. I need to get away from Hedhrawy, not place myself before the whole of the Circle. He's supposed to leave me locked in his office, or a holding room, so I can use the lockpick set I brought with me and find Bren. Although, if Bren truly wants a distraction, perhaps the hearing is precisely where I need to be.

Hedhrawy pushes himself to his feet, smiling. "You will come. You're the slippery type, and I am not about to let you out of my grasp. Not until we've seen to your future."

He walks around his desk to take me by my arm, forcing me to my feet. "Don't think that if you walk into our hearing room crying about snatchers, you'll be heard. You'll be mocked as a madwoman, and sealed up in a cell for the rest of your short life. Dealing with your type is just a necessary evil."

I meet his gaze with the full force of my pent-up rage. "I understand all about necessary evils."

He regards me coldly. "If you cannot hold your tongue, I will provide a spell to help you do so. Do you have a preference?"

"I will keep quiet," I grit out.

"Excellent. I knew you could be made to see reason. Come along."

He drags me through the door, his stride brisk. I half jog to keep up with him, my cane clenched in my hand, my turned foot making me bob up and down at his side. It's enough to make his mouth flatten into a displeased line. By the time we've reached the end of the hall he's slowed his pace somewhat to allow me to walk more normally. After all, he has his dignity to consider.

I drop my chin so he doesn't see the contempt on my face.

CHAPTER

41

Located at the very heart of the building, the council chambers mirror the shape of the larger structure: angled interior walls creating a symmetrical central room with a domed roof from which hangs a truly grandiose chandelier. The opulence in the entry hall was one thing; the sheer weight of cut crystal and shining luminae stones here is another.

I lower my eyes in disgust to observe the dais on the far side of the chamber. A single line of curved wood creates a semicircle of connecting desks, behind which the members of the Circle will sit. A half-dozen mages mill about behind the desks, chatting with each other.

The rest of the room is filled with carved wooden benches facing the dais, except for a small, boxed enclosure directly before it. The walls of the box are carved with sigils or runes, I've no idea which. At its center, seated on a small wooden chair, is Niya. She wears the same clothes she was arrested in, now smudged and wrinkled. Her face is washed, though, and they must have allowed her a comb, for her hair is neatly braided back.

I am marched along the side of the room and up to the first of the benches. They are all elegantly furnished with maroon brocade cushions. As I reach the front, Niya glances toward me and then stiffens, her eyes widening in horror. I offer her my brightest smile. Either this will work and we'll both walk free, or not. I'll be with Niya regardless.

Hedhrawy shoves me down onto the bench, then bends to murmur, "If you move, I will bind you in place. I suggest you stay."

He continues on to the dais, pausing to chat with one of the other mages of the Circle on his way to his place at the very center.

I slide a look toward Niya. From this angle, I have a better view of her face. Her normally luminous eyes are a steely gray today, her expression pinched. She sits stiffly. I imagine her hands are tightly clasped in her lap. Are they bound? I cannot tell from here, though I can see that she wears a short chain of some bright metal, a small red gem hanging from it just below the hollow of her throat.

My stomach tightens. I know without asking that it's the sort of amulet that drains the magic from its bearer. It is precisely what Niya will be made to wear for the rest of her life, one amulet traded out for another, allowing other mages to access the magic that has been stolen from her. It seems the ultimate insult that the chain looks so pretty against Niya's neck, the amulet like a prized jewel on display.

"Let us begin," Hedhrawy says as the final mage enters. The mages by the doors swing them shut, remaining outside as guards. Only the nine mages of the Circle, a scribe in the corner, and Niya and myself remain.

Hedhrawy clears his throat and intones, "We are gathered to rule on the case of Kelari Niyagara ni Ansarim, who has hidden her talent from our purview in clear violation of our laws."

The mages eye Niya speculatively.

"Yesterday, a criminal use of magic was detected, the spell dissolved by the protections that cradle this land, cast by the upstanding mages of our kingdom. That illicit working was cast by the young woman before us."

None of them look surprised, though a few shake their heads in disgust or disappointment.

"It was through this incident that Kelari Niyagara was discovered and taken into custody. She has refused to describe the spell she cast and, unfortunately, no residue of the spell remains to be studied. It is known, however, that only the vilest of spells would activate the protections." Hedhrawy pauses heavily, then goes on, "This morning, the girl's talent was assessed by two of our own." Hedhrawy nods toward a pair of mages seated at one end of the tables, naming them. "If you will share what you found."

The mages discuss in detail their attempts to assess Niya, who had not cooperated at all, "forcing" them to eventually push her into defending herself from a series of offensive attacks. She did well in her defense, suggesting that she has significant talent—which was hardly in question, considering she brought the protections down on her. As one of them points out, the strength of her talent will greatly benefit whoever takes her into their household as amulet bearer.

Never mind that Niya's refusal to speak is her way of protecting that fool Cormorant. As irritated as I may be with the Fae mage who gave her the spell that triggered the protections, my real anger is reserved for the *upstanding mages* before me. My hands curl into fists, my left faintly tender again after all I've put it through. The pain grounds me, keeping me from jumping to my feet and snarling out my rage at these cold-blooded, self-serving, misbegotten swine.

That isn't how this fight will be won. I scan the tabletops before the mages, but there is no sign of any water here, no indication that a servant is expected. If they don't take any refreshments, Bren won't be able to do his part.

I listen woodenly as the mages dissect the assessment of my sister's skills and abilities. The fact that she was able to defend herself at all—released from the amulet that bound her but held, it seems, in a warded room—raises even more interest in those who might qualify to claim her as a slave.

I curl my hands around the edge of the bench, clenching my teeth. Eventually, the mages move on, demanding from Niya an explanation of why she hid her talent.

"It is simple," she says coolly. "When my parents sought the help of a healer mage for my eldest sister's foot, they were turned away. They were too common, you see, and it did not matter that they could pay for any services rendered. My parents had no wish for me to grow into such a heartless boor. So, I remained with them and am what you see now."

"How *dare* you speak so of us?" one of the mages spits.

"Do you consider yourself the equal of that mage?" Niya returns, a sharp smile curving her lips. "I am not surprised. I have certainly not been treated with even a modicum of kindness since I was taken into custody."

Pride lifts my chin as I watch my sister. Niya is almost never rude. I forgot how well she uses words when she loses all respect for those before her. Let her put these mages in their place.

"Be silent," Hedhrawy snaps.

She smiles prettily. "As you wish."

His nostrils flare, and then he smiles, turning to me. "We also have present the sister mentioned by this rogue mage. Kelari Amraeya ni Ansarim, of the twisted foot. Tell us, kelari, did you know of your sister's talent?"

Rage twists inside me at his words, as if all I am is my foot. It is because of a mage like him that my foot was never straightened.

The thought brings me up short: I am who I am because of my foot, and so also because of that mage. I cannot conceive of who I would be without my turned foot, without having grown up as I have. I'm glad of it—glad that I am here, now, facing down these mages, with the body I have grown with and learned to love exactly how it is.

I settle back into my seat, crossing my arms. "It's called a club-foot, though I wouldn't expect you to know such a thing. You don't have any talent for pattern magic, do you?"

Hedhrawy's aspect darkens with fury. "I suggest you answer the question before we lose our patience with you."

I regard him with amusement. "Of course I know of my sister's talent. She has never refused me her kindness."

Glaring balefully at me, he asks, "Do you know the price of hiding a Talent from the Circle?"

"My sister has every right to her own freedom. There is no price to pay that is too high for that."

"Another fool, it seems," one of the mages says.

I catch a faint movement at the other end of the dais. Bren wheels a trolley onto the dais from a hidden door, pausing to shut it behind himself. He is dressed in the quiet brown uniform of the complex's servants, his hair tied back in a tight tail. Relief floods through me as he looks out and spots me, brow furrowing before he catches himself.

"*Kelari*," Hedhrawy snaps.

I startle, dragging my attention back to the Circle, my heart in my throat. Bren is here, and I almost gave him away. "What?" I say roughly.

"You will answer the question."

I am going to be the most obnoxious distraction the Circle has ever seen. Whatever it takes to make sure Bren goes unnoticed. "You'll have to repeat yourself. I'm afraid I wasn't paying attention."

The whole of the Circle glowers at me, utterly inattentive to the servant behind them.

"When did your sister's talent manifest?" Hedhrawy repeats.

"An excellent question. Have you asked her?"

"This is a waste of time," one of the mages mutters, a short man with a balding pate and a stringy beard. "They are both impossible."

"You have given us no incentive to comply with your wishes," I observe.

"Incentive!" Stringy Beard echoes, infuriated.

I slide a quick glance to Bren as he stands beside his trolley, arranging the cups, his eyes flicking to me. He lifts the ladle and then pauses, as if awaiting a signal from me.

Among the mages before me are one or two who have not been fully taken into Hedhrawy's confidence. I have no way to separate the wheat from the chaff, the innocent from the guilty. Still, there are so many wards made by their students, so many ladles from so many saved practice amulets, so much wealth flowing into the Circle. They must either know or willingly keep themselves ignorant, aware that they do not want to find out the details. Either way, they are complicit.

If I have to weigh the possibility of unjustly condemning one or two people to the Darkness, versus allowing the ongoing abduction and enslavement of generations of children, as well as the use of the Darkness against them . . . there is only one direction the scale can tip. I will do this for my friend Ani's sister, Seri, stolen from the streets of Sheltershorn, and Fastu, and every other child snatched from their home. And for Kirrana, abducted for her work in helping me research the snatchers. I have the royals' blessing, and my sister and all my people to save.

Meeting Bren's gaze, I dip my chin, judge to his executioner.

"There seems to be no question as to the rogue's guilt, or her sister's complicity," Stringy Beard says. Behind him, Bren lowers the ladle into the pitcher, stirring.

"Let us finish this and be done. I should like to get back to my workshop," a woman wearing a chain with a great golden pendant says in agreement.

No. I need to keep them here long enough for them to drink, and for the Darkness to come. Once Niya is taken from this room, it will be much harder to steal her away. Perhaps obnoxious was a bad choice—I need to offer an incentive instead, as I suggested to Stringy Beard.

"Surely you wish to—" I pretend to blurt and then cut myself off.

"Wish to what?" Stringy Beard demands, paying no attention as Bren sets a cup of water down before him. As Bren reappears beside the next mage with another cup of water, he meets my gaze, his expression steady, neutral. As if he were doing nothing at all. Then, as he turns away, he winks.

"Well?" Stringy Beard demands.

"I mean, surely you can tell she is not wholly untrained," I say, flagrantly lying. "Do you not care that some of your own might be keeping secrets as well?"

Niya spares me a glance ripe with disbelief. As if we knew any mages we wanted to drag through the fire. Well, there was that one who crossed our paths the winter before last, with whom I *certainly* have a bone to pick, but . . . I shake my head to rattle the thought loose.

Hedhrawy raises his brows. I watch in sickened fascination as he takes a sip of water from the cup before him. He sets it down with a click and says with unmistakable contempt, "Do you expect us to believe you would willingly turn over the names of trained mages who have spurned their oaths and given your sister, what? A set of tips? There are no such people. Your list is, no doubt, a set of loyal mages upon whom you most wish to cast doubt. We are not so easily tricked."

"No," I agree as the final mage turns to accept his cup directly from Bren's hand, drains it, and hands it back to be refilled. "Of course not. No doubt you have found out everything you wish to know. So, for example, you know that my sister has learned to merge her magic with her sewing."

The woman mage with the golden pendant sneers. "Sewing? That is one of the least arts."

"Truly? I thought it quite impressive when she hid a man in her stitches, at his request, and let him out hours later none the worse for wear. Can you all do that?"

Bren has taken up a station at the rear of the dais, standing sentry beside his trolley. I lick dry lips, glancing over the water cups before each of the mages. I can't tell if each mage has taken a drink yet or not. Nor do I know how much longer it will be before the protections are cast. Surely it will be soon?

Ehelar said he casts the protections every twenty hours or so. I've triple checked my calculations, but if the variation is more than I planned for... the Darkness may have already been cast today. Or it may not fall for another hour. There's no way to know, nothing to do but hope and try to prolong this trial as long as possible in the hopes that it will yet fall.

"Hid a *man?*" Stringy Beard demands. "In your *stitches?*" He stares at Niya aghast.

"I like sewing," she says simply.

"A very effective way to transport someone who doesn't wish to be seen," I say, my hands tingling with fear. "I don't suppose that would be a useful skill for you all, though."

Hedhrawy studies me. Perhaps he can't believe I'm suggesting a more effective way to transport slaves. I can't either. My only hope is that no one will remember this conversation in an hour's time.

"Perhaps you would like a demonstration?" I suggest.

Hedhrawy snorts. "Ah, that's your game. You think we'll allow your sister to practice magic unbound before us? That she'll manage to escape us then?"

I roll my eyes so hard Bean would have been proud of me. "Don't be absurd. One untrained girl is going to escape the full Circle of Mages? Even I wouldn't think that. I just thought you might be interested in what she has learned, and how it might differ from what you would normally do. Even if you make her an amulet bearer, she may have some knowledge and skills that could be useful to you."

"You are telling us this because you have suddenly found a well-spring of love for us where before you were nothing more than a rude peasant?"

"No," I agree. "I have only the greatest disgust for you. But I *do* have a deep and abiding love for my sister. Perhaps, if you decide she has something of value to you, you'll be kinder to her."

"Save your breath, Rae," Niya says, her voice cutting across the room. "I would not show these people anything they don't already know. I can only imagine they would use such skills for themselves, rather than for those in need. It is all we have ever seen of mages, and these particular mages set the example for our realm. They will certainly be the most unkind and selfish of the lot."

I stare at my sister in dismay. Perhaps she thinks she has nothing left to lose, that she may as well be clear what she thinks of the Circle. Unfortunately, her words cut short the conversation I was working to prolong.

Hedhrawy slaps his hand against the tabletop. "That is enough. Let us move forward with the sentencing. Any further questions can be answered once the agreed-upon sentence has been carried out."

The mages nod their agreement. I glance helplessly toward Bren, as if there were some way to slow them down. He gives a curt shake of his head, the movement so slight I see it only because I'm looking. He's right; we need to wait for the Darkness without raising suspicions. But if it comes too late, Niya will be lost.

"For the crimes already listed," Hedhrawy says, flicking a finger at the paper before him, "namely, ungoverned use of magic, criminal castings, and a refusal to swear loyalty to the Circle, the standard punishment is lifetime bondage as an amulet-bearer. Let the votes be cast as to the guilt of Kelari Niyagara ni Ansarim."

I bite my lip, listening in growing desperation as the scribe in the corner calls out each mage's name and takes note of their vote.

"Guilty," intones the woman with the gold pendant.

"Guilty," says Stringy Beard, plainly bored.

I knew none of them would take Niya's side, and yet each mage's response rings in my ears like a death knell.

"Mage Hedhrawy," the scribe calls finally. As head mage, he is the last of the mages to cast his vote. He smiles coolly, opens his mouth, and *barks*—a strange, coughing cry that seems torn out of him. It is a horrifying sound, and I am unutterably relieved to hear it.

Across the dais, the mages jerk, one falling out of their seat, then another. Niya springs to her feet, aghast, as the mages succumb to their seizures. All except one.

The woman mage with the golden pendant jumps up. "What is happening?" she cries as the man beside her collapses facedown over the desk, writhing and convulsing.

"Lady Mage!" Bren says sharply.

The woman pivots, her mouth open in horror, and Bren grabs her cup and shoves it to her mouth. She stumbles backward, choking on the water. Bren darts away, throwing himself over the table as she waves her hand, but the protections built into the room take the magic she throws at him and sends it rebounding back at her. It slams her across the dais, into the wall. For a moment, she remains pinned there, her eyes wide and her mouth working. Then she lets out a small, keening wail that trails into nothing, her body seizing as she crumples to the ground.

The only sound now is the sickening gasp and grunt of the mages as the Darkness takes them.

"Rae!" Niya cries. "What's going on?"

Her voice brings me back to myself. I leap to my feet, hurrying toward her. Across the room, the scribe is backing away from the dais, ashen-faced and shaking. Bren already has his sights on the man; I focus on Niya instead. I don't want to see what Bren does, the silver of a blade flashing in his hands as he closes in.

I am almost to Niya's box when I feel it—a flicker of fire at my waist, accompanied by a weight on my limbs, a twinge of pain at the back of my skull.

"Rae!" Niya cries again.

She's so close. I stumble on, one hand clutching at my story sash through the fabric of my tunic. It's hot to my touch, the scent of burned fabric rising, and there's pain—pain in my skull, drilling through my mind.

I thump blindly against the wood of the box that holds her. There must be a latch somewhere—why didn't I look before? My vision is failing, a gray-white haze I can't see through. I fumble at the wood, finding the gap where the door is. She can't reach over it, of course. Damned protections these mages set.

"Rae, it's down a little. What's *happening*?"

"Darkness," I mumble. My hand catches on something. I jerk at it, fingers grasping. Niya shoves at the door, or I assume she does, because suddenly she's through, grabbing me by the arms.

"Rae!"

"Sash," I tell her, my tongue clumsy and my limbs jumping and shaking, no longer in my control. I cannot think through the haze of pain. "Shash . . ."

"Bren!" I hear Niya calling. "Get this off of me!"

And then, farther away, "Hold on, Rae!"

But there is nothing to hold on to in the grayness that enfolds me.

CHAPTER

42

I surface by degrees, aware first of my body, aching but unharmed. Then there's the throbbing pain at the back of my
skull. And then there's the feeling of being cradled in someone's
arms.

I blink open my eyes. Niya crouches before me, her hands
curled around one of mine.

I turn my head slowly to find Bren holding me, his arm supporting my back.

"Oh, thank *God*," he murmurs, resting his head against my
shoulder. His arms tighten around me. I lean into him, vaguely
aware that I'm on the ground in a dim hallway, Bren beside me, legs
splayed as he supports me, his knee against my back. It's all a little
awkward, and yet I don't want to move.

"Rae," Niya whispers. "Are you hurt?"

"Headache," I tell her. Bren shifts back and I force myself to sit
up, take a little more of my weight. "I'm all right. How did we—?"

I look toward Niya helplessly.

"You let me out of the prisoner's stand. Bren got the amulet off me, and I cast my own wards to protect you. Then Bren carried you here."

I rub my face, trying to think past the pounding in my head. That must have been difficult on Niya, with the amulet having stolen all her reserves.

"If you're all right, I need to do something," Bren says, easing away from me. I nod, and he disappears down the dark corridor we're huddled in. I try not to miss the warmth of his arms around me.

"Where is 'here'?" I ask Niya.

"Servants' hallway, behind the council chambers," Niya says. "Rae, you—you planned that, didn't you?"

"You didn't think I was going to let the Circle have you, did you?"

Niya hesitates. "What happened in there?"

She doesn't know. In quick, broad strokes I tell her how the Circle has profited from and aided the snatchers for the last thirty years, as well as how Kestrin and Alyrra gave me their blessing— even if they didn't know what I'd planned.

Bren arrives just as I finish. "Found these," he says, holding out the blue shawl he gave me earlier, as well as my cane.

"Perfect." I pass the shawl to Niya. "Wear this. It should help disguise you at least a little."

Bren offers me his hand. "Can you stand, Rae? I can carry you."

"I can walk," I grumble, taking his hand. "I'm not some fainting city girl, you know."

I pull myself to my feet with his help. Bren catches my elbow with his other hand, steadying me as I waver. I set the tip of my cane down and adjust my balance. Bless Bren for getting it for me.

"No," he agrees lightly. "You're the sort of country girl who chews up mages for breakfast."

My cheeks heat. "Don't we need to hurry?"

Niya eyes us oddly, the shawl now wrapped around her shoulders and draped over her head. "Do either of you know where to go from here? We're going to be caught if we don't move."

"I've a sense of these halls," Bren assures her. "We're headed to a back door; we need to get there before it's closed. There's a carriage waiting for us near the palace."

We walk in silence, moving as quickly as I can shuffle down our chosen hallways, the only sound the quiet tap of my cane. Within three turns, we exit the servants' passages into a wider hallway. The faint sound of a shout echoes from deeper within the building, followed momentarily by a great deal more shouting.

"Secret's out," Bren says mildly.

"What happened to the scribe?" I ask, not sure if I have the energy to care. Would the scribe have known what the Circle was doing with the snatchers? He certainly witnessed other injustices.

"I tied him up before, so I went back and gave him the Blessing," Bren says, shocking me. "Had the cup delivered here this morning in case I needed it. He won't remember what he saw."

Nor does he have to die. "That's good. You took the pages from his ledger?"

"They're in my pocket. You really do make an excellent thief, Rae." Bren pauses, then whispers harshly, "Get to the side!"

We plaster ourselves to the wall beside a doorway, listening as boots pound past.

"Don't suppose you can cast any spells right now?" Bren murmurs, glancing at Niya.

"I doubt it," she says. This close, I can see the exhaustion dragging at her features. "I used everything I had to protect Rae."

"That's fine," Bren says. He guides us through the now-quiet doorway and from there into another servants' passage. The alarm has been well raised and appears to have attracted the attention of the servants who would normally be here.

I've gotten my balance and most of my strength back by the time we slip through the empty room that serves as a preparation station for food sent from the palace kitchens. My head still pounds with the headache left behind by the Darkness—a small price, considering how close I came to losing myself.

"Door's open," Bren says with satisfaction.

No doubt the guards and junior mages are trying to revive the Circle. When they do think of blocking exits, they'll focus on the doors they use most. Which allows us to slip out of this one with hardly a worry.

Outside, it's a stunningly beautiful day, the open spaces drenched in sunshine. Birdsong drifts to us from the trees, and more than a few servants and administrative workers linger together on the paths. It seems worlds away from where we've just been.

Niya and I fall into step together, Bren moving ahead. With his servants' clothing, he would stand out immediately if he were seen walking with us.

I walk as quickly as I can, grateful for my cane. Niya gives me her arm as an added support. We follow the path as it curves past the tax buildings, and I think again of Kirrana, gone now. Abducted and never recovered. Would she be glad of what I've wrought? Is she even alive?

I drop my gaze to the path, blink away a heartache I can do nothing about.

Niya says, thoughtfully, "I know I gave you that story sash as an early present before you left, but happy birthday anyway."

I stumble, my cane sliding over a paver. "What?"

"Happy birthday," she repeats, grinning crookedly. "But in the future, can we lean toward quieter celebrations?"

I hadn't even realized the date, but taking down the Circle of Mages is not the sort of celebration I want to host again anytime soon. I give a choked laugh. Niya giggles in return, and something about the sound of it, light and innocent and ever so perfect, sets me off. A moment later Niya dissolves into mirth as well.

Bren glances back at us in amused disbelief.

"Niya," I gasp, holding tight to her arm. "This birthday—"

"Yes?" She wipes at her eyes.

"Never again, all right?"

"That's what you say now, but if Bean needs saving, I know exactly what will happen," she says, gesturing vaguely behind her, and I lose what composure I'd gained.

Behind us, a bell tolls, loud and rolling. I swallow hard, my laughter falling away. The people around us pause and turn toward it. Bren does as well, so Niya and I do too.

"What's that mean?" he calls to a young woman sitting on a bench. "I'm new, and no one's mentioned a bell."

"It's trouble, I think," she says, rising from her seat. "Best get inside and wait it out."

"Bren," a voice says from farther down the path. Captain Matsin slows to a stop some twenty paces on. He looks past Bren to us. "And Kelari—ah."

I tighten my hold on Niya and limp forward, gripping my cane. If I have to bash him over the head, I will. "Captain Matsin, how lovely to see you."

Bren moves ahead, reaching Matsin a few paces before me. He says, quietly, "We have your prince's blessing. Walk with us."

I twist to wave cheerily at the woman who warned us. She nods and moves on just as Matsin offers Niya his arm and says, "You've a story I want to hear."

"*You* will walk on my other side," I say archly. "Now."

Niya just looks at him, making no effort to take his arm.

"Come along," I say and stump forward when he doesn't move. He catches up to me a moment later, the cane providing a comfortable distance between us. Matsin wears an old, battered set of palace armor, the leather worn and the velvet thin and shiny with use. There's also a faint line of damp along the edges of his hair, pulled up in a warrior's topknot. No doubt he heard the bell tolling and raced this way from the practice fields.

Bren ranges only a few paces ahead now, well within hearing distance.

"How much did Kestrin and Alyrra tell you of my audience with them?" I ask Matsin.

He grimaces. "I know who it was who betrayed you here in the palace. Beyond that, very little. The prince suggested I take this morning to train, and pay attention for any signs of trouble."

"He's a lovely man," I say warmly. Ahead of us, Bren coughs abruptly. "He set you up to meet us. You'll help us get out now, won't you?"

He glances across me to Niya, brow furrowed. "You've rescued your sister."

"Yes, and now we need to leave."

We're nearing the outer edges of the palace. Bren gestures to the side and I follow him, dragging Niya with me. Matsin is quick to keep up, at least. We stay pressed against the low hedges as a group of guards thunder past toward the slow tolling of the bell. Surely the mages have a better alert system than a bell? Or perhaps such a magical system is primarily controlled by the Circle, and now there is no one left to sound it.

"Kelari," Matsin says quietly as we start forward once more. "You need to tell me what you've done."

"I've done what the prince and princess gave me their blessing to attempt. I cannot explain more right now, but Prince Kestrin would not have unofficially stationed you here unless he wished you to offer your aid. At the very least, you must not slow us down."

Matsin hesitates. "Where are you going?"

"To a carriage in one of the outer courtyards. It will carry us out."

"Not now that the bells have sounded. All the gates will be closed."

Bren says, "The carriage will still be fine."

Niya tightens her grip on my arm. "We could try the Cormorant—"

"After he already let you be his scapegoat before the Circle?" I snarl. "It was *his* magic that activated the protections!"

"But he was helping us!" Niya argues.

"We are not going to him, and that's final," I say firmly.

"No one will see you or your sister," Bren assures me. "The carriage will be fine. They'll let us through when the gates reopen."

I'm not sure if he believes that, or if he just thinks the carriage an excellent place to lose Matsin before he leads us out one of his secret ways. Regardless, I trust Bren over the Cormorant without question.

We reach the end of the first palace gallery, pillars raising an arched roof over our heads, an open-air courtyard to our right. We turn into the next gallery, moving fast. Not twenty paces away, another group of eight or so guards hurry toward us. At their forefront strides a man I know well. He is tall, with midnight hair that brushes his shoulders and high cheekbones that accentuate the shape of his long-lashed eyes. He's handsome by any measure, and yet the ugliest man I've ever met.

The ember in my mind roars to life, pounding with my pulse. I push back at the flames, my breath hitching. Alyrra and Kestrin are supposed to take care of Garrin—not me.

"Bren," I croak just as Matsin pauses and then says, his voice tight, "Verin Garrin."

Garrin raises his brows and smiles, a cruel twist of his lips. "Kelari Amraeya, how fortuitous! I was just coming to see you. How *did* you get away from Hedhrawy?"

I don't know how much longer I can hold back the compulsion— or if I should at all. Except that I have only Winterfrost's word that she won't turn on the king once I grant her entry to the palace, and I'm still not sure how much I can trust her. Nor will I have any control over her once she's here.

"Admittedly, I would have preferred you were not here," Garrin says to Matsin.

His men haven't stopped and neither has he. Now he pauses a bare ten paces away, his men fanning out around him in a semicircle, the nearest of them far too close for comfort. The right side of the gallery may open into a wide, mosaic-tiled courtyard, but we're already hemmed in. I can't hope to run fast enough anyhow, cane or not.

"Verin, it is important that you allow us to pass," Matsin says.

"I think not, Captain. You see, I have unfinished business with Kelari Amraeya. I'm afraid you're all involved now."

Bren has moved back until he's even with us. He exchanges a glance with Matsin.

"You're armed?" Matsin breathes.

"Daggers only," Bren returns, the blades already in his hands.

There's no way they can fight off eight armed men.

I feel a strange wetness on my lips and chin, the tang of metal on my tongue, but it doesn't matter—not past the throbbing fire in my mind. "You have a choice," I tell Garrin. "Leave now, or face what justice I bring you."

"You bring me?" he scoffs. "There is a story here, and this is how it will be told: Matsin came across you and your sister attempting to escape the Circle. Sadly, he was attacked by your companion." Garrin gestures with some amusement at Bren. "I stumbled across the scene too late to stop the carnage. My only sorrow is the good captain was killed before I could aid him."

Niya takes a shaky breath, her hands curling into fists and her face strained. She's trying to gather enough magic to do a casting, but she hasn't the strength to fight this.

"I'm not sure who you think is more stupid, your cousin or your king," I say. "Regardless, they already know what you are."

Garrin hesitates.

"Leave now," I repeat, my voice straining with the effort of holding back the compulsion. "I do not want to have to destroy you."

Garrin smirks. "You don't have the ability," he says. "Kill them."

His soldiers leap forward as one, swords sweeping free of their scabbards. Niya grabs me by my tunic and hauls me back as Bren and Matsin join forces before us.

"Let go," I gasp, twisting free. There are too many—Bren blocks a blow, sends another man stumbling, and then leaps sideways to stop a third man from impaling Matsin through his practice armor while he fends off two others. My brain stutters as Bren stumbles sideways, another sword cutting past his side, barely blocked. Matsin slams through another attack, protecting Bren.

They will both die in another heartbeat—

I grasp the ember in my mind and break it free, fire on my lips as I roar the sorceress's name.

CHAPTER

43

The gallery explodes in a searing flash of white light.

I cry out, throwing an arm over my eyes.

I hear Matsin grunt, feel Bren's fingers brush my arm as he reaches for me, but there is nothing else—no shouts, no sound of metal on metal, or flesh.

As suddenly as the light came, it ebbs away to regular daylight. Bren fastens one blood-damp hand around my left arm. I blink, lowering my right arm, and glance toward him. His expression is stiff with pain, but he's focused on the gallery, not me, turning slowly to assess what's happening.

It takes me a moment to see that the guards have all been knocked back against the wall, their limbs stuck at strange angles, so that they look like insects pinned to a fabric display. Garrin stands facing me, his face gray with shock.

"Greetings, my would-be prince," a voice says from my other side.

I turn and find the sorceress standing not three paces past an ashen-faced Matsin. He regards her with blank horror. Behind me, Niya shifts, her breath coming short and fast.

Winterfrost is precisely as I remember her: night-dark hair, alabaster skin, eyes like empty wells. Her clothes are equally as foreign as last time, only now they are a set of layered robes, sweeping and elegant, pale as moonlight. They remind me forcibly of the robes I once saw the Fae lord Genno Stonemane wearing.

"No," Garrin says, panic in his voice. "You cannot be here."

"I was invited in. Did the noble-hearted child I chose not warn you?"

Garrin casts me a furious look, then returns his focus to the sorceress. "I know how your game is played. There is nothing and no one here I would sacrifice myself for."

"Rest assured, little prince, I am aware. If you would not sacrifice yourself for your aunt, you surely would not do so for a girl you threw to slavers."

His aunt—the *queen*? Is this how she died? For a man who sold the children of our land for his own gain? I know nothing of her but that she was spoken of as a gentle woman, both clever and kind. Since her death, it's been said the king has grown harder, colder. Remembering Kestrin's reaction during my audience with him and Alyrra, though, I have no doubt that this is true: Garrin traded the queen's life to the sorceress before me.

Niya steps up silently so that I am bracketed between her and Bren. She slips her hand into mine. She's scared. Perhaps her mage sight allows her to see just how dangerous the sorceress is. Not that I have any illusions on that score.

"Then what game do you play?" Garrin demands of her.

"The game has changed. Did you not see that I let your cousin go?"

Garrin hesitates, brow furrowed. "Kestrin said you tested him."

"I did," she says, baring her teeth in a glinting smile that is all predator. "How unexpected that he passed."

Bren drops his hand from my arm. I glance toward him, take in his uncharacteristically hunched stance, the way he's pressed his hand against his side. He's bleeding, a patch of scarlet spreading down the side of his tunic, staining his hand red. He didn't manage to block that thrust to his side, only partially deflect it. I meet his gaze, eyes wide. He shakes his head at me sharply, casts a glance toward the sorceress.

He'll be all right, then. He must be. I look up, wipe my own blood from my mouth and nose.

Garrin raises his chin. "I suppose you think you will test me as well. I will not grant you that. You've no hold on me, sorceress. I refuse your tests."

Winterfrost laughs, a sound so cold it leaves me light-headed. "Oh no, little prince. I have decided to dispense with vengeance, and you have already shown what you are. So, I will serve you up a taste of justice. For that, I require a different sort of hold."

She turns toward me, a small, dangerous smile playing on her lips. "Amraeya ni Ansarim."

I nod warily, taking a half-step forward. Niya moves with me, her hand tight in mine.

"What hold can you give me on this man who wishes you dead?"

I don't know," I say uncertainly.

"Does he owe you anything, perhaps because of something he has done to you?"

I meet her gaze and think of all that I have suffered because of Garrin. My breath trembles with the force of my wrath. "He owes me a life debt, to be sure, veria. I can give you that debt. I can give you a thousand such debts for every child he has sold into slavery to line his pockets, every young woman he has had stolen from her family. What good will it do?"

"That is for you to decide. What do you want with him?"

I cast Garrin a look of pure contempt. "I want nothing with him. You spoke of justice. Offer him whatever justice you please."

"I prefer to deal in equal exchanges," Winterfrost purrs. "If you do not want him, what is it that you want of him?"

Of him? I look at Garrin, taking in the sick horror with which he stares at me. He's bobbing strangely, and it takes me a moment to realize it's because he's trying to run but his feet are rooted to the floor. Slaver and murderer that he is, he will not face his own reckoning with courage.

I can't bring myself to care about him even now, in the face of his growing terror. I know what he did to me, to the children I shared the hold with, to Kirrana whom we never recovered, to my friend Ani's little sister Seri, stolen from the street of Sheltershorn.

"I want them back," I say roughly. "I want to be able to find every girl, every child, every last innocent he sold into slavery, whether he did it directly or through the channels he profited from. *I want them back.*"

"Ah," the sorceress says. "That is a worthy request. Do you see those flowers growing there? You must bring me one."

I turn, bewildered. Set at the base of each arch, there stands a great stone pot from which a profusion of flowers grow. I let go of Niya and cross the gallery, stepping down into the courtyard and approaching the nearest pot, carved of white stone. Flowers spill over its side, fragile, soft-petaled things. But rising from the center are three taller stalks with sturdier blooms.

I use my bone knife to saw one off. Only when I look up from the stalk do I realize the blooms I hold are asphodel, a pair of star-shaped flowers already open and two more buds above them almost ready to spread their petals. Asphodel. The symbol that first helped me connect Garrin's family with Berenworth Trading Company, and so the slavers.

I carry the stalk back to the sorceress. It is only as I pass it to her that I realize my palm is still sticky with my own blood. It leaves a smudge of red behind on the stalk.

"Perfect," she says, one pale finger brushing over my blood. That's what she wanted, not the flower itself.

"You cannot—" Garrin cries, his eyes bulging with fear.

"Oh, but I can." She raises her other hand, twisting her fingers as if plucking an apple, and a swirl of light closes around Garrin.

He screams. I turn, grabbing Niya and pushing her around so that we face away. Matsin ducks his head, eyes averted. Only Bren remains still, his hand pressed to his side, shoulders stiff. I do not look to see if he is watching.

Garrin screams and screams, and there are other sounds, the ripping and tearing of flesh, his screams descending into a bubbling frenzy that no throat should ever voice. Niya presses her hands over her ears.

I turn slowly, my stomach roiling. I can't hide from this. I *asked* for this; I cannot turn away. If Bren can watch, so can I.

But there is nothing to see past the swirling white light, and now, nothing to hear either. With a final swirl, the light dissipates, and Garrin is gone.

A shudder runs through me as the sorceress glides across the blood-soaked tiles to where Garrin once stood. She lifts something from the ground. It is as long as my forearm, the creamy white of ivory.

She crosses to me, her expression still, and offers me the thing in her hand. A flute. It is the kind a shepherd might hold vertically before them and press to their lips to play a jaunty tune. But this flute is carved of shining bone, engraved with asphodel along the sides. A green gem winks from its throat, set just above the first of the finger holes. It's the same gem that the sorceress once wore on a ring on her finger.

I look from the flute to the sorceress, unable to speak.

She says, "If you play it, it will lead you to the souls you seek."

Slowly, I reach out and take this last, cursed piece of Garrin from her hand. It is warm to the touch, and that is perhaps the worst thing of all.

"I release you of your second debt to me, Amraeya ni Ansarim."

I nod stiffly, barely aware of the pain from the bruises ringing my neck.

"How many debts does my sister owe you?" Niya asks.

"Two, little mage. I bid her call me when she reached the palace, and so she has done and repaid me. The other debt I used to bind her to silence."

"You have released her of that one as well, then?" Niya presses.

Winterfrost pauses, considering me. Oh no.

Niya continues, her voice soft and persuasive. "She gave you the hold on Verin Garrin that you required to bring him to justice. Would it not be best to lay all these debts to rest entirely?"

Winterfrost considers Niya with a hint of amusement. It's bewildering to see that touch of warm humor on her face after what we've just witnessed.

"As you say. I release you of your debts, kelari."

I feel her magic wash over me, gentle as a summer breeze. The faint warmth of the ember-spell fades, and perhaps the life debt in my veins as well. I cannot tell.

Two figures step into the courtyard from the opposite gallery. They are limned with light, their features impossible to see, but I've a hunch it's Adept Midael and Genno Stonemane. One of them says, voice echoing, "Winterfrost, we bid you stop."

He reaches out, and the sorceress laughs, batting her hand through the air and sending both Fae staggering back, their bodies braced as if against a great wind. "I think not."

They attempt to push forward, but the force of her magic holds them at bay, reverberating in my ears like a great howling gale.

Winterfrost smiles, cold and pleased, dips her head to me, and takes three steps into the fall of sunlight from the courtyard. She breaks apart into a wash of golden light that dissipates as easily as a breath in winter.

The gale shatters to pieces, thrown back by the Fae to break itself against the palace walls. Just as abruptly, the guards pinned to the wall collapse to their knees, freed of the spell that held them. Matsin starts toward them at once, a grim set to his face.

And Bren crumples to the ground.

Dropping the bone flute, I lunge past Niya to reach him where he lies on the tiles. "Bren!"

He turns his head toward me, his lips strangely pale. He was wounded—only now does it occur to me that he was hiding the true extent of it.

"No," I whisper, taking in the blood drenching his side. "Bren, please. Niya!"

"That," he says, his voice thin and unsteady, "was quite a trick, Rae."

His hand reaches for mine, wet with his own blood. I grasp it tightly. Niya drops down beside me. She's bundled the shawl I gave her into a thick wad which she presses hard against the wound in his side, trying to stanch the blood. "Hold on," she says.

Bren's eyes roll back for a moment; then they drop down and focus on me, half-dazed and still somehow warm with admiration. "Remind me . . . not to . . . cross you."

"Oh, be quiet," I say, tears spilling down my cheeks. "Don't you dare die. You hear me? You're *not going to die*."

"Trying not to," Bren whispers faintly.

A figure kneels beside me, the flutter of robes reminding me for one uncertain moment of the sorceress. But this is Adept

Midael, the Cormorant, his skin the deep brown of rich earth, long hair gathered in a score or more braids, threaded through beads and glimmering with bits of silver.

"Here," the Cormorant says to Niya. "Let me help."

He sets his hand beside hers, his eyelids lowering as his focus follows his magic into Bren.

"You're going to be all right now," I tell Bren, as if I could see the future. My heart is tearing apart inside of me. He can't die. He *can't.*

He smiles up at me in a haze of pain and says, gently, "Love you too, Rae."

CHAPTER

44

Eventually, Adept Midael sits back and assures me Bren will survive. "He has lost a great deal of blood," he says. "Such recovery will take time, though I am sure the mages here can provide you with a potion to help."

I almost ask, an edge of hysteria to my thoughts, *Which mages?* Then I remember the palace healer mage, Berrila ni Cairlin, whom Kestrin thought the king would favor to step in once the old Circle fell. For certain, she doesn't need to know the role Bren played in that fall. No one does.

I clear my throat. "When will he wake?"

"The sleep I've laid on him will last only a few hours, if that. Anything deeper would be dangerous for him. It's enough to move him and see him properly settled."

I nod, grateful.

"Captain Matsin," a voice says.

I look up, shocked. The king crosses the courtyard at a brisk pace, at least three quads of royal guards striding in his wake.

Matsin rises from where he was bent over the last of Garrin's guards, the man now bound as tightly as the rest. Stonemane stands a few feet away, hands tucked into the sleeves of his robes, his expression neutral. At second glance, not a single one of Garrin's men made it more than a few steps from where they started. I suspect that was Stonemane's doing as much as it was Matsin's.

"These are my nephew's men," the king says as he reaches Matsin.

"Tarin, they turned upon me and my companions," Matsin says, head bowed.

"Where is Garrin?"

Matsin glances toward us, his expression grim. "Tarin, forgive me."

The king moves past him, crossing the blood-spattered tiles toward us. He pauses as his embroidered leather slipper slaps against the puddled blood where Garrin once stood. He looks down, then raises his gaze to focus on me. He *knows*. I can see it in his eyes, however still he holds his expression, however hard it is to read his emotions beyond that single flicker of anguish and sorrow.

I stare at him mutely, holding tight to Bren's hand. I can't think of a single thing to say to save myself.

"Tarin," the Cormorant says, rising to his feet, his robes swaying around him. "The one we have spoken of has come and gone here. Whatever story Kelari Amraeya has to tell, it will be for only a few ears."

Niya remains crouched beside Bren, her gaze flitting from me to the king. *Stay there*, I will her. As if she will somehow escape notice by not moving.

I force myself to set Bren's hand down and push myself to my feet, hoping to keep the king's attention on me alone.

He takes another step toward me, setting his foot down carefully to the side of the puddle. His gaze doesn't move from me. "This hall is bathed in blood though there are no bodies, and the Circle has sounded the bells—something that has not happened in a hundred years. Tell me what you know *now*."

I have to trust that Alyrra and Kestrin spoke to him. They must have, or he would be asking other questions. "Tarin, the sorceress took your nephew's life for the crimes he has committed against our people. In return, she left that." I point at the bone flute where I dropped it on my way to Bren. I'm trembling—the aftereffects of shock, or simple fear of the king in front of me, whom I barely know how to read. "She said it will allow us to find those whom he betrayed into slavery."

The king crosses to it and lifts it up, his expression inscrutable. He looks from me to Niya, still crouched beside Bren. "What of the Circle?"

"It was an unexpected tragedy," I say, spreading my hands to reclaim the king's attention. I will protect Niya with everything I have, always. "The whole of the Circle fell to the Darkness."

His eyes widen as he stares at me.

"It must have been the slavers, for no one else can control whom the Darkness strikes," I add.

"Can't they?" he murmurs, his eyes glinting as he considers my words. "*All* of them fell?"

"Yes, tarin. I hope you will be able to, ah, help the Circle recover." That was perhaps a bit too forward, but my head is pounding and I don't think I have any nuance left in me.

He raises his brows. "I have never heard mention of a cure," he says, deliberately misunderstanding me.

"No, tarin," I agree, and take the opportunity he's offered me. "Although I don't believe the mages of the Circle, or those below them, have ever had such great incentive to find one."

"Indeed. That is your sister beside you, is it not? Who was meant to be on trial."

Niya pushes herself to her feet, swaying slightly. Her hands are soaked in blood, her gray eyes dull.

"Tarin," I plead. "Can you not offer her some small mercy?"

The king considers me a long moment, his grip tightening on the flute, and then he says, "I have heard the girl has been studying in secret with the Cormorant." He eyes the Fae mage speculatively. "Is that true, Adept?"

Stonemane makes a slight gesture, half hidden behind his robes. I glance at him, but he's looking at the Cormorant. The younger Fae takes a quick step forward, beside Niya. "Tarin, it is true."

I take back *all* the terrible things I've thought about him. At least he's here now, doing *something*.

"For more than a week?"

The Cormorant shrugs, an elegant shift of his shoulders. "Time flows differently for our kind, tarin."

He's claiming Niya as a true apprentice, and from the faint smile the king gives him, it is both impolitic and exactly what the king wished.

"I see. You are returning to your lands soon, are you not?"

"In five days, as we discussed," the Cormorant says, sounding faintly hesitant.

"Tonight," the king says. "You are leaving tonight, with your apprentice. Earlier if possible. Now, I must get to the mage's complex." He glances toward me. "Kelari, you are bleeding. I will send Alyrra to you at the infirmary. Your companion will be seen to there as well."

"I—thank you, tarin," I say, and because I cannot possibly curtsy, I ease myself to my knees and dip my head. Even so, my legs nearly give out. Niya dips down into a perfect curtsy beside me.

She will not come home again, not now, and perhaps not ever. But the king has arranged a new life for her: freedom and the chance to learn and grow in her magic. It is both a blessing and a banishment; I do not know whether to smile or weep.

The king holds the bone flute out to Stonemane. "I request your study of this, verin. I suspect you will be able to tell me more than any human mage might."

"Tarin," Stonemane says, gliding forward to take it. "It will be my honor."

The king issues a spate of commands and departs, leaving behind most of his guards to gather up Garrin's men and march them from the gallery.

Only a pair of guards remain behind, along with Captain Matsin. I'm not sure if they're here for the single guard of Garrin's who is too injured to walk, or for Bren, or for me. Perhaps it's all three.

"You are leaving tonight?" I ask the Cormorant, reaching out to grip my sister's hand again. It's a foolish question, but my mind is still reeling from all that's happened. Bren lies quietly on the tiles beside me, his face sallow and his breathing a little too soft for comfort.

"So it seems," the Cormorant says, glancing toward Niya. "Forgive me, Kelari Niyagara. I hope you will find this future preferable to the other fates that might await you here."

"Why?" I ask, before she can answer. "Why did you protect her?"

He hesitates. "I have not been able to verify it, but I suspect that the reason your sister was arrested was because of the spell I gave her, and not her own workings. That was a mistake I should not have made."

He's right. It's also a relief to know he sees this as a repayment of a debt. The Fae prefer their bargains and trades—if Niya incurred a debt to him now without set boundaries or limits, she might never be free of it. Which might still be preferable to the future offered to her by whatever new Circle the king helps to establish, but not by much.

"Thank you," I say, my gaze flicking from him to Niya.

She bobs her head, her cheeks pale. I fold her in a hug, holding her tight. "Will you be all right?" I whisper. The Cormorant helpfully drifts away from us.

She nods against my shoulder. "I think so. But—what about you?"

"I'll be fine."

"But I was always supposed to stay with you," she says, pulling back to look at me. "We were supposed to stay together."

It's the same thought that's given me only one future until now. I didn't realize it was holding Niya back as well.

"I'm glad you have Bren, though," she says, glancing toward him. "He will recover, and faster than you might expect, given the Cormorant's intervention."

"I'm grateful for that. But I'll be fine whether I'm with Bren or not," I say, though I want it to be *with*. I so very much want it to be *with*. "I'm pretty sure I'm the only one who can play that flute."

Niya snorts. "I saw the two of you together. He's not going to let you go around playing that thing without him."

"Niya." I glance toward the Fae, but neither is particularly close. Still, I keep my voice low as I say, "He's a thief lord. You know that, right?"

"It is unfortunate," Niya agrees, with all the optimism of a little sister. "But he's done the kingdom a great service, which means he'll never have a better opportunity to, um, shift his occupational ventures."

"Right," I say, although part of me wonders if Bren might. It's hard to imagine what that would look like.

Niya grimaces, her eyes dropping to the blood-streaked tiles. "Well, I'll hope, anyhow."

"Kelari," the Cormorant says. "We should leave soon. I'm sorry. We do not have a great deal of time to make preparations."

Niya nods.

"I'll see you off if I can," I tell her. "I just need to make sure Bren's safe." The sleep the Cormorant has laid on him will allow him to be moved with a minimum of pain. It also means he's utterly helpless. There's no way I'm leaving him alone in the palace of all places.

Niya smooths her hands over her skirts, leaving behind a smudge of blood. "Tell Mama I love her if I don't see her before we leave. And Bean and Baba."

"I will. I love you too, Niya. So much. I'm so proud of you."

"I know," she says. "I'm proud of you too. A little afraid of following in your footsteps, but proud."

I give a breathy laugh and gather her into a final hug. She squeezes me tight and then steps back, her eyes both sad and bright. She turns to where the Cormorant waits. They leave the gallery together, Niya pausing at the corner to look back at me one last time.

It takes me a moment to realize Stonemane hasn't followed them. Instead, he's standing by one of the arches, to all appearances enjoying the view of the courtyard. I turn to him uncertainly, wishing I could sit down once more beside Bren. "Verin?"

He wears his people's clothes, a mauve robe that drapes elegantly over his form, trimmed with embroidery at the neck and cuffs. He dips his head to me, dark hair falling loose about his shoulders, the locks tousled from Winterfrost's gale. It's his expression I can't understand, his jaw tense and a hint of worry in his eyes, and yet his smile is all court, utterly meaningless.

"You are bleeding, kelari. May I help you?"

I trust Stonemane, and I've met with him on my own before, but I'm a little unsteady now. I glance toward the corner, but my sister is long gone. Bren lies silent and unmoving on the ground. A pair of the king's guards remain, standing stolidly against the wall by the one guard of Garrin's who was wounded. At least Matsin is still here, watching quietly.

"Kelari?" Stonemane asks, crossing to me.

"What will I owe you?" I ask abruptly.

His smile tightens, becomes a sad thing. "We do not all deal in bargains all the time. There would be no debt."

"I—I'm sorry," I say, embarrassed. "I'm not . . . I would be very grateful, verin."

He faces me and places the tips of his fingers against my temple. "First, we'll stop the bleeding. It is almost done anyhow."

A whisper of warmth brushes beneath my skin, traveling along the lines of my cheekbones and across my face, and then sinking deeper. "Ah," Stonemane says, but it isn't a good sound. I open my eyes to find him staring at me, his brow creased, his gaze—it's as if he's looking deep within me, through flesh and bone. "There is some bleeding within, kelari," he says softly. "A very small amount, but it is as if your brain sustained a slight injury very recently."

"Can you help me?" I ask, fighting a chill. Niya did her best to protect me from the Darkness, but now I know why there is no cure for it. There wouldn't be, if it does physical damage to the brain itself. Such healing is nearly impossible, even for the most advanced mages.

"I will do what I can. It is not a dangerous amount, kelari, but you should rest this next day or two. Stay in bed, do your best not to exert yourself."

That sounds next to impossible, with Bren injured and Niya about to leave. But I won't be any good to them if I hurt myself. "I'll try," I promise.

His magic washes through me again. I breathe slowly, waiting as he works. The touch of his magic brings no apparent relief, but I also know this is a type of injury you can't always sense, at least not until it's too late.

"There," he says. His eyes focus on me once more. "It seems the sorceress removed her spell, but there is something else here, a touch of magic in your blood."

The marker the Darkness is drawn to. "Can you remove it?" I ask shakily.

"Easily. It is faded already, barely more than a trace."

I feel a faint twinge in my mind, and then he sweeps his fingers back, brushing over the feathery edges of my hair. A ripple runs through my body, washing through my veins and flowing through my heart, and slides free, like a web releasing me.

Stonemane flicks his fingers, dispelling the magic he's caught.

"Thank you, verin," I say through dry lips.

He nods and steps back. "If you require anything further, I hope you will call on me," he says.

"That flute," I say abruptly, gesturing to where he set it, balanced on the same pot I cut the stalk of asphodel from. "Is it like my knife?"

He stills. "How so?"

No, I decide, I really don't want to know how my knife was made. Instead, I say, "My knife is spelled, isn't it? To always come back to me? I can't understand how I haven't lost it yet—or how it came to my hand once, as if guided."

"Its pattern is linked to yours," Stonemane says. "As is the flute's."

"Then I'm the only one who can play it?"

"For now. You may gift it to someone else, just as I gave you the knife." He moves to collect the flute. "I am sure the king will return it to you shortly. It will be your decision from there."

I nod, glance to the corner. A young medic stands there, watching us with interest. She's brought two pairs of men with her, each with a stretcher. One pair moves over to gather up the wounded guard. The other waits beside the medic, their gazes moving from Stonemane and me to Bren.

"Please," I tell them, gesturing to Bren. "My friend needs your help."

"Of course, kelari," the medic says, stepping forward. "We are honored to be of aid."

CHAPTER

45

T he medics at the infirmary have a room waiting for Bren and launch into action as soon as we arrive. I take up a station in the corner of Bren's room, watching as they transfer him to the bed and cut away his tunic to assess his injury. The wound in his side shows sickeningly raw alongside the web of older scars that crisscross his chest. The gash is the length of my hand, its red edges pulled snugly together by the Cormorant's magic. The skin around it is swollen and shiny, bruised.

I look up from it, toward his face, and my gaze catches on the silver chain hanging from his neck. I blink, focusing on it. Looped through the chain is my grandmother's ruby ring. I stare at it, remembering how Bren would sometimes touch the front of his tunic, the pendant there—not his own sign but my ring.

The thought makes me want to cry.

Once the medics ascertain he has no other injuries, and there's nothing more to be done, they leave. The medic who escorted us here brings me a pillow and a thin mat to rest on, reminds me to call for her if I need anything, and finally departs.

I must be more exhausted than I know, for I slip into a light doze almost as soon as I lie down. The medic pops her head in once to check on us, but otherwise it's quiet.

I sit up on my mat sometime in the late afternoon, judging from the fall of sunlight through the window. Bren has barely shifted in his sleep, the blanket still pulled up to his chest. I lean against the bed and gaze blearily at the wall, thinking of Niya leaving for the Fae lands as the Cormorant's apprentice. It is a much better future than anything I imagined in the last day or two. Gratitude wells inside of me toward the king, who stood there with the flute in his hand and still granted Niya his mercy.

Something brushes the top of my head. I startle, turning, and Bren's fingers slip deeper into my curls, grazing my scalp. His head lies at a tilt on his pillow as he gazes at me.

"Thought you were a dream," he mumbles, running his fingers through my hair. His touch sends a tendril of heat through me, curling down into my belly. "Been wondering what your hair feels like."

"Bren." I push myself to my knees beside him. His hand slips out of my hair to cup my cheek. For a long moment I stare at him. He's alive, his eyes glinting with mischief despite the fact that he can't even sit up right now. He's still too pale, and there are creases around his eyes and mouth that are probably from pain—

"Don't cry, Rae," he says, his thumb brushing my cheek. The mischief in his eyes drains away, replaced by something much deeper.

I take his hand in mine, pulling it down so I can look at his palm, the calluses there. His thumb is wet with my tears. "Look," I say, my voice rough, "I know we come from two different worlds, and a country girl isn't going to know how some things work, but—"

"That's hardly—" he interrupts.

"Just listen," I say, fixing him with a watery glare. "I care about you, all right? And I can't—I *can't* watch you die. So don't you ever do that again."

"Oh, Rae," he says tenderly.

"I know who you are. I know you're used to taking risks. I just . . ." I shake my head, the words caught like a sob in my throat.

"*I'm* used to taking risks," he echoes wryly. "And what of you, sweet Rae? Will you agree to never end up with a noose around your neck again? Because I was too far to do anything, and I don't know what I would have done if your sister hadn't gotten to you in time."

"You know I didn't plan that," I say tightly.

"Just as you didn't plan for your sash to fail against the Darkness today—but you knowingly risked it to save your sister."

"I had to," I say, swallowing back the rising tide of my heartache. I can't save him, or keep him safe, any more than I can build a future in which we might promise our lives to each other.

"I know. I can't swear I won't endanger myself again any more than you can. We each have our battles to fight." He exhales on a whisper of a laugh. "I can promise I definitely don't *intend* to let myself get killed."

I sit back with a pained smile, loosening my grip on him. I have to let him go, after all. I've always known I couldn't keep him. After a moment, he lets me go as well, his hand dropping down to rest on the blanket.

"The medics think you should heal up," I tell him. "The Cormorant did a lot to save you."

"I'll have to thank him," Bren says. He rests his head against the pillow. "I need to get word to my people."

That, at least, is something I can help with. "If I can reach that page of yours in the palace, will he know how to contact someone at your house?"

"That's probably our best option," Bren murmurs, closing his eyes. He looks exhausted. "You'll stay with me?" he asks.

The word at the tip of my tongue is *always*. It's just another promise I can't give. "Of course," I say instead. "But don't sleep yet. The medic has a potion for you."

He grimaces. "I wouldn't have minded if you'd forgotten that."

"Oh hush." I push myself to my feet and limp to the door, my muscles stiff.

Captain Matsin is still outside, though he's given in to his own exhaustion and sits cross-legged on the floor. I'm glad he didn't attempt to stay standing all the while we rested. He leaps up at once to fetch the medic.

Once she arrives, I help her prop Bren up against a wall of pillows so he can choke down the vial of liquid she brings.

"You'll need to stay in bed till tomorrow at the earliest, most likely the day after," she cautions him. "Call for help if you need the washroom. You're still not healed. Don't push yourself. You were lucky indeed to have a healer mage see to your wound." She shakes her head. "All the mages have been called away now. There's some trouble at the Circle."

"That's unfortunate," Bren says, the corners of his mouth dipping down to hide that wicked little smile of his I know so well.

"I'll check on you again in an hour or two." She opens the door and jolts to a stop. I step sideways, trying to see past her, my thoughts on my bone knife and what I can do. She dips a deep curtsy. "Zayyid, zayyida," she says in an awed tone.

Relief rushes through me. I hastily brush out my skirts. They're terribly rumpled from sleeping on the floor. Straightening, I run my hands through my hair, glancing toward Bren.

He's watching me with a faint smile. "You're perfect, Rae."

Easy for him to say. He's got a blanket to hide under.

"Anyhow, your makeup's worn off your throat, and there's blood all over your front. They won't even notice your hair."

I scrunch my nose at him, my fingers going to my throat, not that I can tell how much shows by touch. Regardless, they've already seen that bruise, haven't they? I suspect Bren didn't give me that little pot of cosmetics until after my audience with them for a reason, the cunning goat.

I look down to find that, unfortunately, he's correct: my nosebleed has left a significant number of brownish stains dried over my chest. Lovely.

Alyrra steps through the door. I lower myself into a stiff curtsy. "Don't, Rae," she says and crosses the room to pull me into a hug.

Kestrin discreetly shuts the door behind him, dipping his head to both of us. "Kelari. Kel."

Clasping my hand, Alyrra turns toward Bren, a smile flickering across her face. "I thought it might be you."

"Mmm," Bren returns. "I've a way of showing up, don't I? I've always wanted to meet your husband."

Alyrra glows with amusement. "Of course. Kestrin, I'm honored to present an old friend of mine, Red Hawk. Red Hawk, my husband, Prince Kestrin."

I should have expected Alyrra would know Bren's true identity, but I'm still irrationally grumpy. I even asked her what Red Hawk was like. Come to think of it, her description was just vague enough to leave me in the dark, no doubt to allow Bren to maintain what secrets he thought necessary.

Now, Kestrin raises his brows, every bit the enigmatic and suddenly dangerous prince. Bren meets him stare for stare, as confidently as if he stood in the city streets, his blades at hand, a thief lord in his own right. Even though he's propped up in an infirmary bed, mostly held together by magic.

Oh no, I am *not* allowing this. I clear my throat and say brightly, "By the way, zayyida, I'm sure you've heard we had to break my sister out of the Circle. I do hope our friend here won't face any difficulties leaving, either."

Alyrra gives a little cough of amusement while Bren closes his eyes in a convincing display of despair.

Kestrin flashes me an amused look. "Indeed, kelari. It is good to know who has your protection."

"We'd like yours too," I say humbly. "It just bears mentioning."

He laughs and takes a seat on the bench. From there, no longer towering over Bren, he says, "I understand I owe you a double debt, kel, for your work today, and for what you did for my wife when she was a goose girl."

Now that's much more promising.

"I am honored to be of service," Bren says with only a trace of sarcasm. "Though I did think we were just going to discuss how I returned Kelari Amraeya to the palace. There's a reward for that, I hear."

Kestrin looks faintly affronted, and even Alyrra seems surprised. I smother a laugh.

"It would be the most honest money you've earned in a while," I observe to Bren, hoping to smooth things over. "Can't fault you for trying for it."

"The reward is well earned," Kestrin says finally, glancing at Alyrra. "We'll see it delivered to you. I have spoken with my father and can promise you full medical treatment and a safe departure." Kestrin pauses. "But I wonder if more might be possible. Your services—and loyalty—could be very valuable to us."

Bren raises his brows, then glances toward Alyrra and me. Between all their looks, I'm not sure who's actually directing this conversation.

"With your permission, that may be a discussion for another day," he says.

Alyrra nods. "I thought it past time the two of you met. Now that you have"—she flaps her hand at Kestrin—"we'll leave you to rest. Matsin will stay outside your door to ensure your safety. Should he need to leave, he will introduce you to his most trusted men first. You may dismiss them at any time. Is there anyone you would like us to send for?"

"Rae can see to that for me."

Alyrra nods and turns to me. "I'm sure you've been in all sorts of situations in the last few weeks, Rae, but it's better if you're not keeping company with an unrelated young man in the palace if you can help it. Come along. Red Hawk will be just fine."

"Certainly," Kestrin says with a quirk of his lips that reminds me forcibly of Bren. "I doubt anyone would knowingly cross you at this point."

"I wouldn't," Bren agrees. "Go on. I'll be fine."

I force a smile and move to the door. I want to ask when I will see him again, if he truly will be all right or if I should come back. But those aren't things I can ask before the royals, any more than he could answer them.

"Goodbye, then," I say.

Bren clicks his tongue, clearly aggrieved. "I'll see you soon, Rae."

I can't help my smile as I look back at him. "All right."

Alyrra ushers me out with a shake of her head, but she's smiling too.

CHAPTER

46

Alyrra and Kestrin escort me to my cousin's apartments where I am enveloped in hugs and plied with tea and biscuits.

As soon as the royals depart, I write my messages for Bren's page to deliver: one to my mother, and a second to Kelari Bakira as a backup. Melly bustles around as I work, opening up my old trunks, lined up against the wall, to find me a change of clothes. It feels as if I have somehow fallen back into a piece of my old life, but it doesn't quite fit right anymore. My edges are sharper, and when I turn to give Melly the letters for the page, it feels like I might inadvertently cut through the fabric of this world to a darker, more dangerous one underneath.

"Is there anything else we can do?" Melly asks.

All I want is to lie down again. But as I start to shake my head, I remember a promise I made myself. "Just one thing," I tell her. "Tell Filadon I need him to teach me how to bow."

Then I crawl into bed and there I stay. I get up only once to hug Mama and hear how she saw Niya off at the docks, and then I slip back under the covers and lose myself in a dreamless sleep.

When I finally wake the following morning, I find a small, leather-bound book sitting on the table beside my bed: the archer's journal I traded to Stonemane in return for his aid in trying to trace Kirrana. This is where I first read Winterfrost's name. I give it a long, thoughtful look and then get up to wash my face and eat something with my family.

Eventually, though, I return to the guest room to sit on the bed and flip through the journal. It was this same archer who eventually betrayed her liege to Winterfrost in a bid to end the war. To all appearances, it worked.

The archer herself disappeared into the war-ravaged plains, seeking news of her family, and carrying with her a burden of guilt she could not lay down: she had sworn herself to the king she betrayed. Though he broke her trust, ignored their people's needs, and fought for himself and no one else at the end, still she blamed herself for his death.

I trace her words with my fingers. Both the mages of the Circle and Garrin were sworn to serve our people. They betrayed those oaths, just as this ancient king did. Like the archer, I consigned them to their ruin. I will carry those memories with me, no matter how I try to pretend they do not bother me. They are there when I close my eyes: the mages convulsing on the dais, the gurgling screams torn from Garrin's throat, the feel of the flute in my hand, still warm.

I set the journal down with shaking hands. No, I'm not the same as the archer. I *saw* what my hands wrought, just as I saw what the Circle and Garrin did. Even now, I'm different. The archer went to seek her family, hoping the people of her land would weather what came. But my family will be all right—they're in no danger. It's the people I can't turn my back on, the children still lost, still enslaved in mines or brothels or worse.

I've known this since the moment the sorceress handed me the flute. Niya knew it. But I still need to choose this future for myself.

I look up as Mama peeks into the room. "Mama, we need to talk."

She sits down heavily on the edge of the bed. "What about?"

I take a steadying breath. "I can't go home with you—not to stay. I need to come back here, keep doing this work. Finding the children who were snatched, and bringing those who hold them to justice."

Mama blanches. "I understand if you wish to do something different. But *this*? Rae, you were nearly hanged. You were nearly cut down by that traitor Garrin's guards. You were nearly drowned, nearly sold into slavery. My God, there's almost nothing you weren't threatened with!"

"I know. But I can't walk away from this, Mama. There are still children missing; there are still snatchers doing their work. They'll rebuild their networks without Berenworth, without magic to back them, because even with the risks there's money to be had. I have to help stop them while they can still be found."

Mama studies me for a long time. Finally, she says, "If you cannot leave it, then you must promise to stay off the streets. I can't allow you to risk yourself as you have been."

I shake my head. I'm not going to agree to limit myself when I don't yet know what I can accomplish. I've spent far too much of my life limiting myself as it is.

But I understand. I do. It's the same thing I asked Bren in the infirmary, and so I already know my answer. "I can't promise I'll never be in danger again, Mama. You taught me to fight for what I believe in, to stand by my values. The flute the sorceress made— she gave it to *me*. I'm the only one who can play it. I can't walk away from that. As for the streets—they were no more or less dangerous to me than the palace."

Mama closes her eyes. In that moment, I see the shadows beneath them, the deep creases lining her mouth. She's exhausted and afraid, and much of it is because of me.

"Mama," I say quietly, "I've always let myself settle for what I already had. I don't want to do that anymore. I want this, and I will carry it with me the rest of my life if I walk away from it. Please don't ask that of me."

Her expression falters. She looks suddenly lost. "I'm sorry, Rae. That we taught you to settle. It's the same thing we did to Niya, isn't it? We've held you back instead of helping you forward."

"You were just trying to keep us safe," I say, reaching out to clasp her hand. Because this I know: Mama never meant to harm us.

She shakes her head, her face crumpling. "There's so much hurt in the world, Rae; it seemed that there would be even more for you. But instead of making you strong, we taught you not to try, not to even hope. We thought we were protecting you." She looks at me, her eyes bright with tears. "It's a terrible thing to realize the damage you've done trying to safeguard what you love. I'm so sorry."

"Oh, Mama, I couldn't have asked for a better family." I lean forward to wrap my arms around her. "I'm as strong as I am *because* of you and Baba. I just never wanted to fight for myself before. Now I do."

Mama holds me tight. "Talk to the princess, then," she whispers, her tears dropping onto my shoulder. "Just promise me you will take care of yourself."

"I will, Mama. I promise."

CHAPTER

47

I present myself at the princess's apartment that afternoon. Jasmine opens the door, her expression cool. For a moment, I'm taken back to my very first visit to the royal wing, unsure why the princess would want me as an attendant at all.

"Amraeya?" Jasmine says, her eyes widening. She's dressed impeccably in a flowing burgundy skirt and cream tunic, both heavily embroidered and beaded. She's always been the most elegant of the princess's attendants, tall and perfectly poised, her dark hair put up today in some inexplicable manner involving a pair of hair combs and various gems and pearls.

"Veria," I say, and offer her a bow.

She coughs a laugh. "Bowing now? You can't be serious—oh, this won't do. I was planning to be welcoming to you!"

"It's all right," I assure her as the page gapes at us. "My plans don't always work out, either. May I see the princess?"

Jasmine shakes her head at me, though she does step back to allow me in. "I suppose the bowing is easier on your foot?"

"Much."

She closes the door on the page and says, voice lower, "Amraeya, I don't mean to pry but . . . are you here to ask the princess to reinstate you as attendant?"

"No," I say with some amusement.

Jasmine heaves a sigh of relief. "I'm so glad! You were a *terrible* attendant."

"And you are *ever* so welcoming," I say, trying not to laugh.

"Well, it's true!" Her mouth creeps into a guilty smile. "You were always disappearing places; or the princess would send you off and then act as if it were perfectly normal to be missing an attendant."

"It's because I was helping her investigate the snatchers. She really didn't want me as a regular attendant. I'm sure you've heard as much since."

"One mustn't believe everything one hears," Jasmine says absently, her gaze skimming over me again. "Those are some dreadful bruises around your neck."

"They're barely yellow!" I lift a hand to them.

"Yellow-green," Jasmine corrects me. "I'll send you a cream to hide them. Though I've only ever used it for spots. I don't know how it will do trying to cover so . . . much."

The exquisite Jasmine just admitted to having spots? I've heard everything now.

"Well, come along. The princess is waiting," Jasmine says, as if she wasn't the one to stop me with questions about what I intended.

I follow her across the outer sitting room with its sofas and painted silk screens to the similar but more intimate inner sitting room.

Alyrra sits at a small writing desk in the corner. She rises at once upon our entrance, grinning as I offer her the deeper bow Filadon taught me for addressing royalty.

"Rae! I'm so glad to see you. Please, come sit. Jasmine, will you send for tea?"

"Of course, zayyida." With a dip of her head, Jasmine slips back out again.

I join Alyrra on the sofas, and we spend a couple of minutes on the usual social questions of health and family well-being.

"Zayyida," I say at the first natural pause. "I've come to tell you I wish to continue the work I began with you. Not as an attendant, but working directly on the snatchers."

Alyrra settles back in her seat, studying me thoughtfully. "I hoped you might decide that, but are you sure, Rae? You know better than the rest of us that it's dangerous work."

"I'm sure."

"Your family?"

"Mama and I spoke this morning."

"Hmm." She looks down, her eyes tracing the pattern of vines and flowers on the carpet. "What kind of work do you want to do, precisely?"

"There's the flute, zayyida. It was given to me, which I believe means I will have to be the one to play it."

She inclines her head. "No one else can draw a note from it. However, Verin Stonemane assures us you can choose someone else to bestow it on. You do not have to force yourself to this."

"I don't want to give it away, zayyida. It is what I asked for. I wish to use it to help the children who have been taken." I smile derisively. "I doubt you'll need a go-between with Red Hawk anymore. I need some other role."

"Perhaps not a go-between," Alyrra says with a slight quirk of her lips. "He seems to be quite direct nowadays. You heard he had a private audience with the king this morning, before he left the infirmary?"

I sit forward. "He did? About what?"

Alyrra considers me brightly, then shakes her head. "I'm not sure I can speak of it just yet. If all goes to plan, I expect you'll hear shortly. Are you quite sure about the flute?"

"Yes."

She rises and crosses the room to a console to lift up a long, slim object wrapped in a dark cloth. I know what it is at once.

"When I received your note asking for an audience, I sent for this," Alyrra says, carrying it back to me. "I thought you might ask for it."

She slips it free of its fabric wrapping, the ivory gleaming palely. I stare at it, at the carved asphodel and the embedded emerald that lends the enchantment its store of power.

"You don't have to take it," Alyrra says gently.

But I do. Its pattern is linked to mine, as Stonemane said, our pasts and our futures intertwined. I asked for this, and the truth is, I want it.

I lift the flute from her hands. It warms to my fingertips just as I knew it would. I adjust my grip, arranging my fingers over the holes. All except the last hole, which I'll never be able to cover. I doubt it will matter.

I lift the flute to my lips.

It is no surprise at all when my first attempt draws a single, resonating note from its body.

I return to Filadon and Melly's apartment to find a letter has finally arrived for me through Bren's page. It's from Lirika.

Bren is safe, she writes. *You said you wanted to see me. You can come tonight. He won't be here.*

I consider her words, the slightly disjointed feel of her thoughts on paper, the way the nub of her quill pressed into the paper unevenly, scratching deep and then barely touching in other spots.

I fold the letter carefully and go to find Mama.

As dusk deepens into night, I step into the open-air atrium at the center of Bren's house. The adobe walls glow palely in the faint moonlight, the mosaics underfoot blending into a pathway of shadows.

"You came," a voice says from across the atrium.

I peer through the darkness that envelopes the far corner, made deeper by the high walls. "Lirika?"

She shifts and says, "Aye."

I cross to find her sitting against the wall, her hair unkempt and her hand curled around the neck of a bottle. The little silver flask she had with her on the *Heron* lies on its side beside her. I stoop down to retrieve its cap, and just like that the sheltered halls of the palace fall away from me. "Have you been out here long?"

"You judging me?"

"No." I ease myself down beside her, pick up the empty flask and screw it shut. "Just a little worried about you." Though, now that I've come, I'm not sure how I thought I might be of any help.

She grunts, takes a swig from the bottle, her expression pinched. There are deep shadows under her eyes, dark as bruises. She smells of alcohol and sweat.

"Does it help?" I ask. "Drinking?"

"No. I can still hear him screaming." She gestures vaguely toward the sky. "Hear it in the wind when it blows over, hear it on the edges of everything."

"I'm sorry," I say softly.

"My baba was a piece of filth. I'd have watched him scream and enjoyed it. So, why's it the good men who get hurt like that? Why's it because of me?"

I hesitate. "It wasn't because of you."

She laughs, a bitter, jagged sound. "Is that supposed to help? You don't know anything."

I bite my lip. I don't know what to say to her, if anything I can say would help. Finally, I say, "You should try to sleep."

"Can't. Not drunk enough. Don't want to dream." She tilts her head toward me. "I keep seeing him when I close my eyes: the blood on their blades, and then his eye when they were done. I hear Bardok laughing, and the screaming." She looks away. "Always the screaming."

I look down at my hands, at my missing finger. However bad that was, it was nothing like this. It's only been a few days since Artemian was tortured, I remind myself. Surely it will get better for her.

"Have you seen Artemian since that night?"

"He's here now," she says. "I saw him a couple of hours ago. He's got an eye patch and says the rest will heal up." She gives a dry, pained laugh and looks at the bottle in her hand.

"Does Bren know how you're doing?" I ask, changing tactics. "Maybe you should talk to him."

She shakes her head, takes another gulp from the bottle. "He's a bit busy. You know, between getting his chosen thieves settled in Bardok's territory; working out a split with the Scholar; making sure what's left of Bardok's men don't start anything too bloody; and figuring out how to help the innkeeper's wife, what lost her husband when Bardok came looking for you. Not to mention whatever it is Bren's been up to at the palace." Lirika reaches out with the bottle, nudging my arm with her fist. "You need to slow down, country girl. You're tangling everything. Don't think any of us can keep up with you."

"I'm not doing as much now," I tell her. "In fact, I'm planning to go home for a visit. To Sheltershorn."

She huffs a laugh. "There more girls like you there? Because I don't think the kingdom can handle that."

Slowly, I say, "Maybe you should come and see."

"What?"

"Come with me, Lirika. You can learn how to work the horses with us; I can teach you how to ride, if you don't already know. You'll love my sister Bean. If you think I'm trouble, she once shouted an actual dragon out of the sky."

"A dragon?" Lirika echoes, tipping her head toward me incredulously.

"Bean's a handful."

Lirika laughs. "Sounds a bit like you."

I shrug. "It might help to get some distance from everything that happened here. I need to speak to my parents about it, but I think they'd want you to come. It would just be for a couple of weeks, a month at most."

She stares at her bottle a long moment, her hand tight around the neck. Then she throws her head back and downs the rest. I watch as she starts to set the bottle down, then lets it go a handspan above the ground. It falls on its side and rolls across the tiles toward me.

"Lirika?" I reach out a hand to stop it. At least it didn't break.

"I'll come, if your family'll have me. Can't be worse than here."

"Good. I'll help you to your room." I rise and brush out my skirts.

"I can find my own way." She pushes herself to her feet and pauses, staring across the atrium, perfectly steady on her feet. "I told you to come now because Bren isn't here, but he'll be back later if you want to wait."

I came here for Lirika, not Bren. He said he'd see me again; he'll show up when he's ready.

"I need to head back," I say, but then can't help asking, "Is he doing all right?"

She scoffs. "Cut up but mending. Half as much trouble as you, easily. Glad you're not staying, though. There's some things he needs to figure out for himself."

I watch her move heavily across the tiled atrium, head down, not sure what exactly she means.

CHAPTER

48

Mama is not wholly happy with my tentative invitation to Lirika, but she doesn't demand I withdraw it either. "She helped you come back to us, of course she's welcome," Mama says as we get ready for bed. "I'm just concerned about her drinking. I don't want Bean influenced."

"I'm concerned about it too," I admit. "She's struggling, Mama. She's seen a lot of darkness and not enough light. If you want, I can ask her to keep her drinking behind closed doors. I suspect, though, that she only drinks when she can't handle her memories."

"Invite her," Mama says. "We'll find a way to make it work."

I step over to give Mama a hug.

She hugs me back and says, "Now, tell me about Bren."

I startle. "What?"

"How is he? I assume you've had word of him."

My cheeks warm. I kneel before my trunk and lift out my night shift, better suited to warmer weather than my two-piece night clothes. "Lirika says he's healing. Alyrra mentioned he had an audience with the king, but I don't know what about."

"You haven't heard from him directly?"

I shake my head.

Mama *hmms* thoughtfully.

I stare down at my old night shift, and say softly, "I like him. A lot."

She pauses behind me, and then she turns with a rustle and sits on the floor beside me. "I know, Rae. I've never seen you so comfortable with a boy before."

I sigh. "He's a thief lord, Mama. He told me he cares for me, but he also said he can't offer me anything. I know it. I just . . . I want there to be something. I want it so much." I take a shaky breath and hold it to keep from crying.

Mama looks down at her hands. "I don't know if this will help, my love, but it's the best advice I can give. I've come to believe there are three things a couple needs to make a future together: mutual respect, shared values, and the ability to enjoy each other's company."

I turn this advice over slowly.

"If you're missing any one of those, the relationship can't last. You and Bren clearly respect each other, and you certainly enjoy each other's company," Mama says, and stops there.

Because Bren *is* a thief. Even if I've managed not to think about the ruthless things he must have done to become a thief lord and then maintain his territory, that doesn't mean they didn't happen. Not that I haven't been equally ruthless.

"He has his own code of honor," I say, my chest aching with the words. "I don't agree with everything—I wish he would uphold the king's law and make *it* work rather than making his own thieves' justice—but I respect it."

"What if he steals to enrich himself? Could you live with that?" Mama asks, as if there were a possibility he doesn't. But he does; I know he does. He told me so himself, unapologetically. Even if his home is humble in comparison to the other thief lords. Even if that means he's spreading his wealth out among the networks that serve him.

"I couldn't," I say, my voice small. "Not if we were married."

"Would you marry him if he gave up the unjust aspects of thieving?"

"What do you mean?"

"Beyond stealing for his own ends, are there other major differences in your values?"

"Not really," I say slowly.

"Then wait and see. If he's talking to the princess, or the king, then perhaps things will change," Mama says.

I can't imagine Bren as something other than a thief. It's how he raised himself, the only way he could survive; it will always be a part of him. Which is why it takes me a moment to catch on to what my mother is implying. I cast her an odd look. "Would you and Baba really approve of him?"

She purses her lips, but there's a smile hiding in there. "Truthfully, Rae, if you'd asked me that question before I came to Tarinon, I would have swept in here to catch you by the sleeve and hustle you home again. But I've seen him fight for you, and Niya, and stand by you against your enemies. He *suits* you. I don't know how —I thought your match might be a steady, kind farmer type, not a brash thief-boy, but there it is."

"I don't think there's going to be that many farmers in my life from now on," I say dryly.

"No," Mama agrees. But then she says, "You're only nineteen, Rae. If Bren doesn't come around, give yourself time. You may yet meet someone else in a year or three."

I nod, but I don't want to meet someone else. Nor do I want Bren to give up who he is. Which I suppose makes it a good thing that Bren's making his own decisions.

Mama and I stand at the back of the royal throne room, the dais with its trio of thrones opposite us, and nobles lining the walls to either side. The arched ceiling soars far overhead. The windows set high in the walls are edged with bands of engravings, letting in the bright morning light. Below them, the walls are decorated in carved inscriptions and flowing mosaics.

I drop my gaze back to the empty thrones, wishing I hadn't eaten quite so much breakfast. But the royal summons hadn't come till I was finished.

"Relax, Rae," Filadon says. "If you're worried about the king being angry with you, I wouldn't be."

"Easy for you to say," I mutter. "You didn't kill his nephew."

Filadon studies me thoughtfully. "Do you remember a few weeks ago when you told me how terrifying you found the royal family, after you watched a crown change hands and a prince stripped of his rank and exiled—all before breakfast, as you put it?"

"I remember," I agree, chilled.

"Consider that you brought the Circle's own curse down on their heads while sitting right in front of them, and then traded the king's nephew for an enchanted instrument to save the people he betrayed—all before lunch."

I open my mouth to respond and find I have nothing to say. I close my jaw again with a click.

"Precisely," Filadon says.

"We'd better take our places," Melly says, turning away from her conversation with Mama.

Filadon offers me an encouraging look, and they slip away to take up their station among the lines of nobles. I spot Veria Havila, that matriarch of the court, toward the front of the room, seated on a small but exquisitely designed wooden chair, her cane at her side. I left my own in my room, forgotten in a corner after it was delivered back to me from the gallery where I left it, wiped clean of blood. But seeing Havila reminds me to use it again as needed.

A voice announces the arrival of the royal party. I straighten, trying not to look too tense, as the king takes the great carved throne at the center of the far dais. Kestrin and Alyrra seat themselves in smaller thrones on either side of him.

"Verin Melkior," the king intones. The nobles, quiet already, fall silent. "Approach."

Melkior? I glance to the other side of the door to see him waiting there. He is dressed simply, his summer robe over his tunic and pants elegant but unadorned, and only a single ring on his fingers. He walks slowly up the long aisle to kneel before the king, head bowed. It isn't the stance of a nobleman before his lord, but a petitioner, or something even less.

"Twenty years ago, I appointed you to the post of lord high marshal," the king says, staring down at Melkior. "A month ago, I believed you to have served me and our land well through those years. Now I have learned a different truth: that the rumors of what our people call snatchers were not rumors at all. The slavers they speak of are organized, and have been preying on our youth for decades while we have ignored our people's call for help. It was your responsibility to heed that call, to investigate and learn the truth of it. What have you to say for yourself?"

I lean forward, straining to hear the somber, muted tones of Melkior's voice. The acoustics of the hall, designed to carry the voices of those at the front to even the farthest reaches of the hall, just barely deliver his response to me.

"I have failed you, my king. I have failed you and our people. I heard these same rumors over the years. I did not grasp the corruption that had infiltrated our land, from the lowliest guards, to the courts, to those working side by side with me. In my blindness and arrogance, I failed all who relied on me. I have nothing to say for myself but that I am sorry. Those are paltry words for the sorrow in my heart and the fury I feel toward those who have betrayed me into inaction where I should have stood firm and fought. Even so, I should have looked harder, should have seen past the lies around me. I did not question my own assumptions. I ask your forgiveness not because I deserve such, but because I cannot help but ask. I am surely unworthy."

The nobles shift, a current of unease running through them. Only a few look pleased to see Melkior brought so low. The king gazes down at him in silence, his expression faintly troubled.

"How shall I decide your fate, when it is my people you have betrayed above all?" he asks.

Melkior bends his head farther.

Slowly, the king looks up, his gaze fastening on me from across the hall. My stomach plummets.

"Kelari Amraeya ni Ansarim, come forward."

Mama gives me a slight push as I stand unmoving. "Be strong, love," she murmurs. "Don't keep him waiting."

Her words unroot my feet from the floor. I walk forward, chin raised as the uneven sound of my slippers whispers across the marble. My palms are damp with sweat. I come to a stop before the king, Melkior three paces to my right, and dip into the bow Filadon taught me, elegant and deep as befits one's liege. It is so much more graceful than the best of my curtsies.

"Rise, kelari. Your service to my family and my kingdom in the last month has surpassed all that I might have imagined. You protected my daughter-by-law when our own protections failed, as all our court knows. You stepped in to investigate the snatchers where my own marshal failed. You uncovered a conspiracy of slavers, brought forward your evidence, and then paid the ultimate price through your own abduction from within the palace itself."

The king pauses, allowing his words to settle into the hall. "When you returned, you brought with you all that is required to dismantle the slavers entirely. There is a great deal of work to be done, it is true, but you have given us the key. You have provided us with evidence of all the layers of corruption that surrounded my marshal and have infected our land. All of this, at great risk to your own life and limb. Kelari, the crown acknowledges to you a great debt."

I look up in relief and find the king's gaze warm upon me, his mien unexpectedly unguarded in this most public of moments. He's thanking me—for bringing down the Circle with enough forewarning for him to put his own mages in place. That's the key he means.

Perhaps he's also thanking me for Garrin's fate, so that he did not have to bring his nephew forward as he has Melkior. Or, worse, quietly dispose of him. Looking at the king before me, I've no doubt he would have brought Garrin to account himself. Not only would that have pained the king, it would not have resulted in the other key I now have: the flute made of Garrin's bone.

The king continues, "For your service, we elevate you to the rank of noblewoman. We further bestow upon you from the crown's holdings a villa in the north of the city, that you may always have a home near us. Finally, we will bestow upon you an estate from among our lands, the details of which we will discuss with you that they be to your liking. These are yet small gestures in comparison to what you have wrought. Veria Amraeya, we thank you."

I dip into a deep bow. "Tarin, it has been my honor to serve my people and my king."

I hesitate and decide to stop there. I'm not sure what else to say. It didn't occur to me to have a speech prepared.

The king regards me keenly. "Veria, you have heard the words of Verin Melkior who stands beside you. You know better than the rest of us the depths of his failures to protect our land; it was through his own blindness that you were stolen from us. Tell me, what counsel would you give regarding my high marshal?"

If the hall fell silent when the king first ordered Melkior forward, it is as if I stand in a tomb now. The king has made me jury to his judge. What I say now will influence Melkior's fate, as well as a host of political machinations of which I have no concept.

I take a shaky breath, casting a glance toward the man still kneeling to my right. I found him officious and condescending in the few interactions I had with him while investigating the snatchers from the palace. Had he had his way, we never would have found the children in the slave galley at the docks, for fear of unnecessarily disrupting the business of the local merchants. The king is right: he failed our people spectacularly and consistently for decades. There is no question that he should lose his post.

But . . . I would not see him punished terribly, either. He has done good over the years through his other work, brought stability and maintained order. It was his arrogance and ignorance that cost our youth their lives and freedom, not his loyalty or diligence in the work he did take on. Beside me, Melkior remains on his knees, his whole body tense. I think of the king standing as I saw him last, his slippers steeped in blood and his nephew's bone flute held tight in his hand, listening as I begged mercy for my sister.

"Tarin," I say slowly. "Our land needs a new marshal who will question assumptions, one who will seek out the truth behind rumors and see justice done."

The king dips his head. "Indeed. What fate do you counsel for Verin Melkior, then?"

I lick dry lips. "Mercy, tarin. He too was betrayed, though it was his responsibility to watch for such betrayal and to listen to those who petitioned him. I would see him given the opportunity to make amends as you see fit, under the supervision of your new marshal."

Beside me, Melkior's shoulders sag with relief. He casts me a single, grateful look before returning his gaze to the foot of the throne.

The king dips his head. "Wise counsel, veria. So let it be."

CHAPTER

49

The villa the king has gifted me is Garrin's ancestral home.

I stand in the wide foyer with Mama, Melly, and Filadon. There are mosaics underfoot and shining wood paneling on the walls, and a crystal chandelier with luminae stones straight out of the mage's complex hanging over my head. I cannot imagine sleeping here.

"I am afraid some personal effects are still being removed," the housekeeper tells us. "Perhaps I can give you a tour of the main rooms?"

"That will be fine," I say, ignoring the vase of flowers on the console to the side, stalks of asphodel rising above the other blooms.

The villa is massive. I walk through it in a dream, the whole experience surreal. We pass the entrance to a gallery, a pair of servants engaged in removing a long line of portraits to be sent to the palace.

"Did Garrin live here?" I ask Filadon, voice low.

"No, he stayed mostly at the palace. He came here only sometimes once his parents passed away. It was used more when the family was larger, I believe."

Even so, it is both strange and chilling to walk the halls where he spent his childhood. To see the history of his branch of the royal family, always a step or two removed from the crown, written upon the rooms here. The furnishings are exquisite, even those that are covered in fabric to protect against dust, long out of fashion but still gorgeously made.

We finish our tour in the extensive gardens behind the house, where the housekeeper has arranged an extravagant tea for us. I sit down, grateful to rest after the plethora of stairs we have just navigated. Even with my cane, the stairs get old.

"I beg your forgiveness that the house is not quite ready for you, veria," she says, as if she could have known this morning that she would have a new mistress by the afternoon.

"It is no matter. My mother and I are quite comfortable for the time being, staying with my cousin." I point across the gardens to a low building just barely showing through the greenery. It's clearly not the stables—those, I've been informed, are on a neighboring plot, separated by a wall. "Tell me, what is that?"

"A small guesthouse, veria. It has fallen out of use. It was built some decades ago for an elderly family member who preferred her own space and, as I understand it, found the stairs in the main house difficult."

I take a slow sip of tea. "I should like to see it, kelari, as soon as you can show it to me."

The housekeeper excuses herself at once, no doubt to retrieve the keys and send a handful of servants to sweep out the floors as best they can.

"Why do I have the feeling you're going to want to live in the guesthouse?" Melly asks, grinning at me.

"Let me see," I say, pretending to count out the reasons on my fingers. "It's small, Garrin's never lived there, and, *no stairs*."

Filadon chokes on a laugh. "Rae! You can't accept a royal villa from the king and then stay in the hovel out back."

"He gave me the hovel out back too. He should have thought about that if he didn't want me staying there."

"I can't imagine a royal hovel is too terrible a place," Mama argues. "At least let us look at it."

Melly pats Filadon's arm. "I'm quite certain the king will only laugh when he finds out. Rae handled the question of Melkior very well. The king is determined to be pleased with her for at least the next week."

Filadon moans, well aware he doesn't stand a chance against our united front. "Will you leave the villa empty, then?"

I look up at the towering building—five floors, at least, multiple wings, a great receiving hall for banquets. There's enough room to fit our whole town twice over. While most of it was paid for generations ago, its upkeep must have been funded in part by the benefits Garrin received supporting the snatchers.

Which means it isn't really my villa. It belongs just as much to every child stolen into slavery because of Garrin's actions. A smile touches my face. "No," I tell Filadon. "It won't be empty at all."

Late the following afternoon, I step out into the gardens. They are alive with day-end birdsong, butterflies and bees roaming the blooms one last time as evening sets in. Melly and Filadon spent the day helping Mama and me move into an impressively well-cleaned if eclectically furnished guesthouse. It is the perfect size: four bedrooms to allow for guests, two connected sitting rooms, a small kitchen, and an expansive washroom complete with a heated in-ground bath the likes of which I've only seen at the royal bath-house. My whole family can stay with me as they like, but it won't feel too big if I'm ever alone.

Mama's letters should have found Baba and Bean by now, even in their hidden retreat in the mountains. Filadon insisted we can't leave Tarinon until we've stayed at least a night in the new home the king has afforded us. So, a single night in the guesthouse, and then we'll head home. We should reach the ranch around when they do.

By the time I return to Tarinon in three weeks' time, Alyrra and Kestrin will have brought together a small group of recruits from among the guards to work with me. Matsin has already volunteered to head the special unit. Between them and my flute, we will be able to start recovering the snatched soon.

The only thing missing will be Bren.

I grimace. He's not missing, per se, he just hasn't sought me out as I hoped he would. I know he's busy. The only explanation I can find is that he doesn't realize how soon I'm leaving. That, or he is trying to break free of his feelings for me, hoping to once again escape my orbit, as he put it. The thought hurts to consider, so I try to keep it at bay.

I follow a path through the gardens to a quaint little seating area surrounded by bushes and flowering shrubs and take out my flute. Filadon arranged a flautist to give me a lesson yesterday evening. It was just enough for me to learn the basic mechanics of my instrument and a single simple tune.

I run through the song a dozen times before it begins to feel right. A servant passes by on her round through the gardens, lighting the lamps hanging from their poles. She walks the perimeter of the little seating area, the lamps casting a golden glow over the benches. It's peaceful and quiet now, my only company the chirp of crickets.

I settle more comfortably into my seat and continue practicing until I can sing along in my mind to the tune my fingers play, my eyes closed to the swirling blue magic. It can't find direction here, so far from the rest of the city where there are children to be found. But this song is for them. I will play it for the rest of my life, a lullaby that is more promise than comfort, and I will find them.

Eyes closed, I start over one last time before I go back inside.

Life is a river, it carries you to the sea
Distant is the land that has stolen you away
But I am the wind in your sail
I am the current you ride
So, sleep, my child, with your heart tucked close to mine.

As I begin the second stanza, a surprisingly sweet tenor joins in to sing along with the notes.

Life is a river, it carries you to the sea
Bright is the hope that you'll come home some day
Though you may fear that you'll fail
My love is always at your side
So, sleep, my child, with your heart tucked close to mine
Sleep, my child, with your heart tucked close to mine.

I let the final notes die away and open my eyes. Bren stands by the opposite bench, his eyes bright despite the deepening gloom. My heart squeezes painfully at the sight of him. He wears a well-made tunic and a pair of pants, olive and sand and a hint of shadow. His hair is tied back in its usual tail. He looks utterly normal, his face golden brown in the wash of lamplight.

"Bren?"

He grins and glances around. "I was hoping you'd be on a rooftop, but I suppose a garden will have to do."

I huff a laugh. "Tell me you didn't climb any walls to get in here. Not with that wound still healing."

"It was the strangest thing: I presented myself at the gate and they let me in."

"I was hoping you'd come," I admit.

Bren's gaze runs over me, taking in my sturdy, deep purple skirt and cheerful yellow tunic, as well as my hand, fully healed. Finally, he meets my gaze, but even then, it's as if he's drinking in my features. It's enough to make my cheeks burn.

"Couldn't stay away," he confesses in return.

"I suppose you're going to say something absurd about how you're the moon and can't help orbiting me," I say, and even I can hear the bitterness in my voice.

That familiar line appears between his brows as he considers me, and then he says, tenderly, "It's not that I'm the moon; it's that you're the sun."

"Don't," I say, even though I invited this. "I'm glad to see you, Bren. But please don't say such things."

"It's true, though."

I give a watery laugh and slip the flute into its carrying case. "Doesn't matter." I stand up. "By the way, I'm planning to steal Lirika from you."

"I heard. I still love you."

I flush, my chest hurting. He's said these words before, and each time my heart breaks a little more. This time, I can't help blurting, "Bren! Don't you understand? I have a heart too. I can't go on listening to your words every time I see you and still pretend my heart isn't breaking." I jerk the flute's strap over my shoulder. "I want to spend the rest of my life chasing slavers with you. But you have another life to live. I understand that. You're still Red Hawk, you'll always be Red Hawk, and—"

"That is the single most romantic thing you've ever said to me," Bren interrupts.

"What? That you're Red Hawk?" I ask, bewildered.

"Not that. I'm passing that mantle on," he says, eyes sparkling, brown with glints of gold.

I stare at him, barely daring to hope. Because if he isn't Red Hawk anymore, if that's someone else—

"You said you want to spend the rest of your life chasing slavers with me," Bren says, taking a step toward me. "Why don't we start now?"

"Not until we're married," I say, because this at least I'm sure of.

"Oh, very well. If you insist."

"What?"

Bren closes the distance between us, that mischievous smile of his tugging at his lips. "Honestly, Rae, I thought you'd never ask."

My heart thunders in my chest, and for some reason my fingers seem to be going numb. Except that it's still impossible, this dream of his. Of mine. "Bren," I say, my voice strangled. "I can't marry you."

"Hear me out," Bren says, as if he was the one to propose. He takes my hand in his. "You can't marry a thief, can you?"

I squeeze my eyes shut, then force them back open, meet his gaze. "No," I agree.

"No, because even though you've been a part of thieves' justice, in the end you want the king's justice. You're right, of course. A single system of justice, equitably applied, is what we all need. I didn't think it was possible—I still don't believe it can ever truly be achieved—but I've watched you fight your way out of the darkness and change the impossible because you knew it had to be done. I'm not so foolish as to refuse to follow you."

"What are you saying?"

Bren threads his fingers through mine. "I've spent the last few days having a series of conversations with the royals. What they most need right now is a thief to help steal back the freedom of all the people who have been snatched over the years. Interestingly enough, that's the one thing I *am* still interested in stealing."

"A thief?" I repeat. "So you'll be, what? The king's thief?"

"More like the people's thief. I have to swear a few oaths, Rae, one of which is that I won't steal for myself. In return, I have the king's blessing to do what's necessary to recover those who've been enslaved. I've a letter with his seal, and it isn't even a forgery."

I can't think, not with his fingers twined with mine and everything changing. "Wait," I say and gently detangle my hand from his. I take a careful step back, make myself meet his gaze. He's watching me intently, with the full force of his abilities, because right now, I'm what he wants. But I have to make sure that this isn't just about me. "Bren, would you still choose this if I can't marry you?"

"Why couldn't you marry me?" he asks, his voice betraying his anxiety. "I'll find a way to convince your parents."

I hold up a hand, a tightness building in my chest. "This isn't about my parents. Would you still choose this path, even if we never saw each other again?"

He runs a hand over his hair, tugging at his tail. "Rae, please. If there's something else—"

"There is something else," I agree. It's cruel, but it only has to be so for a few moments. "If I make a different choice, would you still make this one? To be the people's thief, as you call it?"

Bren's shoulders sag. He looks away, and then back at me, the brightness gone from his eyes. "I would," he says quietly.

Relief rushes through me. "I'm glad. Because I need to know that this is from you, and not just about me."

He hesitates. "You said there's something else."

"There is," I agree. "You see, we have this rule in my family: you can't marry someone until you know their name."

He blinks at me. "*Oh.*"

"Oh," I agree, grinning back at him. "I'll make an allowance if you don't actually remember your name, but I've a feeling you do."

"I can't believe you made me think you—*Rae!*" He reaches for my hand.

I stick both hands behind my back. "Names first!"

He laughs but subsides. "It's a little embarrassing."

"It can't be that bad."

He says, with an endearing sort of shyness, "My mama liked these old folk tales. She named me Lukai. It's from this . . . ah . . ."

"From Riha of the Woods!" I crow.

"How did you—"

"It's my *favorite*." I reach for my story sash, only I can't show it to him because I'm not wearing it anymore now that the wards are burned away.

"You're very excited," Bren observes, a smile tugging at his lips.

I stop patting my sides as if my story sash might reappear, and turn an imperious look on him. "Lukai is an excellent name. You're just like him, you know."

"If by that you mean I'm a prince and a mage both, I have some unfortunate news for you."

I give an insulted sniff, but can't help laughing. "I meant that you were going about your life unhappily committing yourself to all sorts of atrocities until someone came along to set you straight."

"As long as that means I get to marry you, I can live with that."

"You're terrible," I tell him as he reaches for my hand. This time, I let him catch it.

He turns my hand over in his, cradling it against his palm. It's my left, my empty knuckle with its missing digit starkly clear.

"You'll have to tell me how to win your parents over," he says, tracing the creases in my palm. His touch does strange things to my insides.

I clear my throat. "You may have forgotten, but you saved my life repeatedly and also rescued my sister from magical slavery. I'm pretty sure if you show up promising to be an honest thief, they're going to love you."

He meets my gaze, his finger still tracing shapes on my palm, sending a flood of sensation through me. I swallow hard, my breath coming a little too fast. He smiles wickedly. He knows exactly what he's doing to me.

"Bren!"

He bends and brushes a kiss over my palm, his lips soft against my skin. I nearly lose my balance, my knees going suddenly weak.

"Come on," he says, tucking my hand through his arm with a supremely self-satisfied look. "I need to talk to your mother."

I take a halting step or two with him, trying to gather myself. He's far too pleased with himself—and there are still a few questions we ought to agree on before racing to get married. I muster my defenses and say, "We should discuss children first."

He stops in his tracks. "What?" There's just a hint of panic to his voice.

I slip free of him and set my hands on my hips, laughter bubbling up in my chest. "I don't know if you city boys quite realize how things work, but we country girls know exactly what to expect after you breed livestock."

"Rae!" he cries, choking on a laugh.

"So you haven't thought at all about the, um, wedding night?" I ask, my cheeks so hot they might as well be on fire.

His gaze sweeps over me, darkening with an emotion I've seen before but didn't know how to name till now—desire. "I have," he says huskily.

I swallow hard, trying not to admit to the very real shivers whispering under my skin. "So you've considered the question of nine months later?"

He hesitates. "You're right. We do need to discuss this."

I gesture to the bench. We sit beside each other. Around us, the faint, heady scent of roses lingers in the air, combining with the first hint of night jasmine.

I tilt myself toward him, so there's a little more space between us, even if our knees almost touch. "Do you want children, Bren?"

He studies me. "Do you?"

I swallow down my unease, knowing the response most girls would give, the answer that's culturally expected. We'll navigate this regardless, but I want to make sure I know what Bren really wants first. "What if I said yes?"

"I would . . . ask for time. It's not . . ." He shakes his head, starts over. "Are you saying yes?"

His answer, incomplete as it is, makes it that much easier to admit my own truth. "I've always wanted to marry, to have a companion through life who was more than—well, more than a sister, however amazing Niya is. But children?" I shake my head. "I've never been sad that I didn't expect to have my own. I've spent my life looking forward to being Auntie Rae, and I still hope for that. But I don't really want children. If you do, then we can talk about it, but . . ."

"No," Bren says a little too quickly. "No, I—you know the life I've lived, Rae. I barely remember my own parents; I can't imagine *being* one. Especially not with the work we intend to do. Even with the king's dispensation, chasing slavers isn't exactly safe."

"It isn't," I agree. Bren exhales in relief. My lips twitch, but I say only, "I guess I'll speak to a healer about what potions to use. Actually, my mother probably knows."

Bren shifts uncomfortably. "There's no need."

"No?" I ask, eyeing him curiously.

He clears his throat, his eyes darting away and then back to me. "A few years ago, I went to a healer mage and bribed him to perform a small bit of magic."

"Meaning?"

"A . . . snip of sorts."

I nearly choke on my own breath. "Bren, when we snip something on the ranch, that's code for castration."

"*What?* No, nothing like that!" The tips of his ears turn pink. It's utterly adorable.

"I didn't think so," I say, my shoulders shaking with laughter. "Could you please be a little less circumspect so I don't tell my parents the wrong thing?"

He rubs his mouth, but he's laughing too. "It's on the inside, Rae. It means I can't father a child, not unless I go back and have it reversed."

"That's handy," I say, impressed.

His shoulders tense. "It—ah. I haven't really been with, um . . . I can tell you—"

I reach out to rest my hand on his. "It's all right, Bren. I meant it's handy that I don't have to worry about potions or their side effects. I know you have your past. As long as you're sure about *us*—as long as you won't walk away from me in a month or a year or fifty —I don't need to know anything else."

He turns his hand to grasp mine. I have the feeling he's holding on to me in more ways than one. "I'm not going to walk away. Ever."

"Marriage is hard," I caution him. "We'll have fights; there'll be times when we do things wrong. We're committing to a partnership to work through all of that, to keep being there for each other even when it's rough."

"I know. I also know how you commit to things. I wouldn't offer myself if I didn't think I could meet you. Can you trust that?"

I nod, my fingers tightening around his.

"Good, then. Let's go talk to your mother." He rises and draws me up with him, heading toward the big house.

"Wrong direction." I turn him to face the guesthouse, amused despite myself.

"You aren't staying in the main house?" he asks, baffled.

"I like the little one. I've got plans for the big one."

"What plans?"

"I've been thinking about all the children we've rescued so far. About how one of them didn't have a good home to return to. And the fact that if we're rescuing children stolen thirty years ago, some of them will be adults with nowhere to go. I thought I might make the house into a home and school for the children whose families can't be found, and those who don't want to go back. Training for the older kids, respite for those who are even older and need to recover before they can find their feet. Set up apprenticeships, that sort of thing."

Bren tilts his head to regard me, his gaze soft. His words when he speaks don't quite match up. "You should talk to Alyrra. The king ought to be paying for that."

"Maybe. I still want it to be here. There'll need to be more such houses in other places. Another one in Lirelei, for sure. They can pay for that."

"That's good work, Rae."

"I figured I'd ask Artemian to help, if you'll let me have him."

Bren snorts. "You already have Lirika."

"I'll need someone I trust here while I'm haring about with the flute. Artemian has a way with children."

Bren pulls me a little closer. "While *we're* haring about, Rae. You bring the flute, I bring my thieves. We'll make the perfect team. Matsin can clean up after us."

I laugh. "That's pretty much why I'm marrying you." We reach the guesthouse door. "Now, in you go. Mama's in the sitting room."

Bren considers the door with trepidation. "Stay with me?"

"You just negotiated your future with a king. This can't be more worrying."

"Oh, it is," he says. "The king couldn't take you away from me."

I keep my hand threaded through his arm, my heart full. "Together, then."

CHAPTER

50

"I can't believe you just cut your hair again," Ani grouses, watching as Mina, my ex-roommate and fellow attendant, applies my makeup.

In the six weeks since Bren proposed—or I did—I've had my visit home with Lirika, and my family and friends are now here in the guesthouse with me to celebrate. Everyone except Niya, of course. Tonight is the sweetening.

"I think it suits her," Bean says loyally from the floor, her arms around her latest rescue project: a too-thin orange striped cat with a torn ear and a particularly malevolent look. Somehow, it has not yet clawed her *or* had an accident indoors.

"It does," Melly agrees. "I'm glad you've kept it short, Rae." She sits on the bed with Ani, resting her arms on the great round of her belly beneath the loose, floor-length embroidered robes she wears. The baby will be here within a couple of months now.

Lirika, crowded into the corner of the bed, rolls her eyes, but the slight tilt of her mouth tells me she's enjoying herself. The weeks on our ranch seem to have done her good, though the horror that she's been through still dogs her footsteps sometimes. Just as my dreams still bring back memories to haunt me. Still, Lirika's here and looking forward to working with Bren and me. We'll get through the dark things together.

"Short hair is easier to care for," I tell Ani now, pushing away more somber thoughts.

"It's harder to do things with," she argues back. "You can't even use a hair comb!"

"Barely need a brush," I agree, despite the fact that I have been pampered, primped, and brushed within an inch of my life. "It's lovely."

"There," Mina says, sitting back to inspect her work. She's used a light amount of makeup to bring out the pink in my cheeks and add a bit of color to my lips. She also lined my eyes with kohl and shadowed them with blue and gold. Even I have to admit the effect is striking. "You will always need a brush, Rae. I do hope you know that."

"Yes, Mama Mina," I say meekly.

Mina huffs a laugh just as Alyrra bursts into the room unannounced in a swirl of embroidered skirts. "Did I miss it all?"

"For the most part," Mina says, as half the room attempts to scramble to their feet to curtsy and the other half just bobs in place, myself included. "I did tell you to come earlier."

"I tried," Alyrra says, hurrying over to grasp my hands. "I'm so sorry, Rae! There were—"

"Zayyida, it's fine!" I say, squeezing her hands. "We've gotten done a little early. Sit with us and have some tea."

Mama rejoins us a moment later and starts serving tea, and the next time I look up, Alyrra is on the floor beside Bean, her skirts spread in a puddle of shining silk, offering her hand to the cat for inspection. It sniffs her once and turns its head away, unimpressed.

"I heard you're going to take Moonflower home with you," Alyrra says to Bean. "She was my favorite."

"She was?" Bean says, sounding as shocked as I feel. Moon-flower is hardly a loving horse.

Alyrra nods. "She just needs a little kindness. I know she'll do wonderfully with you."

"Rather Bean than us," Melly says. "I can't wait for Filadon to finally buy a horse I would *want* to ride."

"Don't hold your breath," I say. "Not unless you're picking it out yourself."

"Of course I'm picking it out," Melly says archly. "I learned my lesson the first time."

"Moonflower is a lovely horse," Bean says crossly. "The princess said so."

Alyrra laughs.

After tea, I step behind a screen and slip into my clothes for the evening, Mama coming with me to help me navigate them. We have to be careful to make sure the tunic doesn't ruffle my hair or smudge my makeup. The skirt is so heavy with embroidery, Mama has to help me lift it. Then there are only the embroidered slippers, lined with velvet and carefully shaped to fit me.

"You look lovely, Rae," Mama murmurs, her eyes bright with tears. I hug her tightly, so grateful for this moment, for this future I never thought possible.

"Are you ready yet?" Ani calls.

I laugh against Mama's shoulder, listening to Mina and Melly chastise her. Then I step out and, at my friends' urging, turn in a circle to show off the crimson tunic and skirt, the sleeves and hems banded with cobalt, all of it heavily embroidered with gold wire and pearls.

As everyone rises and gathers themselves to escort me out, I glance across the room to my cane, propped up in the corner. I don't need it right now, nor do I want it, but there's a good chance I'll be grateful for it by the end of the evening.

"What's wrong?" Bean asks, slipping up next to me.

"Nothing," I say. "Would you mind grabbing my cane for me?"

"Of course," she says, and hurries across the room to fetch it.

She swings it along in her hand as we proceed together through the gardens to the villa and its banquet hall. The rest of our party is spread ahead and behind us, the path too narrow to walk more than two abreast.

"I miss Niya," she says quietly.

I give her hand a squeeze. "Me too."

She glances ahead to where Alyrra walks beside Mama. "I'm glad things are changing with the apprentices."

The Circle has announced an option for apprentices to study from home. They will provide a monthly stipend for families and require only three months a year of study in residence with a teacher until the apprentices reach fourteen years of age. After that, the ratio switches and apprentices will study in the city for nine months of each year, but still have the option to return home the remaining three. It's an utter reversal from previous policies, and the impact is already being felt in new and wonderful ways across the kingdom.

"It's good news," I agree as we cut around the wide open-air tents set up for the men, who will hold their revelries out here. It's one of a slew of changes that have slowly taken shape as the new mages of the Circle have revisited old ways of doing things. Thankfully, the protections have also been changed—Mage Ehelar was instrumental in sharing his findings with the Head Mage Berrila, and those aspects of the protections that once sent out the Darkness have been expurgated.

Though there's still no cure for the Darkness itself—which means every single mage who fell to it has now become an amulet bearer, unable to safely control their own Talent. It's a strangely poetic fate.

Bean purses her lips. "But they haven't changed their policies about hidden Talents like Niya."

Oh, sweet Bean. "Alyrra says the new Circle is discussing them," I tell her. "I expect any kind of change will take some time to be reached. It's hard to navigate because it's too dangerous to leave Talents unregulated."

"Do you think Niya will be able to come home then?" Bean asks, as I knew she would.

"Perhaps," I say gently. "Bean, I don't think she'll ever really come home to stay again. This apprenticeship will open up a whole new world to her. She'll come to visit, I'm sure, but I think she'll want to go back. She'll always still be your sister, though, and so will I."

Bean reaches out and wraps me in a hug, pulling us to a stop in the doorway to the villa. I hold her tightly, and we don't move on until she's ready.

The sweetening proceeds just as every sweetening I've been to before did: with singing and dancing and far, far too many sweets. I enjoy it all, though I can't help watching the door for Bren's arrival, one hand outstretched to have henna applied.

Finally, he's announced. The women immediately adopt the familiar demure attitude required by tradition. Bren enters carrying a silver tray with a medium-sized, engraved box on it. He wears a knee-length tunic of sky-blue jacquard with cream pants and an embroidered cream sash at his waist. Over that he wears a flowing dark-blue open-fronted robe, trimmed with silver embroidery. His hair is loose, falling over his shoulders in a cascade of silk. If it weren't for the look of absolute mischief in his eyes, I almost wouldn't recognize him.

Bren takes the two small steps up to the low dais where I sit with my friends and family around me, coming to a stop before us. Behind him walk Artemian and the thief Edhren, grinning in anticipation. Artemian wears an eye patch of embossed leather. He looks more gaunt than before, but the hollowness of his cheeks is made up for by the pleasure warming his features.

"What have you brought to honor my daughter?" Mama asks.

Bren sets the tray on the table before me and flips open the box. It's filled with gold coins.

For a moment, we all stare. This isn't how this tradition is supposed to work. He's supposed to bring a paltry gift, and then the womenfolk hurl insults and drive him off so that he can come back with something they might deem worthy of the bride. But this— this isn't paltry at all.

"Bren," I say uncertainly. "What are you doing?"

The sly, laughing curve of his mouth tells me he knows precisely what he's doing. "I present to you, O light of my eyes, a poor sum. Truly, I wish it were more, but you must blame the princess for what it is."

"What?" Alyrra says, taken aback.

"And the Circle," Bren adds.

I look from him to the box of coins and say with disbelief, "Are these coins the rewards you collected for me?"

"Fifty gold for your safe return to the palace, another twenty-five for turning you over to the Circle," Bren agrees readily. "Sadly, the additional twenty-five from the Port Authority was given to someone else. I should have preferred an even hundred." To match the bounty he once carried on his own head, no doubt. He goes on, "Still, it seemed like you earned it more than I did."

"What!" Mama shouts, laughter in her eyes and fire in her voice. "You no good, arrogant son of a two-tailed lizard! How dare you insult my daughter so! Have you no respect? Were you raised among rats? Have you the intelligence of a mud-dwelling fish? Begone from here, and do not return until you can make amends!"

The hall erupts into jeers and shouts. Bren turns tail and races out, waving saucily on his way, Artemian and Edhren jogging to keep up with him. I can't help laughing.

"That," Melly murmurs, bending toward me from her place at my shoulder, "was certainly both the best and most inappropriate sweetening gift I have ever even heard of."

"He had *better* make amends now," Mama says, but there's no hiding the laughter warming her voice.

Bren and his little entourage return not twenty minutes later. This time, each of them holds a tray. Artemian carries an ornate silver tray bearing a wide gold belt for me to wear for the wedding procession, the links gorgeously worked. Edhren carries a similar tray, only this one burdened with a fine set of gold jewelry, each piece glittering with sapphires. Bren's, by contrast, appears somewhat bare.

As before, he approaches and sets his tray on the table before me. I reach out with my hand that has not been decorated with henna yet and lift up the small roll of paper threaded through a familiar gold circle.

"That," Mama says with a sharp look, "was my mother's ruby ring. What were you doing with it?"

"But the paper," Bren wheedles. "Look at the paper!"

I swallow a laugh and unroll the paper against my skirt to find the names of six of my father's prize mares, all, the note assures me, properly paid for.

"If you will look out the window," Bren says, gesturing to the wide windows opening onto the garden. There, lined up for all to see, stand the mares, their coats shining in the lamplight.

Mama smiles as I gape. She must have known about this part all along! Six horses is another fortune.

"A worthy gift," she allows. "Though I will require an explanation of the ring."

"Rae will explain," Bren says brightly as Artemian and Edhren deposit their trays beside the first.

"He's a thief," I tell Mama. "That's about it."

Bren sweeps us a deep bow, his laughter sweet in my ears, and a moment later exits once more.

FOUR MONTHS LATER

"Y ou've been sleeping better the last night or two, haven't you?" Bren asks. He sits across the low table from me in our inn room, meticulously polishing his dagger.

"I have," I agree, cradling my morning tea in my hands. My first nights in Lirelei were punctuated by nightmares, and Bren is, unsurprisingly, a light sleeper. He woke with me every time. "I'm not sure how long it will last."

He nods. "Those sorts of things don't ever really go away, but they ease up."

He's right. I've learned not to let my memories drag me down, to steady myself when they come for me in my dreams. Sometimes, they're quieter and I can face them, or simply push them away, and sometimes they hit me as hard as the moment I first lived through them. I've begun to accept that they will always be a part of me, one that I am slowly getting better at navigating.

A quick knock sounds on the inn room's door. "Package!"

Bren looks up, his hands stilling on his dagger. "Are you expecting anything?"

I set my tea down, thinking. "Maybe?" We've only been in Lirelei a week and a half. It seems unlikely that anything would come for me this quickly, but not impossible.

Bren rises and moves toward the sturdy wood door. "Got your knife?"

"Yes." I slip it out and rise to peek out the window, just in case. The inn yard is clear. This is just Bren being cautious, as always. I watch as Bren positions himself beside the door, then unlatches it and swings it open with a flick of his hand.

A serving boy stands on the other side, package in hand, blinking at me. "Kelari?"

He has no idea I'm a lady, and I'm not about to tell him. I set my knife on the low table beside me with a smile—just as he catches sight of Bren, dagger in hand. The boy's face goes slightly gray.

"Is that for me?" I ask brightly, crossing to take the package from him. "You'll have to excuse my husband. He's far too used to people trying to kill us."

Bren sighs, slipping his dagger out of view. "You do make us sound so very normal, Rae." He nods his head to the boy as I hand him a copper for his troubles. "Apologies."

The boy bobs his head and flees.

Bren latches the door behind him. "Who's it from?"

I cross to the table and set it down—it's a compact package, but still bigger than I'd dared to hope. I look up with a smile. "Artemian."

Bren settles across from me on his cushion, his gaze flicking from me to the package, but he doesn't speak his questions. I answer them anyway.

"I was looking into something with him in Tarinon. He promised to send me anything he found after we left." Artemian chose to remain at the villa to care for and see to the education of the thirty or so children we've recovered thus far who either couldn't return home or had no wish to do so. He has help of course, and he's also equally interested in seeing the dozen or so adults we rescued find their own paths forward.

I slice the package's ties open and unwrap a wooden box. It's locked. Bren snorts with laughter as I retrieve my picks and work the lock. Inside are two letters—one for me, and one without a direction on it—set atop two or three small, cloth-wrapped packages.

I skim my letter and then pass it to Bren, watching as the laughter fades from his gaze.

"These are—my mother's things?" he asks, his voice unsteady.

"Take a look." I scoot the box toward him. "I'm going to finish getting ready."

I slip into the connected room, where our sleeping mat has been rolled up and put away, and all our clothes are carefully folded on shelves. I peek through the door at intervals while changing. Bren reads the second letter, slowly, then sits with it in his hand. It's an account of his mother's last few months, spent with a friend—not just the things she did, but the stories and hopes and memories she shared with her friend. A few of which were about her son Lukai, lost so many years before.

As I step back into the main room, Bren gives himself a shake and reaches for the box. The first package reveals an old tin cup, battered and scratched, but still serviceable. The second has a thin handkerchief in it, worn and stained, one corner carefully embroidered with a single red poppy surrounded by green leaves.

"Poppies are for remembrance," I say, pausing at his shoulder.

He runs his finger over the worn stitches. Then he sets the kerchief down as gently as if it were the finest silk and reaches for the third package. It's a small leather-bound book, the cover worn smooth and glossy, the pages within thin. Bren opens it with shaking hands. On the first page, above the type that proclaims it a book of folk tales, is his name written in thick, wobbly letters.

"My mother bought this for me," he says, his voice rasping. "It has Riha of the Woods in it, and she wanted me to have it, to know who I was named after. The printer gave it to her at a bargain because two of the pages were bound in upside down."

His fingers brush over the letters of his name, as hers must have a hundred times before, and then he bends his head and weeps for the childhood he lost, for the mother who never stopped loving him, who kept what she could of him no matter what. This is what she had to her name when she died: a tin cup, a kerchief, and her son's name written in his book.

I kneel beside him and pull him into my arms, and let him grieve the things he has not let himself think of, or hope for, all these long years.

"She never stopped loving you," I murmur against his hair.

"I—I know," he says, and that is all.

Sometimes that is all we need to know.

Eventually, he sits back and wipes his nose with his sleeve. I rise and fetch him a cup of water while he rewraps his mother's things and places them reverently back inside the box. All but the key to the lock, found at the bottom of the box, bless Artemian.

"All right?" I ask, passing him the water.

He nods, his eyes faintly red.

"The others are probably ready. Do you still feel up to going out?"

He glances toward the box, then looks up at me with a fierce smile. "Of course I do. Give me just a moment."

He takes the box to our shared room and returns with his sword belt. "Got your flute?"

"It's here," I say, lifting it from the cushion where I set it earlier. I pass the strap over my shoulder as he tugs his boots on.

As he rises, I ask hesitantly, "Was that all right?" This time, I'm not asking how he is, and he knows it.

He takes a swift step toward me and wraps his arms around my waist, drawing me to him. His face pressed against the feathery softness of my hair, he murmurs, "I didn't know how much I needed that."

I slip my arms around his waist and rest against him, just as he rests against me.

"We should go down," Bren says with some chagrin, easing back.

I reach up a hand and lay it against his cheek, feel the faint roughness of his shaved skin against my palm. "You know I love you."

A gentle glow comes into his eyes, soft and yet fierce at the same time. It makes me want to slide back into his arms. "I know." His lips curve into a wicked smile. "But if you keep reminding me, we'll never make it downstairs."

I laugh and step away, even as my body flushes with warmth. I pat his arm consolingly. "There's always tonight."

"And every night after that," he says.

I catch up my cane from beside the door. "Oh, I don't know. I'm sure some of those nights we'll be sick, or too exhausted to even look at each other, or we'll just want to spend time with a dear friend—"

"Rae," Bren complains, though I can hear the laughter in his voice. He grabs my hand as we start down the hall. I tug him along behind me the rest of the way to the common room where our companions wait.

I know all of them relatively well by now, though Lirika is by far my closest friend among them. She winks at me as we enter. "Got delayed on the way out?"

"Rae would have dragged me here by the back of my tunic if I'd taken any longer," Bren says cheerfully as my face heats. "*You* try slowing her down."

I thump his arm. "You're both terrible. Is the carriage here?"

"Out front," Lirika says. We head out together, the others falling in behind us.

Once the carriage door is closed and the windows curtained, I take out my flute and start to play. The notes fill the carriage, and drifting after them comes the magic I have grown used to seeing, a softly glowing blue, twisting and whirling in the air before spreading out. The carriage rolls forward. We've already cleared out the neighborhoods surrounding the inn—although we saw to the docks first. I keep playing, watching as the magic shifts and reaches, moving through the walls of the carriage as if they weren't there at all.

"There," I pause to say as a thicker tendril forms.

Bren raps on the ceiling and the carriage rolls to a stop. I play a few more notes until the tendril is fully formed. It still shifts and moves, but all the magic that surrounded it has coalesced around it, until it looks like a thick rope of spider silk, glinting and drifting and utterly unbreakable.

We pile out and Bren helps me up to the driver's bench, taking a seat next to me. From here, it's easy enough to direct the driver after the rope. Our course isn't perfect, for the rope gives no consideration for buildings that might be in the way. Inevitably we follow a zigzag route after it, until we come to a tailor's shop nestled into a building. The rope twines up, past the open doors and the prettily embroidered fabrics put on display, to float through the window of the apartment above.

We clamber down while a pair of Bren's men make a quick circuit of the building. I turn to fetch my cane from the inside of the carriage, but Lirika already has it in hand, passing it to me with a nod.

"Stairs around the side," Bren's men report when they return. "A second exit at the back."

Bren sends them to guard the rear and orders another pair to keep a watch on the front while the rest of us take the stairs. I carry the flute in its shoulder bag, and the rope connected to it shifts as we climb. It will always show the straightest path forward, which is now through the door before us.

Bren knocks sharply. One of the two guards assigned to us by Matsin stands just behind him, dagger ready but hidden from view. Lirika leans against the wooden railing by my side. "This is my favorite part," she murmurs.

"What?" I ask bewildered. "Knocking at doors?"

She chuckles. "Well, after this. Seeing them realize that they're about to pay for everything they've done."

Bren knocks again, and this time a woman opens the door. "Who are you?" she demands at the sight of us crowding her stairwell. "What do you want here?"

"We're here on the king's business," Bren says levelly, putting out a hand to stop her from slamming the door. The woman's eyes widen, her gaze darting to the guard's armored leather vest, the insignia sewn there.

Bren says, "You will allow us in."

"There's nothing here for you to see! What do you want, hey? I haven't done anything to warrant your swords! Go away!"

Lirika laughs softly under her breath. "This one's not afraid of anything."

Bren, still speaking levelly, shoves his way through the door. We all follow behind. It's a small, cluttered apartment, the sitting area spread with a trio of ragged carpets and littered with cushions. Bren continues past the woman, telling her to take a seat and wait, though she doesn't, instead following behind him and haranguing him.

"The last door on the left," I say loudly enough for him to hear, my eyes following the rope.

It's locked, of course.

Bren turns to the woman. "Where's the key for this?"

"It's a storage room! I hardly use it. I don't think I even have the key here. You'll have to come back when my husband is home. He'll be able to help you."

"Shall I?" Lirika asks, stepping forward. The lock barely takes her four breaths.

She pushes the door open and steps back, allowing Bren to see inside first. I step to the side to catch a glimpse of four girls gathered together by a single small window set with iron bars. They range in age from seven to thirteen or so. The floor is strewn with half-cut fabric and work baskets; they were sewing. I'm almost used to the faint disappointment I feel as I realize neither Kirrana nor Seri are among those we've found.

"They're visiting from my sister's home," the woman says, changing her story without a hitch. "You leave my nieces alone!"

Bren turns and steps up to the woman, meeting her eye for eye.

"I'm telling you—"

"Please do," he says silkily. "And while you're at it, why don't you tell me what the punishment is for keeping people captive and forcing their labor?"

"I don't know what you mean—"

"There's a newly passed law by the king, not two months ago. Five years imprisonment for each infraction. That's twenty years right there, in that room. And do you know the penalty for misleading and lying to a representative of the king?"

"I haven't done anything," the woman says desperately, real fear in her eyes now. She backs away, her gaze darting from us to the exit.

"That's the look," Lirika says with a dark sort of delight.

"I would disagree," Bren tells the woman.

The guard takes a quick step forward and grasps her arm. "You'll come with us now."

She lets out a shrill scream and attempts to pull away, but with a brutal twist, the guard has her arm behind her back. They march her out past the rest of our number and down the stairs, still crying and shouting.

"She was never going to go quietly," I say as I reach Bren.

"No," Bren says. "But it was extremely satisfying to inform her of her fate. It always is."

I pause in the doorway. The girls are still backed against the window. I take a slow breath; this is where I can help again. I cross the room, my cane tapping softly, and come to a stop a few paces away from them. "My name is Rae. I'm here to help get you out. If you want to go back to your families, we can help you find them. If you don't, we'll find you a place that cares for you. You'll get good food and can go outside when you like and you can leave if you don't like it. Does that sound good?"

They stare at me, unmoving. After months of this same reaction, it still breaks my heart.

"Is there anything here you want to take with you?" I ask, my voice just firm enough to get through to the girls. "Any clothes? Anything special?"

One of the girls points to a larger basket set against the wall. Bren immediately lifts it up.

"Good," I say. "Anything else?"

She shakes her head.

"Come along, then," I say and gesture them forward. It takes a little more cajoling, but they finally start moving, still clinging to each other's hands. I've learned that a brisk firmness joined with a kind look works far better than any other method to get the children out of their prisons. That, and letting them see that I fit certain stereotypes that suggest I'm not as dangerous as other people they know. There's a benefit to having a limp, or using a cane, alongside a kind bearing.

A hand slips into mine, holding tight. I look down in surprise into the gaunt, wide-eyed face of the youngest girl. "Rae?" she says, and my heart stutters.

I drop to my knees, looking straight into the small face before me. Her cheeks are hollowed, her eyes shadowed, and her expression somber. She looks nothing, *nothing* like the bright-eyed, cheerful girl I once knew, and yet . . . "Seri?"

She stares back at me, unblinking, but her hand tightens in mine.

I lick dry lips, wanting to fold this girl into my arms whether I know her or not—but she holds herself so stiffly. She doesn't want to be held. Just the fact that she took my hand is a miracle. Carefully, I say, "Can you tell me your sister's name? Or your mother's?"

"Anisela," she whispers. And then again, so I won't be confused, "Ani."

"Oh, Seri," I breathe. I clasp her hand in both of mine, tears spilling down my cheeks. "Your family misses you so much. I'll get you home to Sheltershorn. It's going to be all right now. We've been searching for you all this time, did you know? Can I—do you want a hug?"

She shakes her head jerkily, her own eyes dry. I'm going to overwhelm her. I swipe my face with my sleeve and stand up. "Come, let's go down to the carriage. There's food waiting."

Bren waits in the hallway, basket in arms. "Rae?"

"I'm fine," I tell him. I wait until the children are settled into the carriage, their captor already seated in the following donkey cart with a trio of guards. She'll be taken straight to a holding cell, and the guards will lodge charges against her.

As I step down from the carriage to speak with Bren, a pair of men come out of the tailor shop, bringing the tailor with them. He's a short, heavyset man with a balding pate. The sight of him sets off a tirade from the woman, blaming him for his bad decisions and insisting she was only doing as she was told. He in turn declares that he has no idea who she is and is *certainly* not married to her.

"True love, don't you think?" Bren murmurs from beside me.

I shake my head, a smile tugging at my lips.

"That little girl, you know her?"

"She's my friend Ani's little sister," I say, my eyes filling again. It was because of Seri, and Ani, that I came to the king's city at all, and set my feet upon the path my life has taken since. "You met Ani at the wedding."

"I remember," Bren says softly. "Why don't we take her home? It's been a few months since you saw your family."

He slips an arm around my waist, drawing me to his side. I lean my head against his shoulder, breathing in the faint scent of soap clinging to him, a trace of cinnamon and cloves. "There's so much more to do in Lirelei," I say uncertainly.

Bren's arm tightens around me. "I think you need to take Seri home, as much for her as for yourself. You have to give yourself space to breathe and rejoice, Rae. After all, we're going to spend the rest of our lives chasing slavers together."

"Promise?" I ask, looking up with a smile.

"Always." He tilts his head to brush a kiss on my cheek. In broad daylight on a public street. Behind us, Lirika hoots.

I slip out of his arms, face burning, and clamber back up into the carriage to sit with Seri and the other children. Laughing, Bren follows behind me, and together we tell them stories of the lives they have before them, all the hopes and dreams that they can lay claim to again.

ACKNOWLEDGEMENTS

This book nearly wiped me out a few times. I am thus deeply indebted to my legion of beta readers, who kept picking me up off the floor, gently brushing me off, handing me a bazillion suggested edits, and telling me how much they loved the story despite the various disasters unfolding on the page. You are all amazing, and I'm so grateful to you for sticking with me and this story.

In order of reading, thanks to: Charlotte Michel, Anne Hillman (twice!), Ashley Lambert, Shy Eager, Suzannah Rowntree, Anela Deen, A.C. Spahn (twice! On deadline!), Tracy Banghart, Elizabeth Kelly, Basma (@bookishbasma), Alura Fogger, Virginia McClain, and sensitivity readers Cara Liebowitz and Lucy-May Galbraith. Thanks to Diana Cox for her proofreading prowess, and an extra shout out to Suzannah and Anela who helped me get a handle on the romance line (as I repeatedly fumbled that), as well as to Alura for the idea of giving a nod to the Pied Piper of Hamelin – that was just the suggestion I needed to come up with the perfect fate for Garrin! Deep gratitude to Batool AlKhawaja, Madolyn Rogers, and Virginia McClain for a final look through after file conversions created unmitigated chaos—your kindness and eagle-eyes made all the difference.

I am equally grateful to all the wonderful people at Hot Key Books in the UK, not the least for stepping up to offer editing when my US deal fell through, and supporting me as I moved forward with Snowy Wings Publishing here in the US. To Maurice Lyon for initial edits on Darkness, thank you for your kindness and incredible support. To Ruth Bennett, who came on board halfway through and yet put your all into this book, I cannot thank you enough! To Dominica Clements for all the behind-the-scenes design work, Melissa Hyder for exceptional copyediting, Talya Baker for all your support, Eleanor Rose for your work in marketing, and Kate Griffiths for helping to make those gorgeous FairyLoot editions a reality, and to the rest of the Hot Key team, many of whom I've never met but have still done so much for this story – thank you.

On the US side, I am so grateful to my agent, Emmanuelle Morgen for continuing to be my champion and a steady support through multiple pandemic releases. I'm so thankful to be on this journey with you! Thanks to Whitney Lee for working on foreign rights, and finding me a home with Hot Key. Thanks to Lyssa Chiavari for inviting me to join Snowy Wings Publishing as an indie author and walking me through my first publication there— you're amazing, as is the work you do. And to Jenny Zemanek, for another stunning cover—these books would not be the same without you.

A huge shoutout to all my amazing backers on Kickstarter! Thanks to your support, we have an audiobook for *Darkness* (narrated by the talented Shiromi Arserio). Further, your backing allowed me to make this book as beautiful as it is, from the gorgeous hand-lettered title, to the art of Rae and Bren on the hardcover by Avendell, to having a special edition complete with gilt foil designs by Kerstin Espinosa Rosero. Thank you!

My family, as always, has continued to be a vital support crew. Thanks to my two young daughters for all the laughs and brainstorming through this book (I promise you can read it when you're older!). And you're right, "Br-Red Hawk" / "Bread Hawk" was a terrible missed opportunity. Gratitude also to my husband, my parents, and my brother and his beautiful family. I'm so thankful to share this life with you.

As always, I am grateful to the wonderful readers and reviewers who have found something to love in my stories and shared them with others. A story is nothing without a reader to give it a home in their heart. Thank you.

Finally, I am grateful to God for all that He has given me, in my writing and in my life.

CPSIA information can be obtained
at www.ICGtesting.com
Printed in the USA
BVHW051410090822
644141BV00021B/1020/J